THE BIRTH OF LEGEND

Dudley Boden

DEDICATION

This book is dedicated to my family who allowed me this outlet when I desperately needed it. Their love and support has allowed me to recreate my life.

1 IN THE BEGINNING

Fenly awoke to a dawn caste in contrast, the rich color of the deep blue sky against the first brilliant rays of orange from the sun juxtaposed against the black hills on the far side of the valley that still lay in darkness. Beside him Ashmere continued to doze though she stretched her legs which told him she knew he was awake. Open to the sky their bed of soft moss provided an unbroken view of the shallow valley. To all appearances they were alone, though in fact the other members of the Natec tribe were never far away.

Ashmere yawned and stretched her long arms and legs to bring them back to life. Fenly watched, admiring her black hair that grew from her head and the back of her neck as far down as midway on her back forming a long thin V of hand length hair that shimmered with dew in the early morning light.

Fenly loved to watch her wake, evolving from the look of a young child asleep to waking cat suppleness and finally to bright eyed hawk. Her narrow face and slanted steel gray eyes completed this impression, though no hawk could stir the feelings that rose in him whenever he looked at her.

Ashmere smiled as she appraised Fenly sitting on the moss carpet like a bent sapling ready to spring straight at any moment to his full height, arrow straight and ready for anything, yet as coiled looking as if the stars falling from the sky could not interrupt his reverie.

Fenly, as with other Jhirum males had the same pattern of hair as Ashmere, though growing farther around his neck, almost meeting at his Adams Apple and continuing down on to his shoulder slightly. His hair was the color of rusted iron.

Fenly caressed Ashmere with his mind. He did not speak; the touch of minds was much more intimate. He felt the warmth of her response, sending a tingle up his spine. The feel of each other's mind was familiar and comfortable, though slightly diminished from when they bedded down.

Fenly's stomach growled reminding him that it was time to feed the body as well as regenerate the threads of life. They would begin this day seemingly alone and likely would spend much of it the same way, only occasionally encountering a few of the members of their group.

All Jhirum, except for the Jhirum of the Sea, lived independent, often solitary lives, with little need for formal social contact or structure. The tide of their lives brought them together because they liked to be close to others of their kind, not out of need for mutual protection or support. What group structure there was allowed for those rare times when collective action was required and in those instances the Natec looked to Fenly to focus their efforts, though not to lead in any normal sense of the word.

Fenly, as with all Jhirum loved his life and his world. He knew each tree branch like he knew his own arm. Though the highest order of creature by any reckoning, the Jhirum no more dominated the land than they did each other. Instead, they were part of the land in more senses than could be imagined at first glance.

Fenly caressed Ashmere's dark mane and in his mind she purred at his attentions. The sun, however, was already warming the ground and with the slow disappearance of the sparkling dew it was time to reawaken and then to feed their growling stomachs.

They both stood and moved out from under the protective cover of the large evergreen, which had been their roof. Fenly took in the umber cliff face which would be their first destination, still dark in shadow on the eastern side of the valley. The cliff fell from a series of rolling hills that issued like the last ripples from a rock dropped in a pond, with the mountains behind them the first waves. These mountains were called The Spine, because they ran through the middle of the land in a narrow strip, occasionally broken by a valley that cut through all the way to the plains beyond.

They set off at a casual pace for them though even that was a good trot for the small dogs that loped off in the distance. Fenly watched the dogs disappear behind some brush that dotted the mostly open field.

As they reached the bottom of the clearing he could sense others of their tribe along the edge of the trees beginning to make their way toward the nearby cliff, though they were hidden from view.

Stepping into the darkness cast by the towering trees Fenly paused a moment to let his eyes adjust, though they were hardly necessary for him to find his way. As they continued on Fenly caught a fleeting glimpse of another member of their tribe, Genlie, converging on to their path. Even in the relative darkness Fenly could see the powerful movements of the young Jhirum. With silent nods they acknowledged one another and continued on the short remaining distance to the rising cliff face.

The cliff face looked like a child had crudely tried to make hair on a clay figure. Gouge marks covered it for a short distance on either side of the main stream, from the ground to just above head high. Cold water trickled slowly down the face from a spring that leaked out of fissures about halfway up the cliff.

Fenly took his Yoruba, a small wooden bowl, from the pouch at his waist and bent down to pick up one of the harder looking stones. Holding the Yoruba to the wall he began scraping the rock face knocking small chips and powder into the bowl. Others from the tribe began converging on the rock face performing a similar ritual.

2

After collecting a small amount in the bottom of the bowl he held it under the trickle of chill water until it was half full of the crystal clear liquid. Then after gently swirling the contents he downed it with one swallow.

The earthy taste and cold made his mouth tingle and he could feel some of the larger rough particles scratch the sides of his throat. In much the same way as the sun had crept up the valley he felt awareness build in him. The minds of each member of his tribe opened up to him as a flower opens with the warming sun. Even the color of the trees grew more intense and the darkness of the shadows less impenetrable.

The other awareness that became more intense was one of hunger. His stomach growled with a gentle pang at being teased by the small amount of liquid. It was time to find food. Before he left the cliff, however he filled the water skin at his waist with more of the water as well as some more powder from the cliff. He then strode away from the wall with no apparent acknowledgment of any of his brethren, although in fact he had greeted and was now saying his goodbyes to all of them.

He knew exactly where he was going though it was different each morning. Working his way alone back through the trees to the edge of the field he walked straight as an arrow to a bush laden with ripe berries. The taste of the berries was sweet and tart at the same time, sweet on the first bite followed by a subtle astringency at the end. By the time the sun had cleared the hills he was sated.

Having eaten, he wiped his sticky hands on the still damp grass and moved on up the valley. Today he was interested in making contact with his neighbors, though he had not seen any one from the Bagnog tribe in months.

They lived on the other side of The Spine and although there was no reason to avoid each other, there was likewise little reason to seek out the members of other tribes. Each had their own territory which they cared for and watched over. These territories were loosely defined and unguarded. There was no sense of ownership, only a sense of responsibility for the territory each watched over.

What brought him to seek this contact were the trees near the shared border of their territories. The border lay past the rolling foothills and through a valley, which cut through The Spine just to the north of where their cliff was located. It would take all day at a good pace to get through the valley to where he could meet with the leader of the Bagnog. There he could get an update on a region within the Bagnog's territory where trees had grown progressively sick and the ministrations of the Bagnog had proven insufficient to stop the pestilence.

Fenly could not recall any time in his couple of hundred years of life that there was a problem that required more than a few Jhirum to overcome. Their power to heal the land and its creatures was great and they rarely failed at healing unless a creature was already too near death, or age was the cause.

3

The last time that Fenly had seen the blighted area, what few leaves remained on the trees were small and withered. He remembered how; as he got closer, he first felt in the pit of his stomach a nausea that grew as he drew nearer. He had gone close enough to see the outline of the damp ground around the base of this grove of trees marking a shallow swamp that had developed where once the ground was dry. He did not stay close long for his stomach twisted in distaste. It was this swamp, he was certain, that was the cause of the decline in the trees.

For him as for all of the Jhirum the health of the land and the inhabitants of that land regardless of species was of as much concern as his own health, for the Jhirum were part of the land and the land part of the Jhirum. The blight was no different than if he had a diseased arm.

He knew that Nomber, the leader of the Bagnog, would be coming to meet him from near the trees, for he had not ventured far from that area since the sickness had begun to grow. Fenly reached out with his mind and found a familiar presence on his side of the swamp, but still far away. He touched Nomber's unsettled mind and asked him to meet him at the end of the valley.

Fenly took in the landscape as he walked with an eye for the smallest changes. He knew this area like he knew Ashmere's body. A piercing screech drew his attention to the top of a huge old oak tree. The giant red tail hawk that he had watched since it fledged nearly ten years ago lifted off its nest and soared into the sky. Any other time he would have stopped and watched for a while, hoping for a glimpse of the newly hatched chicks he knew were hidden down in the heap of tangled branches, but his meeting with Nomber took priority.

He walked steadily through the morning and into the afternoon before pausing along a small stream to have a drink and pick some more berries and gather a few nuts. The Jhirum rarely ate meat. They were protectors of the creatures in this land, not the takers of lives. They did not however, interfere with the natural cycle of life, which brought some creatures to untimely ends to feed others.

He continued into a narrow valley with the high peaks of The Spine on either side. Here the trees crowded in until he was walking in primeval forest, dark and barely dappled even when the sun was higher in the sky than it was now.

He walked all day and as the sun was beginning to wane at his back he reached out to Nomber again, finding him just entering the other side of the valley headed in his direction.

He adjusted his course, angling in the direction that his sense told him would bring him to the leader of the Bagnog. Entering a small clearing he could see Nomber striding to greet him. Nearly as tall as he, though somewhat broader, Nomber had a mane of almost pure white hair though not from age.

Nomber waved and smiled briefly before his face became stern again. Speaking in the quiet voice of one unused to vocal conversation Nomber greeted Fenly, "Welcome neighbor. Seeing is knowing and knowing is being part of."

Fenly completed the formal greeting, "Being part of is being one."

That was the extent of the formalities. "How is the diseased grove of trees?" Fenly began, "Is there any improvement since you brought your tribe together to heal the pestilence?"

Nomber shook his mane. "It seems to me that the water is darker and deeper than before. Each day it grows, whether rain or shine."

Fenly could see the concern on Nomber's face. "It is time, Nomber, for our groups to join in cleaning this blight before the trees fade beyond recovery."

Nomber nodded agreement. "I hope that we are enough, it seems in some way to have great power."

Fenly remained confident, despite Nomber's concern. "Let us set three days from now for the healing. That will give me sufficient time to gather most of my tribe and get them to the swamp."

"That sounds good and thank you for your support, Fenly."

"Anything that confounds the best efforts of the Bagnog is of great concern to all of us" was Fenly's simple reply.

Nomber nodded and then glanced around at the growing darkness. "It is already growing dark. There is a small grove of pines at the base of the mountain there." He said pointing north, "that would make for a comfortable place to spend the night."

"That sounds good," Fenly replied as Nomber moved off.

As they walked into the shelter of the tall evergreens the last of the day sounds seemed to disappear, absorbed by the needles above and covering the ground. Nomber meandered aimlessly through the cushioned evergreens until he found a spot that met his liking. He sat lightly with his back against a weathered giant. Fenly sat to his side facing the valley, listening to the last faint chirping of the day birds.

As darkness settled in around them Nomber shifted his weight and spoke quietly, his brow furrowed, "The darkness of the swamp grows every day. At times I can almost believe it is alive. Just being near it gives me a headache."

Fenly was quiet for a time, listening to the growing chorus of crickets and the occasional howling of a wolf in the distance. "I remember the one time I was near it with you my stomach almost turned over and that was when it was still small. There is power in that water."

"That there is. And that kind of dark power is too near our spring. If it keeps growing who knows what would happen when the two waters come together."

Pondering these concerns they both fell back into silence, listening to the night sounds grow with the fading light. They spent the rest of the night with their own thoughts. They did not build a fire. The Jhirum felt little need for added light or heat, the magic being their warmth and their vision no matter the weather, or the time of day.

Fenly slept soundly on the soft blanket of needles until the first hint of light filtered through the dense canopy. The morning was cool but dry. He needed to get an early start so that he could get back and gather his tribe. Touching Nomber's mind the older Jhirum stretched and opened his eyes. "I suppose you need to be on your way."

Fenly nodded. "I need to meet with my people tonight if they are to be ready in time to arrive at the swamp in three days."

Nomber stood, shaking his legs to get the blood flowing again. "Thank you again for your support. Remain one, though distant."

Fenly nodded and turned back to the valley. As he walked Fenly recalled his clenched stomach from when he had last visited it. Even the natural decay of growing things caused an uneasy feeling in the pit of his stomach, but this swamp was much more. There was some form of magic in those waters and not a beneficent kind. He sincerely hoped that their combined efforts would be sufficient to clear the blight.

As soon as he was about halfway through the valley he began reaching out to his tribe. He had in fact been gathering them near the cliff for a couple of weeks. The Jhirum ranged widely over their territory and so it took time to gather them together, though they all eventually returned to the cliff, which was their only source of magic.

In their sojourns they carried with them leather pouches, or containers made of gourd, with water and dust from the cliff, in order to renew their strength when gone on long journeys. Normally they could sustain their magic for a couple of days with no replenishment, but longer than that and what they referred to as the threads of life would grow weak, diminishing their abilities. If they had to use large amounts of power for some purpose such as trying to heal the fetid swamp, they could diminish their power in hours.

Fenly reached the end of the valley by early afternoon and by late afternoon he was back at the base of the cliff, having paused along the way to feed on some nuts and more berries. He then settled himself in the shade of a giant elm and began to reach out to those of his people that were not already gathered near him.

Though his mind sense was strong and could convey general intent, he needed to gather his people together to explain the situation and the required response. So as he touched familiar minds he simply called for a meeting the hour before sundown to talk of an important issue. To the Jhirum the health of every plant and animal was important and required their concern and efforts when threatened. The Jhirum, however, were not aware of a threat too distant to touch their awareness, a celestial body to small to see, moving counter to the natural paths of the stars.

As the sun began to settle toward the top of the hill and the shadows grew in length, the Natec began to appear around the giant Elm. This had been their prime meeting area for hundreds of years and this tree had been large for all of that time. Ashmere appeared first, feeling for his mind before she was within shouting distance.

Some of the tension that he hadn't realized was there left his shoulders as she approached. Though Fenly was the nominal leader of the tribe, in fact Ashmere was more decisive and better able to sway this strong group of independent minded people to common decisions when necessary. He was glad to have her there for support.

As she reached his side and gathered his hand in hers she spoke. "You have been to the blight?"

"No, but I have met with Nomber, who just came from there. It is clear the Bagnog need our help."

She fell silent as they both sat with their backs to the tree and waited for the rest of the group. He could feel the confidence in Ashmere's mind as they watched their umber cliff turn golden with the setting sun. As the sun crept toward the top of the cliff, thirty adult members of the tribe and eight youngsters had congregated around the tree. There were a few others who walked the edges of their domain and could not be called to return, but Fenly was confident that this would be a sufficient number when joined with Nomber's tribe, to quell the threat. The talk was quiet and relaxed as the day drew near to a close.

When the last to arrive were settled Fenly stood. He surveyed his tribe members. Some were close to five hundred years old, weathered but sitting straight and tall. "I have been to see Nomber. The black swamp is growing and the trees continue to fade. It is clear that Nomber's efforts alone cannot reverse the growing blight. We have agreed that it would be best if we combine the strength of his tribe and ours to stop this pestilence now before it is too late for the trees. We would like to meet at the third rising of the sun to join forces."

He looked around the group, seeking assent, expecting nothing less, not because he demanded it, but because they would all see the need on their own. He could sense through his mental connection to each of them the combination of confidence and consternation, confidence that they could overcome anything together; but consternation that the Bagnog had not succeeded on their own. After a moment of mental assessment each in turn nodded their agreement.

Ashmere rose beside Fenly, "As you all know this is not a simple spring that has suddenly welled up, but a form of magic. I would suggest that you all feast deeply on the wall at sunrise before we journey to the east. Make sure that your skins are full as well."

Without dissent they murmured their agreement and immediately rose and began to disperse, each to their own favorite bedding grounds. As the mental goodbyes diminished Fenly drew Ashmere's hand in to his own and gazed briefly into her face before turning toward their bedding ground.

CHAPTER 2 GATHERING

After leaving Fenly, Nomber had immediately begun reaching out to his nearest tribe members. Most of the tribe by this time was within a day's walk of the swamp. They had gathered here previously in an unsuccessful attempt to beat back the swamp and knowing that there would be another attempt had stayed close.

Though he could still not reach the farthest out of the group they relayed the message from nearest to farthest that there would be another gathering on the morning of the third day from now. Excitement rippled through the connection with his tribe as they learned that the Natec would join them.

After assuring himself that all had been contacted he settled in to what had become his almost constant home, a small knoll overlooking the shadow of the trees and swamp. He had dwelled on this corruption for weeks now trying to come up with a clue as to its origin and cure, to no avail. Now he hoped that sheer strength of numbers would be sufficient to beat back the contamination.

Nomber tried not to imagine what would happen if this fetid swamp merged with their magical spring that bubbled up in another copse of trees only a short walk from this dying one. He could not guess what the result of the two waters coming together would be, but could not risk this vileness contaminating their only source of the magical powers that gave them true life.

As he settled into the soft grass Nomber sensed another Jhirum approaching from the other side of the swamp. It was Bashley, one of the younger tribe members. Nomber liked Bashley and appreciated his support. A tribe of independent people who rarely even consider themselves part of a tribe was not easy to organize into a group to work in concert to accomplish a common goal. Bashley however, helped Nomber to gain their acquiescence and their agreement on how best to fight the evil. This would be his last chance before they would begin to question his ability to overcome this obstacle. If they came to that conclusion he feared that they would begin to work on the task individually, which he was convinced would not yield results.

Bashley waved from the thin shadows of the skeletal trees. Nomber could see the frown creasing his normally jovial face just from passing close to the black swamp.

Nomber returned the wave with a tight smile.

"I think that all of our tribe will be here," Bashley exclaimed, excitement overcoming the nausea. "How many Natec do you think will come?"

Bashley was clearly in awe of the idea that within a few days more Jhirum would be gathered at the swamp than had been assembled in several generations.

"I do not know for certain," Nomber answered him. "But Fenly had already put out word some time ago for his people to be assembled and ready so I suspect there should be at least twenty to add to our number if not more."

"That will give us sixty or more!" Bashley exclaimed, wide eyed. "That has got to be enough to overcome the swamp."

"I certainly hope so," Nomber replied solemnly. "I have never seen any vileness this strong and persistent."

Bashley fell silent, turning to stare at the withered trees. Nomber could see he was wrestling even with the possibility of that many Jhirum not being able to succeed.

After sitting staring silently at the swamp for a short while Nomber pushed himself up off the ground. "We had best gather with the rest of our group at our spring so that we can all be as strong as possible when the time comes," Nomber concluded.

Bashley nodded, never taking his eyes off the swamp until they headed off together to the copse of trees that sheltered and grew from their magical spring. There they would await the arrival of the rest of their group and then the Natec, so that they could make a last assault on the putrid swamp.

Bashley was glad to leave the proximity of the black waters. His nausea had quickly evolved into a headache, making it hard to even think. He could not see how Nomber could spend so much time close to that foul presence and stay sane.

CHAPTER 3 MAESTIC

In the high country north of the valley of the Natec, Endmere looked down from his perch on the sharp cliff above the defile. The day began here quite differently from in the valley of the Natec. The height of the mountains and the shade of the trees kept it cool even in summer. The Maestic would not be described as a tribe even by Jhirum standards. Endmere had not seen a single member of his tribe in several weeks. They each followed their destiny in their own ways, cared for the land through solitary dedication and rarely sought each other's company. The mountains shaped their habits, the peaks throwing up barriers of snow, ice and harsh winds. There was little comfort to be gained in numbers. The comfort they sought came from the land.

This ancient tribe really only existed as a tribe as a means of facilitating procreation. Otherwise it is likely each member would wander the mountains never encountering another Jhirum and the land would slowly become devoid of their care. The only other source of chance communion was their single shared spring, which gave them the magic to survive and heal in these harsh mountains.

Endmere stood over the valley as if cut from the granite upon which he stood. He was of average height for a Jhirum, which was still tall, but broad and solid. Most Jhirum had no facial hair, but Endmere's neck mane grew up almost touching from either side of his neck and chin forming a full mane and beard. Gray streaked the dark hair though not in sufficient quantity to mark him as past his prime.

He was an unyielding man, strong and sure of himself. Though never in his lifetime called upon to lead his people it was clear that if there was a need he would be up to the task. The Maestic, however, did not even make a pretense of designating a leader. Even the old among them could not remember a time when there was a group gathering or exigency sufficient to require a group effort.

Endmere had fathered two children, whom he had not seen in years. He knew they were now eighteen and thirty years old and that is about all he knew. Their mother, he still sought out on occasion, perhaps with the full circle of the seasons. They belonged to each other and always would regardless the distance or seeming disconnection. Endmere was glad just to know she was somewhere and content with that knowledge.

On the other hand, he could not bear to be separated from the mountains. He would whither under the bare sun of the plains, or the vast expanse of the ocean. Here in this cold, though lush mountainside, with snow capped peaks behind him, he felt at one. He knew how to tend to this land and the land to him. The mountains were reflected in his roughened skin and thick black mane.

On this clear late summer day he was working his way back to the tribe's spring after having spent several weeks in the northern reaches of the mountains. Even for him this was a long time to be away from the home range, but though harsh and cold the northern mountains needed care as well. Knowing that few among them ventured that far he made it a point to travel to the northern border of their range a couple of times a year to monitor the health of the land there. Though all of the mountains were rugged and cool, in the far north the peaks reached even farther into the sky, remaining snow covered throughout the summer, frequently cloaked in fog and always, it seems, battered by harsh winds.

These features, rather than being forbidding, appealed to Endmere's character and made him feel more alive than he ever did in the more southern reaches. His trips to the high mountains were like vacations to some harsh wonderland. The length of these trips required him to take significant stores of the precious spring water and to carefully meter his resources to last the trip. Now that he had nearly made it back to the spring he was unconcerned that he had used the last of his special water two days ago and was beginning to feel the magic weaken in him.

He had traveled at a quick pace throughout the day not stopping to inspect the land carefully as he normally did. Though he was not concerned about having used the last of his water he still did not want to spend a night without sufficient magical power to ward the chill that was borne on the winds blown from the high peaks.

As the sun set he topped the last peak which overlooked the small valley where the spring carved a path. He watched as the narrow dark ribbon that was the stream born of his magic spring wound its way into the mountain shadows. It was time for him to visit his spring before sleep. Sliding off the perch where he had settled in to watch the sunset, he picked his way among the small boulders along the edge of the defile then into the darkening woods for a short distance until he could sense the water issuing from the ground.

Endmere approached the clear, ice-cold water which bubbled gently in the small pool and then flowed off into the deepening night, gurgling quietly in the evening stillness. Retrieving his wooden bowl he scooped a small amount of water and drank. His mind seemed to open to the stars that were aborning in the dark blue sky. Used to the feeling, he pulled himself back into his body and turned from the spring, moving off in to the forest. He soon found an overhanging ledge that would afford some protection from the chill night air. He did not fill his skins as he planned on staying near the spring for a few days to rest and contemplate.

Wrapped in his magic cocoon he fell quickly asleep, only giving passing notice to a small tickle at the edge of his magic enhanced awareness, a mere pinprick, too far away to be of concern.

CHAPTER 4 JHIRUM OF THE SEA

Far away to the south the Jhirum of the Sea were preparing to set sail on a voyage to gather food and to explore their world, which although based on the rocky coast, was really a world of water. They rarely ventured out of site of the waves, or even turned to scrutinize the white-capped mountains in the distance. Of all the Jhirum, only the sea people worked closely together in groups on a regular basis and built, collectively, anything but the simplest structures.

The Jhirum of the sea however, built great sailing vessels, not huge, but large enough to convey a crew of twenty for long distances in storm tangled seas. Their ships were built low and long, sleek like a giant canoe though significantly wider in the beam than a canoe even of such size. Propelled by masts fore and aft with surprisingly small sails, these craft could cut through the waves at speeds which defied the limitations of their sails. They were, of course propelled more by magic than by wind, though both were employed together.

On this day a great voyage was about to begin. Shwaren stood, the wind hard in his face watching as supplies were loaded on to the ship. Though the leader of the tribe did not always go on these voyages, the importance of this voyage and the uncertainties compelled him to be at the head. Despite the uncertainties he could not wait to set sail. He had been on land for half the summer, though constantly in touch with the sea and caring for it from the shore.

It had been only a couple of weeks earlier that a crew had returned from the sea with disturbing news. While linked to gather strength to propel their boat they had sensed, however remotely, something wrong. Though they felt only the slightest pinprick on their senses it felt to them like a threat, and dangerous in some way. As they continued their journey they explored the sensation more. Though unable to place it either physically or by its nature they could sense it growing, very slowly, stronger.

Shortening their journey they returned home to share the news. After several days of discussion it was decided to launch another expedition, this time to try to locate at least the general direction from which the threat approached. This journey would have no destination, but would in fact involve meandering in a somewhat planned fashion to try to detect in which direction the sense of danger grew stronger and possibly to pursue and identify it.

For this type of journey Shwaren could not remain on shore. He shook himself from his reverie as Faren approached up the small hill where he stood. The young Jhirum bounded up the hill with the excitement of youth.

"The stores are almost all on board," he announced as he came next to Shwaren and turned to follow his gaze out to sea. "We can sail at any time."

Shwaren looked once more to the horizon, nodded his head as if he had received permission from the waves and began the decent to the docks. Most of the crew was already on board, having assisted in storing the provisions. He walked the gangplank without looking back to land. The Jhirum of the Sea never regretted leaving solid earth and seldom felt the necessity to give it more than a passing thought. The feel of the wood beneath his feet sent chills up his legs which began bending rhythmically with the gentle rolling of the boat. The sails set and lanyards cast, the active crew began to join their minds to drive their ship as well as to sense the remote threat.

Momentarily Shwaren felt the boat drift gently from the dock, the sail turned to deflect the oncoming sea breeze. Then suddenly the drift ended and the boat surged into the breakers driven by the magic of a dozen Jhirum stationed around the railing. Salt spray flew into the air prickling at his skin. Already, even though focused on the task of pushing the ship forward and away from the dock, Shwaren could sense through their joined magic, the remote but sharp pang that was at the heart of this voyage.

Shwaren, at the wheel urged the boat slightly to the south. He had determined to start by following the coast to see if the sense grew stronger in that direction. The wind now caught the sails and the ship listed gently and surged ahead. Several of the linked Jhirum severed their connection and began moving about the deck, adjusting lines and securing items not previously stowed as they cleared the breakers and moved off into the rolling sea.

CHAPTER 5 POWER UNITED

Fenly's group had traveled at a quick pace in the warm summer air for two days, arriving near the swamp as the sun was just setting. They chose to sleep some distance from the swamp to avoid the ill feelings that emanated from it continually. After sunrise they walked the short distance to the swamp. The stand of trees appeared in the early morning light, weeping rather than standing, their branches mere skeletons nearly bereft of leaves. What leaves that remained were a ghostly white in the new sun, curled in upon themselves in feeble attempts at self preservation.

At this distance Fenly's stomach was already beginning to clench from the sense of wrongness which emanated from the direction of the dying trees. As they grew closer the feeling began to build to the point of nausea. Glancing at the rest of the group they all looked distressed. Legolan was looking like a trapped animal. Ashmere, however, had already noticed his distress and gone to comfort him.

Nearly in the exact spot where Fenly had found him those many weeks ago when he first came to consult with him, stood Nomber, though this time with the company of perhaps thirty adults that made up the bulk of his tribe. With the addition of Fenly's group they numbered nearly seventy Jhirum, an august gathering the likes of which had not been seen in the lives of any of those present.

Fenly greeted Nomber somberly. Nomber's brow barely rose out of its scowl for a moment before furrowing again. They each new that the task ahead would not be easy and that should they fail the blight might continue to grow unchecked.

Since it was Nomber's territory he assumed the leadership of the combined group. "We shall space ourselves around the entire perimeter of the swamp. It is not so large that this will weaken our connection."

Tandeir however would not be dissuaded from her questions. "Your objective is to force this back under the earth? Are you certain this is the best approach? Have you studied the power of the swamp closely?"

Nomber frowned briefly, clearly impatient to be on with the work at hand but calmly replied, "I have personally studied this evil for weeks, others have also explored it. We cannot be certain of anything, but based on our past results we feel that this is the best approach, at least for the time being."

Jarine, Nomber's daughter approached the two. "We have already tried to cleanse the swamp and all of us have spent days studying it. My father has spent the most time here and I think has come up with the best approach."

The rest of the Bagnog had already begun to disperse around the grove and the dark black pool, which seemed to give back no reflection of the sickened trees overhead.

Tandeir studied father and daughter for a moment as if weighing their judgment then smiled in reassurance. "If you have already spent so much time studying the swamp I am sure that you would know best."

After a moment of hesitation the Natec began to disperse as well settling into positions almost equally spaced around the perimeter of the dark water. As each one sat they went silent, staring calmly at the dark pool. In the silence their magic strength began to link. Fenly could sense each of the Jhirum individually for a brief moment before they merged into one. A tingling sensation flowed around his body with the growth of their combined power and awareness, as the group grew tighter together.

He relaxed somewhat as the nausea faded under the strength of their magic, but his relief was brief as their heightened sensitivity made the vileness all that more palpable. A battle ensued between the increased sensitivity to and awareness of the vile presence and the increase in their strength.

The sensations continued ebbing and flowing from the euphoria of strength and heightened awareness to a gut wrenching nausea brought on by this increased awareness and sensitivity to the evil presence.

Slowly, however, he could feel their combined energy forming a blanket over the swamp, coming together with a combined pressure to push the vileness back below the surface.

Suddenly in the midst of their heightened awareness a sharp pain ran through the group, the blanket faltered and weakened. It was as if, collectively the entire group's attention was drawn away from the task at hand. It was clear that the distraction arose not from the swamp but from an entirely different source.

Before the joining was entirely broken however, Ashmere and Nomber joined together to bring the group back to the immediate task, though with difficulty since the remote pain remained in all of their awareness. Fenly shook himself to clear his head as the blanket built and strengthened to the point where the dark water began to recede again.

After what seemed like days, but was in fact less than the passing of morning, the last vestige of the darkness disappeared. Fenly noticed that the nausea was gone and the air seemed to be fresher than a moment before. Immediately the group broke their connection. Fenly flopped unceremoniously onto his back breathing heavily. He could hear others around him also collapsing to the ground as well.

Nomber however forced himself erect as he inspected the area. The water was still there though now clear and clean. Though he too was exhausted Fenly could see the look of satisfaction in his friend's tired features.

After almost an hour of no one moving or speaking, one by one they began to stand and slowly regroup at the side of the now pure swamp. The mood however, was subdued, not jubilant. Instead they met each other with questioning eyes and murmured inquiries.

A young Natec approaching Fenly voiced the collective question simply, "What was that?"

Fenly shook his head. "It felt like another threat, but what and where I cannot say."

Nomber's tired features furrowed once more. "It seemed almost as if it came from the sky, but I have never felt such a threat from there. It was apparently, only our collective sensitivity that allowed us to detect it as I have not felt it before."

"But from the sky?" questioned Phalean, one of Nomber's tribe. "I have never even heard in stories of a threat from the sky, how is that possible? Even storms do not show themselves directly from overhead as this did."

Fenly shook his head. "I have no answers, but I feel we will have to think about this another time when we are not exhausted."

Nomber nodded agreement. "In the meantime we have accomplished a great thing here and I thank you all. I think that the swamp will now recede and the land return to health. It is clear that this would not have been possible without our combined strength. Go and replenish yourselves at our spring if you wish. Remain one, though distant."

With that, the historical gathering was over, though there were still frequent almost involuntary glances at the sky. Fenly could see nothing there, however, apart from the dark blue of a clear early afternoon, dotted here and there with billowing white clouds.

Fenly walked slowly in the direction of the Bagnog's spring since he had consumed most of his water right before the joining. The spring was not more than a few minutes' walk from the former black swamp. He could understand why the Bagnog had been so concerned. As he knelt by the spring, which gurgled quietly from a small copse of trees, and drank he could feel the warmth spread throughout his body contrasting with the coolness of the water on his lips. With the warmth his stiff muscles began to relax.

One by one the Natec drank at the spring and turned to head for their home territory, spreading out as they went each with their own destination in mind.

Fenly lingered upon the same path as Ashmere a while as they both began their journey back through the valley. She knew that he was troubled, or they would have parted their own ways as the others had.

As they walked Fenly spoke, "How did that intrusion feel to you?"

She answered uncertainly, "It felt remote but sharp. I have not felt anything like it before."

"It seemed like it was unapproachable. Even when our attention was drawn to it I could not discern it any more clearly than when we first sensed it," he responded.

She nodded her agreement. "There is no doubt that whatever it is, it is new to us. I do not see how we can respond to something of which we know nothing and which we can sense only when in a joined group?"

"My fear is that it will not remain so remote for long," he answered, glancing involuntarily at the sky. "Perhaps another day we will join with just a few others and see if we can sense it and discover more. But for now we must regain our strength." As he said this he veered off their mutual path and set out on his own.

Ashmere likewise turned slightly unto a new path toward food and her own thoughts only glancing briefly as Fenly's form disappeared into the shadows of the towering trees. Perhaps their extremely heightened sensitivity had allowed them to glimpse a presence that was too far away to ever affect them. For now the questions would have to remain unanswered.

CHAPTER 6 DAY OF DARKNESS

Two days after the Natec and Bagnog had accomplished their cleansing; Endmere awoke to a morning cast in shades of gray. A low mist hung over the peaks of the mountains obscuring the valleys below and everything beyond a stone's throw in any direction. This was not a day for major travel though in fact the fog presented no real obstacle to his magic enhanced sight. Today he would continue to rest and contemplate. He recalled briefly the odd sensation of several nights before, though it seemed of little immediate interest. He was simply ready for some time to focus inward rather than labor on the maintenance of the mountain range and its inhabitants.

Heading back to the spring, he refilled his bowl and was soon lost in magic enhanced thought, searching within himself for peace and calm. His drift into revere, however, was interrupted by that pang of unease again, though this time somewhat stronger. He decided to explore it further and reached out to examine it more closely. Unlike sickness, or other blights, however, which could be drawn nearer through focus and identified as to their source and location, this sensation remained distant and indistinct despite his best efforts to bring to bear his full power.

Frustrated after a long time of fruitless seeking he broke off his examination as well as his reverie and decided to seek instead someone with which to discuss this unusual sensation. He decided at once to seek the counsel of Cragen the oldest member of his tribe and the most likely to have encountered something so unusual in the past.

Endmere reached out for Cragen and found his aura two valleys to the east eating the meager breakfast that would start his day. Endmere touched his aura and received a response that Cragen understood that they were to meet. He set out immediately down into the valley lost in mist.

Back in the shallow valley of the Natec, just after breakfast as Fenly reached a small knot of trees, a pain split his skull. Sharp and clear, this was no distant and indistinct sensation, this was an attack, but from where? He shook his head to try to clear it. Opening himself to the pain, he realized that it indeed was still the same sensation as before, only now grown suddenly strong. Involuntarily he looked up at the sky. It was now clear where the threat emanated from, though nothing was visible in the vast expanse of blue.

Shwaren's boat had sailed a day south and east and then had turned and headed north and west, trying to determine in what direction the sensation that they could feel in the distance grew stronger. But it seemed that no matter how they turned the sensation grew stronger, as if it was closing in on them from every direction. Winfew was at the helm, his jaw clenched against the ever increasing pain. Suddenly the pain stabbed out even harder totally breaking his concentration and his connection with the other Jhirum that were driving the boat through the waves.

Shwaren who had been resting near the forward mast looked toward the tiller as he felt the boat lose momentum. He could see Winfew grabbing his head then several of the other Jhirum around the boat also grabbed their heads, some dropping to their knees, obviously in pain. He jumped to his feet and rushed to the nearest Jhirum. "What is wrong, what is happening?" But before the Jhirum could answer the pain stabbed at his own brain even unlinked with the others. As he grabbed his head he looked to the sky.

As Endmere descended the last slope to meet with Cragen the pinprick turned to a pain beyond the point that it could be blocked out or ignored. Glancing involuntarily upward into gray nothingness, his concern increased and he called to Cragen. The old man was bent over on the ground, his eyes glazed. Clearly he felt the same stabbing vileness.

As he approached him, there was an almost imperceptible flash through the fog, gone as quickly as it had come, then nothing but a blinding pain that felt as if it were rending their heads in two. As Endmere dropped to his knees in pain the fog lit up in a brilliant flash. Shading their eyes they stared at each other, dumbfounded, but before they could speak the ground heaved under their feet, throwing them both down the mountain.

Though caught unprepared the heaving ground was not by itself strange to them for these mountains were new and still growing, often through the violence of earthquakes. They gathered themselves to their knees but did not stand, instead waiting to see if there were more shocks to follow. It was from this position that they began hearing what at first sounded like large raindrops. Nomber strained to see in the direction that the sound was coming from. At first he saw nothing but the gray fog. Then streaks began to appear in the fog almost as if someone were rapidly moving the end of a stick through smoke. Before he could voice a question sharp thuds coalesced out of the distant pattering followed immediately by the site of small objects striking the ground with great force, burying themselves or ricocheting off of boulders. A shower of small rocks the size of hail was beginning to rain down on them.

They scrambled for cover under a large tree as the pellets hissed through the fog. Many of them sizzled and smoked as they reached earth. Small curls of smoke began rising from many of the impact sites. Both Maestic had shielded themselves now with their magic, which kept the projectiles from pummeling them.

"What is going on?" Endmere asked his voice unusually tense.

"I do not know? What could cause rock to fall from the sky?" Just then a larger rock crashed through the trees smashing into the ground, throwing dirt in every direction.

Recovering from their stunned immobility they both leapt up and began moving randomly through the trees extinguishing embers which threatened to burst into flames in the dry leaves. Endmere stared for a moment at a small crater from which curled a small wisp of smoke. Then he covered it over with dirt and looked up to see a dozen more just like it all around him. They continued this futile effort despite the dawning realization that there were thousands of these rocks falling all over the mountains.

Endmere was just stamping out a small fire that had already erupted when a rumble like thunder came echoing through the mountains, followed by a sudden gust of wind, which whipped the fog around, blowing it rapidly from the peaks.

Though separated by some distance, both Cragen and Endmere stopped their frantic rush to extinguish the small fires and looked at each other. Endmere could feel through their connection that Cragen and he had a common thought. What next?

Endmere's usually stolid character felt shaken to the core. What possibly could have caused all of these strange events in such a short period of time? There was, however, no time to contemplate the source. He looked around him at the swirls of smoke and immediately resumed his frantic rush to stamp out the fires.

While he worked Endmere ran through different possibilities in his mind. This was clearly no simple earthquake, but nothing he could think of would cause all of these phenomena at one time. Had they taken the time they would have seen the smoke beginning to curl up from their forest in all directions as finer particles and falling dust began to replace the larger projectiles.

The Jhirum of the Sea witnessed the mysterious event from a better vantage point. The boat had little time to drift in its now aimless course before they saw the streak of light leaving a trail of smoke in the northeastern sky. As it disappeared below the horizon they saw a large flash, which seemed to encompass the whole horizon. Shwaren quickly shielded his eyes, but could not fully ward off the searing heat that blasted at their bodies.

When the light faded Shwaren looked at his hands and then at the other Jhirum, they all had what looked like sunburn, accept where their hands or some object had stood between them and the flash. Though the flash of heat was gone his skin continued to burn. He took a couple of steps toward the railing thinking of nothing but extinguishing the flame in his body by diving into the waves, but before he could jump, he heard a rumbling coming from the earth. Looking up he saw a large wave approaching them from the direction of the shore. Behind the wave a huge black cloud was building into the sky and expanding toward them.

The pain of the injured earth continued to sear through him, but recognizing the threat of the wave to their unguided ship, Shwaren quickly linked minds with Winfew and a couple of the other crew members who were not totally dumbstruck by what was happening, to bring the boat about to face the rapidly approaching wave. It crashed into them with fury, casting them up, almost pointed straight at the sky and then down at the depths of the sea. The broadness of their boat helped them as they road over the wave like a cork rather than boring into it. By the time they had emerged from the valley of water in the wake of the tsunami the black cloud was nearly upon them, moving impossibly fast. They strengthened their link, gathering in the last of the stunned crew to ward their ship as best they could against this unknown monster.

After throwing up their shield there was nothing to do but watch, though his head split with the pain of the violated earth. Suddenly Shwaren felt their protective barrier press back against him. With horror he realized that this cloud was not made up of smoke, or even dirt so much as it was composed of sizable rocks. The first impact was rocks ranging from larger than a man's head down to pebbles, thrown at impossible speeds against their magical barricade. Collectively the linked Jhirum flinched against the barrage. Many fell down to the deck with the concussion, but most of the deadly projectiles were deflected.

Their shield however, could not hold back the entire weight of that deadly cloud and soon smaller rocks began whizzing through the air past his head, striking the deck and side of the ship, some leaving holes and smoke streams in their wake. The ocean sizzled as the superheated rocks pelted its surface.

Just when he thought the worst might be over, the wind hit them with a fury that tore through what remained of their magical cloak, instantly stripping the sails from the masts and threatening to topple even their low profile ship. Then the second wave hit them, skulking out of the black cloud, catching them unaware. This one born of the tearing wind rather than the shaking earth was nearly as large as the first. Only the fact that they were fairly close to land saved them. The wave did not have sufficient space to build to its true potential before encountering their boat, which was like a twig cast on this violent ocean. Climbing skyward again and then back into the depths it seemed that they might touch the sea floor before turning to rise again. Shwaren, now on his stomach clung desperately to the railing. They were spun and propelled along behind the massive wall of water for what seemed like an eternity.

Suddenly feeling panic through their tattered link Shwaren looked to his left, Gair was clinging to the railing as water washed over the ship. His heart racing he ran to help him, but could only watch as he was carried beyond his reach and into the tortured sea. Others lay on the deck, dazed and confused, in the deadly calm that blanketed them along with the warm snow of ash and dust that was now drifting from the sky.

Only Nomber and his tribe were closer to the impact than Fenly and his group. Fenly barely had time to glance up at the blazing streak in the sky before it crashed to earth. The only thing that saved him from almost instant death in spite of the strength of his magic was that the pain in his head reached him before the concussion, driving him to the ground in a small hollow. A brilliant flash and searing heat ripped over his prostrate body leaving his back tender and red. Just as he started to push himself up the ground rocked with a loud groan, shaking the trees. A large fracture opened in the ground to his left swallowing trees and grass.

Despite his shock he called on his magic to defend himself from anything else that might be thrown at him. Well that he did, for when he again looked in the direction of the impact a massive black cloud was racing toward him at unbelievable speed. Without hesitation he lowered himself face down in the depression, covered his head and put all his strength into his magical shield. Just as he did so he was hit with the first fragments, he could feel stones striking his shield and glancing off. A deafening roar pounded at his ears as debris was whipped past his body by a hot wind that turned the sand into a flesh-rending gale. He heard the groaning and cracking of broken trees, snapping or ripped from the ground by their roots. With his magic he clung to the earth fighting the pull of the roaring wind. Fractions of a second later the small copse of trees nearby fell around him like sticks dropped on a fire. Covered by the trees, the remnants of the blast blew over him leaving the air unbreathably hot and choked with dust.

His magic though weakening continued to offer protection from the heat and created a shield around his body, though he was already scorched. The blast from the impact took only seconds to blow past him but all was darkness in his mind for what seemed like an eternity. At last, however he managed to lift his head and scrape the dust from his eyes and nose so that he could begin to breathe normally and take in his predicament.

Fortunately, the strength of the blast had stripped the trees and actually prevented sustained fire, which could have finished him off. Instead he looked up through a tangle of dark trunks at a few patches of murky gray sky. His body was aching and raw from heat, but seemed to be intact as he delicately moved his limbs and tried to work free so that he could at least move into a more comfortable position. It was clear that he would have to work for some time to clear himself of the entanglement.

He could still hear the occasional leaden thud as rocks fell from the sky and buried themselves in the ground. Smaller fragments also still pelted the tangle of trees. He could not keep everything out, but between the protection of the tree trunks and what was left of his magic he managed to deflect the worst of the projectiles. The larger fragments diminished as smaller particles, ash and dust settled heavily around him, a warm gray snow.

Though through the lens of history, no one would count them lucky this day, it was in fact only the chance fact that they had completed healing the swamp that saved a few of the lives of Nomber's tribe. For it was directly on the previous vileness that the meteorite struck. It was also fortunate that it was only a small object, or they would have instantly been obliterated.

After Nomber and Fenly's groups had pushed the contamination of the swamp back into the earth, Nomber and his tribe had dispersed from the area for the first time in several weeks. They were, however, still much too close. Too close to avoid the tremendous concussion as well as too close to avoid direct contact with the worst of the discharge from the blast site. The blast immediately annihilated half of the Bagnog, particularly because of their exhausted state after the cleansing.

Time would prove those to be the fortunate ones. The remaining number would often wish they had been the ones to parish. The only reaction time they had was what was afforded them by the prescient sense of an attack that grew suddenly to unbearable levels.

Nomber did not turn, did not look, or run. There was no time. The pain brought him to his knees facing away from the blast. He was in a wooded area just the other side of a small knoll. It was this that spared him the direct fury of the impact.

Searing heat washed over his body as he blanketed himself in his protective magic. He could hear trees and bushes burst into flame around him. The ground heaved under him, throwing him down the hill. As he rolled he glanced around at the nightmare landscape of burning vegetation and animals, ignited like living torches. He caught only a glimpse of the black wall headed at him before he was struck with wind as solid as rock, snapping trees like twigs and throwing them into the air. One huge, ancient tree rolled to a stop just in front of him, turning from a threat to his life into a shield from the next wave, comprised of boulders thrown through the air like pebbles, crashing to the ground with the snapping of broken trees. Along with the boulders came a literal wave of dirt and smaller stones which swept over him burying him in blackness.

As with Fenly, the blast was gone in an instant, leaving behind only the skeletons of trees, animals and some of the widely scattered Bagnog.

Slowly Nomber regained consciousness. As he awoke he choked and gasped for air through the dust clogging every pore of his body. The weight of dirt piled on top of him would have prevented him from even moving without the aid of his magic, which both kept a small space clear around him and gave him the strength to push against it.

The taste in his mouth was foul, not of dirt and charcoal, but something far worse. He dug and pushed his way up through the layers of dirt, ash and stones until his head poked through the surface like an oversized gopher.

He scraped at his eyes and nose finally clearing enough of the coating to gain a breath and the first site of his transfigured world. All around him was black whether from scorching or from the incredibly dark soot which seemed to cover everything.

He groped to understand what had happened, but found no clues. He reached out with his sense and could barely discern a couple of life forms that he could identify as the remnants of his tribe. The only positive thing about the layer of dirt as tall as he was that had been deposited was that it had extinguished most of the fires, though smoke and ash swirled in the air as thick as the thickest fog.

He struggled to gain enough of a purchase in the shifting powder to pull himself free. Soot and ash clung to his body everywhere as he stood erect for the first time. His mind reeled trying to grasp what could be the cause of such a cataclysm.

He climbed slowly in the debris, which he sank into nearly up to his knees, toward the top of the knoll where he hoped to gain a better vantage and perhaps some answers. He found his way blocked by a tangle of stripped poles that used to be trees. Only the fact that few if any branches remained and that half of the trees were buried under newly deposited dirt, allowed him slow passage.

Looking up from toiling over several entangled trunks he gazed down on a dark valley cast in the gloom of the towering black cloud overhead. This had been his valley that he had cared for and which was now a blackened crater.

Nothing below him could have survived. He knew this by sight and by his sense, which normally was like listening to a gathering of many people in a nearby clearing, a constant low babble of life force. Here, there was almost complete silence. He could neither see the far side or the bottom of this crater, only the near edge. He then turned frantically, reaching out in other directions for signs life and survivors of his tribe. Then all he knew became searing pain and darkness.

Meanwhile, Endmere and Cragen continued to try to put out the small fires that had erupted all across the mountains. Though many of the trees were stripped of leaves, Endmere soon realized that whatever had happened had done more damage elsewhere and that most of his distress was the pain that the earth itself was feeling.

Remembering Cragen, he glanced around, finding the old man busily running about the forest trying to quench fires just as he was. Though old, Cragen was still as strong as the mountains that spawned him and the seemingly endless task had not daunted him.

After confirming that Cragen was fine, Endmere surveyed what little he could see from the deep valley they were in. Looking up to the top of the mountains he could see gaps in the tree line where exposed forest giants had been toppled. What force had caused such a shock wave and such pain in the earth Endmere could not imagine, but he knew that the earth had been changed in an instant, and not for the better.

Shwaren finally came back to his knees as the boat bobbed aimlessly in the now quiet waters. As soon as his head cleared he realized that there would have to be a return surge of water to replace what had been pushed out to sea and that they had better be prepared. Reaching out with his mind to his remaining crewmates he slowly gathered their scattered attention to focus on bringing the boat about to face what would surely come.

Come it did, in the form of a monster swell borne out of the deep ocean, born of the need to replace the huge volume of water washed away in the giant waves. Though not as steep as the parent, the child still came on with a fury, a long rolling wave of massive volume. This time, however, their collective minds controlled the boat, facing the wave and riding up over it with little trouble.

With this wave past the crew began to rise, though still in a daze, lacking understanding. The Jhirum of the Sea, were the few who had witnessed from a distance the entire episode, so understanding came more quickly to them than to the land-bound Jhirum. It was clear to Shwaren that an object from the heavens had crashed into the earth somewhere inland. As his crew began to gather around him with similar stunned expressions on all of their faces the realization suddenly dawned on him, they had been in about the safest place possible, but their brethren back in the village were in one of the worst possible locations. Almost at the instant this thought crossed his mind, others reached out to connect to Shwaren.

With the thought instantly shared with all the crew they were immediately galvanized with the same realization. Scattering to positions around the boat without any discussion Shwaren guided them to swing the boat about despite the continued echoes of the monster wave. He hardened his mind against all the questions and uncertainties and began to drive the boat back toward their village with as much speed as their magic would allow.

Those not directing the ship began to hurry about the ship looking for leaks caused by the pummeling of the rocks from the sky.

CHAPTER 7 SURVIVORS

Fenly began extracting himself from the jumble of trees, squeezing through openings nearly small enough to be bars in a prison. As he worked his way toward freedom, his mind turned to his mate. Pausing in his climb, he reached out for her with his mind. He flinched involuntarily at the incredible silence that lurked immediately below the continuing scream from the earth. Picking through the silence he began to detect small, isolated signs of life, mostly small plants and animals surviving in protected areas. Then he detected it, the thread of life of one of his own. Thin and wavering to the point of being impossible to place more of an identity than that it was a Jhirum. The weakness of the thread caused his heart to pound in his chest but he forced his concerns aside to focus on the task of freeing himself from the tangle.

As he was about to stick his head out of the last branches, the silent fall of dust and ash which blocked out nearly all vision was disrupted by a series of high pitched whistles followed by loud thuds. Though Fenly could not see what was happening small fireballs that had been thrown to the heavens with the initial impact began to pour from the sky, some no larger than the end of a finger, others the size of a man's fist, all in flame as they lashed out at the raw scar that covered the land.

Where piles of trees that were not completely vaporized in the first impact were touched, fires ignited sending new plumes of smoke into the already black sky. A small rock fell just behind him. The impact shifted the trees dangerously, threatening to pin him for good. Fortunately, by the time they had resettled a slightly larger opening had appeared in the last bit of tangle that remained between him and freedom. Wriggling through the newly opened gateway he emerged into a netherworld of warm snowflakes composed of ash and dust descending on a blasted landscape where moments before life had teamed.

Looking in every direction yielded the same image, tangled trees, sandblasted and scorched earth, everything in shades of gray and black, including the sky. He had to duck back under the last tree in the pile to avoid being pummeled by the smaller projectiles that now rained down like deadly hail. One of these was large and hot enough to ignite the pile of trees he was in, forcing him from his protection.

His mind swirled in confusion. He could not grasp the obvious fact that his world had been destroyed, altered beyond recognition. He stood there not knowing where to look, or what to do. Only the weak call of the Jhirum's thread of life stirred him to action. He turned with as much certainty as he could muster in the direction from which the thread issued and set off immediately, his heart pounding in his chest.

Where there had been scrub fields on the rounded hills of this region the going was completely clear with the exception of the concealed ruts and holes covered now in the ash snow. Breathing was difficult in the putrid air, choked with smoke and sulfur. Several times he was brought to a complete stop by coughing fits which brought out nearly black phlegm, but he forced himself on, coughing and gasping. His seared magical sense guided him, for his eyes were of little use in the blackness that had fallen like a basket trap on a frightened rabbit. His eyes teared as the stench burned them and the ash invaded every orifice. He was soon walking in near knee deep powder; snow that burned. He could see fires blazing in every direction casting a ghostly glow through the nearly impenetrable atmosphere. The only fortunate consequence of the strength of the initial blast was that all the underbrush had been vaporized instantly so there was no means for the fires to spread quickly or broadly.

After walking for a short time he could sense the life thread more clearly, he was now certain it was Ashmere. Though it was clear her condition was not good, she was at least alive. His pace quickened as he reached out to comfort her. He topped a barren knoll, which looked down on the valley and cliff where they usually began their day, though it was an unrecognizable wasteland now.

The thread came from a cluster of fallen trees, lined up in perfect rows as if combed into place by some giant. Hurrying now, his heart in his throat, he reached the jumble as he realized that it was the remains of the copse of trees, including the huge evergreen where they frequently bedded together. Ashmere had apparently returned here after eating, to renew herself with a nap. Calling out now with his mind, but receiving no response he honed in on the spot where she must lie.

Just beyond the pile of trees he saw her body. Covered in ash, it was merely an undistinguished lump in the blanket of gray but his magic could not be fooled. Hurrying over, he quickly brushed away the dust from her face. The hair on her head was mostly singed away, but she seemed not to be otherwise damaged on the surface. Reaching in to her with his sense he found her in pain with some broken ribs and internal bleeding, but not in danger if attended too quickly. She too must have been able to throw up a shield of magic in time to ward off the worst effects of the blast.

First attending to the bleeding, he carefully sealed the wound and began to knit the ribs. Once the most urgent damage was healed he reached again for her mind and found her there waiting for him. Though not fully conscious she had become aware of his ministrations, but lacked the strength to pull herself out of her slumber. He left her there to rest and recover before trying to revive her.

His hands shook with the effort of healing Ashmere and the relief of the tension he felt when he did not know if she lived. While he waited he began to search with his sense for others of his tribe as well as animals and plants that had survived. While no strong responses greeted him, he could sense in the distance a small group of individuals. Some of his fellows must have found each other. At least they were not alone. He sensed Ashmere stirring in the back of his mind and glancing down saw her begin to open her eyes. She slowly tried to sit, cringing as the bruises around her damaged ribs made themselves known. Fenly supported her as the next flinch came from the pain the damaged land inflicted on her sense.

Spitting dust from her lips she asked, "What happened and what is that screaming in my head?" Fenly paused and looking around at the wasted landscape. Following his gaze Ashmere stared unbelieving at the moonscape that had been their beloved, lush home.

"I don't know what caused this, but the land has been nearly destroyed. There are a few of our clan gathered near the cliff. If you are able, I think we should try to make our way there."

She sat dumbfounded for a moment clearly trying to come to terms with the horrible truth. Finally she glanced again at Fenly looking for reassurance and then gingerly pushed herself up, leaning heavily on her mate. "I am fine, I too would like to get to the wall, and I need its strength to complete my healing."

Setting off at a measured pace with Ashmere leaning on him for support they made their way in the direction of the wall and the group of remaining tribe members, all the while searching with their sense for other signs of life.

With each step Fenly's mood darkened. They traveled over a once teaming field without him sensing a single living creature. A sudden tingle at the back of his mind turned his head. He could just sense a small life struggling against the suffocating dust.

"Can you stand?" He asked Ashmere without explanation. She nodded uncertainly.

Fenly immediately dropped her arm and bounded a couple of steps to the left. There was something still living here. He knelt and carefully scooped away the light top layer of dust and ash. Finally his finger brushed a soft furry body. He could still sense its struggle for breath as he gently scooped the rodent out of its tomb. The small body did not at first move so he gently stroked it and infused a little of his weakened magic into the fragile body.

With a shake of its head the small mouse began to breath. Fenly gently set it back down in the dust. It looked around, unsure of what to do next then scurried off, burrowing through the ash, toward a tangle of fallen branches. Fenly could not contain a small smile. In such destruction, the smallest life seemed a great blessing. But the smile faded as he hurried back to Ashmere's side.

As he retook Ashmere's arm he shook his head. "One small life, but how many lost?"

Ashmere nodded, a small shiver running through her body. Fenly could not tell if it was from the thought of all the lost lives or because the sun had seemed to vanish, no longer giving warmth and less light than a half moon.

Fenly guided Ashmere on. He could tell that she leaned on him less and seemed to be regaining her strength as they went. Suddenly his foot failed to find solid earth and he lurched sideways letting go of Ashmere as he fell into the powder.

"Are you alright?" Ashmere asked her concern clear on her face.

"Yes, it's just this powder that covers everything. You can't tell when there is a hole or drop off. We are going to have to be really careful or we will break a leg."

Fenly stood and dusted himself off before taking Ashmere's arm again and resuming their trek, though more slowly and cautiously this time.

The desperate reality of the situation sank into Fenly's sole like the chill of a midwinter's night. The berry bushes were gone, where they had feasted only yesterday. No clean water flowed anywhere along their path. At best, ash choked mud pools formed, where clean springs had emerged from far underground.

By the time they arrived at the edge of what had once been the forest near the base of the cliff wall they were panting from the exertion of pushing through the deep powder. Now with the trees nearly all on the ground they had to slow their pace further to climb over piles of broken trees aligned perfectly with the direction of the blast. It was slow going, particularly with Ashmere's bruised body, but they knew they were now near to the small group from their tribe. Even as they walked Fenly could feel his magic weakening from all the use he had made of it already.

As they approached the now choked stream that led away from the cliff, Fenly could see four tribe members huddled by the stream intent on one another's injuries. Fenly's remaining magic helped him identify them as Genlie, a young adult, Minere, one of the older female children, Tandeir, an elder female of the tribe and Pendolin a contemporary of Ashmere and Fenly.

As they approached he could see that Tandeir was attending to Pendolin, who lay on the ground, eyes closed. Meanwhile, Genlie and Minere crouched together, inspecting each other's wounds. Minere sobbed quietly, occasionally looking around bleakly at the blasted land.

Ashmere sat down beside Genlie and Minere, while Fenly moved to see what Pendolin's condition was. He could sense the healing extension of Tandeir's sense as she sought out and healed wounds that she found. It appeared that one side of Pendolin's body had been seared badly, but there were other injuries as well, internal and critical.

Tandeir looked up at him and asked. "Please bring strength from the cliff so that I can sustain the healing that is needed. Pendolin is in bad shape, she has several broken bones and internal injuries."

Fenly moved quickly to comply. "We all can use some fresh strength to face what must be faced."

The cliff was only a stone's throw from where they stood. His heart skipped a beat as it became clear that the concussion had loosened large sections of the cliff face bringing it down in piles of rubble at the base. His heart sank further as he realized that the spring, which issued from the cliff, no longer trickled down the exposed face, but came out at the bottom of one of these piles of rubble.

Fenly hesitated, unsure of where to extract the rock powder, which enhanced their magic. Through long history it had been told that it was the combination of the water from a deep source, which contained concentrated magical essence with the cliff rock of this particular location, which gave the cliff its particular strength. Now the nature of this combination had changed. How it would change the effectiveness of their ritual he could not guess.

Leaning down to where the spring emerged from the rubble, he chipped off some powder from the rocks fallen there. After gathering them he swept the top of the pool with his hand trying to find some clear water. The finer ash had thoroughly mixed with the spring however, so after several attempts he just scooped some of the gray sludge into the bowl.

He stood and stared for a moment before turning back toward the small band of Jhirum.

Without taking any water himself he handed Tandeir the Yoruba grimly. She looked at the gray sludge, clearly uncertain herself what the effect would be, but needing to move with haste to aid the stricken Pendolin. Drinking a small amount from the bowl she nearly choked on the small pieces of grit and dust contained in the water. All the gathered Jhirum paused to look at her and measure its effect. Tandeir could feel the glimmer of the magic begin to fill her veins, but then fade before its full measure could be felt.

They all sensed the weakness of the effect and the concern radiating from Tandeir. "It has almost no power. Are you certain you gathered it from the right spot?"

"I am certain of nothing. The cliff face has fallen where our spring was. The water is still there but I had to get it from a pool near the fallen rocks."

Tandeir stared at the empty bowl before handing it back to Fenly, "perhaps if you try another spot?" She did not wait for his response but turned once again to Pendolin to continue what healing she could with the small addition to her strength.

Fenly took the bowl from her and stared, searching the residue in the bowl for an answer. "I will try some different locations in the jumble, perhaps I have just picked a rock fallen from an inert section." His confidence all but gone he turned and walked back in the direction of the cliff.

All but Tandeir and Pendolin turned to watch his return to the broken cliff with a new and more fundamental concern added to their sorry state.

Fenly climbed carefully over the detritus, sampling here and there, bits of dust and small rivulets. Occasionally he would get a glimmer of the old sensation, but never more than that. Finally, nearly frantic he scrambled to the top of the pile of broken rock. He reached out to touch the newly exposed cliff face and chipped away in several places. Here no hint of magic existed.

He could feel his stomach turning over. He sat down heavily on one of the jagged boulders. Never had he been without magic. The loss was more than the loss of a limb, or a loved one. It was nearly the loss of who he was. He stared down at the few feeble samples he had collected suddenly feeling more alone than he ever had. He fought down rising panic, but knew he needed to be near his tribe members. Standing up in a daze he climbed back down the defile and through the tangle of trees back to his small group. All the while he tried to stave off panic, knowing that they would all be looking to him for stability and strength.

Those left waiting did not have to ask, they still had enough of their sense to know from a distance his failure and their potential doom. His legs shaking he distributed what he had of the feeble poultice.

Trying to keep the shaking out of his voice he turned to Genlie. "Where were you when the blast struck?" Genlie looked away from the still quietly sobbing Minere. "I was just north of here, not far from where the cliff disappears."

"Were there any others near you that are not here?"

"No, I was alone and I was not aware of any accept those you see here."

In turn he asked the same question of the others as to where they had been when the blast struck and where there might be other survivors. Already with the effort of their own survival and the healing that they had done, his sense was diminished to the point that he could hardly detect life beyond the boundaries of the group seated together.

Pendolin finally began to stir for the first time. Fenly watched her restless movements and the creasing of her brow each time a stab of pain shot through her body. Once again steeling himself, he shifted the discussion, "What should we do now? There must be other survivors."

Ashmere nodded. "Perhaps we should fan out over the remains of the valley to look for other survivors in the morning. It is already too late for us to accomplish much today."

Genlie looked around the group anxiously. "But what if there is another explosion? We do not know what caused this? It could happen again."

Tandeir paused before responding. She looked exhausted from her work healing Pendolin. "I do not know what we can do if there is another blast. I think that none of us would survive in our current state."

"Shouldn't we find shelter?" Genlie asked the strain in his voice clear.

All of them looked around for a while at the bleak landscape as if asking it for guidance before Fenly finally responded. "Where would we go? The cliff is the only shelter nearby and you see what happened there. I do not think it is a good idea to be too close to the rocks."

The others nodded agreement except for Minere who suddenly stood with fire in her eyes. "Should we not spend more time trying to find our magical source before doing anything else? What can we do to find or help others without magic?"

Ashmere shook her head. "We still have our eyes and our ears. There may be Jhirum out there dyeing right now which we must find as soon as possible. We have no way of knowing how long or if we will be able to find the water of life."

Minere turned on her, astonishment in her eyes. "What do you mean if? Surely all we have to do is find the right spot again. It might be buried under some rubble but it must still be there." A racking cough stopped her outburst as her body tried to eject the accumulated soot and dust it had inhaled.

Tandeir, still tending to Pendolin looked at Minere. "We do not know that. You may be right but it may take days or weeks for us to find a spot with magic again. Ashmere is right we cannot wait. I will stay behind with Pendolin who cannot be moved at this point. I can continue to search for our magic while you are looking for survivors."

Minere was clearly not happy with this but restrained herself since it was clear she was alone on this issue.

As they settled in to sleep the only benefit of their slowly diminishing magical awareness was the lessening of the pain in their heads from the screaming earth. But the complete quiet, devoid of animal noises, or the constant sense they carried in their heads of life all around them made sleep come slowly. Though they did not often seek physical contact with other Jhirum, tonight they all sought the reassurance of having another body near them. Fenly and Ashmere curled up together, Tandeir stayed cradling Pendolin's head in her lap and Genlie and Minere slept with their backs pressed against each other. But even the closeness could not diminish the sense, when their eyes were closed and calm just beginning to come over them, that they were floating in a void, alone and lost.

CHAPTER 8 THE SEA TAKETH AWAY

The sea continued to roil about the boat as the Jhirum of the Sea fought their way along the coast. The waves were thick with debris which scraped and banged against the hull of the boat. Shwaren was barely aware of the noise however, only occasionally taking notice of a particularly large piece of debris that might endanger the ship. His mind was on driving the boat as quickly as possible to their home.

As they drew closer he kept reaching out with his sense to see if he could contact their brethren. However, as they were turning into their bay there had still been no response from the shore.

During the trip the sky had progressed from a murky gray, echoing the color of the sea, to the black of a thunderhead that bore no rain. Instead ash and particles as big as small stones slapped against the deck and splashed in the waves. Some of them hissed and left steam trails. The crew sheltered themselves as best they could while scurrying across the deck to knock any still smoking debris from the deck and into the waves. Their bay was even more choked with debris than the open sea had been. The constant scrape of tree trunks and smaller sticks grated on Shwaren's nerves.

In the preternatural darkness it was impossible to discern the condition of their village, so Shwaren guided their joined magic to reach out to their kin. Silence answered them, a silence so complete that for a few seconds the boat foundered as all concentration left the crew.

Finally Shwaren called them back to their duty and with renewed vigor again focused their efforts on speeding the boat to the dock.

Connected as they were Shwaren could sense the tension and near panic running through the crew. The remaining distance was gained before the shrouded sun had moved perceptibly in the sky, yet it seemed like days had passed to the anxious voyagers.

As the shore took shape out of the darkness, the first thing that was clear was the lack of a dock. Only the last set of posts remained standing sentinel over the wave line.

"Throw out anchors." Shwaren called out without taking his eyes off the shore. Several crew members scrambled to heave the anchors over the side. Because they had sensed no one it should not have been a surprise, but still Shwaren only now was struck by the fact that no one came to greet them. The waves echoed against the hillside as if in call to a people who had left long ago.

Already the two small dinghies that they carried were being lowered over the side and rope ladders dropped. They would have to ferry the crew ashore since not all of them fit in the small boats at one time. Within a few minutes the first wayfarers arrived on the shore and the boats returned to bring the remaining tribe members to their home away from the sea. The first to arrive just stood, staring into the silent hills until the arrival of the final group with Shwaren on board.

As he climbed from the boat into the now docile froth along the rocky shore he assessed his remaining crew. Eighteen of the original twenty stood silently on the shore staring inland. Of these, eight were women and ten men. Seven were older than he, six about his same age and the remainder in varying ages of young adulthood. A good crew for any adventure, but never planned for what was to face them now. His eyes swept past his crew to the broken rocks of the slow incline which rose from the sea and then more steeply to the hills beyond. Tangled amongst the rocks far beyond the normal high tide mark were the remains of the lower hillside and most of their village.

Striking near midday few of their tribe would have been in the higher caves where some of the tribe lived. They would have been near the sea where they belonged and would have been vulnerable both to the initial blast as well as the backwash of the Tsunami. He imagined in his mind how the volume of water, already enormous would have grown in height as the harbor tried to swallow it whole. The result was a surge brought to all but the highest abodes.

He forced the bile that rose in his throat back down with effort and strode hurriedly up the hill, with the realization of what would have happened threatening to overwhelm him and only the desperation to prove himself wrong driving him on.

The rest of the crew stood for a moment waiting his orders until they realized he had completely forgotten them. Finally they fanned out, each toward where their small stone and thatch huts had once stood. Hurrying, but scanning the rocks they walked past for any signs of their former lives. Occasionally some small remnant would catch their eye and they would pause, pick it up, and then hurry on.

Shwaren had lived with his mate and a few family members in one of the lower caves. As he arrived at the mouth of the cave the piles of debris that choked the entrance were evidence enough that his life here was now a part of history. Even so, the need to call out, to reach out with his mind overcame him, and he picked his way into the cave to the point where it was clear that nothing and no one could have survived here. After pausing for a moment with the seaweed and sticks tangled around his ankles, he moved back into the gray light.

Looking out on the dark desolate hill side he could see his crew, like ceremonial statues standing at the site of their former abodes, frozen erect and unbelieving. Through the link of their magic he could barely distinguish his own anguish from that of his crew.

Finally, shaking himself out of his stupor he called to his shipmates, "Come up the hill! We must check the higher ground for survivors."

He then turned and walked from his cave toward the higher levels of the hill where there was less and then no debris, Madrien joined him silently. Suddenly, they both jerked their heads up, staring in the same direction. Life called out to them, panicked and forsaken, but nonetheless life. As one they raced off in the direction of the herald.

It was soon clear that it was Toren the young daughter of Danfere one of the women who had remained behind.

They entered the uppermost cave in a rush that ended in frozen silence as they stared down at the broken child. Tears etched jagged lines down her soot covered cheeks. Her jet black hair was a tangle of twigs and grime. Her clothes were smudged and disheveled. Beyond that she looked whole in every physical respect. But as Shwaren stared into her eyes he could see there the reflection of the destruction she must have witnessed.

He gently reached out to her mind, but she cowered and closed herself off. Then he gently reached down and picked her up. Though she was not a baby she was clearly in need of a lifetime of succor. She felt limp in his arms unable even to cling to him for comfort.

Carrying the compliant child he turned and moved back out of the cave, though their young charge seemed none too eager to leave her protection.

As they emerged back into the gray twilight Shwaren could see that the others had fanned out through the hill, looking for other survivors. All the others, however, found nothing but empty caves and silence. They all turned back toward the shore where some were already congregating.

As Shwaren and his precious cargo reached the group, no one jumped to ask the child what had happened. Those questions would have to wait for another time, for it was clear that no response would be forthcoming this soon after the terror, most likely of watching her village and her friends being washed out to sea.

The others turned to Shwaren. Bandai spoke, "We could shelter in the higher caves. There are few enough of us to easily be accommodated."

"No," Shwaren growled more harshly than he intended, "there is nothing here for us. Our best shelter is the boat and our only hope of finding more survivors is the sea which took them."

Most nodded agreement. Even when not venturing abroad they were most at home and secure on their boats. Even Bandai on hearing this suggestion readily agreed, though he was often hard to sway.

"Let's get back aboard," Shwaren ordered.

Immediately several Jhirum clamored aboard the dinghies. By the time full darkness arrived they were once again gently rocking at anchor, eating and resting. The now calm wash of the waves on the rocky shore belied the recent violence.

Shwaren watched his silent comrades drift off to different spots to sleep and dream restless dreams. He did not think that sleep could overtake him this night, the night the world changed, but eventually he did drift off into haunted dreams.

CHAPTER 9 THE MOUNTAIN PROTECTOR

The initial blast had done little damage in the upper reaches of the mountains that the Maestic called their home. However, Endmere could tell that this was not the end of it. During the time that he and Cragen had been madly trying to stamp out the small fires that seemed to be everywhere, the sky had continued to darken even though the sun had not yet reached its zenith.

Cragen finally stopped running around madly and approached Endmere holding his head. Endmere could see the question in his eyes, but only shook his head. "It appears that the earth has sustained some incredible blast, but from what source it is impossible to tell."

"In all of my years I have never felt such a hurt from the very rock of these mountains," Cragen replied. "What could possibly have such power?"

"I do not know," Endmere answered him, "but I fear that we did not suffer the worst from whatever it was. I think that we must try to gather as much of our tribe as we can to ascertain what they each saw and try to determine what has happened and what we should do."

"I agree with that," Cragen nodded. "Do we have enough strength left to call them to the spring?"

"I think that is best," agreed Endmere. "If we can at least reach the closest in and then perhaps they can reach others."

Before they could begin the attempt however, Endmere was distracted by a series of concussions. He immediately grabbed Cragen's arm pulling him down under an overhang just as the sky began to rain down a second wave of stones the size of a fist and smaller. Some blazed orange in the darkened sky setting new fires in the forest. Cragen and Endmere watched in horror as the black day lit up in wavering orange light.

Cragen looked at Endmere. "Will this never end?"

Endmere ignored the question since he had no answer. "We have got to try to contact the rest of the tribe."

Cragen nodded as they turned their attention to joining their strength. As Endmere opened his mind to join with Cragen a stabbing pain seared his skull. He could see Cragen flinch as well from the same experience. The earth and its damaged denizens continued to cry out to them.

Forcing his concentration back while trying to suppress the screaming inside his skull he finally found Cragen. As they joined their strength together they focused solely on finding other Maestic.

It did not take long to find the nearest of their brethren. Jasper and Thespan were the first that their minds encountered. Shock and dismay was the feeling shared through the link. Endmere did not waste time trying to calm them however, he pressed on with the necessary business, calling them to the mountain spring that was their source of strength and asking them to call on others that they could reach.

Endmere and Cragen then went on to search for others. Lamsil was almost out of their reach, but with their combined efforts they reached her several valleys away. She was already headed in their direction and had been in touch with several other tribe members.

The last of their tribe that they could reach was Bastile. She seemed weak in her response as if she was not entirely focused. It was clear that she suffered mildly from shock. Endmere and Cragen had to take some time with her to extend some calming and to help her focus on their request. Once she was clear that there was action to be taken she seemed to gain heart and indicated that she knew of several others in her area that she would contact.

It was difficult to say how long it would take for all of them to be gathered at the spring. Those they had been able to reach would possibly be there before night, if they were not waylaid by the fires, but the others would be farther away and unlikely to be able to traverse the mountains for at least another day.

After breaking their contact with Bastile they slowly stood, staring out into the gloom. "We might as well start for the spring," Endmere practically whispered. Cragen nodded as Endmere headed up the mountain. He could see the ominous orange glow of small forest fires in several directions. They came across a couple along their path that they quelled with their magic, but he knew there were others growing larger beyond their reach.

As they climbed through the trees a low rumble swelled through the ground. They each kneeled preparing for what was inevitably to follow. Within seconds the ground heaved, sending rocks from a nearby defile tumbling down into the valley. These mountains were not old. Several times in Endmere's life he had experienced growing pains as the mountains pushed toward the sky. Seldom did they result in major destruction except for those unfortunate enough to be at the bottom of the wrong valley when a landslide ensued.

The rumbling stopped briefly and the trees slowed their swaying, but Cragen and Endmere remained in place. Sure enough a second wave swept through the valley sending more rocks down the slide and this time bringing several trees to the ground with a crash. Birds emerged from trees all over the forest scared into the secure airways by the insubstantial earth.

A few forest animals called out in alarm as well but most were silent as they waited out the tumult. A few moments later the ground grew silent again, leaving the crying birds to fill the void left in its wake. Endmere glanced at Cragen then rose slowly scanning the surrounding hillsides for further activity.

By this time Endmere's normal confidence was thoroughly shaken. He could not imagine what could have set off this series of events and dreaded what might come next.

Steeling himself against his fears he reached out and patted Cragen on the back. "We should get moving," was all he said and they once again set out on their course.

Clearly, whatever had caused the blast was powerful enough to have triggered the release of the mountains' pent up energy. As they emerged into a clearing at the top of the ridge they again scanned their surroundings, noticing instantly, enlarged bare spots where slides had toppled trees. The crest of one adjacent mountaintop had a new shape to it, where the jagged peak had broken and tumbled into the valley, carrying with it hundreds of trees and who knows how many forest creatures.

In other times they would have hurried to these areas to see if there were any creatures needing healing, or rescue, but today there were more urgent issues to attend to, so Endmere started off again, following the ridge to the valley of the spring.

Though they could not see it, by the time their path along the ridge brought them to a point where they could look into the gathering darkness at bottom of the valley the sun was nearing the tops of the mountains in its descent. The growing darkness seemed alive with dancing orange specters cast by the fires dotting the valley. Soot, heavy in the air burned Endmere's lungs as the desiccated ash and dust snow continued to fall.

This was their nexus, in all of their wanderings this valley was the center that they always returned to at regular intervals. Even Endmere's stolid demeanor faltered as he looked into the smoke choked valley.

Endmere pulled his eyes from the fires following the valley up to where the secluded basin turned into a sharp deep scar running to near the top of the mountain. From their position on the eastern side of the valley he could see that one side of the steep embankment had slid into the streambed leaving an open section where before there had been trees. It had not even occurred to him until now that their spring might have been affected by the catastrophe.

Cragen must have seen the same thing. In tandem they surged forward hurrying into the wavering glow of the burning trees toward their spring.

With all that had happened, Endmer's only concern now was to see the spring unchanged and pure as they had left it. This side of the valley was not steep and they moved with haste to the bottom of the mountain just reaching it as an aftershock shook the mountains again causing them to stumble and pause. Birds that had just been settling in for the night flew up in clouds again with raucous cries. The rumbling passed with only minor shaking and they resumed their course toward the scar.

As they began to ascend, the well worn trail that they had each traveled hundreds of times, disappeared in places blocked by fallen rocks or trees. In other places it simply crumbled into the stream bed which ran beside it.

With each rock that they had to climb over or around Endmere's tension grew. By the time they reached the spring the last of the natural light had disappeared from the highest peaks and the sky was turning black as midnight.

Unable to contain his anxiety Endmere tried to run the last stretch to the spring, but the frequency of rock barricades grew, forcing him to jump and dodge around them. He could see a new slide that had reached to the edge of where the spring was. Thus impeded they could not see the spring itself until they were within a few feet. There they stopped, faces frozen as if etched in stone. Welling from the ground was a grey, bordering on black liquid with a light steam rising from the surface.

Cragen kneeled beside the fetid pool, dipped his hand into the water and lifted it to his nose. The quick turn of his head and shaking of his hand as if to rid himself of every drop of the dark liquid confirmed Endmere's fear. Their pure beautiful, powerful spring was dead, contaminated by the opening of some fissure far underground, which had released the noxious liquid into the pure spring water. Suddenly a remote occurrence of some violence but only casual concern had become a catastrophe beyond measure.

Endmere stood, frozen where he was staring at Cragen and the spring, unable to move or think clearly. In all their travels in all of the mountains that they cared for, no other spring of power had ever been discovered. Their source of magic, power and communion with the earth was cut off. He felt as if half of his family had just died. With a groan he sat heavily to the ground.

Cragen turned and sat facing him. "What can be done?" Cragen beseeched.

"I don't know," was Endmere's only reply. Then with a slight brightening he continued. "Perhaps when the others arrive we can use our remaining sense to try to seek out the source of the foulness and see if it can be healed."

Cragen continued to stare at the dark pool. "Perhaps; our only other hope is that the spring clears on its own after a time."

Silence fell between them as dark as the night which now shrouded the valley. They would have to wait for the others, and hope.

CHAPTER 10 THE BLACK EARTH

The blackness held Nomber for what seemed like an eternity. The first sensation that returned to him was pain, splitting his skull as if cleaved by an ax. Then his eyes flickered open and struggled to focus. For a moment he could not comprehend his surroundings, thinking himself still lost in a nightmarish dream. Then it came back to him, the explosion, being buried alive and then something had struck him hard on the head. Fortunately a glancing blow or he would not have regained consciousness.

He reached for his head and felt the crusted blood clotting his hair as he struggled to sit up. After several long moments he recalled his original intent, before he was struck. Again he tried to reach out to find his kin. He felt, not far from where he sat, Bashley, a young tribe member. He could tell he was hurt, but alive.

He stood, taking a moment to let his unsteady legs regain some strength and began to work his way through the tangle of tree trunks in the direction of the young man.

The going was torturous. His legs sank into the debris up to his knees at times. As he heaved himself over a large oak a wave of nausea washed through him causing him to settle back to his knees. Was he injured more than he thought? Taking precious moments he used his sense to search through his body looking for damage. Then he took a long pull on his water skin to renew the magical strength that he had nearly depleted in his defense against the blast. Nothing appeared to him accept for the bruise on his head and an overall sense of wrongness. Even the flush of the magic strengthening in his body seemed somehow weaker than normal.

He could not waste time now on speculation; however, he needed to try to put his tribe back together. Pulling himself back up and over the trunk he proceeded onward. As straight as possible he made his way toward the young Bagnog.

He encountered one pile of trees burning brightly, casting an eerie orange glow against the shifting gray-black fog of soot and ash. Twice he sank nearly to his waist where lighter ash had filled a depression, forcing him to almost swim out of the powder.

It was not long however before he could see Bashley pinned under a medium sized birch. He was moving slightly but clearly not with great strength. Approaching he reached out with his mind, but could not seem to enter the other's thoughts, so instead he spoke to let him know help was at hand.

"Bashley, it is me Nomber, can you tell if you have any bad injuries?"

Dazed eyes looked through him from a blackened face. One side of his face was severely burned while the other looked whole except for the black soot. Clearly Bashley was in no condition to respond so Nomber reached out with his own sense again to test the integrity of Bashley's body.

Where he was pinned under the tree he could feel a bone fracture, though not severe. He would first have to try to dig him out from under the tree before attending to the injury.

Digging with both hands as well as pieces of stone he began to loosen the dirt underneath Bashley's legs. Suddenly the young man began to thrash wildly. Nomber paused and again tried to reach into his mind to calm him, but found nothing.

Exhausted after only a minute Bashley settled back down allowing Nomber to continue, though his mind now wandered from the immediate task to his lack of ability to contact Bashley's mind.

After digging until his fingers were bloody he could tell that the legs were free enough to be worked from under the tree. His fingers were scraped raw by the stones and sand, but he gently pulled on the legs together, working them out while trying not to cause further damage.

Bashley lay limp though still with eyes wide and staring. Nomber sat to rest a moment before trying to repair the broken bone and the burns. His strength was not great given the earlier effort to cleanse the swamp as well as the effort to protect his own body from the initial assault of the concussion. He had to do his best, however, as he was sure this would not be the last tribe member that would need his help.

Concentrating on the wounded area he began the healing process. As he searched the wound it felt like he was pushing against a barrier where normally there should be no resistance. Within a few minutes however, he managed to stitch the bone back together sufficiently that it would stand pressure and movement.

Still he had not been able to reach Bashley's mind. Exhausted he tried the direct approach, picking up his head and speaking slowly to him. "Bashley, do you hear me. You had a broken leg but I have healed it well enough to walk. Can you speak? I need you to walk with me so I can search for others."

Bashley's eyes focused momentarily on Nomber and then he shuddered again. Trying to conceal the growing panic that was building with each passing moment Nomber tried again. "Bashley, please help me, you must try to bring yourself back."

The eyes focused again and this time held as Bashley struggled to regain full awareness. Nomber lifted his rapidly depleting water skin and forced some of the precious liquid into Bashley's mouth.

A moment later he managed to softly mutter, "I am here Nomber, but I feel disconnected from the world, something is wrong."

Nomber shook his head "There is not much left of our world to connect with, but for now we must try to reach others of our tribe who are in need of help. Can you stand?"

"Yes, I think so," he said as he tried to lever himself up with one arm.

Nomber reached under his arms and pulled him up to a sitting position where he stayed for a few moments before pulling his legs underneath himself. Nomber helped to lift him, leaning him against the tree trunk. Bashley stared around in horror at the site of the blasted woods, shrouded in a fine snow of ash and dust that was now falling from the sky.

While giving Bashley time to stabilize, Nomber reached out again to see where the next victim still alive might be. Though he struggled to sense anything through the growing haze of his weakened magical sense he soon found another tribe member. He reached for Bashley who numbly responded by pushing himself off the tree in the direction that Nomber indicated.

When he and Bashley had managed to pick their way through the fallen forest to the location that his sense told him held the next survivor they found Gromand. Gromand was in his early twenties, strong and tall. At first glance he seemed a man, but on closer examination it was clear that he was still young. His eyes were the eyes of a child, bright and open, ready to be entertained or to learn. But now his eyes only held pain and confusion. He stood, so he could not be hurt too badly, but a bloody bruise had closed one eye completely and the other just stared dully as if he were staring out of a dream.

Nomber helped Bashley over a final tangle of fallen trunks and approached Gromand with a gentle voice, "Gromand, are you ok?"

Gromand started as if expecting to be pounced upon by a vicious beast. Seeing Nomber though, life came back into his single good eye and he limped in their direction with some certainty.

"Nomber, what has happened?" Gromand pleaded.

"I do not know Gromand, are you well?"

Gromand nodded. "I guess I was lucky, I was behind the boulder mound over there when the blast hit, only a falling rock caught my head. Is Bashley OK?" He motioned toward Bashley, who had kneeled to the ground as soon as Nomber had left him.

"Yes, he had some broken bones and other injuries, but I healed the worst of them. Let me see your eye. Do you have any of your sense left?"

Gromand almost whispered, "Yes, but I can hardly stand to use it. There is vileness everywhere that screams from the very ground."

"I know," Nomber reassured him, "but for now you must try to use it to help me heal your eye. I do not have the strength on my own. Turn it inward and the pain will be less."

Nomber reached for his shoulders, which were nearly as high as his eyes and with a gentle push indicated that he should kneel or sit.

Gromand complied without hesitation and soon their minds had joined in seeking out his injuries and healing them. Fortunately Gromand had not expended much of his magic as Nomber was greatly weakened at this point from healing Bashley and protecting himself. He exerted most of his effort in keeping Gromand calm and focused on his own healing.

The wound to his eye was the only one of significance and not bad enough to be beyond healing. Together they quickly stitched a small crack in the eye socket and staunched some bleeding beneath the skin. His eye would remain puffy and bruised for some time but should soon be back to normal.

What disturbed Nomber more, however, was an odd darkness, which seemed to be lurking in the back of Gromand's being. He dismissed this however as the fear and trauma of what he had just witnessed.

After separating, Nomber looked deeply into Gromand's good eye and as calmly as he could, commanded, "Gromand, my sense is weak already. I need you now to reach out to see if you can find other survivors of our tribe."

Gromand physically flinched and glanced at the ground.

"You must do this though I know it is painful and frightening."

Gromand glanced back up at Nomber. "I will try, but isn't there any way to lessen the pain?"

Nomber looked directly into his eyes trying to sound confident. "You must focus exclusively on your tribe members, do not let the earth's pain distract you, or pull you in."

Gromand nodded, though his brow remained creased with concern. As he reached out, Nomber could see the waves of pain flow through him as he fought for focus and control. He was young and his mastery of magic, though a part of him since birth was not that of an adult. Nomber could see him slowly gain some calm and then withdraw his sense and come back to himself. Nomber looked at him with anticipation.

Though he still grimaced at the pain he finally spoke. "There is a small group of our tribe over the hill to the south and two others just to the east. I think I detected one very weak brother just at the bottom of this hill, though his life force is fading."

Nomber nodded. "We should go to the weakest first, are you well enough to help me with Bashley?"

"Yes, I am fine now, but what is this black soot that covers everything?"

"I don't know," answered Nomber. "It must have been blasted from the earth when the object from the sky struck. I do know, however, that it is something foul and unhealthy. I would suggest that you clean as much of it off yourself as possible."

Gromand nodded. "I felt it as soon as I regained consciousness. I cleaned it off, mostly, but I still feel vile from its touch."

Nomber moved back to Bashley who was still seated where he had set himself down when they first found Gromand. "Come Bashley, we must go help others. Are you feeling better?"

"Yes, a little," he replied. "I think that I can walk on my own now, just not too fast."

Nomber brightened a little. "Good, then Gromand can lead the way to our next brother."

The next victim that Gromand had located was Floan. Like Bashley, she was pinned beneath a tree, which had fallen across her abdomen. The only reason she survived at all was because of a small depression that her luck or magic had lain her in as the tree came down. Knowing that Nomber though the better healer was very weak in magic Gromand kneeled beside her and began to probe with his sense.

"She has many injuries, a broken rib and several internal wounds. I will try my best to heal her."

Nomber could see the uncertainty in his eyes. "I think I am still strong enough to help guide your work if you will let me?"

Gromand nodded and relaxed a little. Nomber knelt beside him and they began the process, gently probing for the most serious injuries and delicately rejoining broken bones and lacerated flesh. After they had finished with the worst they reached into Floan's mind to see if she was aware, or could be reached. Though clearly alive, her mind was not accessible so they withdrew for the time being.

"I think she should live now, but I don't think we can get her out from under the tree by ourselves." Turning to Bashley Nomber asked, "Bashley, can you stay here while we search for others?"

"Yes, I would only slow you down anyway," Bashley answered. "I will wait here until you get back. Perhaps some more of my strength will come back to me by then."

With a moment's hesitation to reassure himself that his two weakened charges were well enough to be left he motioned for Gromand to lead the way to the next tribesmen.

Gromand winced as he reached out with his sense into the broken land. Soon he nodded and started off with Nomber following.

The way they went this time was considerably easier because it was in the direction leading away from the blast so they could simply walk between the lined up trunks of fallen trees buried in the debris.

Gromand did not pause as he filled Nomber in as to what he had found. "There are two more tribe members in this direction".

Suddenly Nomber stopped dead in his tracks and doubled over as a wave of nausea washed over him.

Gromand turned in alarm. "Are you ok? Perhaps you need more healing yourself?"

"No," Nomber replied in a strangled voice. "This is not from an injury, but something else that I cannot quite grasp. I am fine now."

Gromand hesitated a moment and then turned and walked on. Though the wave of nausea had passed, the taste of bile remained. Nomber dwelled on the feeling of wrongness for some time, trying to identify its source and whether it had a connection to the nausea.

By the time they were nearing where the two tribesmen should be, it struck him, this sensation was not new to him, he had felt a similar sensation only a few days before, the day they had cleansed the swamp. His certainty of the source of his ill feelings was reinforced as he considered where the impact crater lie, directly on the site of the fetid swamp that they had banished back beneath the earth.

His mind began to race trying to grasp the implications. Then he was struck by another sinking feeling which shook him to the bottom of his feet. He stopped again stark still holding his hands up to stare at the midnight black soot that was still lodged in his fingernails and streaked on his skin.

Reflexively he scraped at the soot trying to rub it off in a frenzy of revulsion.

Noticing that his companion had stopped again Gromand turned with concern on his face, expecting retching again. But the look on Nomber's face and then his frantic scratching at his skin only confused Gromand and made him even more concerned.

Finally stopping his attempts at purification, and noticing the look of concern on Gromand's face Nomber took hold of himself again. "Gromand, I think I know the source of the ill feeling of the land. The swamp, we didn't destroy the vileness we only pushed it under ground. I fear the blast released the black swamp water."

At first Gromand stared uncomprehending, then as understanding spread, he too looked down at his own hands in horror, at the same black stains and grime.

Nomber could not contain the panic in his voice. "We must find water as soon as possible to get this poison off of us. Who knows what it is doing to us already. We must find our other tribe members and get them all to water quickly."

As the sun was setting in the west, apparent only by the blackness fading into an even deeper gloom, they came upon the two tribesmen they were looking for. It was Thane and Jarine, Nomber's daughter. Both were seated. Jarine appeared to be tending to Thane who was watching their approach with blank eyes. Like all of them, they were covered in soot, which they had not even attempted to scrape off. Gromand knelt beside them as Nomber approached.

Jarine appeared to be relatively unscathed but for a few scrapes and bruises. Thane's arm was lying limply across his lap.

Jarine looked at her father with puzzlement in her eyes. "Thane's arm was badly broken, but it still should not have been difficult to heal. But I was barely able to complete the task. It seemed like I was fighting against a current the whole time."

Nomber's look of concern deepened but he did not waste time with explanations. "All of you must go to the river now, before we rest! Wash every bit of this soot off of you. Have you had any contact with others?"

Jarine, looking confused and concerned replied, "I sensed a small group not far from here, but could only identify Tamber. They were headed in our direction."

"Good," Nomber replied, "be off with you. Gromand and I will go to meet them and lead them to the river as soon as we can."

As he and Gromand set off in the opposite direction another wave of nausea overcame Nomber, but he fought the urge to double up on the ground.

Gromand, though still moving with the strong gate of the young looked more and more haggard as the gloom of evening set in. Fortunately they had barely left the others when they could sense and see a group of five tribe members headed their way at a measured pace.

By the time he could make out their faces he could see that they were a haggard group with various levels of burns, bruises and probably some poorly healed broken bones and internal injuries.

As soon as they reached Nomber they began to settle in, as if ready to spend the night in that spot.

"You must move on to the river," Nomber urged, "This black soot must be washed off of us before we rest. Any of you that are well enough I need you to come with us to help dig out Floan from under a tree."

With many groans and questioning looks they lifted themselves back on to weary legs.

Two of them followed Gromand and Nomber back to where they had left Floan and Bashley. By the time they got to the fallen tree Bashley was slowly digging around Floan's legs. She was now conscious though still weak, brightening only slightly at the site of her rescuers. They joined Bashley digging around the tree which was too large to move, particularly with debris nearly covering it.

It was so dark they could see nothing with their eyes by the time they pulled Floan free. Only their remaining magical sense allowed them to finish the work, provide some small additional healing to Floan and find their way to the stream.

By the time they had joined the rest of their tattered group by the river the first to arrive were emerging from the river having scrubbed each other raw. Even in the flickering light of the fire that they had built Nomber could see that black stains remained on all of them.

"Into the river, all of you," he said to the new arrivals. "Get every bit of that soot off that you can." At first the group did not respond only looking at him with incomprehension on their faces. Jarine finally voiced the question on all of their minds. "Why must we be so concerned about washing off the dirt we will only be covered again soon?"

Nomber realized then that in his distraction he had not explained his belief to most of those gathered there. "I believe that this dark soot is from the vileness that we just cleared at the swamp near our spring. It appears that there was an explosion, or something struck the earth right where the swamp was, spreading the black contamination all over our territory."

Many of them glanced at their hands as Nomber had when the thought first occurred to him. Thane raised his eyes to study Nomber. "Are you certain? This could just be some soot from the fires."

Jarine answered for Nomber, "No, it makes perfect sense. Haven't you all felt the nausea? Is it not like the feeling we got when near the swamp?" She looked from face to face. "How many of you have had headaches?" Many nodded. "I think that Nomber is right we should get as much of this off of us as we can, and quickly."

The weary group looked at one another briefly and then began plodding into the shallows and scrubbing themselves with sand and water. Even some of those that had already been in the stream, now understanding the importance, joined the group in the water, putting a little more effort into the task.

Nomber joined them in the cold stream. The normally refreshing bath did little to renew his strength and the scrubbing only removed the loose crust of soot without lightening the stains on his skin. He glanced at the others to see if they were having more success, but they all remained tainted with dark stains.

Chilled and exhausted they emerged from the cool river to sit by the fire to dry and drive the chill from their bones. Nomber could tell even without his magical sense that the reality of their situation was settling in on the group, a reality too heavy to bear in their diminished state.

For now sleep would have to suffice and here their exhaustion served them well as they soon drifted off to face their personal nightmares.

CHAPTER 11 THE ALTERED LAND

The land had been irrevocably changed in an instant. Gone was the benign, lush valley habitat. Blasted skeletons of once verdant giants covered the ground like the graying hair of some monster. The mountains, however, except for the lower slopes near the blast were not obviously damaged. They were however, altered. Earthquakes, a not uncommon occurrence normally were released in rapid succession from the trigger of the massive concussion. These brought down towering peaks and caused massive slides that cleared the sides of mountains of everything in their path. In addition, for some significant distance beyond the immediate blast zone the shower of debris cast into the stratosphere pummeled the earth with fiery brands, igniting secondary fires throughout the forests and grasslands. These fires added to the gray clouds, shrouding the land in the colors of mourning. Mourning for the lost peace that the surviving inhabitants had not yet realized was gone forever.

The fact that there were survivors at all was a credit to the strength of the magic that lived in the Jhirum. The size of the blast would have annihilated all but those in the farthest mountains in the first concussion were it not for their magical strength. But though more than half of their numbers would be counted as lost on that day, they survived to face a world and a people changed forever.

The sea, with the exception of the flotsam clogged beaches pounded on as if nothing had happened. Shwaren awoke to the lulling roll of the waves under his battered ship. He awoke to the all-encompassing gray of a dawn that would never break. Unlike almost every morning of his life rather than turning first to the sea, he gazed instead at the land, silent but for the sea gulls and other birds picking through the wash of debris along the beach and amongst the rocks.

He had harbored no real hope of seeing any of his tribe materialize amidst this wreckage, but he still looked, unbelieving, disheartened. He steeled himself as his crewmates began to rouse around him, each to stare as he had done with the brief hope that it had all been a nightmare, hope that rapidly faded to disbelief and despair.

Toren was the last to rouse. Only she did not turn to the land, disdaining to acknowledge the terror that had visited her there. She had not spoken since they found her, but she walked to Shwaren and stood near him staring out to sea, gaining some small comfort from his nearness and his strength yet still refusing to emerge from the defensive cocoon she had woven around herself.

Shwaren reached out with his mind gently to her, but sensing her immovable barriers instead called in his mind to gather his crew to him. Then he turned to Winfew who stood nearby. "It is clear that there is nothing left of our people on land. I believe, however, that we should not yet give up all hope of survivors. It is still possible that some who were washed out to sea are still alive."

"A slim hope," Winfew responded, "the waves that cast our boat about like it was a twig would have thrown any one in its wake to the bottom of the ocean in an instant."

"Still, I am not prepared to abandon all hope," Shwaren replied. As the others gathered around he raised his voice, "What think the rest of you. We must determine what to do now."

Waymeir, after a brief pause where glances were cast uncertainly between many crew members answered, "If there is any hope at all, we must pursue it and if there is any hope it is in the sea."

A few others nodded agreement. "Is there any among us who would pursue a different course of action?" Shwaren asked.

Madrien answered for the group, "What would we do but go to the sea in any case?"

Winfew scowled and replied shortly, "Were it not for the possibility of survivors at sea, we should rebuild our shattered homes. But I think that we must first search for survivors."

With nothing but a small shake of the head from Madrien in response, the crew moved away to their posts, inspecting the damaged ship and the repairs required.

By midmorning teams were beginning to assemble the necessary material on the beach with which to repair the ship for its new mission. A new mast was the biggest task. Strong, straight trees did not grow this close to the coast, so the largest work party set off, inland to a valley beyond the hill, which protected the harbor. Here they found that part of the work had been done for them by the blast, which had stripped many of the giant trees in the valley of all their branches and brought several of them down. All that was left for them to do was to cut off the roots of one of the straighter trees and then begin the arduous task of hauling it to the sea.

By the end of the day the giant pole lay on the beach ready to be trimmed and mounted. Another day would be spent mounting the mast and what was left of their sails, precious time for any survivors, but necessary if they were to have any chance of covering the large amount of ocean necessary to ensure that they had given their brethren a chance at rescue.

Shwaren surveyed his crew as they settled in around the fire. He could see the weariness on their faces and could tell that it was not just from the hard work of the day. He too felt beaten down both mentally and physically. They fed on the provisions that were still stored on the ship, dried salted fish and a few berries. They would also have to replenish these before they set out.

Shwaren was determined to be out of the harbor before the sun set on another day. Though exhaustion pushed him to sleep quickly he woke to the dawn still tired, but aching more than ever to be back at sea where the evidence of catastrophe was less visible.

The mast was small enough that the Jhirum had little trouble securing it in place. Magic as much as wind propelled their boats, magic that they found in the sea. Throughout the ocean they had learned of vents that laced the waters in their vicinity with magic from deep in the earth. Even eating the fish in the area of these vents brought strength beyond mere sustenance. Though the nearest vent was some distance off shore, they had renewed their strength on the return trip and so were not in danger of being too weak to propel and control their craft.

By noon they had positioned and secured the mast and had made significant progress on the other repairs. They took a brief break for lunch then quickly resumed their tasks. Shwaren sent a small group back to shore to work on restocking their supply of freshwater and food. He was determined to be out of the harbor before dark even if they were only able to just clear the harbor. Sitting here working on their boat felt too much like they had already abandoned any hope of finding survivors.

The gray day was just beginning to show signs of fading into night when all was ready. Shwaren placed watchers on all sides along with those who would help power and steer the boat. As the anchor was heaved up the side of the ship the boat eased forward, pointed toward the open sea. He did not have a firm plan as to where they should look for survivors, but they had agreed that they would sail to either side of the opening to the bay and then double back, each time moving farther out to sea. They would not get far today, but any movement would relieve the tension of doing nothing.

As the boat glided toward the mouth of the bay in the gray gloom of early evening the eyes of more than the assigned watchers swept the waves and the rocks of the distant shore hoping beyond hope for a glimpse of life.

Rounding the mouth of the bay they headed south close to the shore. Though still early evening, already the day was as black as midnight. Only their magic enhanced site allowed them to search for a short while before anchoring for the night. Their short search fruitless, they settled in for a small meal and early bed.

Madrien sat by Shwaren. "Shouldn't we head north tomorrow? The current from the south brushes the coast outside of our bay perhaps any who were washed out of the bay were picked up by the current."

Shwaren thought only a moment before answering. "You are probably right, that would be the most likely direction to find survivors."

Madrien studied him for a moment before continuing. "I wonder what it is like further inland, closer to where the earth was struck."

In concentrating on his own people Shwaren had given little thought as to other parts of the land and other Jhirum. He glanced sidelong at Madrien, a frown on his face. "I do not know, but it cannot be good."

Madrien nodded. "There is just too much we don't know."

Shwaren pulled away from his own uncertainty. "In good time we will learn more. For now we should probably turn in. We will want to start with first light."

The Jhirum who had been listening all rose, heading to where they would sleep still able to cling to the hope that a new day would bring more of their kin back to them alive. This would have to sustain them for now, but for how long Shwaren could not know.

CHAPTER 12 SURVIVORS

Fenly opened his eyes after a restless night's sleep. He felt that it must be morning though the sky gave little indication; still set in darkness that he feared would barely pass even at midday. He glanced around at his camp mates. All were covered in the fine dust that blanketed everything, huddled together in pairs like lovers. He could not know how lucky they were that the dirt and soot that covered them was no more than that. The heavy black contamination that covered the Bagnog had been deposited only near the blast leaving the rest of the Jhirum lands choked in soot and dust, but not in the vile blackness.

Smoke still stung his nostrils and made his eyes burn. He tried to reach out with his sense, but already he could barely sense anything beyond what his eyes, ears and nose told him.

An involuntary shutter ran through his body at this realization. Some of his camp mates were beginning to stir, shaking the dust off of their bodies and scratching at their faces to wipe away the grime accumulated overnight. None of them had eaten anything since the cataclysm. Fenly's stomach, groaned in complaint. He decided they would have to find food and clean water before doing anything else this morning.

By the time everyone was awake a discussion had already begun about where they would have the best chance of finding food.

"Water should not be a problem," Tandeir stated flatly, "We should be able to clear out around the stream enough to get some drinkable water even if it is without magic."

Ashmere nodded somberly. "But what about food? Where we walked there was not a single bush surviving yet alone one with berries."

Pendolin though still unable to stand followed the conversation from where she had slept. "There is certainly nothing around here, where can we even start?"

Fenly knelt beside her trying to quell his own uncertainty. "We must not falter; we do not know the full extent of the damage. Perhaps there are places that were sheltered enough."

His attempt at reassurance, however, lacked conviction as he was close to panic himself. The loss of magic made it feel as if all his senses had been cut off wrapping him in a smoky cocoon.

Ashmere, however, seemed undaunted. She turned the conversation toward what they should do first. "We should first clear out a pool at the base of the cliff where we can get some clean water and fill our skins. Then we can look for food."

"But where shall we look?" Tandeir asked, looking from face to face.

Fenly stood. "I believe that we should stay close to here. Clearly Pendolin cannot be moved yet. There must be some food that we can find near the cliff."

Ashmere looked around at the bleak landscape. "I think that we must look for a more sheltered place. Perhaps the small valleys on the other side of the cliff where perhaps some bushes survived."

Fenly knew that time was wasting. The Natec were not used to making group decisions and although not an argumentative people, they were independent and had little social structure to help in such situations.

"Well let's start clearing the stream, we will need water first.

As they worked on clearing a pool they continued to discuss what to do next. By the time a pool had been cleared and the muddy water had settled to near clarity they were no closer to a decision. Finally as she filled her skin Ashmere said in exasperation, "Fine the rest of you do what you want, I am heading to the other side of the cliff," and with that set off along the cliff face without glancing back.

Fenly, looking unsure finally shook his head and set off to follow her. Genlie also followed Ashmere and Fenly. Minere, however, looked to the cliff, and after some hesitation set out on her own, clamoring up the pile of debris, though she frequently glanced at the backs of the receding Jhirum.

Weary and hungry, Fenly, Ashmere and Genlie trudged along the cliff face. They would have to work their way around the end of the cliff to where it descended to the valley floor and they could ascend the hill from the side. Much of the cliff face had crumbled leaving piles of debris that had to be circumvented. But this pushed them out into where the forest had been thick and where now there were either smoldering heaps of branches, or twisted tangles of tree trunks.

Several times they also had to jump, or walk around jagged cracks opened in the ground by the earthquakes. The short distance that would normally have taken them little time to traverse turned into a tiring half morning. By the time they got to where the cliff face shortened and disappeared they had to stop for a time to regain their strength. These were a tough, strong people, but the events of the past day had already taken their toll on their bodies and their psyches.

The way up the hillside was no easier, though there were some places that were almost blasted clean of any debris. The thick ash and dust made it hard to tell where depressions lay waiting to twist an ankle or wrench a knee. Several times Fenly felt his foot fall below where he expected hard earth, jarring his bones and threatening to topple him.

As they neared the top of the hill and began the descent down the other side they encountered more trees still standing though stripped bare of leaves and most branches. The open areas were still wiped clean by the blast and fires.

They did manage to gather a few recently dead animals that had enough meat left on them to provide some nourishment. They also came across a small fawn, alone, bleating at the darkness for its mother. Half of its hair was singed off its body though it stood erect and ready to run. Instinctively it knew the Jhirum presented no danger and allowed them to approach closely. Fenly looked it over carefully to see if it was hurt beyond the burns, but it seemed otherwise sound and soon bounded off into the dark.

Finally, almost at the bottom of the hill Fenly spotted some color amidst the gray. Growing close to the backside of an escarpment were a few haggard bushes with at least a few berries left on them. The berries were covered in dust and ash, but each of the Jhirum still put a few directly in their mouth so depleted were they. Then they gathered what they could to take back.

When the last berry had been picked they all turned to Ashmere clearly wondering what she planned next. "I think that we should head back but we should fan out for the return to cover as much ground as possible."

Fenly nodded without thought, happy to have someone else make a decision, but as the other two diverged along separate paths and he was left alone the fright returned. Never had he felt afraid, but the lack of magic made him feel more alone and vulnerable than he ever could have imagined. He discovered himself standing still, alone in the semi-darkness and finally had to force his legs to move forward.

Meanwhile Minere had spent the morning on the jumble of rock at the bottom of the cliff from where their spring flowed. She could not imagine that no one was making more of an effort to resurrect their only source of magic. This was more important to her then food at this point.

She tried to identify the point where the spring should be flowing from the rock face which was now buried in rubble. Here she began to dig.

In no time her fingers were raw and bloody from tearing at the rock and dirt almost frantically. Many of the rocks were too large for her to budge so she tried to dig around them and roll them away, but it soon became clear that there was no way that she could do this by herself. She sat heavily on one of the obstructing rocks and sobbed, her tears cutting lines through the grime on her face.

As she was beginning to feel that all hope was gone she heard Tandeir picking her way up the pile of rocks. Already Minere could not sense her even at close range. She could not bear the emptiness of the feeling.

Tandeir looked down on her from the edge of the small depression that she had managed to clear. "You cannot move this mountain of rocks by yourself. Even with all of us working together it would take days or weeks to dig deep enough and you still do not know if it will be of any use."

"What would you have me do?" Minere sobbed.

Tandeir stared down on her, unsure how to react to her sorrow until Minere finally looked down in shame. "I would suggest that we try to clear away where the stream exits the pile. Perhaps we can work our way back to some point where it retains its magic."

Minere stood and stared at the small dent she had made in the mountain of rock before answering, "I guess you are right I am getting nowhere here." Minere scraped a sooty hand across her face, smearing the tears with the dirt and then began to pick her way back down the slide to where the stream flowed out of the rock pile. Tandeir followed joining Minere as she began to pick rocks out of the stream trying to clear a way further into the pile.

Tandeir's thoughts drifted as she worked. The last day seemed a dream, could it possibly be real? Her body ached from bruises and burns, but more so from the yearning to be filled with magic. She understood what drove Minere, she too longed for the strength and confidence that only the magic could give. Could they, and would they really have to figure out how to survive without magic?

It was mid afternoon by the time Fenly arrived back at their makeshift camp. Tired and weary, he dropped to the ground and laid down his meager collection of food. Though they usually ate more berries and plants than animals, today would be a meat day. Vegetation was scarce but the blast had left many dead animals some of which were still edible.

Pendolin still lay where she had been left, though she was now fully awake and alert. "Is the other side of the hill as bad as here?"

Fenly could not look her in the eyes, the fear and longing for miracles he saw there was too strong. "I am afraid it is not much better, though on the far side of the hill there are some living bushes and a few trees that may survive."

Pendolin stared at him in disbelief and fear. "How is it possible? What could have caused all this destruction? And how will we survive without plants or animals, or magic?"

Finally Fenly looked her in the eyes. "I frankly don't know. All we can do is try to survive another day and see where that takes us."

As he looked at her he could see that she was shivering and not just from fear. For the first time he noticed the chill in the air. Though it was now well after noon, it was still dark and had warmed little from the night before.

Fenly knelt down beside her. "You are cold. I will find some coals from one of the fires still burning to start a fire here to warm you and to help us cook the meat." Pendolin managed a weak smile through her chattering teeth.

As Fenly started off in search of wood and hot coals he mused that in many cases it would be to re-cook the previously charred meat.

Genlie arrived as Fenly was getting the fire started, a deer over his shoulders, yes they would have plenty of meat for today, before it started to rot. "How was your return Genlie?"

"It would have been easier if I had found this closer to the camp." He dropped the deer beside the fire.

"I guess we need to clean and skin that," Fenly replied as he placed a few more sticks on the smoky fire.

"Yes, I suppose. Is your stone any sharper than mine?"

"I think it may be. It has stayed sharp for a long time. Here, you can get started. I will help you as soon as I get the fire going well."

Fenly reached to his belt pouch and pulled out the hand length stone blade. Though rough it was actually fairly sharp. Fenly had rarely used it since for most things magic was better than knives.

Tandeir returned as Fenly was finishing with the fire which left Ashmere and Minere still away. Fenly knew that Minere was still working at the stream. He did not know what to think of her determination to find magic. He only knew that they were all hungry and tired.

They had already begun eating and drinking by the time they heard Ashmere approach. Fenly could see that she had discovered another survivor, which must have slowed her return. He dropped the piece of meat he was gnawing on and ran to help her.

It was Legolan who was about the age of Fenly. He was leaning heavily on Ashmere and Fenly came up to his other side to help her support him.

"I think his leg is broken, I could not summon enough strength to heal it," Ashmere panted with concern in her voice.

Fenly glanced at her, she was not yet completely whole from her own injuries and supporting Legolan had nearly exhausted her strength. As he wrapped his arm under Legolan's he gently pushed Ashmere away. "Go, eat and drink, I will bring Legolan the rest of the way."

Ashmere was too exhausted to argue, slipping out from under Legolan's shoulder and stumbling to the waiting group. Fenly encouraged Legolan who had not yet spoken. "We have food and water. You can eat and rest now."

Legolan nodded disconsolately. The side of his face was seared and much of his body was covered in bruises. Clearly he had not had enough of his own strength left after the blast to repair any of the damage to his body.

Fenly eased him to the ground by the fire. Tandeir handed him a drink of still slightly murky water and a few berries, until more meat could be cooked.

After some moments of drinking and eating in silence he found enough strength to speak. "I have been lying with my leg broken by a falling tree since yesterday. I could not understand why I could not contact any one and that no one contacted me. I feared that everyone else had perished. I could not even heal myself as I had used all my strength during the blast. I was very glad to see Ashmere, but I would like to be healed now."

Everyone looked at each other in despair. Tandeir finally spoke. "Legolan, I fear that at least for now we have no power to help you. We have all used what magic we had, during the cataclysm and in healing afterwards, and now as you see, our cliff has been shattered and it appears, the magic lost."

Legolan looked from face to face in disbelief, somehow hoping that someone would argue that this was not their fate.

Ashmere added, "It is true, though I think that we can form a splint to help secure your leg. Perhaps in time we will find some power. Genlie can you find two straight sticks about an arm's length long?"

Legolan continued to look at each of their faces in turn, searching for answers to troubling but unvoiced questions. "What can we do now?" He finally pleaded.

Fenly, forcing calm into his voice that he did not feel responded, "First we must make sure we have found all of our surviving tribe members. Between us we have encountered only five bodies, some which were not identifiable. That leaves many more unaccounted for. We must hope that more of them have survived. We must each try to remember the last contact we had with any of our tribe not here, where they were and if we knew their intentions."

Tandeir was the first to respond. "I was at the far end of the valley with Chastine the morning of the blast. She was following the river toward the sea. She could not have gotten too much farther before the blast."

Legolan chimed in, "Five of the boys were headed to the far side of the valley the day before yesterday. They said they wanted to go to the foothills of the Western mountains."

By the time they had all accounted for their last contacts they had clearly identified three directions they had to explore and had some knowledge of everyone but Gloren one of the tribe's elders. This did not surprise Fenly. Gloren was a loner and had not been seen by anyone for some time. In fact he was one of the few that missed their meeting with the Bagnog.

"It seems that there is more food and shelter on the far side of the cliff," Ashmere began, "I think that we should move Pendolin and Legolan there and leave someone with them to help find food and attend to other needs until they are stronger. The rest of us will divide up to look for the others."

"But without our sense our chances of stumbling across anyone in this murk are small," Pendolin stated flatly.

"True enough," Ashmere responded, "but we must try. We also have to find out more about the conditions outside this immediate area."

As Ashmere was concluding Minere rejoined the group catching only Ashmere's last sentence. "What is going on? Is someone going somewhere?" She looked from face to face.

Ashmere repeated her suggestion. Minere continued to look around at the group. "Are you kidding? We cannot get our magic back unless all of us work together to dig at the cliff! We cannot continue without our magic.

Tandeir and I have been working to uncover the stream, but some of the rocks are too large and the pile is huge."

Ashmere looked her in the eye. "Minere, we cannot afford to spend the time necessary to dig through that whole pile of rubble in the hope that we can recover some magic. There may be more Jhirum who need our help now or they may die."

Planting her hands on her hips Minere stared back at her. "So we are giving up on our spring completely? How can you even consider this?"

Tandeir stood to command Minere's attention. "We are not saying that we are giving up on our magic, only that it must wait for a while."

Minere looked defeated, she expected Tandeir at least to understand. "How can any of you stand to be without magic? I feel like I am only half alive. Can't you see that we cannot help anyone without it?"

Ashmere had enough of this debate. "Our decision is made Minere, you can help us or not, but we cannot waste any more time."

Minere glanced involuntarily back at the cliff. "I will go with you, but as soon as we have accounted for the living I am coming back to continue digging."

Without further discussion they gathered up their few belongings, the remnants of their meal and with Legolan and Pendolin each with a tribe member for support they headed off back to the far side of the cliff where they had found the berry bushes.

Minere walked behind the rest, still reluctant to leave the area. The air was still warmed somewhat by the many fires burning in the valley, but there was beginning to be a hint of chill in the air, chill that should have been lessened by the midday sun, which instead was hidden behind black clouds of soot and ash.

With their injured charges Ashmere knew that it would be near the end of the day by the time they could establish a camp on the other side of the cliff. They would have to wait until the next day to set out in their search for survivors. But they must know that they have a safe camp for their injured brethren and a safe place to return from their journeys.

CHAPTER 13 RETURNING WANDERERS

Endmere opened his eyes, but it was still dark. He soon realized however that it was indeed morning but the sky was still shrouded in soot and ash and a gray-black smoke clung to the mountains. Everything existed in shades of gray. Even where leaves remained on the trees they were smothered in dust and ash muting the verdant green.

Here in the mountains at least, much of the vegetation as well as the animals, survived. The mountains were scarred by landslides and fires, which still burned, but there was no immediate struggle required to survive. True, Endmere knew they must hunt for a clean source of water, but there were many clean springs in the mountains, just not any others with magical power. He could not help himself from staring once again at the black pool which used to be their spring.

Endmere could already feel the strength of his magic waning and his contact with the world diminishing to the near blindness of his five basic senses. No loss could compare to this in his mind. How could they heal the broken land without their magic? There was never a doubt in his mind that they could survive without it, but who would they be. They would no longer be the tenders and caretakers of the mountains. They would merely be another of its denizens, surviving day to day like the deer or bear, subject to the vagaries of nature's opportunities and disasters rather than the protectors of all creatures.

The mere possibility of being diminished to this state made his mind go black as the soot clouds overhead. From the scowl on Cragen's face as he awoke it was clear that he felt the same, but they forced themselves to prepare a meal before setting out to find fresh water.

They had just returned with their water skins filled, around mid morning when Jasper arrived, winded from setting a rapid pace to return to their home valley, thinking that here would be some comfort and peace. Jasper was an adult, though half Endmere's age, his youthful steps brought him quickly to the side of the spring.

"Hello Cragen and Endmere. It is good to see you," Jasper began lightly. But then he noticed Cragen and Endmere's faces and his face dropped. "What is the matter?"

Endmere nodded his head toward the spring. Jasper turned, stared for a moment then hurried to the side of the pool. He crinkled his nose at the foul smelling liquid that oozed from the earth.

He jerked his head around looking at Endmere with horror on his face. "What is wrong with the spring? Can we still drink from it?"

"No," Endmere answered. "It is poisoned, at least for now."

Jasper stood rooted in place and stared from man to man.

"Jasper, we do not know what the future holds," Endmere counseled. "Perhaps the spring will clean itself after a time. Perhaps the shaking of the earth released this rancid liquid into the spring but it will be washed clean again. We cannot know, so for now we must learn what we can and do what we can. Do you have any spring water left in your skin?"

Jasper, brought back to himself with the direct question responded, "Only a little."

"Well, save whatever there is for a time when we really need it," Endmere sighed. "We must wait for the others to see what news they bring. Did you have any recent contact with anyone else?"

"Early this morning shortly after I started out I had contact with Thespan," Jasper replied. "I think he was close behind me."

Thespan was only slightly younger than Endmere and his equal in strength and determination.

The three men sat down a short distance from the spring to discuss what had happened and what each had seen in more detail. It was clear that Jasper was thoroughly shaken by the condition of the spring. He kept glancing back at it, shaking his head and frowning each time.

Before the shrouded sun had moved to its zenith, Thespan could be seen picking his way up the broken path to the spring. He waved from a distance to the threesome seated by the spring. The tepid response he received made him almost stop in his tracks and by the time he reached them and they stood, concern was etched in his face.

"What is the matter?" he began. Are things worse than they seem?"

Jasper could not contain his anguish. "It's the spring, look at it."

Thespan, as Jasper had before him turned to look at the dark pool. His normally jovial face darkened with what he saw. Then he caught the sulfurous scent in the air that was evident even over the acrid smoke that shrouded everything. He turned looking for the source, and then stared at the dark liquid oozing from the spring again.

"It is poisoned," Jasper nearly wailed in answer to his unspoken question.

Thespan walked to the edge of the pool, bent and dipped his hand in to lift a palm full but quickly shook it off and wrinkled his nose in disgust.

"Do you have any spring water left?" asked Endmere.

"A few drops are all. I have been out for weeks and was on my way back when this all started to happen. Does anyone know what exactly did happen?"

"It is not at all clear," answered Cragen. "I have never experienced anything like it."

"We were hoping that some one of our group would have seen something that would provide us with some insight," Endmere added as they drew away from the fetid spring and sat to continue their discussion.

"I saw nothing that could explain all of this. It was too foggy and I was in the middle of the woods where I could not see far even if it had not been foggy."

Endmere nodded, "I am afraid that most of us were in the same situation. About all we can do is wait for the others."

It was just after midday when Lamsil arrived, looking haggard. She had seen many more turnings of the seasons than Endmere and at this moment looked twice her age. The gray streaks in her hair were barely distinguishable from her dark brown hair because of the covering of ash. She too went through the shocking introduction to their contaminated spring.

As they sat Endmere drew her out of her stunned silence. "Were you able to tell what happened?"

"No, I was further north than you were here. I was on the side of a mountain when the earthquakes started a landslide which nearly buried me. My magic saved me but I used the last of my water to strengthen myself enough to heal my injuries."

"What was it like in the north?" Endmere prodded. "Were there fires there as there are here?"

"There were fewer fires and less damage in general. Whatever happened must have been farther away there."

They all nodded at this small piece to the puzzle. Endmere's mood darkened with each confirmation that something terrible had happened, and that none of them so far had any water left to sustain them until the hoped for clearing of their pool.

Cragen looked thoughtful for a moment. "From what we have each seen in our journeys it appears that the blast must have originated somewhere south and east of here. But there is no clue as to how far away, or what the origin."

Lamsil nodded agreement. "Where I was there was no fog so I could see the huge black cloud approaching from that direction. I could also see the rain of smaller rocks well before I had to find shelter."

The perpetual twilight was fading into blackness by the time Endmere heard Bastile coming up the gorge. Middle aged and strong she appeared unbowed by the events of the past days although obviously tired from pushing herself to get back to the spring as quickly as possible. She did not even notice the spring in her exhaustion, she simply collapsed with the group around the fire they had built to ward the darkness and chill.

Lamsil handed her some food and water before any one spoke. After some time during which she ate and drank in silence she finally paused, looking around at those gathered around the fire, "May I have some spring water, I need to renew myself."

The answer, however, was slow in coming and was preceded by glances and silence. "We cannot," Cragen offered. "The spring has been contaminated."

The blank stare that each of them in their turn had worn in response to this statement swept over her face. Endmere continued, "We have only the remnants that some of us carry in our water bags."

"Then what are we to do?" Bastile responded in astonishment. "Will it clear?"

"There is no way to tell," Endmere answered. "It could clear in days, or never. What did you see in your travels?" Endmere continued, trying to move past the painful issue of their spring. "We are trying to piece together what has happened and the extent of the damage."

Bastile, still trying to assimilate what she had just heard hesitated a moment before gathering her thoughts. "I was near the sea in the western mountains" she began, "tending to a grove of evergreens that had been attacked by a boring insect which threatened to kill many of them. I felt a searing pain in my head and moments later heard the rumble and felt the ground shake. I was on the western slope of the last mountains before the sea so I could see little, until the black cloud swept over the top of the mountain blowing down many of the trees on the peak and darkening the sky. I was frightened and hid in the deep protection of the evergreens. I did not move until I was contacted to return to the spring.

By the time I reached the top of the first peak, I could see that there had been much scattered destruction. The earthquakes had begun and I could see scattered fires in the distance as well as large slides. It also became obvious that my most direct route back was blocked by a large fire, so I headed north along the ridge where I could continue to see what was happening. However I eventually had to head east into the valley and that is where I began to have problems.

I had traveled until dark with little difficulty and I found a quiet place to bed down for the night." Here she paused to cast an uneasy glance at the spring before returning to her story. "Before dawn however, I was awakened to find myself nearly surrounded by fire. I had to run for my life in the dark. Thank goodness I still was strong in magic, or I may not have survived. I worked my way to higher ground around the edge of the blaze to where I could wait for dawn. Of course dawn did not add much light but I continued on through the day working around slides and fires at every turn until I got here."

Though her trip was longer than most, there was no new information, nothing that could shed light on the source of the catastrophe. Finally Endmere concluded, "We must take some time to decide what to do next. We can just sit here watching to see if the spring clears, or we could go in search of the source of the disaster in hopes that it might yield information that would help us decide what to do."

"There are other possibilities we should consider," Cragen added. "If our spring is truly contaminated for good, we need to find a new source of magic, or we will be no better than the other animals that inhabit these mountains."

"We know of no other source in all of the mountains we have traveled," Lamsil countered. "Where would you have us look?"

"Go to the source," Cragen responded. "The spring originates deep in the ground. Obviously somewhere beneath these mountains is where the magic comes from. I suggest that if we are convinced our spring will not clean itself, we should seek to find the source itself, which lies, beneath these mountains. There are many caves we have encountered. Some were explored in times past. Some go nowhere while others lead deep beneath the mountains and their ends have never been found. Perhaps one of these leads to the source of our magic."

"That seems a slim chance," Lamsil responded. "We have only found one spring in all of these mountains. What makes you think that there is any reasonable chance of finding the source of our magic in a cave which meanders aimlessly through the rock?"

"There were stories," Cragen began, "from times past, that have been handed down to us, telling of some of the deep caves and of mysteries that occurred in them and of clearly magical places. Admittedly there is no certainty, but some hope is better than none."

Endmere interjected, "I agree it is a remote chance, but one not to be completely dismissed until we have had time to consider the alternatives. We should sleep now and discuss what we should do next in the morning."

This, they all agreed to because they were exhausted from the events of the past two days and the strain on their psyches. They spread out away from the fire and settled in to a restless night's slumber. Endmere could not help noticing the chill in the air that had never touched him before.

CHAPTER 14 THE DAWN OF MIDNIGHT

Nomber awoke to a gray dawn, soggy, with a light mist. His muscles were tight and his head ached as if he had eaten rotten fruit the night before. He looked around at his sorry companions, in various states of ill health ranging from a few remaining bruises, or burns, to poorly repaired broken bones.

Never had any of them experienced this type of misery. The Jhirum were born to magic and healing. Occasionally one of them would be injured through accident, or being careless around a wild beast, but their wounds were quickly healed. Their magic in general protected them from the elements and discomforts of living without shelter and they had little need for extensive clothing. Now, there was little hope of more healing and even the discomfort of the cool summer rain ate at his patience. Worse than any of these discomforts was the constant headache, which gnawed at his nerves and troubled his sleep.

Others in the group began to rouse themselves, each in turn reaching for their head as they sat up with groans and winces. Apparently, the headache was a common theme amidst their diverse injuries. Nomber stirred the fire to try to raise a flame in the dampness. It was unusually cool for late summer and with no sun to warm their bones they had need of the fire.

A reluctant coal stirred to sluggish life with prodding, sputtering weakly against the fine mist falling from the sky. Soon though he had a steady flame and though smoky it cast some warmth. The others quickly gathered around huddling as close as possible.

Nomber stood to stretch his back, looking for the first time at the stream. Bobbing along the edge in the back currents created by boulders were the silver bodies of several fish. He could see that the water was choked with ash and mud, making it the same color as everything else in the blasted landscape. The fish apparently unable to breath had quickly expired in this flowing cesspool. Well they would have a fine fish breakfast, which might be the last fish they would have for some time if all of the streams were like this one.

Nomber glanced around the fire at his beleaguered charges. "Bashley and Gromand, let's grab some of those dead fish to cook for breakfast." They responded with unenthusiastic nods.

The water was cold as it swirled around Nomber's legs and so chocked with ash that had the fish not been on the surface they would have been impossible to see.

In a few moments they each had a couple of large fish to bring back to the fire. Quickly gutted and skewered they were toasting over the fire before the chill had left Nomber's legs.

By now everyone was awake and huddled by the fire in the semidarkness that passed for day. As the fish cooked, Floan looked to Nomber. "Why do I have this constant headache? Is it just from my injuries, or this ash and smoke? I don't think that I can stand it much longer." There were furtive glances around the fire. Then several of them at once commented on having the same headache.

Nomber, trying to sound unworried responded, "I have a similar headache. I think it must be from all the smoke and soot in our lungs. Perhaps this rain will wash some of the contamination out of the air."

"But now what," Jarine asked, having been silent up to this point. "What are we to do? Without our magic we are cold and miserable. It is hard to tell how long we will have food if we stay here. There is nothing left growing, the fish are dying and soon the animals that are left will die too."

Nomber straightened himself, trying to look more confident then he felt. "You are right Jarine. We must make some decisions now, before all hope is lost. I think that we should consider moving at least to the edge of our territory to see if we can find a place with less damage, where we can still find food and shelter."

Thane's scowl took in the whole group before landing on Nomber. "Shouldn't we first get to our spring and replenish our water bags and ourselves?"

Nomber looked at him a moment in silence then replied, "I have been to the edge of what appears to be a great crater in the earth. It looks to me that this crater has completely swallowed our spring. I fear there is little hope that we will find any magic water to replenish ourselves." He looked around at the silent blank faces until Bashley shook himself before responding, "Are you certain? Surely the water still flows somewhere?"

Others joined in, the question passing many of their lips until Nomber motioned for silence. "You have not seen the crater, nothing there is as it was. Wherever we go, however, I agree that we should investigate the area to see if we can find any trace of our water."

Thane stood, staring at Nomber, the scowl deeper than ever. "The question is where should we go? The east is wild and unknown to us. That leaves the Spine to the west, or the mountains in the south."

Nomber paused in thought. "The Mountains might have provided some protection from the blast and still harbor life, to the south is mostly open country until you get to the black mountains which are far away. On the other hand the further south we go the warmer will be the climate. We are not far from fall this far north and I would not like to deal with cold weather on top of our other problems."

"The west is our best chance," Thane quickly countered. "There are sure to be more of our tribe still surviving to the west. We can be in the Spine in a day. The Black mountains are many days travel."

"Thane has a good point." Nomber admitted. "But I think the greater distance to the mountains in the south is a benefit. We are more likely to find food and shelter. We are also more likely to find more of our tribe along that path. I think that it is best if we have as many of our tribe as possible together at this time. We can forage as we go for anything edible."

Thane's lips tightened but he remained silent. The fish crackled on the fire, interrupting the discussion. Their grumbling bellies demanded immediate attention.

Nomber pulled a piece of meat off one of the fish juggling the hot morsel from hand to hand until it cooled. As he took the first bite he could not help but wince at the taste and feel of grit which still covered everything including the food. But his hunger won out and soon they were all eagerly devouring fish and ash.

As Nomber licked the last morsels off of his fingers he could not help wondering when their next meal would come and from where.

The rest of the tribe was just finishing up when Nomber heard a call. All their heads snapped up at once. Through the gloom of ash and rain Nomber could just make out the shadows of several more Jhirum trudging through the black mud that had developed as the rain strengthened.

"Bashley, Gromand, go back to the stream and see if you can find a few more fish," Nomber immediately exclaimed. The rest of the tribe solemnly walked to greet the newcomers.

As they came into the light of the fire Nomber could see that Dankin was leading the way, waving disconsolately. They had clearly fared no better than the group around the fire and were in fact still covered in the black soot. A couple of them were supported by others and nearly all of them hobbled to one degree or another.

Nomber hurried up to Dankin. "I'm glad to see you Dankin. Come sit we have a fire and fish."

Dankin nodded solemnly. "It is good to see you to Nomber. We had nearly given up hope of finding other survivors." The new members moved around the fire as Bashley and Gromand returned with more fish.

But before they could settle in Nomber reconsidered. "Before you eat I think that you should go to the stream and clean yourselves thoroughly. The stream itself is filthy but I fear that this black soot that covers everything may partially be the same filth that we cleared from the contaminated swamp. It appears that whatever struck the earth did so right where the swamp was."

He could see confusion turn to wide eyed fear as they all reflexively looked at their hands and bodies. Without further urging they moved quickly to the stream cringing from the cold but plunging in regardless, scrubbing as quickly as they could.

By the time they emerged from the stream, even colder than before, but somewhat clean except for the lingering stains, the fish was ready.

Gathering as close to the fire as possible they ate ravenously. Only after the last bit of fish had disappeared did Nomber ask, "Where were you when the blast occurred?"

Dankin finished licking a stray piece of fish off of her fingers before starting. "After cleansing the swamp all that you see here had headed off to the west, scattering from there. When the explosion occurred a couple of us had just been together and so we quickly found each other amid the rubble. From there we were able to seek out the others as we had fairly good stores of magic water between us, although several of us had lost what we had. We collected every one we could from near the mountains before heading back in this direction in hopes of finding others. We have found little to eat along the way although we were able to heal most of our wounds. We still have a little water left. The only thing that we have not been able to cure is a headache that we all seem to have to some degree or another."

Nomber paused and shook his head as he replied, "We have a similar ailment although few of us were able to save any of the healing water and so were not able to heal all of our injuries completely."

Dankin cast and assessing eye over Nomber's group, "we should attend to those that need further healing now." Immediately, Dankin and a couple of the others began ministering to those who still clearly had unhealed injuries.

As best as he could guess it was nearing mid day by the time they were all resting by the fire in what was now a steady cold rain. The stream had turned into a roiling gray entity, carrying away volumes of the dark gray ash and the bodies of countless dead fish and other creatures.

Nomber recounted for the new group their discussion regarding what to do next. Dankin nodded in agreement. "I agree that the south is our best chance. We were either in or near the Spine and there was just as much damage there as here. But from what we saw there is not likely to be much food until we are far from here."

"Then we had better be on our way," Nomber said without hesitation. It would be a slow journey at least until they cleared what had been the forested areas and reached the more open plains to the south. There the tangle of fallen trees would not hamper their way at every turn.

Though they all felt better with full bellies and their bodies almost fully healed, the headaches persisted and the cold rain and ankle, or knee-deep ash mud sucked at their feet and their moods.

In fact, though they still traveled in what had been sparsely forested land as they moved south, the obstacles thinned as if all evidence of every living thing, large or small, had been simply vaporized. Soon they were traveling through a gray-black muddy moonscape where nothing lived and there was no sound but the sucking of their feet from the mud and the drops of rain splattering in the gray puddles.

Nomber looked around at the group. Their eyes were vacant and haunted. With each moment that they walked revealing only more desolation his own heart had sunk to a depth he would not have believed possible. He heard a quiet sob escape Floan's lips. Bashley put his arms around her as her shoulders shook.

They had traveled most of the afternoon when they topped a small ridge and looked down a steep slope, which seemed to have no bottom. It was difficult to tell where exactly they were with no landmarks and even the terrain altered beyond recognition, but the whole area had been a plain with no point being much lower or higher than any other except for a few small rolling hills in some sections. This slope, Nomber was certain had not existed before the blast.

With some trepidation Nomber led them down the slope, subconsciously avoiding heading directly into its depths but skirting the edge as much as possible. Here there was much less ash and mud. Instead there were large stretches of almost glassy rock that the rain had washed clean of any loose debris. Nomber had never seen anything like it. They all walked gingerly; as if at any moment it might turn to water beneath their feet.

Though they could not see far in the gloom Nomber could tell that they had descended quite a distance before he began to sense the ground turning and beginning to rise again. It was as if they all held their breath for the entire sojourn into the strange valley and back out again, so foreign and altered was the place. Finally cresting the far rim, as one they paused and turned to glance back at the strange valley. Whatever had created this odd landscape had incredible power the likes of which they and probably their ancestors had never encountered.

Nomber shook himself free from contemplating the possibilities. "It is nearly night; I think that we should stop for the day."

Thane looked around and then back at Nomber, his perpetual scowl still on his face. "This is no place to camp. There is no water, no shelter and nothing but mud to lie in."

Jarine drew up beside her father. "And where would you suggest we would find a better place Thane?"

"I don't know but if we kept on we might find something." He looked around to the others for support.

Dankin looked around at the bleak faces. "It is not a good place but we are all too tired to go on. I don't think we have many choices right now."

Thane just shook his head and moved away from them. Number knew that Thane could be negative and was determined not to let him drag the tribe down even further. "If we all huddle together we can at least share some warmth. Perhaps by tomorrow we can find more shelter and food."

As the group settled in, huddled close together, Number sat next to Jarine, leaning close so that only she could hear. "I am certain that somewhere within that basin we just traversed used to lie our spring."

Jarine looked thoughtful a moment. "Yes, you are probably right. That means that our spring is no more." A shiver ran through her body as she said this. Number put his arms around his daughter's shoulders, holding her close as a tear trickled silently down her cheek.

It was nearly impossible to find any comfort in the mist which continued to fall, chilling them to the bone as they tried to settle in for sleep. Finally they all huddled into groups, tight together, sitting up. Number sat on the outside of a small group with Dankin, Jarine, Thane and a few others. Thane looked like a thundercloud with rain running down his scowling face.

Dankin shifted her weight trying to find a comfortable position. "I hope that this rain does not keep up for long, we could use some sun."

Number nodded agreement. "Hopefully there will at least be more shelter as we get farther away from the crater." Jarine looked at her father across Dankin's back. "How far do you think the destruction reaches?"

Thane just grunted. "Feels like it must be the whole world."

Dankin glanced sideways at Thane. "It must get better the farther away from here we get."

Number bent his head down to shelter his face from the rain. "That is certainly true, so we had better try to get some sleep so we can move on as early as possible."

The next day arrived much like the one before it, dark and gray. Their headaches continued and their tempers flared easily as they roused themselves, ate a small amount from their meager provisions and resumed their journey.

They had encountered no life for some time. However, after topping a knoll with a steep southern slope Number thought he saw a dark shape moving near the bottom of the hill. Though the drizzle and haze that still clouded the air made it hard to see, by the time they were halfway down the hill he was sure that it was a Grall.

Gralls were beasts, which normally walked on four legs. The front feet, however, rather than being heavily padded for walking like the hind legs, were instead crude hands with long claws that were used to dig insects from trees or roots from the ground. In order to reach fruit and anything else that they could get from trees, including the eggs of birds, they could stand on their rear legs and reach easily the height of two Jhirum into the air.

With a porcine face and entirely covered in course dark brown hair the Grall cast a frightening visage, but was normally shy and avoided confrontation.

This Grall, however, upon seeing the large group of Jhirum immediately rose up to its full height and bellowed so loud the Jhirum drew back. Its hair was matted in the black soot that covered everything and half of its body was devoid of hair completely where it had sustained burns from the blast or subsequent fires.

The Jhirum, some of whom still had magic at their disposal immediately spread out in defense. Nomber and those without magic held back a little allowing the others to take the fore. Without hesitation the Grall attacked as if possessed, splattering mud as it charged. The Jhirum had never presented any danger to the Galls, but it was clear that this one intended to destroy them.

Those with magic immediately reached out to try to calm the beast. Their first attempts were rebuffed by a violence of spirit they had never before encountered even in the most aggressive beasts. Finally as the Gall neared them they had to attack it with the full strength of their magic. This brought the Gall to a stunned halt, but still it sought to tear at them with its claws. Using all their combined strength they finally brought it to the ground unconscious and panting.

Stunned by the violent attack, the Jhirum stood motionless for several moments before exhaling and moving to the side of the beast. As a people they were used to caring for the animals in their world not defending themselves from them. Even the aggressive large carnivores seemed to understand both the strength and the benign intentions of the Jhirum and would never attack them unprovoked.

Nomber could tell that some of his tribe were probing the beast with their magic trying to understand and perhaps heal what was wrong. "We cannot afford to waste what little magic we have on the Grall," he exclaimed a little more sharply than he intended. Several of the tribe jerked their heads around to look at him blankly a moment before comprehension softened their faces.

Dankin was the last to withdraw from the beast. She flinched involuntarily as she pulled away from it. "This beast has nothing but hate and aggression seething through its mind," she said in a tone of bewilderment.

"Even the catastrophic events that it has been put through should not have created this state." Nomber replied. "It is strange, but we can't spend time on the beast while our own survival hangs in the balance. We had best just put some distance between us and this creature before it recovers."

Nomber turned to leave, but glanced back over his shoulder at the sleeping giant. Several of the tribe were still lingering, shaking their heads in confusion before finally turning to follow.

As they walked Nomber continued to ponder the actions of the beast. Could the black soot that seemed to be giving them their headaches have something to do with its strange reaction? If so would it have more serious effects on them as well?

By mid afternoon they had cleared what had been heavy forest and were encountering fewer obstacles. Their pace picked up considerably, although their moods improved little. At one point one of the tribe that had come with Dankin stumbled and had to be helped back to her feet. She seemed groggy and disoriented. They spared a little of the remaining water to help her regain her senses.

Nomber, himself had settled in to a black mood driven by the oppressive headache and gloomy weather. As the day wore on uncharacteristic bickering broke out periodically between tribe members. By the time it was apparent that what little light there was had begun to fade he could barely focus on putting one foot in front of the other.

Nomber called them to a halt in a ravine that offered only small shelter from the wind. However, they gathered some of the fallen trees that were scattered on the ground and propped them up to make a crude lean-to which offered some protection from the rain. With the help of some magic they were able to start a fire in the soggy wood they gathered which threw a febrile warmth amidst the clouds of white smoke it generated.

As they crowded in close to the fire Gromand almost knocked Dankin over where she sat, she glared at him and stood. "Watch what you're doing you oaf!" She pushed him with all her might. Stumbling backward, a clearly startled Gromand fell across Thane who unceremoniously threw him on the ground.

Nomber nearly growled at them. "Let it be, stop acting like children!" Although in fact he had never seen a Jhirum child act in this manner. He was certain that they had many more difficult days ahead of them. How was he going to keep the tribe together if they were already at each other's throats?

Along the way they had picked up small bits of food wherever a plant had been sheltered or where an animal had recently died. Much of it was tough or partially rotten, but it would sustain them. Two of the Jhirum almost came to blows over a particularly fresh rabbit. Nomber once again had to intervene, separating them with a shove and a glare.

It seemed somehow that even the food, did not renew either their strength or their mood as they huddled around the smoky fire. The rain continued to fall, turning everything into mud and making it impossible to find a dry or comfortable place to sleep, so they slept sitting up again, huddled close enough together to support each other and to provide some additional warmth. Only through sheer exhaustion did any of them find a few moments of sleep.

By morning their senses were so dulled that no one noticed that the tepid light of morning had returned until it was well past dawn. They ate a small amount of their remaining food and pressed on.

About mid day they came across an entire herd of grassland buck dropped dead in their tracks, exposed to the full force of the blast in the open plains. At this Number called a halt. "We cannot continue in this way unprotected, we will die of exposure. If we gather the skins from these buck we can use them as cloaks until we can find better."

Dankin turned to him with a look of disgust. "I would rather freeze! You expect us to wear the hides of buck without treating or drying them?"

Number shook his head. "I know it is not a pleasant prospect but we are freezing in this cold rain. Few of us have any magic left. We need something to protect us from the elements."

The Jhirum rarely wore more than loincloths in any season, because their magic protected them from the elements, but without the magic they were quickly realizing they were ill prepared to face the unusual late summer chill.

Blinan wrinkled her nose. "Will bloody skins really help us?"

Floan also looked distressed. "Surely there is a better way for us to survive. We can take some meat, but leave the rest for the vultures."

At this point Bashley forced his way into the debate, "I for one am already freezing. Untreated skins are better than no skins at all. These beasts have no further need of them. I agree with Number, let us take what we can."

Thane countered, "We could be in The Spine by now if we had gone west. I see no reason to continue to blindly follow Number's lead on this or any other matter."

Though unaccustomed to group decisions, the Jhirum were nonetheless normally civil to each other, but this discussion was becoming heated.

Number, momentarily taken aback by the confrontation finally retorted, "I do not claim to tell anyone what they must do. I only suggest what I think is best. I also am sure that it is best that we stay together to survive whatever we must face."

Jarine nodded agreement. "Any who do not wish to wear a raw skin does not have to, but I for one could use the protection from this damp cold."

Dankin turned her back. "That is fine but I am not waiting around for you to butcher these animals while I could be further on my way to the mountains. Any who care to join me are welcome." With that she strode off into the rain.

Kang, a young man who came with Dankin to the group and Blinan strode off with her followed by a few others. Thane started to follow, then hesitated and remained in place.

Nomber shook his head. "Fine then let's be about it before we waste more time."

They set about methodically removing skins from the buck with their small stone knives. Though dead for a couple of days the stench was not too strong, but the thought of eating the meat turned Nomber's stomach. He knew though that they were not likely to find anything better in their travels.

He had just peeled back the skin of a buck from the belly to the backbone and was rolling it over to the other side when someone in the group let out a piercing yell that brought them all upright from their labors. Bashley was running away from the buck that he was about to skin. The rest hurried in his direction.

From some distance Nomber could see one of the buck writhing, its skin rippling and jerking. As he came closer he could see that there was some sort of animal inside the belly of the buck disemboweling it with relish. He approached with caution until a head broke through the skin to look at them. The head looked something like a badger but was covered in blood and black soot. The vile black soot had actually been less apparent for some time now. It must have been heavier than the ash and had mostly fallen nearer to the impact site. This badger, however, had either traveled a good distance from the direction of the impact or had found a pocket of the putrid slime. But this was not what made it appear a monster in spite of its modest size. In its eyes Nomber could see madness. It took only a moment to glance at the gathering Jhirum and then resumed ripping and tearing at the buck, this from an animal that normally subsisted on roots and grubs.

One of the tribe attempted a closer approach and without warning the badger shot out of the carcass with gnashing teeth and snarls that sent the Jhirum scattering in every direction. Just as quickly it turned and tore back into the buck. After that the Jhirum kept their distance, working on skins that were far from the maddened badger.

It took them till after mid day to complete their bloody task and by that time none of them complained about the stench or the bloody slime as they gladly threw the skins around their shoulders. They immediately felt the warmth return to their bodies, though being undried and untreated the skins weighed as much as a young child.

They ate some of the meat around a quickly made fire of bushes and small trees and then moved on into the plains. They were still some distance from the protection of the mountains, and if the rain kept up it would take them even longer than they had anticipated to get there.

CHAPTER 15 FLOTSAM

The gentle rocking of the boat on the sluggish waves made waking up slow for the Jhirum of the Sea in the gloom that now passed for dawn. But as soon as consciousness grew to the point of remembrance the laziness quickly was overcome by anxiousness. The possibility that survivors still floated somewhere on the vast sea drove them all to the deck despite their lethargy.

They had hardly begun their search for survivors that may have been washed out to sea when darkness had overtaken them the night before, so they each had a quick breakfast from the fresh food gathered the day before and a small amount of fresh water. The anchor was raised and they began their search in earnest.

If there were tribesmen still alive it was a good chance that they could find them. They still had their magic, which would mean they would only have to be in the general vicinity to make contact. In addition they had an intimate knowledge of the sea, its tides and currents, so even though the tsunami was an unusual event they could surmise where anyone cast adrift would most likely have been carried by the currents.

As once again Shwaren took the helm. Melding his power with those of the crew that were assigned to drive the ship he swung the boat about to head north toward the current that brushed the coast and would probably carry any debris from the bay. Joined as they were he noticed the lack of the painful sensation that they now knew came from the object which struck the earth.

They sailed until nearly midmorning with no sign of life apart from the normal sea birds and an occasional porpoise. The wind had begun to build and occasional downpours washed across the deck from the rapidly passing clouds. They were about to stop at one of the locations where there was an undersea release of magic when they came upon a debris field, which indicated they had caught up with some of the wash from the tsunami. With this encouragement they decided to press on instead. It was impossible to tell from where the debris had originated but Shwaren was certain they were at least in the general area where there could be survivors.

The hull of their boat periodically echoed with the sound of a tree trunk slapping against the side and there was almost a constant scraping of smaller debris along the hull.

Still short of midday the watchers in unison let out a cry. Linked as they were through magic to strengthen its reach they all felt the contact as one.

Without having to exchange words the boat swung slightly to the east and soon Shwaren could see a large tree floating on the waves with one of their kin hanging on to the side. As the boat drew closer Shwaren could make out through the tangled and matted hair the face of Maerl. She was one of the female contemporaries of Shwaren. As they eased alongside she pulled herself up on to the trunk of the tree and reached for the ladder, which was thrown over the side. Hugs and grins greeted her on board, not only because of the relief of finding her, but the hope, which she brought that there might be other survivors.

Shwaren eased through the crowd around her. "Take her below, dry her off and give her some food and water. The rest of you back to your posts. There may be others nearby."

The cold water had chilled her even with her magic and she shivered as a couple of the Jhirum escorted her below deck. The crew quickly returned to their positions around the boat, anxious now to find others. Shwaren could feel the excitement through the bond. Everyone knew that if there was one Jhirum alive here there would likely be more.

Before noon they had plucked three more from the debris, which was now beginning to thin as they reached the edge of the tsunami's waste. After clearing the remaining debris they circled around moving further from the coast to head back south in hopes of finding others farther out.

Only one other survivor, however, was retrieved before darkness began to settle over the water. A light rain had begun to fall again and a chill wind was blowing off the shore. Since they could sense their location and the presence of survivors as well at night as in the day they continued on until they were nearly back at the mouth of the bay. There they laid anchor to rest, eat and discuss what to do next.

Maerl and the others had recovered sufficiently to join them at their meal, which they took below deck since the rain was now pounding in sheets across the deck. The belly of the ship was one large room, though low enough to require them to bend over, it easily accommodated the present crew and castaways with supplies stacked all around the periphery. Magic provided light as they began to query the survivors about their ordeal.

"I was on the dock," Maerl began, "bringing supplies to be used in repairing one of the other boats. I felt a searing pain and looked to the east. I could see the black cloud growing over the tops of the hills and spreading out. Then the earth shook knocking me to the ground, destroying several of our houses and nearly emptying the bay of water. Although we were concerned we did not imagine that we were in imminent danger. Those of us on the dock stopped our work to watch the approach of the black cloud. Not until it was very near did we begin to realize how quickly it was moving. By then it was too late and the blast swept over us where we stood.

Most of us were blown into the water like leaves in a fall wind. This is what saved several of us. The blast pushed us out into the harbor with the retreating water. When the return surge came we were far enough out that we were not immediately crushed against the rocks. I think all but one of us that you have rescued were saved in this way. We were however thrown into the midst of the debris washed from the shore, which battered us, and I fear killed some."

Her story was interrupted by the quiet sobs of Toren. Waymeir drew her aside, taking her to the front of the boat where she would not hear the remaining details.

Quieter now Maerl resumed, "In the chaos we all lost track of each other and then by the time we could make contact there was nothing we could do to get closer together. All we could do was float along hoping for rescue or an opportunity to be carried closer to shore."

"What of those on shore," Winfew prodded. "Could you tell what became of them?"

Maerl stared at the floor her eyes haunted. "Almost everyone was working near the shore. I saw some of their bodies float past me. They were battered so hard first by the blast and then by the return surge that it would be amazing if any survived, though I see two here that were on the shore." She glanced hesitantly at Toren.

"We rescued Toren from her cave," Shwaren explained. "Only Zifere is a survivor from the wave."

Zifere looked away momentarily then began almost in a whisper, "Several of us clung together for a few moments before we were torn apart. After that I saw only bodies."

Madrien prodded gently, "When you were able to try to make contact with others did any of you have contact with any one that we have not already rescued?"

Each in turn shook their heads, Maerl finally filling the silence, "We were not that spread out when we began to make contact. I do not think that there were any other survivors."

A long silence followed as each measured their loss, tried its weight and let go the hope they had carried the past couple of days.

After many moments Shwaren lifted his head as if in defiance of the future thrust upon them. "We must begin to decide what lies ahead for us. We are few in number now. We have been inland for a small distance. There is great destruction there which must only grow worse the closer to the blast you go."

Waymeir spoke for the first time, "It will be hard to rebuild our village, but the sea will continue to provide our food. We should start at once to reestablish our lives."

Winfew looked almost curious, or excited. "We are rootless now. We could start a new village anywhere, not necessarily where the old stood."

Waymeir shook her head. "The bay is good and the caves provide shelter. Though the sea is our home, I see no reason to abandon what has for most of our lives been a good land base."

In the brief silence while they pondered the alternatives, a small voice said simply, "I for one will not return to that place." Their heads turned to stare in silence at Toren, who looked at them in quiet defiance. "There is nothing there for us but bad memories and death."

Uncomfortable silence settled over the group, thinking of their losses and for the first time, seriously of perhaps not going back to their home off the sea.

Finally, looking away from the haunted eyes of the girl Shwaren broke the silence. "If we believe that further searching of the sea is of no use, then I think whether we rebuild in the bay, or elsewhere, we must return there to allow ourselves time to make plans, investigate the disaster further and if we decide to leave, to stock up for an extended journey."

To this they all nodded agreement, all accept Toren who now stared blankly off into a vision none of them could share.

After a few more moments of silence each in turn moved to find a place to sleep, or to go back on deck to attend to the ship. Occasionally they cast glances at the small girl who still sat near the front of the boat, silent and locked inside her own visions. Soon all that could be heard was the pounding rain the building wind and the creaking of the boat.

By morning the wind was nearly at gale force. The boat, though broad in the beam bounced roughly on the waves. None of this had disturbed any one's sleep. The Jhirum of the Sea were more comfortable sleeping to the sound and motion of waves, even large ones, than they ever were on land. That was not to say that some did not pass a restless night, but restless with thoughts of what lie ahead not of the storm.

With the onset of the gale the temperature had dropped significantly. The pounding rain threatened to suck all the heat from their bodies as they prepared to haul up the anchor. Their magic, however, kept them comfortable in their small jerkins and their magic would power the boat into port as their small sail would not stand well against the wind.

In the midst of the activity on deck Toren stood staring out to sea, her hands locked on the railing and her damp hair trailing in the wind. Though land was not in view in the near darkness of the tumultuous dawn she as any of her brethren knew with certainty which direction lay the land and with equal certainty chose to show it her back.

It would not take long to reach the bay and the remains of their village. They had anchored just north of the bay's mouth the night before. With the anchor raised, the boat eased forward against the wind, riding the waves at an angle toward the bay. Though by the time they reached the mouth of the bay and were within earshot of the rocky walls which guarded the entrance they could still see nothing but sheets of rain, they knew as certainly as if it were a clear sunny day where they were and how to proceed to the mooring.

They would however, still have to traverse the shallow water to shore with their small dinghies. That would be the most challenging part of the trip in the pounding surf. But again their skill and magic would see them through.

There was no anxiousness at the prospect except for the building tension that could be felt emanating from Toren. Zifere went to her to try to provide some comfort. She knew that he too had experienced the horror, perhaps even more than her and she allowed him this access, though she did not turn to the land or loosen the set of her jaw. "You understand that we must go back to our bay before we do anything else, don't you Toren?"

A slight nod was all that he received in response. "I know that you have horrible memories from the blast, but avoiding the bay will not assuage them."

"I just do not understand why anyone would consider staying here. Why force us to face the memories every day?"

"No decisions have been made as to our long term plans. Allow every one time to consider the options. Perhaps we will all agree to leave. For my own reasons I would just as soon we find a new home as well."

"I hope so. But I still will not set foot on the land. I will stay and tend the boat."

Zifere studied her for a while before answering. "All right, I will tell Shwaren. Perhaps someone else will stay with you." Receiving no answer he turned to inform Shwaren of her thoughts.

Shwaren looked away from the bobbing dinghies that were near the shore with their first load of passengers as Zifere approached. "Toren will not go ashore."

Shwaren glanced at the back of the young girl then called out to Waymeir. "Waymeir, may I see you a minute?"

Waymeir who was tending the ladder turned and joined Zifere and Shwaren. "Toren is going to remain on the boat. Would you mind staying with her?"

Waymeir glanced as the others had at Toren's back. "Certainly, she will need help in tending the boat in this storm anyway."

Shwaren nodded and returned to the railing. He knew that he would have to somehow get Toren past her horror if they decided to stay in the bay but that could wait until they had agreed on what course to follow.

Shwaren dropped over the side of the boat with the last group headed for shore. Precariously bobbing about next to the large boat, which threatened to crush them at every swell, the dinghies seemed as secure as a leaf blown in the wind as a means of transport. However, everyone in turn lowered themselves carefully to the small boats and cast off for shore. By midday everyone but the two who were remaining on the boat were ashore and trudging up the hill to find a cave or caves, which could be made suitable, as shelter.

Two of the larger caves, one, which was filled with debris, and another that was fairly clean just a little higher up the hill were appropriated as the resting places that they all would share. First though they all gathered in the higher cave to decide what to do next.

After everyone settled in to the cave, Winfew who was anxious for decisions began, "I think that we should explore inland for some distance to try to understand what has happened and the condition of the land a little more before we do anything else."

Maerl responded, "I agree, we must know more about what has happened before we decide what to do."

Zifere though shook his head. "What do we care of the land? Our concern is with the sea which has not been harmed."

"We do not know that the sea has not been harmed," Shwaren cautioned. "Who knows what affects this cataclysm has had, or will have on the whole world?"

Chastened, Zifere fell silent, but Madrien resumed, "Perhaps you are right, we should know more about what has happened and the effect it has had on the land, but after that I think we should go to sea and seek a new base from which to sail."

Maerl persisted, "We can only decide if this is the best course after we learn some more. I think it is a waste of time to discuss what we might do beyond investigating the damage to the land. Our decisions will most likely be different when we know more."

Shwaren stood. "I agree, but with the weather, I think that we should take this time to clean out the other cave to make it livable for however, long we will be here."

Most of those present nodded their agreement and began standing and moving out into the continuing downpour.

The other cave was only a stone's throw down the hill, but the elevation change was sufficient that here debris had been pushed far into the cave and was piled high. Sand, small rocks and tree limbs had to be removed in order to return the cave to a livable state, particularly if they were to fit ten or more people here.

Though the rocks and branches took effort to remove, it was the sand that proved most difficult. They made make shift scoops from bark, flat stones, or anything else they could find, scooped up the small amount of sand that they could hold and carried them from the cave.

The rain continued to pound down. The dim light was fading by the time the cave was cleared sufficiently to build fires and begin to prepare some dinner. A couple of the tribesmen volunteered to go back out to the boat to make sure everything was all right and to see if Toren and Waymeir would join them in the caves.

They returned shortly indicating that all was well, but both were determined to stay on the boat, which should be tended to at any rate in this stormy weather. After a warm dinner they settled in for an early sleep to the sound of the continuing downpour.

CHAPTER 16 DECISIONS

Endmere awoke to another dawn much like the last. They had slept, exposed to the elements, by their former magical spring. The dawn was marked by only a slight increase in light coming from no particular direction. It was a cool morning, one that would normally make him think of rain, but with the current conditions he could tell nothing for sure. Some of his camp mates were already up, the fire blazing against the gloom. Endmere joined them by the fire trying to drive the chill from his bones. One decision that would be made with little argument would be the need to search for food.

It had been some time since most of them had needed to search for food without the aid of magic. The magic and their world were so intertwined that to remove it from their beings was like removing another animal's eyes or nose, it was an incapacitating and potentially deadly weakness. However, he also knew that they had other senses and that they had used only them at times to survive, and could do it again.

As they stood by the fire shifting their feet in rhythm to try to get their blood circulating again Endmere began, "We should all go out and gather what food we can so that we have enough to sustain us for today and if possible tomorrow. By then more of our tribe should be here and we can begin a council."

They all nodded agreement and began to gather some meager belongings that would help them to get or carry food. Each set off in a different direction. Endmere headed on up the gorge toward the top of the valley, as much to get another look around as to look for food. About half way to the top he encountered a charred stretch that had fortunately burned itself out quickly. The acrid smell burned his nose. He looked sadly at the scorched berry bushes, which just a couple of days ago would have been laden with fruit. Shaking his head he continued on his way. He was now high enough that he could look back on their valley. He could still see the smoky fire on the other side of the valley. Fortunately it was not dry so the fire spread slowly and already appeared to be dying down. The valley air was in fact a little clearer than it had been the day before, but there was still little light.

Continuing on he soon came upon another patch of berry bushes, which had not been destroyed and began to gather what he could. There were also some nut trees near the top of the mountain that while early in the season might have some edible nuts. He proceeded to the top and gathered what he found of the nuts that looked like they could be eaten though they would be green and bitter. He then gazed out over the tops of the surrounding mountains. More accurately, he gazed out over perhaps one set of peaks. The others were still shrouded in haze and darkness. As he stood there a light drizzle began to fall. It was a cold rain, which quickly chilled his exposed skin. Normally his magic would have mostly kept him dry and certainly would have kept him warm, but not today. They would have to be more conscious of their clothing and the weather, or they would all die of exposure without their protective magic.

He bowed his head and began the decent back to the spring considering what other problems awaited them that he had not yet anticipated. Perhaps the caves would not be such a bad idea after all. At least they would afford some shelter. They would also have to begin the task of trying to contact the rest of their scattered group. Surely there were more survivors than this small band, but they were unreachable with magic. At some point most of them would return to the spring as it was their common source of magic. But many of them stayed away for long stretches at a time and were frequently a month or more away from the home base.

As Endmere arrived back at their camp, only Jasper was there ahead of him. He had also collected a large number of nuts, a small batch of berries and some fruit, which he must have gotten from the valley floor. At least some of the fruit trees had escaped the fire so far.

"Do you really think it might be possible to find the source of magic in the caves?" Jasper asked as he laid down his burden.

"I do not know, Jasper, it is at best a poor chance, but poor chances may be all we have. Did you check the spring?"

"No change," was Jasper's glum reply.

"I think that we have many things to consider, only one of which is the caves," Endmere counseled. "There is much we do not know about our current situation and much we must learn."

"But why have we not explored the caves recently," Jasper prodded. "It seems that we have ignored them completely."

"There is little life in the caves," Endmere replied. "Our business is with living things, so there seemed little reason to spend time there, and few of our people would willingly give up the fresh air and sun for the eternal blackness of the caves. In fact, now without our magic, exploration would be much more difficult since we could not use our magic to provide light."

"Are there any caves that were explored in the past near here?" Jasper continued undaunted.

"I do not know the old stories," Endmere explained. "Cragen would know better than I. But long ago I explored the cave on the other side of this very mountain, but not very far."

At this point Lamsil and Thespan joined them, each with small collections of berries and nuts and before long the whole group was back together. They reviewed their food and began to eat breakfast, setting aside a large portion that would hopefully last them a couple of days.

Jasper could not contain himself any longer. "Cragen, Endmere says that you know stories of when caves in the mountains were explored?"

"I spoke last night of the caves," Cragen's voice grew quiet. "I have been thinking on this all night. There is an old story about the cave that sits on the opposite side of this mountain. It was explored millennia ago, though an end was never found. The stories say it winds far into the mountain. There are hints in the story of springs and happenings along the way that speak of magic.

Since this cave is part of this very mountain from where our spring issues I think there may be some real chance that we could find a new source somewhere in this cave."

Lamsil spoke up, her dark eyes full of concern, "But it could take a lifetime to explore the cave, with no guarantee of success, or of even surviving the trip. Would there be food there? And what kind of dangers would we encounter. I too have heard some of the ancient tales, which include the mention of fell beasts living in some of the caves, dangerous and dark. I think that there are too many dangers and too little promise of success."

Bastile who had been quiet up to this point pushed wet air out of her eyes and suppressing the urge to shiver responded, "There are few of us at this time, if we go in many different directions there will be too few of us to guarantee our safety, without our magic to protect us."

Endmere shook his head. "I fear that there is no safety for us in any case at this time. Our world has been badly injured, who knows to what effect. Our magic is gone. We have not had to survive without magic for millennia. We must think on things that we have not had to concern ourselves with in our lifetimes, clothing warm enough to protect from the elements, perhaps weapons to help us defend ourselves, shelter that is more than an overhanging bough of a tree. We must relearn how to survive."

Lamsil nodded. "We must at least address some of these basic issues before we do anything else. We must improve our clothing, it is clear that even this summer rain is uncomfortable, not to speak of what will happen when the snows arrive."

Cragen spoke again, "I agree, that these basic needs must be attended to first, however, I think the cave can serve us here as well. It will give us protection, for now at least, that we sorely need."

Jasper eagerly added, "We should go there now and set it up as our home camp, we can leave some one here at the spring during the day, it is only a short hike from here to the cave."

"That is exactly what I was thinking," Endmere concluded. "The cave would certainly provide shelter close enough to the spring. From there we can work on clothing and other needs that we will have. Who would like to remain here at the spring for today while the rest of us go see if the cave will suit our needs? This is another adjustment we must make. We have never worked together as a group except for short periods of time. We must think more as a group now, for our own survival."

Bastile quickly responded, "I will remain here today."

Cragen nodded. "Good, come to the cave before dark, there is no need to be here all the time, anyone who returns here will remain for some time before leaving and as long as we monitor the spring regularly we will detect any changes."

The rest of the group began gathering up the food they had gathered in the now steady rain, anxious for enough shelter to get dry. They said goodbye to Bastile who was settled by the sputtering fire and moved on up the valley.

CHAPTER 17 SEARCH FOR SURVIVORS

After spending the morning and early afternoon moving their group to a place that they agreed could serve as their new camp on the other side of the hill from their cliff, the Natec constructed some crude shelters in the late afternoon darkness, built a fire and went to sleep. The short night ended with a whimper as the feeble light fought its way through the soot and cloud filled sky.

During the night rain had begun to fall and with the dawn it turned into a deluge. Rivulets ran everywhere cutting crooked lines through the gray encrusted land and turning the thick layer of gray ash and dust into a gray sucking mud.

Cold, unusual for late summer penetrated their skins as for the first time in their lives they noticed their lack of clothing. The only positive result of the rain was that it had begun to extinguish the remaining fires and wash some of the dust from the air.

The night having been much too short and uncomfortable had refreshed Fenly little but he spent a little time rebuilding the fire and directed others to shore up their lean-tos so that they would provide more protection for Legolan and Pendolin. They added layers of pine boughs to the rough branch structures, though the boughs were stripped of many of their needles.

Although they were all anxious to be off, before leaving Fenly also had them search the area for dead animals so that they might be able to collect some skins that could be used as blankets or clothing as needed.

They succeeded in finding a couple of buck, which they skinned, and prepared as best they could. Then they hung the skins in the shelters to dry.

Fenly had to stop several times, wracked by coughs. Others had to do the same, their bodies trying to clear the smoke and dust that had settled into their lungs.

Through it all Minere remained pensive, talking little, clearly impatient with what she still saw as pointless activity. Finally, Fenly was satisfied that they had done as much as they could for the time being.

Tandeir was trying to rearrange some evergreen boughs to use as a more comfortable bed for Legolan and Pendolin. "Tandeir, are you sure that you will be able to manage by yourself?"

Tandeir had agreed to stay behind to nurse Pendolin and Legolan and take care of ensuring they had food and the fire was kept going.

"Yes, I will be fine, and I am sure that soon at least Pendolin will be able to help some."

Fenly nodded and turned to the rest of the tribe. "We had best be on our way then. We will not stay away too long Tandeir."

They were now on the eastern side of the wide valley that lay between The Spine in the east, so called because it was a relatively narrow band of mountains running down the middle of the Jhirum's territory, and the Western mountains, many days hike to the west. The Frun River divided their valley though as far north as they were it was but a large stream coming out of the mountains just to the south of their encampment. They intended to fan out, all headed generally west and to travel for no more than a week to see what they could learn and to see if they could come upon any other survivors. Genlie was to take Minere and head northwest, Fenly west and Ashmere nearly more to the south.

They walked together back around the hill to the other side of the cliff, said their goodbyes and set off in their separate directions.

Fenly was confident that there were more survivors if this number of them had found each other in such a short period of time. The problem was in being able to locate them without the magical connection that they relied on to stay in contact over larger distances. Their territory was big enough that they could wander it for months and not come across one of their brethren. He knew that those healthy enough would make their own way back to the cliff eventually. They had left messages in their cryptic language of piling rocks in patterns to indicate that they had been there and where they had set up camp. His concern was more for any who were badly enough injured that they could not travel. For these Jhirum, the longer the delay the less the chance that they would be found alive.

With this in mind he set a brisk pace for himself, slowed only by the fact that much of the territory near the cliff had been forested and so was now a tangle of fallen trees and smoldering fires.

The rain continued to fall, cold and windblown. It was as if the sun had been swept from the sky leaving the land to cool indefinitely. Fortunately the direction he was going in was close to parallel to the direction the blast had come from so at least he did not need to cross every fallen tree he came to. Still, progress was much slower than he would have hoped, especially since he was still in territory where they had most likely already found all the survivors.

To keep his spirits up he focused on the prospect of finding more of his tribe, although trudging through the sucking gray muck threatened to quickly erode his mood.

Even walking, he was noticing the chill, an unusual sensation for one almost continually protected by magic. He wondered if this kept on how long they could survive without better shelter and clothing than they had ever produced. Under the best circumstances the summer was drawing to a close and fall would soon be upon them, making it too chill to survive as they were.

A moment of panic swept over him as he thought of all the dead larger animals that could provide hides for shelter and clothing, which were even now rotting in the mud. Had he failed already by not thinking of this and having them collect as many hides as they could before they rotted away? Who knows how many animals large enough to provide hides of any worth had survived.

He steadied himself, determined not to panic despite the feeling of being suddenly thrown helpless as babes into this harsh land that had only a few days ago offered them nothing but succor and life.

He decided then that if he came upon large dead animals he would attempt to take their hides and briefly prepare them so that they might at least last until they could be given more attention, even if he had to leave them along his trail to be retrieved later. He did not need magic to know this land like his own body and could easily find anything left upon his path at a later date excepting for any which might be pilfered by animals.

It was not long after this that he came across his first large dead animal. Unfortunately it was one of his tribe, Noran one of the strong young men. He paused momentarily. The Jhirum for the most part did not have death rituals. They were a long-lived people commonly seeing a few hundred seasons before the magic and their benign environment could no longer sustain them. Death however was still a natural, uncomplicated part of life. They were no different than the fallen deer or squirrel. They died and became food for the beasts that continued to live, their bones marking their passing for a while.

For some reason though Fenly found it hard to look on the mangled body. Noran had been caught squarely by a tree blown down by the blast. Fortunately for him he had probably not survived the initial impact.

With a solemn nod, Fenly finely moved on. His efforts and mental focus were reserved for the living. He was certain there were living that needed his help and he was determined to find every one that needed him. These thoughts helped him fight down the fear and panic that lay just below the surface; fear of this new hostile world and panic at having no magic to help sustain and protect himself or his tribe.

He was just getting beyond the shallow valley where the group he now headed had been when he came across a dead Borog. The Borog was a large creature; perhaps five arms long and weighing more than five or six Jhirum. It had thick black fur and an almost pointed snout meant for ripping and digging in carcasses.

Primarily a carrion eater, if pressed it could be a formidable adversary and hunter. This one had lost a good part of its fur though the hide looked like it could be salvaged.

Impatient to seek the rescue of his clan, Fenly now questioned his decision regarding hides. Short term survival, however, would do them no good if they could not face the winter with protection, so he set about the arduous task of skinning the beast with his crude stone knife.

He was not overly careful, but made sure he got mostly undamaged hide. He then found a depression filled with the gray ash mud and submerged the skin in it, weighted down by stones. This would not be a bad treatment for the hide and would at least preserve it for later retrieval. He marked the spot with a pile of stones, which clearly indicated the location and what was hidden there for anyone to find. He then quickly cleaned his hands of the blood and set off again.

Fenly had not seen any living animals except for a few small rodents scurrying into new holes dug in the mud. Of plants there were few as well. Here and there a small bush partially buried in mud, or the broken stump of a tree with a few branches left.

Now that he was in territory beyond where any of the survivors in his group had come from, he began to call out periodically so that he would at least improve his chances of finding someone, even if only slightly.

He continued on this way until past midday when he finally found some protection under a small cliff face to eat a little and rest for a few moments. The rain continued to pound down, but he fought off the nagging doubts and concerns that boiled at the edge of his consciousness. A couple of young buck passed by him like wraiths in the downpour fighting their way through the deep mud. Already they looked gaunt and haggard, much as he felt. With a little nourishment to lift his spirits he set out again.

Having only just started out as he was crawling over the trunk of a large tree he saw footprints in the mud, recently left and though nearly obliterated by the rain, clearly Jhirum. His heart leapt as he turned in the direction the footprints pointed. It appeared that whoever left the prints was headed generally back in the direction he had come from, but not in a direct path. The Jhirum may in fact have gotten past him during the short time that he was quiet, eating lunch. This could have been a tragic coincidence. It appeared that the person was walking at a reasonable pace but meandering almost aimlessly.

He quickened his pace concerned that whoever it was might be injured. He strained his eyes trying to penetrate the curtain of rain until finally he thought he saw a shadow fading in and out of the mist ahead of him.

He called out, but at first whoever it was did not hear him and continued on. He broke into an awkward trot and called again. This time the figure froze in place turning their head to find where the sound had come from. As he neared, what he now new to be a woman, he soon recognized Glandine.

At first she stared without response, apparently caught unaware, not expecting to find any one, then her eyes brightened and she called Fenly's name. He came to her and uncharacteristically embraced her warmly, so happy was he to have found another survivor.

She, like he was covered in streaks of mud, hair hanging in wet tangles. Scrapes and bruises covered much of her body and she coughed harshly as he surveyed her condition.

"Are you well? Do you have any injuries that need to be attended to?"

She shook her head to indicate that she was well but then cast her eyes to the ground and was silent. Fenly lowered himself to look up into her downcast eyes. She stared unseeing for a moment and then brightened again.

Her strange reactions told him that she must be suffering from shock. He took her arm and led her back to the cliff where he had eaten. There he got her to sit and began to relate his tale of the group that he had just left and that he was here to help her. He spent time telling his tale, hoping to bring her back to herself somewhat so that he could ask her some questions.

She seemed to follow the story though at times she drifted away to some distant place and then would follow his voice back to where they were.

As he ended his tale he asked her once again, "Are you injured?" She slowly looked over her own body as if inspecting it for the first time to see if there was damage. She shook her head negatively. He continued, "Can you tell me what happened?"

She faded away into her other world for a time. Fenly waited patiently for her return. "There was a huge blast, black clouds and warm snow," she began tentatively, staring at nothing, "and pain, the earth hurt terribly; so much death." She fell silent again.

Fenly kneeled and took her hand drawing her eyes back to him. "Yes, then what do you remember?"

"I blacked out for I do not know how long. Since then I have been trying to get back to the cliff."

Suddenly Fenly's eye caught something it had not before. "You carry your water skin. Is it still full?"

Once again she glanced down as if seeing her own body for the first time. "Nearly full, but it is ruined, I tried to use it once but the pain was too much, I will not touch it."

Fenly's eyes lit up. "May I have the skin?" She looked at him as she began to take it off of her shoulder. "But I said it is of no use?"

"I must try," Fenly replied gently. "It is the only way to be sure that we find all of our kin who might be lost or hurt out here."

Still looking doubtful she handed the water skin over to him.

Fenly hesitated, momentarily weighing the value of what he held and its long term potential against the immediate need to be able to reach out and locate more of his tribe. In the end he decided its value would mean little if it was not used now to save lives. He held it up and swallowed a small mouthful. It was wonderful, like going home. He could feel it suffusing his body with warmth and strength. He felt better than he had since the catastrophe. Then the pain began, reaching out to him from all directions, plants and animals, Jhirum all in pain, starving and dying. He gripped his head for a moment, then realizing that Glandine's eyes were on him, he focused all of his strength on blocking out the pain of those around him with the exception of the Jhirum.

He could identify four within the range of his senses. He marked the locations carefully, touched the minds of those he could, to call them to a meeting place if they were able to move. Then he met Glandine's eyes again. "There are a number near us that need our help. We must go to them, you must be strong and you must help also."

Her back straightened a little. "I will do what I can."

With this little assurance they set off toward the nearest Jhirum that Fenly had located.

CHAPTER 18 NO HARBOR IN A STORM

Morning came for the Jhirum of the Sea with a slight lessening of the rain to a cold drizzle, which did nothing to improve their moods. They ate a quick breakfast, and then began planning their day. Waymeir returned from the boat while they ate although Toren remained behind alone.

While they were finishing their food Shwaren stood. "I think we are all in agreement that we should investigate inland some more to try to assess the state of the land. I think that it is best that we travel in groups of two or three in order to ensure our safety as much as possible. Once you have selected traveling companions come to me and I will tell you what direction to travel in so that we cover as much ground as possible."

The tribe members began shifting around looking for partners. Shwaren spoke above their quiet murmurs, "Do not go so far that you cannot return here before dark and be careful, we do not know whether there could be another such blast, or what else might happen that could endanger us."

Based on the grim faces it was clear that none of them looked forward to a day sloughing through the mud and the cold rain. The temperature was unusually chill for late summer making the dampness all that more penetrating. As groups were formed they came to Shwaren and he sent them off, each in slightly different directions.

Waymeir and Donley were the last group to approach him so he decided to join them for the day. Donley was one of the elders of those remaining. They set off Northwest which would put them along the river Frun before midday. The river flowed into the sea just to the north of the bay. It was not a huge river, but too large to be crossed without a boat except for in the far north. One could never tell what would come down the river and given the circumstances Shwaren hoped to find more evidence of what was happening inland by what the river carried down its course.

As they crested the hill above the bay Waymeir stopped with a quiet gasp. "So many of the trees are broken or uprooted! How could anything survive out there?"

Shwaren looked over the rolling hills which were mostly grassland, but with many small groves of trees spread widely over the area, most of them now a tangle of broken tops and branches. "Yet I can sense that there are survivors. That at least is some small hope."

Donley nodded, and started off across the grassland. Apart from the damaged trees, the open country bore little evidence of a catastrophe. But as they crested a smaller hill they stopped again. Shwaren's stomach turned over at the site before him. Over 50 dark objects dotted the next hill. He did not have to look hard to tell they had been a herd of buck, dropped in their tracks with the initial blast. The smell that reached them on the gusting wind confirmed the carnage.

"Clearly, despite the survivors there have also been losses," he said quietly.

Waymeir held her nose. "They were caught in the open with no chance to escape."

Donley stared bleakly. "I am sure this is not the last we will see of death. Perhaps the resources are too depleted near our harbor to provide for us anymore."

Waymeir glanced at him with concern but said nothing. They altered their course a little so that they would not have to go through the heart of the dead herd, but just skirted the edge so that they could try to confirm what had killed them. Shwaren could see burns covering many of the bodies. There were also many with bloody heads or backs, probably struck by the larger flying stones.

On the other hand shortly after they left the dead herd they came across an area with many live animals. Whether, survivors from the larger herd or a separate herd that had been in a more protected area it was impossible to tell.

Bolstered by the small living herd, Waymeir continued to pursue her interest in convincing them that they should only consider rebuilding their homes where they had been. "What is to be gained by leaving where we are? The bay is sheltered; there are caves as secure homes and a good port for our ships."

Donley stared ahead continuing to scan the hills. "Our people have known many homes over the years. We have never been tied strongly to any piece of land. Perhaps it is time for us to seek out new territory where we can explore seas beyond our reach here?"

"Perhaps," Shwaren responded. "Especially if we find the land here badly enough damaged that it can't provide what we need."

Undaunted Waymeir continued, "We have already seen that some animals survive as well as some trees. We need little from the land." She received no response as they walked on in silence for some time, Waymeir casting sidelong glances at the two men.

As they crested a hill still short of midday they looked down on the Frun. It was however, like nothing Shwaren had ever seen. There was no evidence of its former banks. Below the hill the shallow valley boiled with gray liquid mud, dotted with darker objects. Glancing at each other, without words they descended the hill to get closer to the river's edge.

They soon wished they had kept their distance. By the time they were close enough to see what the black objects were it was too late to retreat.

From near the water's edge Shwaren could only too well discern the hundreds of bodies of dead animals, Jhirum and trees, as if the valley were trying to expel by force the detritus left by the calamity.

In that instant the three of them were brought to understand the scope of the blast and its consequences. Bloated bodies floated past as common as leaves on a fall day, washed away by the pounding rain in the valley to be deposited into the ocean, joining their own dead in endless repose.

Waymeir turned away, having learned more than she cared to know of the circumstances inland. Shwaren steadied her. "We need to continue along the river. Although it is repugnant we can learn much from what the river carries."

Waymeir glanced at him as if he had struck her and began sobbing with her back still to the river.

Donley nodded agreement, "Shwaren is right Waymeir. As hard as it is we must see this, for it tells us more of what has happened inland."

He then reached for her arm guiding her along the water's edge. Here and there they had to walk around a body washed ashore by the waves, putrid but untroubled by flies, which normally would have quickly infested the remains, but were held at bay by the cold and the rain.

After walking for some time they came upon the washed up body of a Jhirum. He was covered in black even with having been in the river, which should have washed him clean. He was not stiff with rigor mortise so he must have only died recently, perhaps surviving in the river torrent somehow, but only reaching shore in death.

Donley reached down to touch his skin curious to see what the black was. His hand flinched back instinctively. Looking at his hand in bewilderment none of the black had come off.

"What is it?" Shwaren asked.

"I don't know, it makes no sense, but I could sense something wrong; powerful and wrong, when I touched him. I think that this coloration is no ordinary stain from mud, or ash."

Shwaren reached down gingerly to touch his arm. A tingling coupled with nausea crawled up his arm making him quickly withdraw it.

Waymeir did not need her own confirmation, "What could it be?"

"I don't know," Donley answered. "Perhaps something either unearthed by the blast or the substance of the blast itself."

"We should move on," was Shwaren's only reply. "He will give us no answers."

They continued along the river seeing nothing new, only more bodies of animals bobbing in the waves like grotesque corks.

By midday the rain had increased again and they decided it was time to begin the return journey. "Let's head straight back from here," Shwaren said pointing at an angle away from the river.

He then headed up the hill setting a steady pace. As they crested the hill beside the river, they paused, looking back at the troubled river and its silent cargo. Shwaren could only guess at the scope of the tragedy to have turned the river into this angry funeral procession.

Shaking his head he again turned his back on the remains of the inland catastrophe. Silently, lost in their own thoughts they headed down the hill toward the remains of their own lives.

The return trip was relatively uneventful. More blasted trees and dead beasts along with the constant cold rain. Waymeir resumed her argument for staying in their harbor, "I think that the condition of the land here is more reason than ever for us to stay where we are. This land will need our attention to recover from the catastrophe."

Donley stared straight ahead. "This land is of little concern to us. Our concern is the sea. There are others to care for the land."

Shwaren interceded, "There are reasons to consider both options, I do not think that either is clear at this point. Let us wait to see what the others have found."

At that point they topped the hill looking down on their bay as hints of increasing darkness haunted the corners of their awareness. Hints only, for the day once again had been as dark as twilight at its brightest. They could not see the shore in the dark rain as they continued on to the larger cave, only their magical sense assured them that the sea pounded on, seemingly untouched by recent events.

Most of their companions were already back, warming and drying themselves by fires, talking in subdued tones. Shwaren could tell that the mood of the tribe was deteriorating with the continued cold rain and the constant reminders of death at every turn. Only their magic and the society of the other survivors kept them from breaking down. Shwaren listened as a couple of the other groups who had encountered the river along their paths described similar scenes to what he had seen, their eyes haunted in the same way as Shwaren's group. The rest had encountered nothing that they did not expect; a lot of downed trees, some dead animals and at the farther reaches of some of their journeys the remnants of fires.

After each recounted their tales in detail over the evening meal it was once again time to turn the discussion to the future.

Shwaren began, "It is clear that inland things are even worse than here. The amount of dead and the ash in the river speak of a conflagration that may have wiped most of the life closer to the blast completely away. However, we still have our ocean which is alive and healthy as far as we can tell. Close to the bay it appears that some life survives, including some trees and food sources though many have been destroyed. It appears to me that we could remain here if we desired, although I do not say that is what we should do."

Madrien, his eyes alight stood, clearly excited. "I see nothing to keep us here. It is time to start anew where we do not constantly have to face the loss we suffered here."

Maerl spoke more quietly, "I think that for those who were here at the village when the blast hit we would not miss being reminded of that experience."

Waymeir stood clearly agitated. "Why are you in such a hurry to abandon our home? The area has sustained much damage, there is much that we could do here to help heal the land and return it to its former condition."

Shwaren frowned before adding, "I agree that our bay does not offer us what it used to, but how do we know that any other place has been less affected. At least here we know the protection we have and we still have the caves as shelter. We would have to start from nothing in a new place."

Winfew joined the discussion. "We have explored as far as we have traveled in many years inland from here. I think that it is time for us to sail along the coast to see what the conditions are there. If we find somewhere better we can stay there, if we do not we can return."

Many of the group murmured their approval of this idea. Even Madrien who seemed anxious to find a new base nodded his assent. Waymeir sensing that this was a reasonable compromise stayed silent until it appeared that there was general agreement.

Finally Shwaren spoke. "Then we will sail the coast to see what we can find. Zifere and Maerl can you go out to the ship to check on Toren and to inform her of our decision?" They both nodded and turned to leave.

The waves in the bay had settled somewhat from the day before though the rain continued to fall. With little difficulty Zifere and Maerl forced their small boat into the waves and out to the ship.

Sensing their presence Toren cast the rope ladder down to them as they pulled alongside. Climbing aboard, Toren motioned them below deck. Maerl noted the dark circles under the young girl's eyes which made her look twice her age.

As they sat by the glowing pot fire she could also sense that Toren was still tense and distant sitting in the shadows cast by the small fire. She glanced at them briefly and then back at the fire.

They first recounted the findings of their inland explorations briefly and then the discussions that had just concluded. Toren listened though she rarely looked at the speakers, only an occasional nod indicating that she followed their words.

Maerl looking directly at Toren concluded, "We have agreed to sail the coast to see what the condition of other ports might be. If we find one more suitable we will attempt to establish our base there, if not we can always return here."

At this last statement Zifere glanced at Toren who visibly tensed. Maerl continued, "You have what you wish Toren, we are leaving this place, only if we find no other suitable base will we return. I think that is unlikely."

Toren's tension eased a bit and she looked directly into Maerl's eyes. "You think then that we will find a place less damaged?"

Zifere seeing an opportunity to relax the girl somewhat responded, "Yes I do. Surely the coastal areas protected by the mountains have sustained less damage. There are several places that may have good harbors at the base of the mountains."

Maerl moved closer to Toren. "Zifere, I would like to remain with Toren tonight if you would like to return to the caves." Zifere nodded his acceptance and turned to climb back up the ladder.

Maerl and Toren stared in silence for a time at the flickering fire contained in the pot, which shed a fleeting light inside the nearly empty belly of the ship.

Finally Toren spoke as if from a distance, "Maerl, are you in favor of finding a new base?"

Maerl nodded. "Yes, I would just as soon put behind me the memories of what happened. I do know however, that simply moving our port will not erase what we have been through or the memories of those we have lost."

Toren, continuing to stare into the light, paused a moment then responded, "I know, but I think it will be easier to not wake up every day and look at this place. I see the images in my head all the time without having to see the real place."

They each returned to their private images for a time, staring silently at the fire, then Toren began again, "Maerl, I sometimes see a place when I stare out to sea. I believe that it is far away, perhaps on the other side of the ocean. It is beautiful. I think it is where our new home should be."

Maerl looked at Toren, she could see that even now her eyes stared at some private vision, not the images of horror, but of something which smoothed the creases on her dark face and almost brought a smile to the turned down mouth.

"It is good to have dreams, but that is all it may be, a dream of what you wish for and nothing more. On the other hand perhaps you see our future. Let us hope that you do."

They sat in silence for a while longer before moving to find a comfortable corner to sleep the night away.

Morning brought another dark overcast day, but with only a light mist in place of the pounding rain. The chill remained in the air but this did not slow breakfast or the beginnings of preparations to set sail. Several tribesmen went directly to the ship to assist Maerl and Toren in preparing it for departure, although those that had stayed on the ship had already done most of the work. The others began collecting supplies as best they could.

Their biggest need was for berries that were now in very short supply. The sea could provide most of their needs but the berries helped to ensure their health on long voyages, and they had no idea how long their journey would be or where they might find better conditions along the way. They still had, however, most of the supplies aboard that had been originally stocked for the voyage they had just begun when the disaster hit so they did not spend long looking for additional provisions.

By Midmorning they were ferrying out to the ship and preparing to weigh anchor. As the last group climbed up the rope ladder the anchor was hauled up and without a look back they left their bay not knowing if it might be for the last time.

CHAPTER 19 RETCHED REFUSE

To the north of where Fenly searched, Genlie and Minere had also reached the point beyond where they had previously collected survivors. They were in rolling hill country, just on the border between forest and open grassland. To this point they had encountered little of note; the occasional dead animal, two dead Jhirum and endless fallen trees, which they mourned as fully as any of the other dead. Finally free of the fallen trees they were starting to make better time, although still slow, with the rain and sucking gray mud.

Though they frequently walked some distance apart in order to increase the area that they covered, Genlie occasionally pulled Minere into conversation, just to try to keep her from falling into sullen silence, which slowed her pace and caused her to fall behind.

During these times when they were together, Minere became animated as she repeatedly lapsed into a discussion of the reasons why they must focus on recovering their magic. "Surely you see that we cannot survive long with the land in this condition without our magic."

The urgency of her plea drew Genlie to look into her deep green eyes. Before responding he almost lost himself. She was beautiful and though young, she was not a child.

Recovering himself he looked ahead again. "I agree with you and am certain that Ashmere and Fenly both intend us to work on recovering our magic once we have found as many of our tribe as we can."

"But we could do so much more to find and to help heal our people if we had magic," she pleaded.

"You really miss our power don't you?" Genlie gently replied.

Taken off guard by the tenderness of his words Minere looked at the ground. "Yes, I can barely stand to go on. I feel as if I am empty and alone without magic."

"You are not alone," Genlie replied briefly looking at her again. "We may not feel our connections as strongly, but we are still all here for each other."

Gentleness entering her voice for the first time Minere returned his glance. "I know. It is just so hard not to be able to feel the connections inside me."

They walked on in silence for a while, Genlie feeling awkward for no apparent reason. But soon they separated silently to walk alone just within eyesight of each other.

The rain was beginning to slow somewhat, though the raw wind continued to blow into their faces. With the lifting of the clouds Genlie began to see vultures circling periodically. Some of those had survived, perhaps come from far away to feast on the destruction.

More than once, Genlie had considered stopping their search for the living to find something that they could cover themselves with to keep warm. But the thought of taking that much time when lives could hang in the balance kept him moving on. At least now with most of the trees gone and the rain slackening they could see a little farther.

He still occasional angled to intercept Minere, trying to divert her attention from her own thoughts by focusing her on scanning the ground around them as they walked. He could not stand the thought of walking near someone without finding them.

As they were climbing one of the low hills Genlie thought he saw the shadow of a figure ahead of them near the crest of the hill. In a few more moments it coalesced into the solid form of a Jhirum headed directly toward them, or more likely toward their cliff.

The Jhirum noticed them as well and called out. Their steps quickened and they closed the gap quickly. He could soon identify the overly large form of Gloren, beaming uncharacteristically at them. They approached, held their palms up and touched them together in greeting.

Gloren began without hesitation, "I am glad to see you. I feared that I had already found all of the survivors there were to find."

"There are others?" Genlie interrupted glancing behind Gloren, "Where are they?"

"I gathered a few together farther north of here, but they were not all in good enough shape to travel so I set off to bring some more water back to heal the rest."

Genlie's face whitened. "Our spring is ruined," he said without trying to soften the blow.

Gloren's face darkened. "Are you certain? What happened?"

As Minere joined them Genlie related briefly the story of the group that had gathered at the cliff and what they had discovered of their source of magic.

Gloren looked pensive for a while before nodding his head as if he had made a decision. "So, now we must return to the survivors and bring them home and nurse them as best we can without magic. Had I known I would have used my water skin more sparingly."

"Yes, we must return to them at once," Genlie replied. Placing a hand on Gloren's arm he continued, "We are on a search for survivors. You have covered an area in your travels, we should return to the group by a longer route so that we can cover new ground."

"That would take us well out of our way for my awareness has been only slightly weakened, though I do not use it continually because of the pain.

At any rate I have searched a wide swath. Still, I see your point. I left two among those in good health. They should be able to take care of themselves until we arrive in any case."

With this they turned and set out again angling south of the path which Gloren had trod.

As they walked Genlie asked, "So you have had water recently?"

"Some time ago now, but after the explosion," Gloren replied. "My awareness is barely still alive." Genlie shook his head.

Minere, however asked, "Is there not any other place in the land where magic is accessible?"

"Not in our territory," Gloren responded. "The Mountain Jhirum have a source as do the Bagnog. It is said that the sea people obtain their magic from the sea."

"So then there is hope of again finding a source of magic." Minere brightened. "We can simply ask one of the other tribes to allow us access."

"True," Gloren responded. "But none of their sources are close to us. We would have to transport water over many leagues."

Genlie, seeing a chance to bring Minere out of her dark mood added, "But you are right Minere we should be able to share the resources of other tribes, even if it is not quite as convenient."

Minere's step quickened noticeably at this thought, easily keeping pace with the long strides of Gloren.

They continued on angling to the south well into the afternoon, finding little of note with the exception of a few small animals and a badly injured plains buck. They then began to turn back north toward the point where Gloren had left his charges. With time to their own thoughts Genlie began to ponder the chill in the air and its effect on him.

One of the times when he walked nearer to Gloren he had to bring it up, "Gloren, without magic I am chilled by this cold mist and stiff breeze. This is still summer. How will we be able to survive when fall and then winter come if we have not recovered our magic?"

Gloren proceeded on in silence for some time, and then with a sigh acknowledged "Yes, I can already feel it myself. I have often ventured far from the cliff and have on occasion gone beyond the resources of my water bag. One time in the fall I nearly died of chill before I was able to get back to the wall."

They each once again fell silent, pondering this thought. When Genlie shared these same thoughts with Minere a short time later she responded, "Even more reason to go to the other tribes as soon as possible to obtain water. Perhaps we should set out even now. By the end of our search we will be well on our way to the northern mountains where the Maestic make their home."

Gloren had walked up beside them while they talked. "For now," Gloren cautioned, "we must focus on gathering our tribe together and ensuring we have saved all that can be saved. Then we can attend to finding a new source of magic."

Though she did not respond Minere fell into dark silence again.

It was nearly dusk; the spare light fading to darkness, when Gloren stopped short, turning his head to the south.

"You have sensed some one?" Genlie asked expectantly.

"Yes, I cannot tell who, or exactly how far, but there is definitely a Jhirum in that direction," he said pointing the way he faced.

With renewed vigor they altered their course in the failing light. They had just crested a hill and could see a copse of trees at the bottom; apparently sufficiently protected that most of the trees had survived the blast. They headed toward the trees certain to find a brother sheltered there.

Approaching the edge of the wood, Genlie heard a call. It was Casmor a female slightly older than himself. She came to them looking spry and healthy. Her chestnut eyes however were bloodshot from recent tears that betrayed a shadow behind the happiness of finding friendly faces.

They greeted each other happily. "Come, I have a fire and some food," she offered.

They followed her back into the trees to where a tree had fallen making an opening. A fire blazed there and a couple of large leaves held piles of berries. They sat and passed the food as Casmor asked them to tell her their stories and what they knew of the situation.

After repeating their tales she then offered hers. "I was almost to the base of the Western Mountains, when the blast occurred. It caught me in the open, but not completely unprepared. The concussion knocked me down but I only suffered some bruises, which were easily healed. Afterward I began immediately to make my way back to the cliff. I was happy to find this grove of trees still standing. I have not seen many along my way."

Minere's face lit up, "You have water left in your skin?"

"Yes I do," Casmor responded matter-of-factly. "I have not used any since right after the blast. The pain of the land was too much to bear. I have only sipped sparingly to keep some awareness. That is how I could sense you coming but did not know who you were."

Minere leaned forward with urgency. "May I have some?"

Gloren Held up his hand. "We must conserve any water that we have for when there is real need." Minere started to protest then leaned back again, remaining silent and pensive.

Gloren after a short silence looked at Minere again. "Tomorrow when we continue on one of us should hold some small amount of magic to help ensure that we do not pass by any of our tribe who might be in need. Perhaps in the morning, Minere that person can be you."

Genlie nodded and smiled slightly when he caught Minere's eye. Minere also smiled, though more broadly.

After completing their simple meal and discussion, they settled in to the relative comfort of the pine needle covered forest floor and went to sleep with the dripping of the mist off the leaves of the trees the only sound.

Morning dawned again with a feeble lessening of darkness. They each roused at about the same time. The Jhirum were attuned to the land even without their magic. Minere, however, was already up when the rest of them roused. Genlie smiled at her knowing it was the anticipation of holding magic again that had Minere up early.

They ate a sparse breakfast of the remaining berries and a little of what they carried with them. As Gloren wiped his hands in the pine needles to try to remove the last of the berry juice he asked Casmor, "Would you mind continuing on to the cliff rather than backtracking with us? There is really no need for all of us to be together and you could carry some of the water back to the injured at the home camp to help heal those still suffering from injuries."

"That makes sense, though I will miss the company. Perhaps Minere could join me?"

Minere scowled at her. "I think I can be of more help with those that are injured. I would like to continue on if you don't mind."

Genlie nodded knowing that it was mostly Minere's desire to have the chance to be the one to hold magic while they continued on that made her protest. Gloren also glanced at her briefly, but did not press the issue.

They said their goodbyes and Genlie instructed Casmor on the paths that they had already covered so that she could try to travel new ground on her return. She left a small amount of water in her skin and transferred the rest to Gloren's. She also took a small sip as did Minere so that they could detect any brethren that they might miss otherwise.

As soon as she had taken the small sip Minere's forehead creased in pain. "The land still cries out with the deaths and injuries of thousands of creatures! How can you stand the pain?"

Gloren faced her squarely. "You must attempt to focus your energy only on signs of our kin and block out all the other cries."

She nodded though the creases in her forehead only deepened. A look of concern crossed Genlie's face. He was afraid that she was too sensitive to stand the pain.

At last she nodded. "I think I am OK," though she no longer seemed overjoyed at having magic again. With one last reassuring nod to Minere, Casmor turned toward their home. Gloren turned to lead Genlie and Minere back to his charges facing directly into the cold mist that seemed to perpetually fall from the gray skies.

By noon they were nearing where Gloren had left his group without having found any more signs of survivors. They did not stop to eat until they reached the group camped in a small copse of trees at the base of a hill much like the one where they had spent the previous night, except that this was just a few small trees grouped together.

Waves and greetings were sent and received. Only one of the two healthy tribesmen came forward to greet them. It was Norwood. "Welcome Gloren. I see you have found more of our tribe." He beamed at Minere and Genlie.

"Actually it was they who found me. They were venturing out with others in search of more survivors."

Norwood studied them for a moment. "How many more do you know have survived?"

Genlie looked into Norwood's anxious face with a frown. "So far we only know of eight of us besides your group." Then he forced a smile. "But we are just beginning to look for others."

None the less Norwood frowned in turn. "So few. Let us hope that the search discovers many more." He then turned back to Gloren. "I did not expect you back so soon. Have you been all the way to the cliff and back?"

It was now Gloren's turn to frown. "I met these two on the way there. They brought bad news. Our spring is destroyed."

Minere practically pounced into the discussion. "We do not know that it is destroyed. Only that there has been a rock slide and for now we cannot get to a place that holds magic."

Gloren who almost stepped back at the ferocity of Minere's reaction recovered himself. "In any case there is no magic for the time being and therefore no reason for me to continue on to the cliff so I turned around and brought Minere and Genlie back here. We are going to have to do the best we can with the little water that we got from Casmor."

Throughout this interchange Norwood stood dumbstruck staring from face to face. Finally he spoke. "No magic? How is that possible? We have people here who need to be healed and a whole land that needs our healing."

Gloren firmly grasped Norwood's shoulders. "As Minere has said, perhaps our magic is not gone for good, but for now at least we must go on without it."

Norwood looked into Gloren's dark eyes. "Then it is good that Engin has been out searching for dead animals from which we might collect skins. We may all need them to stay warm if the sun does not return soon."

"Yes, that is a good idea," Gloren replied. Come let's join the rest of the group and share news with everyone. We must also provide what healing we can for those most in need."

CHAPTER 20 TRACES

By morning the chill in the air had deepened and though some one had stayed awake to tend the fire during the night it was not at full strength, leaving them shivering and huddling as close as they could to the smoky coals. Minere woke and moved close to Genlie. He could feel her chill fade to pleasant warmth as they huddled together next to the fire. She was still far away in her thoughts, though she smiled at his efforts to help warm her. Others were rousing and gathering around the fire however, so Genlie reluctantly stood and stretched his stiff muscles.

He looked around at the gathering Jhirum. They were a haggard looking group, most with significant bruises mottling their skin, many limping. He shook his head again at how quickly things had changed for his people.

After they finished their meager breakfast, they gathered up what little they had and began the march back to the cliff. As they set out Minere left Genlie to approach Gloren. "Is there water left?"

Gloren glanced sideways at her. "Just a few drops."

"Should I use it to help us find others along our way?" There was hope in her eyes, but Genlie knew what the answer would be.

"No, we must save whatever we have now. We have enough people to spread out and cover a large area." Minere could not hide her disappointment as she drew away from Gloren who sadly shook his head.

They had only just set out when the rain began anew, chilling them even more. Between the mud and the still limping injured among them progress was slow. Gloren had the healthy Jhirum spread out so that they could cover more territory on their return although they did not stray too far from a straight path back to the cliff because of the injured.

The morning wore on slowly, the rain continuing to fall chill and relentless, backed by a gusting wind. The occasional small rodent or bird was the only sign of animal life. Nothing broke the monotony and only the hard work of walking through the mud kept them at all warm.

Because of the continued weakness of the injured they had to stop before mid day to rest and eat a little from their meager provisions. They had still found no signs of additional survivors. Without a fire to warm them they were soon all shivering and so decided it was best to press on rather than freeze to death.

As they once again spread out Minere was on the end of the line of Jhirum and could just barely maintain visual contact with Genlie walking across from her in the mist. The afternoon wore on and Minere's mind began to drift. No longer constantly scanning for survivors she frequently found herself staring at the ground in front of her. It was during one of these lapses that a jet black object caught her eye, half buried in the mud. Just larger than her thumb, she immediately reached down to pick it up and resumed walking while examining it.

It appeared to be rock though she had never seen anything like it. Smooth, almost glassy, yet so black, it seemed to suck all of the light near it into its depths.

It drew Minere's attention as well. She found herself caressing its smooth surface and staring into its depths until she finally shook herself free only to realize that she had wandered off in some direction to the point that she could no longer see Genlie. For a moment she panicked and then called out to see if someone could hear her, but did not immediately receive an answer.

Then she noticed that the stone had grown unnaturally warm in her hand. Staring at it again, yet still concerned about where the rest of the group was she noticed that as she turned, looking for Genlie, it grew cold accept in one direction where it warmed and almost seemed to glow dimly.

For no reason other than the fact that she had no better alternatives, she began walking in the direction where it gave off warmth and within a few minutes the shadowy form of Genlie appeared out of the mist.

Momentarily she froze again, staring at the object in her hand. Then shaking herself she began to walk in step with Genlie so that she would not lose contact again. The stone cooled in her hand as she held it. Had she really felt a change in warmth? Had the stone actually responded to what she wanted or needed? Only questions came to mind with no answers. Now, no matter what direction she turned the stone remained cold.

But there was something more as well. While the warmth had been welcome, it had not been an altogether pleasant feeling and now, cold, the stone seemed to cast a feeling of mild nausea, or discomfort into her mind and body. She continued on, puzzling over the strange rock until she finally changed directions to come up beside Genlie.

"Look what I have found." She held the black object out in her palm.

Genlie glanced at it as they continued on then picked it up. A frown crossed his face. "It feels wrong in some way."

Minere slowly shook her head. "I know it does almost seem to give off a bad feeling. But I swear I drifted away from you and it lead me back to where I could see you. Do you think it contains some magic?"

Genlie rolled it around in his hand. "I have heard of objects imbued with magic, but I have never seen one. If this is magic I fear it may be of a bad sort by the way it makes me feel."

Minere nodded again. "But it still helped me. I am sure, so it cannot be all bad."

Genlie was not so sure but he handed the mysterious object back to Minere. "I would just be careful of it at any rate."

"I will," she said and a smile that looked brighter than he had seen for some time crossed her face.

They parted again for the rest of the afternoon, but Minere continued to hold the rock and puzzle over it, occasionally trying to reach out to it in some way.

Only after the day had worn into evening did she relinquish the object to the small pouch at her waist. There it was forgotten for a time.

As the light of day began to fade the shadow that was Genlie waved her in his direction. Tired and chilled to the bone she welcomed the thought of a fire and hopefully a dry place to sit.

Unfortunately the fire could be had, but not the dry seat. Gloren had found a rock outcropping that topped one small hill affording some protection under an overhang, but hardly dry. They were, however able to find some wood to start a fire and drive away the worst of the chill. Thankfully the drizzle had stopped and there was actually a hint of the moon skirting in and out of the fast moving clouds.

They ate a meager dinner and were talking quietly around the fire before Minere thought again of the stone. Taking it out in the firelight it seemed to actually cast darkness around it sucking in the unsteady light of the fire. For a time she stared at the blackness, turning it over slowly in her hand feeling the cool smoothness of the stone against her skin.

Finally Gloren noticed her distraction. "What do you have there Minere?" he asked across the flickering flames.

Momentarily she closed her hand on the stone. "Just a stone I found today."

Gloren stood and circled the fire to where she sat. "May I see it?" Minere opened her palm slowly and held it up to him. Gloren hesitated momentarily before picking up the odd rock, surprised by its blackness and something else that he could not describe.

Minere did not take her eyes off of the rock while Gloren studied it. Its weight was normal, but the smoothness of the surface and the fact that it was blacker than black made Gloren puzzle. After a few moments however, he handed it back to Minere. "Quite a strange rock," was all he said as Minere closed her hands around it once again. She quickly deposited it back into her pouch and Gloren went back to his seat.

CHAPTER 21 BENEATH THE EARTH

Cragen and the rest of the group arrived at the cave before midday, though the interminable darkness continued to hide the fact that there was any sun in the sky. The cave was located about midway down the mountainside nearly opposite to their spring, which had probably given additional hope to some that it might lead in some way to the source of their pure magical water. For now however, it was to be a shelter from the elements and little more. Though they all knew of the cave and felt it would provide some suitable shelter, the entrance was not obvious as they approached it from above. In fact, coming down the mountain it was simply another outcropping of rocks.

However, after circling around the outcropping to the lower side and facing back up the mountain they could see a dark shadow about midway up the jumble of rocks. As they approached it, even from this vantage, anyone who did not know the stories would still have thought it nothing more than a small den for animals.

Endmere remembered the first time he had approached the cave many years ago. Cragen had told him one of the ancient tales about the cave when they were together but for a long time he had not thought of it. Then one day after having returned from a long trip he was taking a few days to stay close to the spring. It was during one of these days that he remembered the story that Cragen had told and decided to investigate.

He remembered bending down to step into the small entrance feeling like there could not be much of a cave there. But soon the small entrance opened into a large cavern which ignited his imagination, leading him to explore the cave for a short while.

As he now took his first step into the small entrance these many years later the memories returned to him of his adventure long ago. With the darkness inside it was still impossible to see how much it opened up, for all was blackness, but the blackness echoed in a way that spoke of space. He could see the same skepticism on each of the faces that he had once felt until they stepped into the echoing cavern.

As Cragen approached this black opening with the remnants of the tribe behind him, he recalled the stories of Maestic from the distant past who had ventured in to this and other caves in these mountains. He knew that this particular cave had been explored to considerable depth without ever finding an end. The stories told of many branches which to this day remained unexplored. The stories also mentioned unusual creatures, some with limited magical capability.

They had brought some fire brands to provide light in the cave so that they could comfortably settle in and arrange a place to camp. As Cragen squeezed through the tight opening Endmere was just blowing one of these brands back to fire. They had no idea how long this might be their home, but understood that they must make it into a place of shelter and safety which could withstand the winter if they did not get their magic back by then.

Before they had all gotten into the cave Cragen stopped the last couple of Jhirum. "We need some wood so that we can start fires, or we will not be able to see in here." The Jhirum nodded and turned to look for wood.

The cave ceiling was high enough and in fact seemed to have some fissures open to the sky from which small puffs of fresh air could be felt. Endmere hoped that these would provide sufficient ventilation for smoky fires not to suffocate them. The few brands that they brought in cast a ghostly light on to the nearest walls, but above and deeper into the mountain the feeble light failed before reaching rock.

The air was not dry, but not so damp as to be uncomfortable and a welcome respite from the rain and dampness which surrounded them the last couple of days.

Thespan and Jasper returned from gathering wood and after squeezing through the narrow opening, dropped armloads of branches on the floor of the cave. Jasper's eyes glowed as much from the excitement of the prospects of exploring the caves as from the flickering brands.

As Endmere knelt down to place the smaller sticks in a pile that he could ignite with one of the brands Jasper spoke over his shoulder. "I would like to take a brand and explore a little in the cave."

Endmere glanced at him as he was blowing on the small spark that had caught on the damp wood. Between puffs he responded, "That will have to wait Jasper. We have a lot of work to do just to make it so we can sleep here tonight."

A small flame began to build, sputtering as it tried to spread to the wet sticks. Jasper looked crestfallen, but Endmere did not have time to spare at the moment.

Soon there was a glowing fire casting light deeper into the cave. Others returned with more wood, which they piled along the wall.

"We have to try to make it more comfortable in here," Cragen announced, "We do not know how long we will be here. I would suggest that some of us go in search of food that can be kept for some time and others look for anything, which might make it more comfortable to live and sleep here. Once we have the basic necessities in place we can discuss what to do next."

They quickly divided themselves up between those who would look for food and those who would look for other necessities and began filing back out, grudgingly into the damp, dark day.

Endmere put a hand on Cragen's shoulder as they were walking toward the entrance. "Cragen why don't you stay here, tend the fire and look around to figure out what the best way to organize the cave would be."

Cragen nodded. "All right, I won't complain about not taking these old bones out into that cold and wet." A wry smile briefly crossed his lined face. "When we had our magic I never felt as old as I feel today."

Endmere smiled back at him. "The tribe needs your age and experience, so wear it proudly."

"I know, but that does not stop the creaking of my bones."

Chuckling quietly Endmere ducked through the cave entrance. He had decided to search for food, preferably food that would keep more than a day so that they could build some reserves.

The ever present darkness seemed to press down upon him as he ventured on in to the valley. Darkness never bothered the Jhirum. Even now without magic, they could see well enough and knew the land well enough to get around almost as well as in full daylight. It was just the unnaturalness of the constant gloom that made him uneasy. Endmere could feel the ash and dust floating above the clouds as if it were a physical weight on his shoulders. He wondered how long this unnatural night would continue. It seemed to him that by now the bulk of the ash should have been blown away by wind or washed from the sky by rain. He knew, however, that the fires, some of which still burned hotly might cover huge swaths of the land and would continue to add to the unnatural clouds.

Shaking his head he brought himself out of these gloomy thoughts. They had more immediate and pressing needs and the unnatural chill in the air emphasized their need for good shelter and perhaps even clothes beyond what they had ever used in the past.

The valley they were in now was relatively unscathed by fires, or the initial blast. It was a deep valley, well protected and though ash and dust had covered everything in a gray blanket most had been washed from the trees by the rain. He could almost imagine here that the past few days had been nothing but a fever induced nightmare. Animals scurried away in his passing and though most of the birds still sought shelter, he could occasionally hear the chirp of a small wren hidden in a bush.

He also found that there were many surviving berry bushes, full of late summer fruit, which he collected in a large skin he had brought for the purpose. These could be dried in the sun, if it ever returned or perhaps in the cave by the fire if tended carefully to prevent rot or cooking.

As his skin began to weigh on his shoulders his spirits began to lift. Perhaps this would not turn out to be such a tragedy for his people after all.

With these positive thoughts he turned to head back up the valley to their new home.

Arriving at the cave he saw that several of the others had brought berries and nuts back as well. In addition there were the beginnings of crude mounts for fire brands around the cave and piles of evergreen branches presumably to be used as bedding to soften the hard rock floor. Cragen was directing people as to where to put things and what to do next. This activity only served to reinforce his improving mood.

After Endmere deposited his haul, he and Cragen decided to enlarge the cave entrance to make bringing in supplies easier.

By mid afternoon they had succeeded in making a small enlargement all the way through the wall, just making a noticeable difference in the ease of egress from the cave. As they were working they heard Jasper call out to someone.

Pausing from his work Endmere came out of the cave and followed Jasper's eyes up the mountain to where he could see a Jhirum approaching.

It was Gabin looking hail and grinning at Jasper. They greeted and Endmere immediately lead him in to the cave. Gabin gazed around at their work. "It looks like you are planning on staying a while."

"Yes," Endmere answered proudly. "I think this will make fine shelter even if we do not get our magic back before winter. But come, sit by the fire and tell us your tale. I need a rest anyway."

Cragen joined them by the fire as Gabin began. "I was at the eastern edge of the mountains, overlooking the central valley when the object hit the earth." Cragen and Endmere looked at each other. None of them had with certainty seen what had caused the explosion.

Gabin saw this in their eyes and explained further, "There was a streak of fire in the sky just as the pain began stabbing through my head. It disappeared over the horizon far away. Next there was a brilliant flash, lighting up the sky, then there was nothing but more pain for some time followed by a giant cloud growing into the sky, higher and higher. It grew at a tremendous rate, but was so far away that it still did not seem to be of any concern to me directly.

Then, as I watched I realized that the cloud was growing at an alarming rate, and the ground shook and rumbled. Before I knew it the outer reaches of the cloud were upon me in a hail of pebbles followed shortly after by a hot blast of wind. A few of the pebbles were hot enough to ignite fires which I tried to put out until I realized that they were everywhere."

Here Gabin paused, allowing his words to sink in, and then resumed, "I can tell you this, I could not see much after the cloud reached me. The air was full of dust and smoke. But I do know that not much could have survived on the plain nearer the blast. The black cloud had thinned noticeably by the time it got to me and it was still bad. On the plains it looked like a solid black mass which must have blasted and smothered most everything in its path."

Endmere was the first to stir. "We were hoping to go to the tribes in the valley to see if we could share some of their magic water. It seems that this is a frail hope now."

Gabin nodded his agreement. "I think we are safest and best cared for here in our mountains."

"We should get back to work," Endmere continued with a sigh. "It is clear that we will need preparation to face whatever this world brings us now."

Slowly, as if stirring from sleep they each rose, returning to their work, understanding that perhaps their mountain world was an island surrounded by desolation. An island, itself wounded and in need of succor.

By the spring Bastile was spending a quiet day in the damp rain. There was no real protection from the elements, so she sat with her back to a tree staring down the small gorge that led to the valley floor trying not to think about how cold and miserable she was. Occasionally she glanced briefly at the spring hoping to see some change in its effluent. It remained, however, black and lugubrious, flowing in slow motion over the rocks. The thick liquid coated the rocks along its way leaving them black and slimy.

Bastile had managed to keep the fire burning while she maintained her vigil, though each time she added new damp wood it guttered and smoked until it could drive the dampness from the fuel.

Finally tired of sitting, she walked over to the spring to look more closely at the strange liquid. She grabbed a stick by the side of the pool and swirled it in the thick soup. It came up dripping black in strings that tried to cling to the wood. She brought the end of the stick near her nose and cringed at the stink.

Disgusted she walked back to the fire casually dropping the stick in the flames as she passed. The fire flared immediately, flames jumping and throwing a black puff of smoke into the air. Startled she paused staring at the fire which quickly settled back to normal.

She sat down once again with her back against the tree puzzling over the reaction of the fire to the black liquid.

Bastile let her mind drift again for a while thinking about the changes to the world and life without magic. She still sorely missed the intimate connection that the Jhirum always had with the surrounding world. At any time they could see the world through the eyes of a bird high above the trees, or feel the contentedness of a baby bear snuggled against its mother's breast. Having experienced these types of connections, it was a mortal loss to have them taken away.

Finally her mind returned to the spring. She rose again, picking up one of the small logs that she had stacked by the fire, carrying it to the pool. This time she dipped it in repeatedly, covering as much of the wood as she could in the thick liquid. She studied the coated log as she walked back to the fire and carefully laid the log in the flames. She barely had time to jerk her hand away as flames leapt to the log engulfing it and throwing off thick black smoke.

Just as the black smoke was beginning to abate and the fire return to its normal level, she was startled out of her reverie by a call. Looking down the valley trail she could see Zeeta waving through the mist.

They embraced and Bastile motioned toward the fire. "Come; sit with me for a while."

As Zeeta sat Bastile studied her. She appeared to have no injuries. Apart from dripping hair she looked like she always had, jet black hair and eyes to match, as hard as mountain rock both in character and in physique. She was a good head shorter than Bastile, but gave up nothing in strength or endurance.

Zeeta wasted no time. "What do you know of what has happened?"

Bastile nodded her head toward the spring. "The first thing you must know is that our spring is contaminated and useless."

Zeeta followed her eyes to the dark pool. "I saw the black liquid flowing down the streambed, but could not imagine that it was coming from our spring?"

"It has been this way since the explosion."

Zeeta shook her head, looking at her deflated water bag sadly. "What do you know of the rest of our tribe?"

Bastile brightened a little. "Most are here. They have moved to the cave on the other side of the mountain to see if it can be used as shelter."

A frown briefly crossed Zeeta's face. "They plan on living in the cave?"

Bastile recognized the consternation in Zeeta's voice. "Endmere thinks that we will need to stay together now without our magic and that we will need shelter and clothes to face the winter if our spring does not clear."

Zeeta silently stared into the fire, clearly unhappy and concerned.

By nightfall the change in the cave was miraculous. Though still a cave, it no longer seemed dank and musty. The burning fires, fresh food and boughs that covered parts of the floor had dried, freshening the air despite the smoke. The mood of the group had also improved significantly. Cragen sent out a replacement for Bastile, who arrived with Zeeta. Zeeta was Endmere's mate, though they rarely traveled together. She liked to go her own way and did not often seek out company.

Endmere on seeing her enter the cave stood to greet her. "Zeeta, it is long since our last meeting. As always you are good to my eyes."

Zeeta smiled warmly. "You are good to my eyes as well my mate." She swept the cavern with her eyes. "It appears that you plan on staying here for some time."

Endmere nodded, knowing what her thoughts were. "I think that we need this as a haven until we can get our magic back or make some other plan."

Zeeta studied him a moment, her dark eyes boring into his. "And why should we need such shelter now when we have never required it in the past?"

Cragen joined them. "The air is chill and our magic fails us. We cannot survive without shelter or magic."

Zeeta nodded in understanding if not acceptance. "Would not some better clothing be sufficient?"

"Perhaps in time, but I still feel for now we need to have a safe base to work from," Endmere countered. He could see the distaste in Zeeta's eyes. Though they spent little time together he understood her well and knew that staying with a group in a closed shelter would be the last thought to appeal to her.

Rather than argue so soon after her arrival however he gestured toward the fire. "Come join us and share your tale."

Zeeta relaxed visibly and smiled once again at Endmere before taking a seat near the fire. The warmth and dryness of the cave was certainly welcome for the time being and there was plenty of food.

As she chewed on some berries she began. "There are some huge fires still raging to the east. However, it appears that the many small fires have started to die out in the rain."

Zeeta fell silent clearly keeping a lot of her thoughts to herself so Endmere picked up the conversation. "We are trying to fix the cave up so that we can find shelter here when we need it. We are also trying to gather some provisions so that we do not constantly have to forage for food. We had also thought of venturing out into the plains to investigate the disaster and perhaps get some water from the Natec, but that does not look like a good idea because it appears the plains took the brunt of the explosion. We are in no condition to help others and I doubt that if they even survive they can be of much help to us."

Bastile then spoke for the first time. "I have thought long on the suggestion that perhaps magic can be found in these caves. I think that possibility as well as our need to know of the place that has become our home would dictate that we should at least begin some exploration here. Who knows what might be here that could either help or harm us. In either case we should know rather than guess."

Lamsil who had joined them to hear Zeeta's story stared at the fire. "Some of the old tales tell of fell creatures and other dangers in these caves. There were those who ventured in and never returned."

Cragen countered, "I know also of these tales, and of those who did return. In any case we find ourselves in the cave for better or for worse, it would be best if we knew our home well."

"Speak of it as home if you wish," Zeeta said firmly, "but I for one will not be here long enough to be concerned with what the cave holds."

Endmere with clear concern in his voice responded, "Zeeta, though I know your distaste for living like this, I think that we need to stay closer together until we know the full extent of the catastrophe and what lies ahead for us."

"We will learn nothing, hiding in a cave," she retorted. "I do not plan on hiding,"

Endmere forced calm into his voice. "We are only using this as a safe base from which to venture and a place of shelter in bad weather. Surely even you recognize that when winter comes if nothing has changed we will need a shelter from the cold."

Thespan wishing to return to the topic of the cave jumped in as soon as Endmere paused. "Do any of the tales speak specifically of this cave?"

Cragen and Lamsil cast a quick glance at one another to determine who would speak first. Cragen began, "In fact this cave is one of which the most tales are told, almost all from one expedition millennia ago."

"And it is from this one cave that both the promise and the pitfalls were revealed," Lamsil added. "Here was one of the few places that the Maestic explored as a group rather than just as individuals. It began after one of our ancestors decided to explore the cave alone. He was gone for almost a month and returned with stories of hidden caverns where the walls glowed with their own light, of underground streams that flowed so deep that no bottom could be found. He also told of strange creatures that dwelled in the caves, never seeking the light of day."

Cragen picked up the tale. "It was from his telling of this adventure that it was decided that a small party should be joined to explore the cave further, for in all of this time, he explored only one branch of the cave and even there found no end.

Because of the apparent extensiveness of the caves it was decided that an organized group would be best, armed with a plan to methodically map out the caves. They would explore each branch to a certain distance then return to the main cave. All along the way they would leave signs telling of what they found and of where each branch seemed to lead. In this way the knowledge could be passed on and built upon as people went farther into the depths."

As Cragen paused Lamsil continued. "Five Jhirum made up the party which was gone for seven months. Only two returned to tell their fraction of the tale. Little is left of the details from so long ago. What we do know is that they followed their plan going deeper into the mountain. One of their party perished in a clash with some form of huge beast that resided in one of the passages. Two of their number separated to go down a side passage and never rejoined the main cave.

Though the remaining two searched for them for some time, no trace was found except for the first few runes left to mark their passage. The last two journeyed on a while before turning and heading back to the surface where they told the tale of fell beasts, bottomless waters, glowing walls and jewels."

Silence settled over the group as they stared into the fire, eyes periodically flickering to the darkness of the far reaches of the cave, imagining what had been seen or what was still there.

Endmere finally broke the silence. "I agree that soon we should explore the cave at least some distance in, to ensure our security and to understand our home, but for now there is much work to do to make this cave comfortable. We must ensure that we have food and perhaps warmer clothing and to explore the damage done to our mountains."

Jasper, staring into the deep darkness of the cave could not contain his disappointment. "I still think that there is time for a couple of us to venture at least some distance into the cave just to ensure there is no danger, or no better place to settle down nearby."

Endmere reluctantly nodded. "Perhaps we can ask a couple of volunteers to explore a short distance inside the cave, just to ensure we have the best location and no beasts are bedding down near us."

Bastile looked almost as excited at the prospect as Jasper. "I agree, perhaps in the morning a couple of us can investigate the nearby chambers."

With this the group broke up and spread out to sleep on the beds of needles and leaves that had been prepared. Zeeta made her bed as near the opening to the cave as possible, as if finding even the idea of spending one night inside, suffocating.

CHAPTER 22 THE YOUNG SHALL INHERIT

After parting at the cliff, Ashmere headed south until she encountered the Frun, which at this point was a small river fed by the mountain springs deep in the Spine. It would be joined by other streams as it wended its way south until it became a considerable river, requiring boats, or at least floats to cross.

For the first time in her life Ashmere was actually uneasy about being alone. The Jhirum from fairly young ages spent most of their time alone and Ashmere was strong and confident, well able to take care of herself. But with the frightening happenings of the last couple of days and the total lack of magic, something that she had never before experienced, she was uncharacteristically anxious. With a conscious effort she forced the unease to the back of her mind and proceeded on with some semblance of her normal confidence.

Already here near the source of the Frun the water was beginning to clear. Though still tinged gray it was at least translucent and she could see a small distance beneath the surface. The bank was littered with dead fish and animals tangled in washed up branches cast aside by the rapidly flowing water. The combination of the choking mud and the hot debris had taken a considerable toll on the denizens of the river. Already the stench of the dead permeated the air.

She needed little time to decide not to walk the bank as she had planned but to move some distance away from this river of death. She then paralleled the river as it headed south and west toward the ocean.

Ashmere had already forgotten her uncertainty, refusing to acknowledge her new sense of aloneness when she encountered the body of a dead Jhirum, one of the older children of the tribe; she lay in the open with no obvious injuries. Had she simply succumbed to the elements? It was a puzzle, but not one that Ashmere could dwell on. She moved on down the river in search of the living, leaving the child to the carrion eaters, if any had survived.

Periodically she would call out, trying to prevent as much as possible walking past a victim who was injured and possibly invisible from where she walked. The country was very flat along the river, but there were many trees, and the tangles that they created could easily hide an injured tribesman.

Her spirits sank with the setting sun having still not found any signs of living Jhirum. She had however, seen some signs of animal life which lifted her spirits somewhat. A young Borog was feasting on the ample carrion washed up at the river's edge and as the rain lessened she began to see a few birds flying between the tangled masses of fallen trees. Whether they had survived the blast, or had come from far away she could not tell, but they were welcome companions none the less.

She decided to stop for the day before it got too dark so that she could find some shelter from the pouring rain. What she found was a single large tree that had survived the blast, though stripped of its leaves it afforded a little protection. Curling up against the rough bark, she slept fitfully through the cold night.

The morning brought only slight relief from the rain. It was no longer pounding down in torrents but was instead a mist, which connived to keep everything wet throughout the day. She had found a few berries along her march the previous day, which she ate slowly for breakfast, scattering the seeds that she spit out in her hand in the hope of spreading new life in the desolate wasteland.

She then set out once again in the dim light of morning. As she began her search anew she passed a small herd of Buck, their ribs already exposed from finding too little to eat.

After traveling for only a short distance she heard a call, drawing her attention to the right just as a form emerged from the mist. She answered the call and hurried in anticipation of company.

It was Harib a young adult woman. Despite the rain and chill they smiled broadly in greeting. "I felt like I was alone in the world before I felt your presence," Harib began.

Ashmere quickly glanced down at her water skin, which though sagging was obviously not completely empty. "You have water?"

A puzzled expression crossed Harib's face. "Yes, I have been far to the south, but I have been using my water sparingly so that it would last until I got back to the cliff, but why do you ask?"

Ashmere then retold the story of their lost spring causing Harib to glance forlornly at her nearly empty skin. Ashmere realized that Harib had become very quiet as she concluded her tail.

"But that is in the past. Now we are searching for more survivors. I am headed south. Others have gone west and north. Have you been on this side or the other side of the river in your travels?"

Harib glanced at the river. "I crossed from the other side just below here yesterday."

"Good, then I will continue on this side. Would you join me?"

Harib hesitated a moment, still thinking of the cliff. "Yes, of course. Have you found any food?"

"Only a few berries here and there."

Harib nodded. "I had a fairly good meal of fish before I crossed the river, but have seen little else since I crossed."

Trying to keep her stomach from growling Ashmere shook her head. "I am afraid that is going to be the story from now on, since the animals killed by the blast are too old to eat." With this she started off, keeping the river a short distance off to her left.

As they walked Harib continued to relate what she had encountered on her journey. "Most of the territory I covered was grassland which was buried in ash. I came across one herd of buck that looked in bad shape, they were having difficulty finding food which was edible, and several had been injured by the blast. I had some meat from one that had recently died. It was clear they were on the move, looking for better grazing but I do not know where they will find it."

Ashmere nodded as she scanned the horizon. She no longer felt the need to call out periodically because Harib still held some magic, which would alert them to any of their kin. "Yes, it seems that the blast reached throughout a large part of our range. Perhaps there is less damage near the ocean."

They continued on until midday and then stopped briefly for some lunch, which was a sparse sampling of what they each carried with them, some dried berries, a few fresh berries and a small bit of meat that Harib had kept from her previous meal.

After lunch they set out again, continuing to follow the river, some distance from its bank to avoid the stench as much as possible. As they began walking Harib looked at Ashmere quizzically. "I sense something."

Ashmere stopped. "Can you tell, is it one of us?"

"I think that it is, but it is very weak, with my weakened sense and the continued crying of other animals in distress I cannot be sure. I think it is off in this direction." She pointed back toward the river.

They changed their course and shortly she confirmed, "Yes, some one is near the river but they are not in good shape and I cannot tell who it is."

They quickened their pace. As they approached the riverbank a piece of the bank seemed to move as if coming to life. Ashmere ran to investigate, followed closely by Harib.

As soon as she got near the form she realized it was a Jhirum, covered in the gray mud from the river to the point of being unrecognizable. Kneeling, Harib could only tell who it was through her magical sense for sight could hardly bore through the caked on slime. "It is Mashnine!" she cried, "She is barely alive."

Without thinking of the preciousness of the remaining water in her skin she quickly reached for it and poured a small amount into the slack mouth of the unconscious Jhirum.

Mashnine coughed nearly expelling the precious fluid, then stillness settled around her again. Her breathing, ragged at first, calmed a little as the magic suffused her veins. She still lay unconscious and unmoving.

121

Ashmere knelt beside them, concern etched in her face. "She must have been in the river," Harib murmured. "She is cold as ice."

"Perhaps I should gather some sticks for a fire," Ashmere replied.

Harib nodded. "Yes, perhaps you should. I am not sure that the magic alone is enough."

Ashmere trotted off to a tangle of fallen trees and began breaking off small branches from underneath where they were somewhat protected from the rain. As she brought an armload back to where the women lay she asked Harib, "Do you have enough magic left to start the fire? Everything is so wet I do not think we can start it otherwise."

Harib motioned her to pile the sticks near her and holding her hand near them she ignited a small flame. "That is the best I can do and still reserve as much of my power as possible to help Mashnine."

Ashmere nodded and set about arranging the sticks so that the fire could build slowly. After she had gotten a small but sustainable flame she returned to the fallen trees to gather larger sticks.

It took some time but eventually she was able to build a substantial fire, enough to cast some warmth in the dampness. Harib had, in the meantime given Mashnine more water, which she again threatened to cough up.

"We will have to remain here for some time I fear before we will even know if she will survive," Harib explained.

"You think that she might not live, even with the magic in her?" Ashmere responded her face full of concern.

"I am truly not sure," was all that Harib could answer. "Why don't you check the area to see if you can find anything for us to eat."

Ashmere added some more wood to the fire, which spit and guttered from the soaked fuel then set out along the bank. She had gone but a short distance down the river when she heard a cry, quiet, but desperate in the dim light. Her heart pounding she found herself running again until she came upon a small form in the mud, it was Voral, the youngest member of their tribe, just barely more than a full turn of the seasons old. She lay weakly thrashing in the cold gray mud. Ashmere scooped her up and hurried back to the fire.

Harib jumped up as soon as she drew near. Hearing the small cries she hurried Ashmere to the fire then snatched the baby to sit in her lap by the warmth.

"How did she get here?" Harib asked, astonished. "And why so near to Mashnine?" For though the tribe as a whole took care of all their young the mother, who was Radine would take the most interest and always be near to a child this age.

"I don't know," Ashmere replied. "The last I saw them was many days ago, they were still not venturing far and were headed to the river north of here." They fell silent, both in wonderment and thankfulness for the apparently healthy though weak baby.

Ashmere came to herself again, remembering her forgotten task she rose to look for food once more. Harib was giving the baby a small amount of water to strengthen her, with almost immediate effect. The little girl quieted then fell into a restful sleep.

Ashmere once again, picked her way down the bank, encountering at regular intervals washed up fish or animals that had died in the river. Most were already bloated and stinking even in the chill air. However, after picking through dozens of these rotting corpses she was able to find a couple of fish and a ground marmot that were still in a state to serve as food. Returning to the fire she found the three as she had left them, Harib cradling the baby, Mashnine still unmoving beside her.

"I have found some food, it will take me a little time to clean it and cook it," Ashmere offered. "I will save the skin of the Marmot. Perhaps we can use it as a blanket for the baby." Ashmere took her stone knife and began to work on the food.

When she was nearly finished, Mashnine suddenly began to thrash and then cough. Then just as suddenly her eyes opened. "Where is Voral?" she practically yelled. "Where is Voral?" Harib held the baby in front of her eyes. Immediately, Mashnine lay back down with hooded eyes.

"What happened Mashnine?" Harib queried gently. No answer came for some time though Mashnine's eyes flickered open.

Then she pulled a ragged breath in and began, "I was hurt here by the river. There was no one with me." She paused again trying to gain the strength to continue. "Suddenly I heard the baby crying in the river. I dove in but was so weak I just got the baby near shore and lost her. I was barely able to crawl up on the bank. I was sure that I failed."

"You did not fail," Harib reassured her. "The baby must have been near enough to shore that she washed up and crawled a short distance up the bank."

With this Mashnine again fell silent and closed her eyes. The little water that Harib had was nearly gone. She dribbled a little into the corner of Mashnine's mouth to no visible effect.

Ashmere and Harib ate a gritty though sustaining dinner of fish and marmot while discussing how the baby might have gotten into the river. There were no real answers to be had however.

After dinner they built up the fire as much as they could. They decided to take turns watching the baby and Mashnine. Harib took the first watch and though uncomfortable lying in the mud, Ashmere fell quickly to sleep from exhaustion.

The night passed slowly with little change apparent in Mashnine. Some time near the middle of the night Ashmere awoke and convinced Harib to get some sleep while she watched their charges.

Harib was sleeping fitfully when Ashmere heard a growling noise in the darkness. She stood slowly reaching for her small stone knife. The growling was followed by a crunching noise. Apparently some animal was searching the night for the dead, or dying that it could use as a meal.

Ashmere peered into the darkness trying to make out what was there. She yearned for her magic again which would have allowed her to easily see and sense whatever was in the dark. The growl was not the sound of a Borog, but there were wolves and foxes as well as Plains Cats that would make the sort of sounds that she heard.

She quietly grabbed a couple of more sticks to put on the fire, hoping that it would keep whatever was there at bay. Suddenly a pair of eyes glinted in the darkness, reflecting the firelight. By the distance between the eyes she could tell it was a large animal, which most likely meant a Plains Cat, or worse a Whorzen, the huge plains wolves. But Whorzen hunted in packs, almost never alone. Either way, without magic they were a danger, though Ashmere had some time ago put away her fear of being without magic. She stood close to the fire, knife in hand, crouched facing the gleaming eyes.

Regretting that she had to do so, she poked at Harib with her foot, startling her awake. "What is it? Are Mashnine and the baby ok?"

Ashmere motioned her to silence and pointed out into the darkness. Harib followed her glance seeing the pair of silent embers at the edge of the darkness. She slowly got to her feet beside Ashmere and in front of the two sleeping patients. A low growl came from the darkness and the eyes moved closer. A form slowly took shape around the glowing eyes, a Whorzen, but alone. Perhaps this was the only survivor of a pack.

Teeth bared he slowly crept into the light never looking from the two Jhirum. Ashmere crouched, knife in hand. Harib had not even a knife to use as a weapon and so reached slowly down to pick up one of the longer sticks that lay by the fire.

Seeing Harib with the stick a better thought leapt into Ashmere's mind. "Harib, can you get a burning stick out of the fire?"

Harib bent down slowly, drawing another growl from the wolf. She found a stick, shorter than she would have preferred, but with a brightly glowing end. The Whorzen was now almost within lunging distance of the Jhirum. Bold with hunger or the reaction to being alone he looked ready to pounce.

Ashmere never taking her eyes off the giant animal whispered to Harib, "When I yell, we rush him." Harib glanced uncertainly at Ashmere, but nodded. As soon as she saw the nod from Harib, Ashmere let out a blood curdling yell and rushed straight at the Whorzen, her knife in front of her. Harib followed her example the brand held out as far as she could reach as she yelled and ran.

The Whorzen, caught off guard by the sudden attack seemed to just as suddenly come to the realization that he was alone and not in a pack where he would have felt nearly invincible against any foe. His eyes widened and with a yelp he turned and headed off into the night.

Panting with excitement and the brief but extreme exertion Ashmere and Harib looked at each other, small smiles creasing their faces briefly before Harib said sardonically, "I thought you were losing your mind."

"We had little else we could do, but I thought he might be uncertain since he was on his own," Ashmere responded. They then turned back to their fire and after Harib had checked on the baby and Mashnine, neither of which had moved during the brief encounter, she settled in to sleep while Ashmere resumed her watch.

The first hints of light were just appearing in the gray skies when Ashmere, who was still on watch, noticed a quiet that was unusual. She rushed to Mashnine's side, but the stillness of her chest merely confirmed that the morning quiet was due to the cessation of Mashnine's rasping breath. She had passed like the retreating darkness in silence and calm.

Ashmere woke Harib who immediately rushed to see if there was any more to be done, but it was clear she was gone. Harib looked lost as if she forgot what she was doing or why. Ashmere put her arms around the younger woman. "You did everything you could. She was just too far gone."

Fortunately with the commotion the baby awoke and cried for food breaking through Harib's abstraction. Starting as if woken suddenly she gave Voral the last drops of water from her skin, which would quiet her for a while, but they would have to find something that the baby could eat soon.

"I think that we should turn back to the camp now," Ashmere said finally after a small breakfast. "We cannot continue on with the baby and I am not sure that one of us alone can care for her under these conditions."

Harib considered this, thinking of the others that might possibly be out there in need of help. Ashmere, sensing Harib's confliction reached gently for her arm. "If I can find some food for the baby," Ashmere ventured, "perhaps you can continue a while on your own back toward camp while I look at least a little farther down river. Then I will catch up with you perhaps by nightfall."

Harib considered this a moment. "That is fine as long as you can find some food so that I do not have to hunt for food with the baby."

Ashmere agreed and set out to see if she could find some berry bushes that survived which could provide some nourishment for the child.

After looking for some time, she was able to find a few berries at the bottom of one bush and then a few left on another bush, otherwise stripped of leaves. Eventually she was able to produce sufficient berries to sustain the child for a day or more, which should be enough until she was once again with them, or they were at the camp on the other side of the cliff.

She brought her meager treasure back to Harib. "Are you sure you will be OK with the child until I rejoin you?"

Harib did not look up from the baby cradled in her arms. "Yes, we will be fine for a day or two."

Ashmere watched the two for a moment. "Take good care of her, I will catch up to you as soon as I can."

Harib glanced at Ashmere, her eyes still watery even though she knew that Mashnine had been in very poor shape. "I will. She is even more precious now. Don't go too far, but I hope you find some more survivors."

Ashmere smiled gently. "I hope so too." Then she turned and headed off into the gray morning.

For Genlie's group the several days after they started their return trip passed slowly. The summer was turning into fall earlier than normal, and it was a damp cold fall with at least some rain most days and none of the clear azure skies typical of fall in the Natec lands. The wounded among them had started to gain strength though they still slowed the progress of the group somewhat.

Minere continued to periodically study her stone while she walked alone. Several times she was certain when she wished for something or felt a strong need the stone had warmed in her hands, but little else unusual had happened.

It took them almost six days to get back to the spot where Pendolin, Legolan and Tandeir had been left. By early afternoon on the sixth day however, they rounded the side of the hill and approached the crude encampment. Smoke rose slowly from a fire, fading into the gray sky.

The first to spy them coming up the hill was Dorla who came running at the site of the fairly large group with Gloren. He smiled broadly at the youngster, though he noticed the slight limp as she hurried down the hill. After hugs and brief welcomes they continued on to the lean-tos that had been added to since Genlie had left.

Though some of the healthy adults were out gathering food and searching for hides, those left behind greeted the newcomers warmly. The evening would be spent catching up on every one's story, for a short time forgetting about their uncertain future.

CHAPTER 23 LIGHT FROM THE PAST

Morning dawned as the last several had, dim and damp. A hard rain had begun to fall again during the night making every one thankful for the relative dryness of the cave that the Maestic had occupied. Over breakfast they discussed what needed to be done next and divided up the chores. Someone needed to relieve the watch at the spring. Others could continue looking for food.

Jasper, looking patiently for the assignment he was interested in finally could wait no longer. "I would like to volunteer to go into the cave and explore," he hesitated uncertainly, "at least the nearby sections."

Endmere was about to object but was cut short by Bastile. "I think that is a good idea, I will go with Jasper."

Endmere sighed and looked at Lamsil briefly for support, but then relented, "all right, but no deeper than half a mornings walk in. Remember that we do not have our magic to aid us. You will have to bring fire brands and perhaps will even have to build fires along the way at intervals to light the return trip. You cannot afford to get deep into the cave and then have no light to guide your return."

"Perhaps we can have one or two people build the fires and maintain them along the way carrying wood and brands in to stations deeper in the cave?" Lamsil suggested.

"One other person, but no more and only for a short time. Remember this whole venture should not take longer than the morning at most. We cannot spare three people from the other important tasks for long."

Bastile and Jasper nodded eagerly. They quickly found another volunteer and began to collect dry wood and sap-laden branches that would work as brands.

The rest of the group scattered to their chosen duties. Gabin had volunteered to help with the exploration. "Perhaps two of us should gather as much wood as we can carry and the third carry a couple of brands to provide light."

Jasper nodded his agreement. "I will carry wood."

"As will I" Bastile added.

This left Gabin to carry a torch to light the way. They decided that they would go as far as they could until the brand was dimming and then would stop and build a fire. Then they would have to return for more wood and brands to push beyond the first fire. It would be a slow and tiresome process and they certainly would not get far in the time allotted, but there was little else they could do without their magic.

Gabin and Bastile smiled at each other as Jasper arrived with an armload of wood so large he could barely see over the top. Bastile peeked at him around his burden. "Are you sure that you can carry all of that as far as we need to go?"

Jasper responded without hesitation, "I will be fine. We need as much as we can carry."

Without fuel of any type the brands cast an uncertain light, which guttered and threatened to die to embers at every step. But despite not having their magic the Jhirum were still a people of the land, with good eyes and good senses to find their way so they proceeded without hesitation despite the dim glow.

"Do you think that we will find the runes left by the early explorers?" Jasper asked from behind his arm load of wood.

"It is unlikely," Bastile smirked in the dark. "The runes probably will not begin until deeper in the cave than we will be able to explore on this short expedition."

"And with this poor light," Gabin added, "we could walk right past them and not know it."

Jasper's look of disappointment was hidden by the darkness but his enthusiasm was not dimmed for long as he took the lead. Gabin and Bastile cast knowing smiles at each other.

In the first section of the cave past their camp they saw several signs of animals that had used the cave for shelter in the past. Scat from bear early on, a little farther in a makeshift den for wolf or some other canine. The air grew damp again as they moved away from the mouth where their fires had dried the cave to some extent, though the ceiling was still the height of several Jhirum and the air not as stale as would be expected.

The light that the temperamental brand gave off was orange and dim, occasionally flaring up as a piece of sap caught flame only to gutter again back to mere embers. They had gone only a short distance past the last animal sign when the brand threatened to extinguish and they decided they had better stop and build their first fire. With the dry wood that they had brought from inside the cave it did not take long to get a good fire burning with wood left over.

"Now what," Jasper asked expectantly across the building fire?

Bastile glanced at the remaining pile of wood. "Perhaps one of us can carry on with what remains of the wood as far as possible while the other two return for more wood?"

"I will go on," Jasper practically yelled in his excitement.

Gabin frowned at Bastile. "I think it would be better if I was the one to continue on. We do not need you going so far into the cave in your excitement that you lose your fire and get lost."

Jasper pouted like a child. "I would be careful."

Again Bastile smiled indulgently at Jasper. "I think that Gabin is right. Come, Jasper, we are wasting our precious time talking."

As Bastile headed off back the way they had come with Jasper trailing, Gabin gathered the remaining wood and drew a burning stick from the fire to light his way. It was already becoming difficult to judge how long they had been in the cave, but it certainly could not have been long. Gabin could not help his heart from racing a little between Jasper's enthusiasm and his being alone for the first time, deep in the unknown cave.

He had not ventured more than two long casts of a stone, though it seemed much farther in the darkness, when he came to a branch in the chamber. To the right a lower tunnel not much higher than his head angled down into the mountain. Straight ahead the larger cave continued on barely deviating from its straight though also slightly declining path.

He decided that this would be a good place to build another fire. He was only just one small turn in the tunnel beyond the dim light of their last fire, but he resigned himself to slow, but secure progress and began to build his fire. After igniting the smaller twigs with his brand and waiting for the fire to build to where he could add more substantial branches he finally had enough light that he could look around at the walls of the cave.

It was then that his eye caught a reflection off the wall near the entrance to the more rapidly descending branch. He moved to get a closer look.

Clearly etched in the dark stone was a series of runes. In the dark gray stone they were hard to see in the dim light, yet they were etched deeply and cleanly as if done yesterday. They were clearly made with magic, sharp edged and precise.

Unfortunately the Jhirum had never used a written language. The runes had been created specifically for the exploration of the caves and their meaning had been lost to time. He gently touched the runes as if to coax from them their meaning.

With the first gentle touch a faint glow leapt from the stone, startling him into pulling his hand away. Almost immediately the almost imperceptible glow dimmed again.

Cautiously he reached out again and gently caressed the abstruse message. The light immediately began to build again. He moved his hand back and forth slowly. The more he caressed them the brighter the light emanating from the rock became until it challenged the light thrown from the fire.

Now it was clear that not only had the runes been left to inform other adventurers about what was known of the caves, but also to make it easier to navigate them should others follow the ancient path. The fire sputtered behind him and he turned to feed it the remaining wood.

It was time for him to return along his path so that he could help with the next step. But he kept glancing back over his shoulder at the brilliant light cast by the rune as he ventured back into the darkness.

By the time Gabin drew close to the light of the first fire, he began to hear the voices of his approaching companions. He quickened his pace as his brand darkened to mere embers, but he could see his destination in the flickering light dancing in the dark ahead. He reached the fire just after Bastile and Jasper arrived with their armloads of wood.

Though by now Jasper was tiring somewhat his enthusiasm had still not dimmed. "Have you seen anything of interest?"

Gabin smiled broadly. "In fact I have found something most interesting." He quickly explained what he had found where he built the next fire.

Now Jasper was completely beside himself. "If there are more runes we may be able to explore farther without the need for fires."

Bastile laid a hand on his arm as if restraining an excited child. "That may be true but it is too soon to know if there are other runes that will glow, or how long they will continue to glow."

Gabin agreed with Bastile. "For now we must continue as we planned. If you two can handle the wood you have I will continue back to bring some more. I would suggest that we stay with the main cave for now."

Jasper did not even wait to respond, but headed off down the tunnel at a frenetic pace leaving Jasper and Bastile once again smiling and shaking their heads.

Jasper could hardly believe that they had already encountered signs of the original explorers from thousands of years ago. His astonishment only grew, however when they rounded the last small curve in the cave before reaching the fire and saw the glow cast in the passageway ahead of them which was as bright as ten fires, though slightly green in hue.

He redoubled his pace leaving Bastile to hurry along behind him. Quickly dropping their bundles by the fire, Bastile added wood to the diminishing flame. Jasper gave no thought to the fire but went immediately to the runes, glowing as bright as a setting sun, though the color was closer to moonlight.

He gingerly reached out his hand to touch them as if expecting to be burned. They were however, cool to the touch, as cool as anywhere else on the cave wall. With his touch the intensity increased yet again, till he withdrew his hand out of fear of blinding them.

Bastile joined him, staring at the incompressible script which was still evident as shadowy lines surrounded by the brilliance. After staring at each character as if willing them to speak their meaning aloud, they finally withdrew, returning to the meager fire, which paled, in the dazzling glow.

"Do you think that we will find more runes?" Jasper asked in a voice filled with awe.

Bastile glanced at the brilliant wall again. "There is no way to say. I think we were lucky to find this one in the dark, it is probably unlikely that we will find others even if they do exist."

Remembering their task she threw some more logs on the fire. "Come on let's see what else we can find."

They each took a small amount of the wood that was left and set off deeper into the larger cave, which was aglow for some distance now.

As they reached the far limit of the light cast by the runes they were reminded how tepid the light of their brands was. With a slight hesitation they journeyed on into the looming darkness.

Jasper's brand guttered and died to embers first leaving Bastile's lone torch to light their way. This deep in the cave they had not seen any other signs of animal life except for an occasional small rodent or spider. Clearly they had passed a divide where creatures from the surface did not normally venture. They were now in the demesne of the cave and only creatures that made their lives here would be found.

The Jhirum were not a timid people, they were used to being safe and at home in a world full of all sorts of creatures apparently stronger or more vicious then they. Their magic was a large part of this inbred confidence, which for better or for worse was not lost by most when the magic was lost. So they continued on undaunted.

Finally the second brand threatened to expire. Here they stopped and started to build another fire. As Jasper began piling the smaller sticks Bastile asked, "Do you think it is worth even building another fire? We are not going to be able to continue much further anyway."

Jasper paused for a moment to look up at her. "Gabin will be along soon with more wood. We might as well do one more fire, then we can go on as far as another set of brands will take us."

Bastile thought of all the work they had done that would be abandoned as soon as their journey was done. Any future group would have to start the whole tedious process over again.

Regardless Jasper carefully built the fire, for they at least needed to reignite brands that would light the way back to the fire by the runes.

After putting nearly all of the wood on the fire it was burning brightly. They took the two sticks that they had preserved for torches and got them burning as brightly as possible then set out back down the tunnel to see if they could meet Gabin. They had not gone far before Jaspers brand, which was held near the wall, caught a reflection that was unusual in the great expanse of dull gray rock walls. Jasper's heart pounded as he quickly realized there was another very simple rune etched in the wall of the cave. A single symbol comprised the entire message, though it could speak a thousand minute details for all they knew.

Jasper quickly reached out to it, touching its glazed surface delicately with his fingers. Immediately an orange light leapt from the rock.

Jasper and Bastile stared at one another in wonder. "Do you think that these runes run throughout the cave?" Jasper asked.

"Perhaps they do, but it's hard to tell from just two."

Jasper bent his tall frame to stare Bastile directly in the face. "But if it is, that would mean that we could travel the tunnels without fire."

Was there magic still available to aid them even in their current state? Bastile reflexively reached out to touch the rune and it glowed with increased radiance though still orange in color.

"I wonder if we might find these runes at regular intervals." Jasper asked.

"I bet that within the glow of one rune there is another," Bastile answered without hesitation, "Though with magic they could navigate these caves without light, it is my guess that our ancestors preferred to have the light available."

"Let's try it," Jasper responded excitedly, setting out on down the cave toward the entrance.

As they got near to where the light from the rune was fading they slowed and began examining the walls. Sure enough the glimmer of a glazed surface shown in the fading light of the last.

Bastile passed her hand over the rune and a brilliant blue light exploded from the rock lighting up the cave in a ghostly hue.

"Let's see if we can find another," Jasper said excitedly as he headed down the cave. Bastile was now almost as excited as Jasper so she followed him as fast as she could, anxiously searching the walls as they drew near a turn in the tunnel, which would block the blue light.

Once again they were not disappointed, a flash of blue reflected like the moon off the smooth surface of a lake. Jasper nearly jumped to place his hand on the simple rune. Pure white light broke from the surface of the rock sending vermin scurrying for shelter.

They looked at each other grinning like fools. From here they could see the light of the original rune that Gabin had found with the fire burning meekly in its formidable glow. They set off toward it keeping their eyes to the walls in case they should pass another sign.

They did not, though this only reinforced the theory that the runes had been left at regular intervals along the caves to light the paths of those who passed. The light had dimmed slightly from when they had left but still cast more than sufficient light to guide them and to allow them to see obstacles in their path.

They arrived at the fire and casually threw the remaining logs on, though they were now certain that it was unnecessary. So certain were they at this point that they dropped their brands in the fire and after touching the rune to once again increase its output, continued on unencumbered. They were still within the light of the last rune when they encountered Gabin returning with wood and torch.

Jasper, too excited to explain took the wood from Gabin's arms. "Put this down, come on follow us."

Gabin, looking confused watched as they worked their way along the walls. Shortly, Jasper called out and as Bastile and Gabin turned in his direction a blaze of yellow light shot out from the wall. Jasper stood there grinning for ear to ear.

Gabin turned a questioning glance to Bastile.

"It seems that our forefathers have prepared the way for us," Bastile said quietly. "I think that we should return and tell the others."

As they set out for the camp Jasper and Bastile filled Gabin in on their discovery and what they thought it meant. He agreed that this made sense and that this would totally change their perspective on the deeper caves.

When they arrived back at the cave entrance there were only a few people around who had just returned from foraging for supplies of one sort or another. Cragen was still there guiding the organization of the living space and the placement of provisions.

When he saw them come into the light he left what he was doing and approached them expectantly. "How was your investigation?"

Bastile responded, "Extremely interesting, we have found signs of our ancestors."

"Not just any signs, we have found magic that they left behind," Jasper added, unable to contain himself.

Cragen looked quizzically at all of them, and then beckoned them to the fire. "Now, can you start from the beginning?" Cragen asked patiently.

Bastile briefly recapped their morning's experience. As she concluded Gabin jumped in. "This means that we should easily be able to explore farther into the cave without the need for fires and brands."

Cragen stared into the fire for a while. "Tonight when we are all back together you can tell the tale again and we can discuss what this means."

By the time it was growing dark again and the Maestic were beginning to gather for the evening, bits and pieces of the story had spread. Several more Tribe members had joined the group during the day and were getting caught up on the stories.

As the last Jhirum returned everyone gathered anxiously at the fire, ready to hear the entire tale. Only Zeeta did not rejoin the group. She had spent part of the day helping to gather food and then without ceremony had left, clearly with no intention of returning by nightfall.

Though this concerned Endmere the news about the caves distracted him from his worry. As they ate their evening meal, Gabin, Bastile and

Jasper retold the tale in as much detail as they could. By the end the group could hardly contain their excitement.

Lamsil however, quieted them with a cautionary glance around the fire. "This is good news, to know that we have a means of using the caves beyond this immediate area if the need arises. This does not mean that we have the time, or the need right now to go on a major expedition into the caves."

Jasper responded incredulously, "We can't just go on as if nothing has changed! There is magic in the runes, who knows what other forms of magic there may be deeper in the caves. We need our magic back, we cannot ignore this chance," he practically pleaded.

Several of the others murmured their agreement. Endmere now spoke for the first time. "This is indeed good news. A world, which has been unknown to us, is now opened, at least to some extent. However, we still have much to do just to get our new home livable. I do not think that we can spare effort at this early stage to go on a major exploration of the caves and I do not think that it is wise for a single person or too small a group to embark on deeper explorations. We have learned something very important from this first glimpse deeper into the mountain and there will certainly be a time when we can explore further, but that time just is not now."

Lamsil nodded her assent. "I agree. There is no need to risk lives that are too precious to us now when the earth is in such a state."

Jasper could not hide his disappointment. "I would go alone, gladly. No one else would have to be risked."

This time Gabin stepped in on the side of caution. "Jasper, having seen what you have seen I am as eager as you to see whatever mysteries lie deeper in the caves, but I agree that now is not the time. Have a little patience. We will make our discoveries in due course."

This was enough to quiet Jasper though frustration still drew furrows across his forehead. There was a little continued discussion about what the runes could mean and if there was any way to decipher them, but the main decision had been made. Every one began to drift off to their sleeping bowers content to rest and build their strength to face the new day.

CHAPTER 24 WALKING WOUNDED

Since Fenly had found Glandine wandering aimlessly and in shock she had gained some measure of herself, becoming surer of foot and alert with each step. Fenly had located an injured Jhirum just north of where they were. The three others he had detected were all somewhat mobile. These he had directed with his sense to meet him where the more seriously injured Jhirum lay.

They were in an area clear of trees so the walking was easy apart from having to fight the mud with each step. The hill they climbed was slippery with the sodden coating of gray slime that covered everything. Frequently they slipped and had to push themselves upright to continue on.

As they crested the small hill in the lowering mist he could sense the Jhirum close by, down the other side of the hill. By now he was close enough to know that it was Ramolin that he was looking for. The life force of the young woman was very weak and he knew that there was no time to waste. He hurried off down the hill with Glandine following behind.

Halfway down the hill an immobile mass that could only be the injured Jhirum lay beside a jumble of rocks. A quick glance told Fenly that she had been near the large outcropping when the blast hit shaking loose some large boulders that must have fallen on her. They must have continued on down the hill for she was not pinned underneath anything but smaller rubble, still she lay without moving.

Kneeling beside her he reached out with his weak senses to search for damage. What he felt made him wince. Both legs had been broken, one with the knee bent back unnaturally. On top of this one of her hands was crushed. Fortunately there were no serious internal injuries.

Fenly hesitated only a moment as he lifted the water skin to her mouth. She needed its strength and he would probably need some as well in order to heal her enough to survive.

The small amount of water that he initially emptied into her slack mouth lay there a moment before she involuntarily swallowed. He could sense the strength building in her. He then placed the skin to his own mouth, taking a good swallow. The warmth suffused his body, heightening his senses and building a sense of well being until his awareness touched the broken body next to him.

He did not at fist notice that while this was going on, Andorian had joined them. He stood in silence watching Fenly and Ramolin as Fenly began to probe the damaged body, gently stitching together the worst of the wounds.

He gently tried to straighten the leg with the badly damaged knee so that he could heal it in its proper alignment. Even unconscious Ramolin flinched with the pain. Fenly knew he could not fully return the shattered knee to health, but had to do what he could.

The little magic that he had taken in was nearly exhausted when he finally withdrew from Ramolin. She breathed easier however and was beginning to show signs of rousing.

As Fenly sat back on his heels he noticed Andorian for the first time. His jet black hair was streaked with gray, not from age but from the ash and mud that was everywhere. He was of average height for the Jhirum and very slender. He looked to be in reasonably good health with the exception of a few bruises and a burn down his one arm.

"And how are you Andorian? It seems that every one is injured, but at least you stand on your own."

"I am fine," Andorian responded with a quick glance at his arm. "Just a few scrapes and bruises. Why did you not take more water in order to heal her more completely?" he asked with a quizzical look.

"There is little enough water," Fenly replied casting a concerned look at the diminished water skin. "Our water source seems to have been destroyed in the catastrophe. There is no more when this is gone."

Andorian stared in shock. "No more water? How can that be?"

"I don't know how it can be, but it is," Fenly replied flatly.

Ramolin stirred slightly, showing signs of gaining strength. A storm was blowing in on strong winds, chill and gusty. There was no place nearby affording any shelter so they stayed where they were; not wanting to move Ramolin yet.

Just as the mist began to turn to pounding rain, Laim appeared like a wraith from the gloom. He was haggard and limping but seemed otherwise to be fairly healthy despite his years. Laim was one of the elders of the Natec, numbering his years in hundreds, he had seen much and survived difficulties many times over.

He gazed down at Ramolin after inspecting the rest of the small group, "She is still weak, why don't you help her more?"

Fenly's shoulders sagged a little in repeating the lament another time, "Our resources are limited. We have only this one small bit of water in the skin and our cliff has collapsed rendering the source unusable."

Fenly could tell that for a moment Laim looked at him as if trying to judge if he was sane, but then looked away. "I thought it was as bad as it could be; the blast and now this infernal chill rain, but our water gone as well? I still have half a skin, but you are right to use as little as possible. Who knows what need we will have the way things are."

He then knelt beside Ramolin; Fenly could sense him probing her further and lending a little more strength. The rain was coming down in sheets now chilling even Fenly, with magic still in his veins. "There should be one more tribesman joining us. I could not tell who it was with my weakened sense and because he was some distance away."

Laim nodded. "It is Findal. She will be here in a few minutes then we should try to find some cover."

The immediate danger for Ramolin past, Fenly's thoughts returned to his mission. "I was heading west when I came upon all of you. From what direction have you come and how far?"

Andorian, shaking off the remaining shock from the news about their cliff answered first, "I was in the west all the way to the Western Mountains. That is what spared me the worst of the blast."

Laim responded, "I was south of here, not far from the river, I encountered one dead Jhirum, but none living."

Glandine looked up as if startled as they all turned their gaze on her, realizing for the first time what Fenly was doing. "I think that I was also to the west, I must have been just south of Andorian, I saw no one until you came along."

Through the pounding rain Fenly's weak sense finally touched the last approaching Jhirum just before coming into view from down the hill. Findal, strong and beautiful even though drenched and bruised smiled weakly at the gathering. She had emerged from a slightly northeastern direction. She must have been closer to home and had turned around when she sensed Fenly. The question was repeated and the answer came back the same.

"We must find a little shelter," Fenly sighed, disappointment on his face. "Andorian, can you help me with Ramolin?" Together they lifted her limp body, though as they did so she moaned slightly and flinched.

"At the bottom of the hill and just north there is an area that was protected enough that a few broken trees still stand," Findal offered.

After adjusting their burden they set off down the hill, knowing that there would most likely not be a better place.

It only took a short time to get to the trees despite constantly slipping and sliding in the cold grey mud. Ramolin remained only mildly aware during the trip although even this was an improvement.

Just as Findal had described it, the battered handful of trees stood ragged in the pounding rain looking like jagged broken bones pointing into the grey sky. Their remains, did offer some small protection, however, and it was certain that they could not look farther as the light was fading into a sodden dusk.

Since most of the group was bereft of magic the chill rain was taking a toll on their unprotected bodies. Fenly asked Glandine and Andorian to gather some wood from the tangled broken branches to use for a fire. He would have to use his waning magic to start the water logged wood, but he could still at least do that.

His magical sense, though weak could still hear the cries of the broken world and its inhabitants, though the cries were growing weaker as those in pain past out of existence.

He had to concentrate hard to bring the soaked wood to a smoldering blaze, smoking and sputtering with moisture, but he succeeded in the end.

They had built the fire under a leaning tree that crossed branches with two other trees, both of which had been topped, but still had some branches remaining. One of them was an evergreen with needles still in abundance, so they had protection from the direct downpour and the fire could sustain itself against the mist and drips that made it through.

They had only a few bites of food between them to settle their rumbling stomachs. Fenly realized that whatever their direction tomorrow, they would have to focus some effort on foraging.

After sufficient wood to keep the fire blazing through the night had been brought near the fire they each found a spot to settle, as close as possible. The ground though having been covered in soft needles at one point, now had a layer of the omnipresent gray slime, making for uncomfortable sitting.

Once they were settled Laim asked for their attention. "We need to decide what to do in the morning. Fenly, you were heading west toward the mountains, in search of survivors. Now, however, we have Ramolin to care for, who clearly is in no shape to continue on. Many of you have also come from the west, so have covered the territory intended. Is there anywhere to the west that one of you has not recently passed, or is there someone you knew was out there that is unaccounted for?"

Each of the companions fell silent reflecting on their past few days. Andorian broke the silence. "I was not aware of any one in the area that I covered, besides those found dead."

The others nodded their agreement. Laim concluded the discussion, "I think that between us we have covered the territory as well as can be expected. I do not think there is anything to be gained by journeying further west again."

Fenly, reluctant to abandon his task so quickly looked from face to face before answering. "You are probably right, I cannot think of any likely places that I would look that you have not journeyed through between you. In that case we should all turn back toward our encampment, though I would still like us to break up into a couple of groups so that we can cover additional ground on the return trip.

Laim and Findal, perhaps you can arc slightly to the north on the return, Andorian, Ramolin, Glandine and I will go slightly south of my outward track."

"Do you think that wise with Ramolin in this kind of shape?" Findal asked. "If she is not able to walk herself all of you will need to help her back as quickly as possible. I would suggest that you head straight back. We will head north as you have said but that is all we can do."

For the first time Glandine stirred. "If you and Andorian can handle Ramolin I will cover the southern return alone. It is not so far now at any rate."

Fenly studied her carefully, thinking of the disoriented woman he had found wandering aimlessly earlier. "Are you sure you are up to this on your own?"

"Let me go with Glandine," Laim interjected. "Findal can go alone the northern route more quickly without me anyway." Fenly nodded approval, waiting for Glandine's response.

"I am fine, though if you think it better I will not argue the point."

This settled they each tried to find a spot comfortable enough to sleep near the fire. The rain continued to fall as Fenly counted over and over in his mind the Jhirum accounted for and those known lost, wondering how many more had been found by the others. It was becoming clear that their tribe was considerably diminished and he could not imagine what their lives would be like without magic. These thoughts as well as the dampness kept him awake well into the night.

He did finally find a restless sleep, but woke to water dripping on his face from the overhanging branches. The rain had lessened somewhat though the air was still damp and chill, with little light in the sky.

Laim was already awake, stirring the fire back to life. Smoke billowed from the damp wood he had added to the coals. Soon though flames blossomed throwing enough heat to drive the night's chill from their bodies.

They each picked through their remaining food and ate what little was left. Ramolin was conscious and able to sit up. Fenly gave her some more water. "How do you feel?"

She tried to move her shattered leg and grimaced. "I feel much better, but I still cannot bend my leg."

Fenly feared that there was little any one could do to help her regain her full mobility, but at least she would not have to be carried prostrate the entire trip. They did not waste time with further discussions. They simply said their brief goodbyes and set out on their separate routes.

Fenly and Andorian each with one of Ramolin's arms across their shoulder headed directly toward the camp from which Fenly had left a few days earlier. The return trip would be much slower, for Ramolin would not last long even being carried as she was now, until she strengthened more.

It took them a while to find a gate that they could maintain without constantly pulling against each other, but then the going became somewhat easier. Fortunately the ground was relatively even, though slippery, which made the going easier and there were not too many downed trees to negotiate.

By the time midmorning had arrived Fenly could see Ramolin's eyes drooping and she had stopped any attempts to talk. Fenly stopped. "I think we had better stop for a while." Ramolin was clearly exhausted, not even responding to his suggestion.

Andorian looked at Fenly, his brows furrowed. "Is she all right?"

They gently sat her on a fallen tree. "I think she just needs to rest."

Finally she roused a little. "I am fine; just very tired." She could hardly complete the sentence. Fenly held up the water bag which he had taken from Glandine and poured a small amount into her mouth. He then reached in his pouch and brought out the few berries that remained, gently putting them to her lips one at a time. After a few moments she began chewing with more vigor and some color returned to her cheeks.

"I think that we should let her rest a while and then take turns carrying her on our backs," Fenly suggested. Then he gave her a little more of the water to rebuild her strength, though the skin was nearly empty.

They had still not found any food so they did not rest long before setting out again. Andorian took Ramolin first. Fortunately she was not heavy though only a head shorter than Andorian, her weight was not difficult to handle. Fenly knew that neither one of them could carry her for long however.

The gloomy gray day wore on with focusing on putting one foot in front of the other and picking out the easiest paths that did not deviate far from the straightest line back to the camp.

While Andorian was carrying Ramolin Fenly spotted a small knot of berry bushes at the bottom of a hill. "Andorian are you ok to carry Ramolin for a while yet?"

"Yes, I am fine."

"Then continue on while I see if I can get some berries from these bushes. I will catch up with you shortly."

The tops of the bushes were stripped of berries and leaves, but the bottoms were such a tangle that many of the berries there still clung to the plants. Crawling on hands and knees he forced his way into the bushes picking as many berries as he could find. By the time he emerged, scratched and with his knees rubbed raw, his pouch was about half full. Though it was not nearly enough to provide a good lunch for all three, at least they would have something.

By the time he caught up with Ramolin and Andorian, he could see that Andorian was tiring, his legs unsteady and his face set. "Let me take her now."

Andorian did not argue, gently lowering Ramolin to the ground. She actually stood on her good leg and though still tired Fenly could see that she was feeling better.

"Here, both of you take a drink from my skin. I filled it at the stream we passed; it may even have a small amount of the magical water left in it."

They both drank deeply, Andorian sitting squat on the ground in exhaustion. Fenly also gave them each a few of the berries which they chewed quickly. Then they rested for a short while before Fenly picked Ramolin up and they continued on.

Later they came across a dead fox, which seemed to be fresh enough to be eaten. This Andorian slung across his back.

By late morning Ramolin at intervals walked between the men, with their support, though her knee still did not bend.

They stopped well before dark because of exhaustion and the fact that they came across a copse of trees, which afforded some shelter and an opportunity to build a fire. At least it was no longer raining.

Though still damp, they were able to start a smoky fire. Andorian skinned the fox, keeping the small skin for whatever use it might be put to.

He then placed the meat on a stick which he held over the fire. They were all too tired to even talk while the meat browned the small amount of fat crackling in the flames. By the time it was done they were all ravenous. Even so, Ramolin cringed at the strong taste and stringy texture, but they all ate until the last morsel was gone, too hungry to complain.

As he chewed the last bits of stringy meat off of a bone Fenly studied Ramolin. She had bags under her eyes and was clearly exhausted, but she ate with relish, despite the strong taste of the meat. She also seemed to be somewhat more animated than this morning. As she stopped to lick her greasy fingers he asked, "Ramolin, how are you feeling?"

Wiping the grease from her face with the back of her hand she looked at Fenly. "Actually I feel almost normal except for not being able to bend my one leg and not being able to use my one hand. I think that you were able to use enough magic that I am nearly healed otherwise."

Fenly relaxed visibly. "That is good. Perhaps tomorrow we will let you walk a little more on your own."

"I am sure I will be able," she replied casting the bone she still held into the fire.

Fenly and Andorian stripped some lower branches from a couple of evergreens, laying them on the ground to provide a dryer and somewhat softer bed and the three curled up as close to the fire and each other as they could.

As they drifted off to sleep Ramolin quietly asked, "What is going to become of us? Are we going to be without our water forever?"

Neither Fenly nor Andorian responded for a moment. Finally Fenly sighed, "I do not know. Right now I would have to say that it is possible that our water is gone forever."

Andorian lifted his head. "How can we possibly survive in this tortured land without magic?"

Fenly turned to look at him. "I cannot say how we will do it, but we will have to learn. We have little choice."

Andorian stared into the fire for a few moments in silence before lowering his head again. Fenly closed his eyes. How indeed could they survive like this?

The next several days were much like the first, though Ramolin continued to gain strength, each day she could limp along on her own for a little longer before needing support. Even in the rain they began to encounter more birds, though there were still few signs of ground animals.

By the fifth day they came to the sloping hill that descended to their cliff, though it was almost unrecognizable having been transformed from a lush meadow dotted with brush into a blasted waste land with only a few torn and twisted small trees still standing.

Fenly did notice however, that he was now beginning to see a few small green plants emerging from the gray muck that was everywhere. Signs that life would return to their land in time even without the aid of the Jhirum's magic.

Fenly had to nudge Ramolin and Andorian into motion, for they had frozen in place upon cresting the hill, confronted with their decimated home. Though they had been walking through their land, all of it in this same damaged condition for days, the site of their cherished valley in this state closed the final door to their old lives. Finally goaded on by Fenly they slowly descended into the valley toward the broken cliff.

Before turning to go around the cliff to get to the encampment they stopped again, in front of the Jumble that had been their source of magic. Ramolin shook her head. "But the water still runs, is there no magic in it?"

Fenly still staring at the pile of rocks and debris nodded. "Something changed. The water has no power. I found a few rocks with a remnant of the magic but not enough to do anything with."

Andorian could not bear to look any longer and turned with his eyes downcast and trod onward. Fenly watched after him for a moment before urging Ramolin on.

As they rounded the hill and climbed to where the encampment had been made they could see smoke rising against the gray sky. By now weary of trudging through the thick gray mud, half the time dragging Ramolin along with them, they were happy to see the crude lean-tos that had been built. Many of the able bodied Natec were out foraging for food but both Legolan and Pendolin were sitting up, tending the fire in the larger lean-to. Though the smoky fire made their eyes burn, the warmth and relative dryness inside the crude shelter more than made up for the stuffiness.

Legolan stood to greet them, though Pendolin remained seated, still nursing her injuries. "Welcome back, I see that you have found others, it is good to see you Ramolin and Andorian."

Ramolin smiled broadly, though she quickly found a log to sit on with her injured leg outstretched before her. "I am glad to be here."

Pendolin's eyes went to her damaged leg. "How bad are your injuries?"

"Not so bad any more, I can at least walk some though the leg does not bend well."

Legolan gestured to a small pile in the corner. "Would you like some food, we do not have much, but there are some berries and nuts that the others have been able to gather."

Andorian nodded. "Yes please, we have not eaten since this morning. I will help myself."

Fenly looked Legolan and Pendolin up and down, "and how are the two of you? Are you getting stronger?"

As Legolan sat he replied, "Yes, I have actually started to help the others forage, though I cannot go for more than a short distance before I tire still."

Pendolin stared at the fire. "I am feeling some better, however I am afraid I am still not much use around camp. The others should be back shortly. They have been out since this morning trying to find some meat, which is still hard to come by."

Fenly suddenly realized what she had said. "Others? Have the other groups already returned?"

Then Pendolin and Legolan brought them up to date as to who had returned to the camp before them and Andorian, Ramolin and Fenly related the tale of their travels and the others that they had found who were also on their way back.

In fact, before Tandeir returned all of the others arrived as well, glad to be in a place where they might not have to travel for a while and glad for the dry lean-to as well, though it was small for the growing group.

CHAPTER 25 DANGEROUS WORLD

The Maestic's plan to focus on gathering provisions and improving their shelter did not progress without interruption. In the predawn darkness Endmere woke to pounding rain. They would not be able to accomplish much outside as long as this kept up. For the first time in his life he recognized the warm comfort of a home beyond the simple shelter it provided. The cave still held a slight dampness, but compared to the downpour it was warm and dry, fragrant with the scents evergreen boughs and the glowing embers of the fires.

He stirred the coals to life and placed some small wood on the fire to light the darkness. It was still some time till dawn and most of the rest of the clan was still sound asleep. The light from the fire was swallowed by the depths of the cave. Endmere grabbed a stick that was burning brightly from the fire and walked into the darkness.

The air became cooler and staler as soon as he reached the point where the high ceiling of their warren came down to form the lower roof of the cave as it began its journey into the mountain.

He continued on. It had been many years since he had been in this cave. Even with the great expanse of their mountain range his couple of hundred years of constant travel made it all seem very familiar. This cave, however, was a new wonder that he had long ago stopped thinking about.

As he walked he remembered back to when he was a very young man deciding to search the cave as far as he could to see what he could find. With his magic he could maintain light and travel unencumbered, but somehow he had missed the runes carved in the walls. In reality, he had lost interest after a day of exploration, longing for sunlight and fresh air.

Now, however, his interest was renewed. Despite his own admonitions to focus on the task at hand, he took this little time before dawn to search the cave wall until he came upon the first of the runes. In the dull glow of the remaining embers of his brand he stared at the simple rune polished to the point of shining in the light. He reached out and gently traced the outline. A glow began to build from the rune, spreading to the surrounding rock until the cave was alight with the amber glow. Could it be that their ancestors had unwittingly opened the way for them to recover their lost magic this many millennia later?

After staring in wonder for some time he began to retrace his steps with the light to his back. He could clearly make out the fires and his tribe mingling around them by the time the light had faded and disappeared. He thought it curious that there were no runes to provide light in the giant chamber. But then again these caves had been explored, but without intent of ever living here. Only now, thousands of years later could such lights be of great value.

Several of the tribe glanced his way as he emerged from the darkness, curiosity, or puzzlement etched on their faces. Jasper, however, cast a knowing smile his way as he drew up to the fire.

Several of the Jhirum were just beginning to bring out some food from where it had been stored in crevices and small chambers in the wall when the sound of pounding feet and heavy breathing at the cave entrance stopped them in their tracks.

Doran and Gladborn stumbled into the cave breathless and disheveled.

Endmere was pleased to see his two children alive and well but at the same time was worried by their harried appearance.

Doran looked around the cave and seeing Endmere came to him directly, not pausing to acknowledge the welcome of those he passed. "A pack of Whorzen has entered the forest," he panted. "We were on the edge of the plains after the blast and went out to see if we could see what had happened. This band of Whorzen came out of the north headed straight at us. We have been trying to evade them and work our way back here since then."

Momentary silence pervaded the cave. "Are you certain they pursued you into the mountains?" Cragen asked incredulously, "I have never even heard stories of Whorzen entering the mountains."

"There is no doubt," was Gladborn's response. "We barely survived their pursuit. Were it not for their uncertainty with the terrain they would have fed on us."

Doran nodded. "We hurried to the spring as fast as we could only to find it ruined, we were told we could find you here. We tried to confuse them on the way here but I am not sure whether we have lost them or not."

Endmere considered this dire news. "Perhaps the migration of the buck was cut off by the catastrophe leaving them hungry to the point of seeking better hunting in the mountains. How many were there?"

"I think only five or six, their pack must have been either thinned or scattered by the explosion," Doran responded.

Suddenly new footsteps pounded down the mountain toward the cave. Zeeta rushed in, drenched and panting. "The Whorzen are on their way, they are only moments behind me! I tried to lead them away but could not stay ahead of them so I finally had to turn back here."

Zeeta had gone back to the spring and had volunteered to stay there as watch for a while. It was she who had sent her children to the cave while leading the pack away.

Endmere rushed to the cave opening, he could see that Zeeta had a gash on one arm but could not pause to give it attention now. "Quickly, roll some of these rocks back in front of the opening then grab the longest, strongest sticks you can find!"

Every one rushed in different directions, quickly returning to the cave entrance. Some began rolling the stones previously removed from the entrance, back to the opening while others grabbed whatever strong looking sticks they could find.

The sound of the huge beasts crashing through the forest drove them all back inside the cave where they arrayed themselves in front of the opening with their crude spears forming a pointed barricade.

The first Whorzen came bounding down the mountain completely overrunning the cave entrance in his haste. The beasts were clearly out of their element, not used to the steep pitch of the mountain or the poor footing. They crashed and banged their way through the trees like an avalanche.

Realizing its mistake, while the others bounded past, the first beast turned, discovering the open cave mouth. Its eyes gleamed even in the darkness of the early morning rain. Clearly hungry to the point of brashness it leapt at the mouth of the cave, huge jaws snapping at the pointed barricade. With one snap it seized the sticks from two of the Jhirum, throwing them aside. But while it cleared a small gap the other sticks were jabbing at it with all the force the Jhirum could muster.

Though not sharp enough to pierce the tough hide they nonetheless battered the creature causing it to yelp and fall back. The others had now joined it, a ravenous gang though thankfully smaller than a normal pack.

Cragen dropped his stake and lifted the two Jhirum who had been tossed to the ground. "Grab burning stakes," he panted. "Try to burn their eyes or anything else you can get to".

They rushed to the fires grabbing lit sticks, burning their hands but hardly noticing. The Whorzen were fighting each other over the entry way which could not allow more than two to stand side by side at a time.

Cragen, Thespan and Bastile rushed to the door where the others made room for them to get their brands to the forefront. Saliva raised by their anticipation of food flew about splattering everything and everyone.

Cragen jammed one brand into the open maw of a huge golden beast which clamped down on the stake before realizing its mistake. With a howl it fell back snapping at the air only to be replaced by another ravenous hulk.

Thespan and Bastile managed to get their brands into the eyes of both beasts even as they tried to back away from the glowing stakes. Whines and howls beat against the sound of the rain.

Now wary the unhurt pair that remained kept their distance though planted firmly in front of the entrance. They eased their way forward. The Jhirum with brands retreated slightly, hoping to lure them closer. Then as one they lunged at the animals, singing hair and blistering noses, though doing no serious damage. In anger they lashed out at each other snarling and snapping.

At least two of the injured beasts had pulled away, losing interest in this rather prickly feast. The others however had not yet given up, though they were reconsidering their approach. Settling down on their haunches just out of reach they looked to be setting siege to the cave, waiting for any opening to attack again.

Several of the Jhirum ran back to the fires grabbing more brands. This time however, they hurled them at the Whorzen causing them to jump up and retreat down the mountainside. The tide had turned at this, the Whorzen were beginning to think on easier prey as they drifted away with an occasional snarl or wary look back. Finally they broke and trotted off down the mountain, crashing as they went. They would find it difficult to corner any prey with the racket that they raised.

The Jhirum held their positions even after the Whorzen were beyond view, shaken and uncertain that they had permanently chased them off. Finally Endmere lowered his stake, still staring into the rain. The others followed suit. Some with brands suddenly realizing their fingers were burning from coals they had grabbed quickly threw them back in the fires.

Endmere still gazing out into the rain called to Jasper, "Jasper, can you stand guard at the entrance in case they return?" Jasper picked up one of the stakes again and moved back to the entrance.

Endmere moved to the fire motioning for Doran and Gladborn to join him. Others gathered around as well. "Can you tell us what happened?" he asked his two children.

Gladborn began, "We had been out near the edge of the mountains for a couple of weeks when the explosion occurred. We spent the next couple of days trying to put out fires and heal injured animals and birds. We kept working our way closer to the plains because it seemed that was where most of the damage was.

We had nearly exhausted our magic when we encountered the Whorzen. Fortunately we still had some strength left or we would not have survived. We were not able to calm them or turn them away entirely but we did manage to distract them long enough for us to head back into the mountains."

Here Doran picked up the tail. "We set a good pace, but did not think that the Whorzen would return to pick up our trail. Nor did we think that they would follow us into the mountains.

We were barely half way back to the spring, thinking that we needed to replace our water, when we heard them crashing through the forest. It was fortunate that they are so inept at negotiating the terrain so we could hear them from some distance.

We began to climb steep hills and tangled thickets, whatever we could do to make it more difficult for them. We managed to keep them off of us all the way to the spring. Then when we came to the spring we had just enough time for Zeeta to tell us the spring would be of no help before the beasts sprang on us. We beat them off briefly with sticks and stones then Zeeta began to lead them off into some difficult terrain after telling us to head here. The rest of the story you know."

Endmere looked around the small group gathered in the cave. There was a haunted look about their faces. He did not need to ask the source, for he felt the same. It was not so much the threat of the Whorzen itself, but the change in circumstances that it represented. Without their magic they were just another animal to be hunted and to hunt. They now had to think every moment of their own safety and not just about what they could do for the land and its denizens. Thinking of the sticks and fire brands they used to fend off the Whorzen, he realized they would have to develop weapons and would probably not be able to travel alone as often. Everything had changed in that one blinding flash.

Mustering his own courage he stood to gather everyone's attention. "I do not think the Whorzen will return any time soon. It is clear, however that it is no longer safe to wander alone in the forest without thought for our own protection. I think that as part of our preparation, we need to consider constructing better weapons. If one of us is alone and confronted with one of these beasts we would not be as lucky as we were this morning."

Zeeta's face had passed resignation and had hardened into steel. "You are right. We must have weapons and be on our guard. You were also right to come to this cave and establish a safe camp here. It is clear that we will need a refuge, although I am still not certain that I can make it my permanent home."

This was a huge concession for Zeeta, which focused the rest of the group even more on their dire circumstances. Gladborn had begun to shake as her body came down from the adrenalin rush of the past several hours and her mind began to grasp the situation.

Bastile recognized an opportunity to press her position. "I think that this only serves to illustrate that we cannot go on without our magic. Who among us wants to live like any other animal, hunted and afraid? Look around us. We are in a cave that harbors magic. The runes have magic, surely somewhere in this mountain the pure source of our water remains to be found. Yes, we need weapons for now, but that is not the answer, the answer is in this mountain. We must reclaim our magic."

Jasper immediately pronounced his agreement. Most of the others waited, still considering the situation. Finally Lamsil responded, "We are still too ill prepared to go venturing under the mountain or over it for that matter. We should first build up our reserves of food here and try to fashion some weapons and other tools that we might need. Once we have these necessities, then we can consider what to do next."

Cragen, cutting in before Bastile could respond added, "I agree with Lamsil, since there is no guarantee if or when we will find magic even if we do go looking under the mountain. We must at least have some basic weapons, clothes and a defensible shelter."

During the discussion Gladborn had been working on trying to stop the bleeding of Zeeta's arm, which was not badly damaged but needed attention. Zeeta cleared her throat to draw their attention, Endmere tensed slightly not knowing what to expect from his mate.

"The last thing I want to do is spend more time around here making weapons and gathering food, but I think after seeing what happened with the Whorzen we must prepare ourselves for our own survival without magic before we can do anything else, or all could be lost."

Zeeta's words carried weight, because everyone knew at what cost to her own preferences she made this statement. Jasper started to protest then sensing the mood of the group relented, though still unhappily.

Since the rain was still pounding down outside and they were uncertain what the Whorzen might do, they determined to focus on doing what they could inside the cave, only venturing out for short distances to look for wood or other things that they needed.

As a first priority Endmere directed several of the Jhirum to work on a door for the cave entrance. Although they could only make a very crude one made of stakes tied together with vines and strips of bark at least it might give them some protection from another attack. The result was more of a set of bars than a solid door, but the main purpose was to keep animals out, so it would serve the purpose for now.

Others of the group set about trying to construct weapons. Having never made or used anything but simple stone knives this proved to be a slow learning process. They did manage to get some crude spears made of stakes either sharpened, or with sharpened stones tied to the end. In the search for good stones to use as blades several Jhirum ventured some distance into the cave using the runes for light but never going far.

As the day drew to a close Jasper could see that it was going to be a long time before they would be prepared enough that Endmere would allow anyone to explore the cave again.

CHAPTER 26 SEARCH FOR A HOME

The Jhirum of the Sea set sail to the north in search of a new harbor, thinking that the mountains would have sheltered the land there, although they knew that there were not many good ports along the rocky cliffs. In most of the northern reaches the mountains came right to the sea dropping precipitously from towering heights to the sea floor with little but sheer cliffs to welcome sailors. There were, however a few places where there were small harbors, somewhat sheltered from the worst of the sea's battering. It was these that they would seek out to see if any of them could offer a comfortable land base with sufficient provisions to stock their ships for journeys.

The sea was calm relative to the froth that had been churning up for most of the time since the calamity. Shwaren stood at the helm, the wind stiff at his back as he guided the ship out of the harbor. As he swung north the offshore breeze battled to push them out into the open ocean, forcing him to constantly adjust back toward shore. He felt almost as if nothing had changed. That the last several days were only a nightmare from which he had finally awoke.

With the swift progress of the boat the low hills around their harbor soon climbed toward the peaks of the western mountains. He could sense, even from the distance off shore that they traveled that the land protected by the mountains had suffered less damage. There were, however, signs of recent fires on the sides of the mountains leaving the charred remains of trees clinging to the steep slopes. Already, with the hard rains that had occurred since the blast there were mudslides on the unprotected slopes leaving scars of brown amidst the green.

In this stretch of coast there were no harbors, only the seabirds could find footholds on the cliffs large enough for nests. Their cries echoed off the sheer rock face mingling with the rhythmic crash of the waves against the rocks. They would have to journey another half a day at least until they could find some purchase on the shore.

They sailed without stopping, rotating shifts, driving the boat with their magic. They stopped briefly for lunch at one of the places where magic welled from the bottom of the ocean through vents, which spewed hot alkaline water along with the source of their strength. The vents were deep, however, so the only way to obtain the magic was through the fish that thrived in this area. The fish seemed to store the magic, building it up in their bodies and making them potent enough to sustain the Jhirum for many days. Storing this much magic, however, had strange effects on the fish, which emerged from the depths in a rainbow of colors and shapes.

Zifere stood on the bow with a spear as a small flash of brilliant red flashed near the surface. He flung the spear, but just missed the creature, which promptly surfaced, sprouted wings and flew off toward the cliffs.

Shwaren could not help but smile at his consternation and several of the Jhirum laughed openly at the comical sight.

Suddenly a yell rose from the stern and Shwaren turned to see two Jhirum hanging on to the end of a spear while several others rushed to their aid. It took some time for them to finally wrestle the beast aboard where it thrashed its single horn about madly.

Shwaren always loved to see what they would find near these vents. No two magical fish were alike. This one, besides the large horn was purple and almost the size of a Jhirum, swirled with colors that glowed from the depths under the boat. They were fortunate to land it so easily.

This one fish would provide them with sufficient magic to last many days, so they wasted little time butchering it and packing it carefully in a special container they kept in the storage area packed with salt. They each shared some of the flesh raw and then were on their way again.

For this whole time Toren stood at the bow of the ship, scanning the mountains and the sea as if willing there to be a good harbor that would finish any thought of returning to their old home.

Several times Maerl joined her and attempted to engage her in conversation, but though they shared a bond through their survival of the tsunami, Toren quickly lost interest and returned to staring at the shore.

Faren had just finished a shift, linked with six other Jhirum prior to them stopping at the vent. Now, having eaten lunch and the magical fish he felt reinvigorated and alive. He almost regretted not continuing to be part of the crew propelling the boat. Instead he settled in to a careful inspection of the shore and mountains. His heightened senses allowing him to see as well as connect with birds and animals a hawk would have difficulty seeing.

He found it odd that they had not sensed the presence of any other Jhirum so far in their journey. Though small in number, the Maestic normally were spread out over these mountains and were detectable at even greater distances than the animals because of their magic. But no sign of them appeared anywhere. There was not sufficient damage to the forests here to imagine that they could have been killed or had reason to flee, but they were absent nonetheless.

As he pondered this mystery Waymeir drew to his side, also staring at the mountains. "Have you noticed that there are no Jhirum?" he asked without taking his eyes off the peaks.

"Yes, I think that they must have gathered inland after the blast," she responded. "At any rate I hope that is the explanation."

"That makes sense," Faren responded nodding his head as if relieved and satisfied with the answer, "how long until we reach some possible harbors?"

"We won't be beyond the steep cliffs until tomorrow I suspect," she said thoughtfully.

Faren stopped scanning the hills long enough to glance at Waymeir. She was many years his senior, though not yet middle age by Jhirum standards. There was barely any trace of age on her face and her brown mane had a blond streak down the middle without a touch of gray. She was, in fact striking. Though shorter than Faren by a head she stood straight and steady on the rocking deck as if no storm could budge her from the spot.

Noticing his attention she smiled and glanced at him sideways. A smile reflected on his face before he turned back to his study of the shore. Waymeir frequently considered Faren a mere boy, though in truth he was not so very much younger than she. Tall and muscular he had sandy blonde hair in striking contrast with jet black eyes. They had teased at affection many times, but never seriously.

She followed his eyes back to the mountains. Tall and rugged, some of the far peaks were capped in ice. This did not seem a likely place to find a good harbor, but further north the mountains retreated slightly from the shore allowing for small sandy inlets that might offer them the shelter and the resources they needed to maintain their boats.

They sailed on through the afternoon with one more shift change, and then anchored offshore for the night. The weather had improved somewhat over the past couple of days. Though still cool for late summer the drizzle and rain that had fallen constantly for several days had lessened. Still the sunset burned in strange hues through the thick haze that refused to give way to the normal early fall blue.

Taking advantage of the better weather the Jhirum congregated on the deck for their evening meal which was composed of fish, freshly caught, cooked lightly over pots with coals in them along with a few berries.

Winfew sought out Shwaren, clearly with something on his mind. As he settled cross legged on the deck he did not hesitate. "We have sailed these waters many times, I do not recall any harbors that would be worth stopping at for more than a short stay. The mountains are too close, with very few sheltered coves or horizontal land to build houses on. I no longer see any point in this journey."

Shwaren continued to chew a bit of fish before responding. "I agree that there is unlikely to be a great spot for us, but, perhaps at least an acceptable one can be found. If not, we may have to sail beyond our normal range though I would not like to go too far north because of the cold."

"But why go at all," Winfew responded looking directly at Shwaren. "Our old home may have been damaged, but it would still suffice as a usable base."

Others were listening as they ate, though Toren was not among them. "And it may still," Shwaren reassured Winfew. "We have not abandoned the possibility that we will return there. Regardless, I think it is a good idea to explore the land to see what we can learn of its condition after the blast."

Waymeir interjected herself into the conversation. "I agree with Winfew, the best way to learn about the blast and what its affect on the land was would have been to stay in our home and journey farther inland, closer to the source. I see no point in wandering the shores."

"We have been through this," Zifere answered impatiently. "We journeyed inland far enough to know that there is terrible destruction in that direction, we need to know nothing more of the land. We also know that many of our sources of food and lumber have been badly damaged and that we will have a difficult time sustaining ourselves in the old harbor, so why not look to see if we can find a better base. Besides, what else would we do now but sail?"

Donley who had been silent set down his bowl. "We sail, it is what we do, now especially since we are few enough to be sheltered together on one boat. I do agree however that there is unlikely to be a better harbor further north. I think that we should consider other destinations. Perhaps even into the deep sea. We know there are islands, some large that we have not explored far out at sea. Surely some of these would provide shelter for us away from the devastation."

Maerl shook her head. "But are there magic sources near these islands? We know of some far out at sea, but the nearest large islands are beyond any of these that we know of."

Donley picked up his bowl again. "There are stories from generations ago of voyages far out to sea, beyond where any of us have gone in this generation. Some tell of a beautiful island several days walk across surrounded by upwellings of magic. We do not know precisely the location, but the stories have enough in them to guide us in the general direction."

Shwaren was impatient with the quick abandonment of their current search. "It is too early to talk of what we might do if. We still have a lot of shore to cover in this direction and if necessary to the south of our harbor. If we find no better shelter then we can return to our old harbor."

Toren who had joined the group flinched visibly at this thought, though Shwaren pretended not to notice. The others fell silent and then began to drift off into less controversial conversations. As darkness stole over the ocean they began to settle in various corners of the boat to get some sleep. When the weather allowed they would always choose to sleep on deck rather than in the stuffy hold.

A watch was posted to keep an eye on the boat, insuring that it did not break free from its anchorage and to warn if storms approached. Shwaren circled the deck one last time careful not to step on the Jhirum scattered about, then found a spot to settle in to a restful night's sleep.

He replayed the arguments in his mind. Being at sea had reawakened his itch to travel and see new places. Perhaps it would be best just to sail off into the deep sea in search of an island refuge.

Despite the turmoil brought to their world by the object from the sky, a day on the seas both exhilarated and exhausted, so his internal debate did not last long as sleep overcame him leaving nothing but untroubled dreams.

Morning dawned grayer then the last. Low clouds clung to the peaks of the mountains and fog drifted in the steep valleys. They could well be in for more of the cold damp weather that had become the norm since the catastrophe.

As each Jhirum awoke they ate a light breakfast of fish and a few berries along with some of the magic imbued fish from the salted barrel.

It was not yet full light when they were ready once again to set sail. The anchor weighed, they continued north, though Shwaren had to agree with Winfew that there would be no point in going too much farther in this direction, for any harbor they would find would be too cold to call a home year round and in fact far enough north the harbors would be closed with ice in the depths of winter.

CHAPTER 27 CASTING THE DIE

By the evening of the day that Fenly and his charges had arrived back in camp the rest of the wandering Jhirum also returned, though no new survivors had been found. With the return of those who had been out foraging the survivors of the Natec tribe were all together.

This was the first joyous occasion the Natec had experienced since the disaster. For the first time they felt as if they were not alone and that there were enough survivors that they could carry on. There was little talk of the future however. Instead they continued to share the details of what they had experienced since the catastrophe. By the time they went off to find places to sleep they each had a good picture of the extent of the devastation and the dire circumstances that they now found themselves in. They were, however, also reassured by each other's company and most slept better than they had in many days.

When the dawn broke, the sun actually visible through the thinner than normal gray shroud that covered the sky, Ashmere who had for the first time since the disaster spent the night with Fenly almost like old times, studied his face for a time then spoke. "We need to discuss the future. We have no magic and the fall is coming on faster than normal. There is little to eat and we have no way of keeping ourselves warm."

Fenly nodded. "Yes, we must begin to plan. Let's gather every one and discuss what to do next."

Since not everyone was yet awake, Ashmere first revived the main fire in the camp, building it against the chill of the early morning.

With the warmth calling them, soon everyone who could move on their own was gathered by the fire. Ashmere, noticing that Pendolin had not made it to the fire asked a couple of the Jhirum to go help her to come join the group.

As they settled her on a log by the fire Ashmere began. "We need to begin planning for the future. We have not had to do this in the past, but it is already getting chill and without our magic we will need shelter and warmer clothing as well as a plan to feed ourselves. Since many of us have not had a good meal in some time let's take the morning to forage and gather back here at midday then we can discuss what to do next."

With little additional comment those able, set off alone or in pairs to look for food. Several set out toward the mountains where the protection of the hillside had left more of the vegetation alive and probably more of the animals as well.

Minere traveled with Glandine. She remained quiet and aloof as they set out. Glandine frequently glanced sideways at her but could see that she was not interested in conversation and so remained quiet.

Frequently her hand strayed to the object in her pouch, the strange black stone, which almost seemed to call out to her at times. One of these times as she held it a thought crossed her mind. Checking to see that Glandine was not looking she held the stone and concentrated on the idea of food. For a while nothing happened. She was almost ready to give up when she thought she noticed the stone growing warmer. Trying not to draw attention to herself she held her hand out in different directions. Just like before the stone grew particularly warm when held in one direction. She put the rock back in her pouch thinking about what to do next. She did not want to look foolish if the stone turned out to be useless, but she felt very strongly that it was responding to her need.

Finally she looked at Glandine. "The other day I was near the base of the mountain in that direction," she said pointing slightly north in the direction the stone had warmed. "There were some nut trees over there that might have some nuts on them." Why she chose to say nuts when she had no idea what might be there even if the stone did work she could not say.

Glandine stopped. "Why didn't you say something before?"

"I was only able to get to the edge of the area and have not been able to get back to see if any nuts actually survived, but I think we should look there now."

Turning and staring in the direction Minere had pointed Glandine frowned for a moment before turning back to Minere. "I guess it is as good a direction as any. Lead on."

Minere nodded and headed off in the direction she had pointed, already unsure of her decision.

It took them until mid morning to reach the base of the mountain. Still they saw no nut trees or any other food except for a few berries remaining on some bedraggled bushes. Minere stopped and looked around uncertainly.

"Well, where are these nut trees," Glandine asked, "Is this the area that you meant?"

Not liking that she had lied to Glandine she still tried to carry on the ruse. "I was sure it was near here, maybe just a little further up the mountain."

"Ok, lead on."

As Minere began uncertainly to head up the mountain she once again reached into her pouch and withdrew the stone holding it surreptitiously in front of her, moving it from side to side. Just to her right it became almost hot. She fumbled it for a moment before sticking it back in her pouch. "I think maybe a little in this direction."

Less than a stone's throw further they came upon a large grove of nut trees still heavily laden, having been protected by the steep slope of the mountain.

Minere stopped dead in her tracks with this seeming confirmation that there was indeed magic in the stone, but still she kept silent.

It did not take them long to gather all the nuts they could carry in their pouches and hides that they had brought along for the purpose.

Glandine hefted the hide full of nuts on to her shoulder and they began the trek back to camp. After walking a short distance Minere could not restrain herself any longer. "Glandine, I have to confess that I did not know that nut grove was there."

Glandine looked back at her. "Then why did you say you did?"

"I used the stone. When I concentrated on food it grew warm in one direction. I thought that it was responding to my needs, but I was not sure so I didn't want to say anything until I was sure."

Glandine stopped, looking squarely at Minere. "Are you certain?"

"This time I am positive, it even grew hot when we were close."

Glandine studied Minere for a moment but could see that she was absolutely convinced. "Well then this could be very important, with all our other sources of power gone we need to see what else this rock can do."

Minere nodded. "I knew that we could find our magic again."

Glandine was still restrained though. "We will have to see if it is something that will be strong enough to be of real use, but at least it is something. For now though we need to get back to camp." With that she swung the sack over her back and continued on with Minere behind her still studying the black rock.

By the time the sun stood nearly directly overhead most of the Natec had returned. Some with little more than a few berries and some with fairly respectable quantities of nuts, berries and in a couple of cases fish or animals that had recently died from the aftermath of the catastrophe.

As they gathered around the fire after depositing their harvest and selecting something to eat from the various piles Fenly stood. "It is time for us to talk about the future. Up to now we have focused on survival and rescuing our injured brothers and sisters. It is unusually cold for this time of year and in any case it will soon be fall and then winter. Without our magic we will need shelter, warmer clothing and food. This will all require planning."

Ashmere interrupted, "It is my feeling that the first thing that we should decide is whether this is a good place to establish a more permanent encampment, or should we relocate somewhere else?"

As often happened Tandeir was the first to state her opinion. "I have not traveled the land as much recently as most of you, but from what I have heard there are not many better places than where we are now. We have the start of shelters, there is still some food and living trees and bushes close by and there is water. I would suggest that we stay where we are."

Gloren stood, commanding attention by his size. "I have traveled a good distance in the north and can say that I saw no better place than where we are, although I have not been into the Spine at all, perhaps there is better shelter in the mountains."

"I don't think that it would be wise to go high into the mountains for it would only be colder and more difficult to find comfort," Ashmere interjected, "Where I was, near the base of the mountain I did not see any better places. What about the rest of you?"

Several Jhirum started to speak at once, most confirming that they had not seen a better place. Engin finally cut in, "There was a place at the base of the mountain near where the Frun enters the valley that seemed to be well sheltered, suffering little damage from the blast. There were berry bushes and the river nearby for food and water. Perhaps we should consider this place."

During this discussion Minere sat quietly chewing on some nuts while absently fingering the black stone but suddenly she could hold back no longer. "Why are we only talking about what to do without magic? Why are we not talking about how to get our magic back?"

Silence fell over the group, both because they were all surprised to hear such an outburst from the young woman and because many of them had never considered anything but going on without magic. Tandeir though smiled knowingly. "I agree. While we certainly must make provision for survival without magic we should not abandon all hope of regaining our magic."

Glandine looked at Minere. "Go ahead Minere tell them about your stone."

Once again all eyes turned on Minere. Hesitantly she stood and reached into her pouch withdrawing the black stone and holding it out in her open palm. "I found this on our journey back to camp. I do not know what it is, or what it might mean, but it has shown me that it has some power."

Those closest to her stared at the midnight black object in her hand, drawing closer in interest. Pendolin who could not see since she could not easily stand spoke above the murmured comments. "Step back so that we all can see. Minere, in what way has this rock shown power?"

Minere's eyes lit up with excitement as she brought the stone closer to Pendolin. "It helped show me the way back to the group when I wandered beyond eyesight during our trip back here and it helped me to find food this morning."

Ashmere stepped closer to Minere. "Can you show us anything now?"

Minere looked at her uncertainly. "I don't know. What could I try?"

Tandeir who was about to put some more wood on the fire paused then brought the sticks to Minere. "Here see if you can light these sticks."

Minere held the stone uncertainly, and then closed her hand around it, concentrating on the couple of sticks that Tandeir had dropped on the ground in front of her. Nothing happened for several moments, and then a small trail of smoke rose from the sticks, fading away after a short while.

"Well there is something to that stone, but making a little smoke is not of much use," Ashmere said as she stooped to pick up the sticks and return them to the fire.

"It is not much, but it is something," Minere pleaded, "and I have not had time to try to learn how best to use it."

Ashmere returned to her spot. "There may indeed be magic left in our world somewhere, but this one stone is not enough to do us much good and we do not know where or how to look for more magic. We could go to the Bagnog, but the blast seems to have come from that direction so I fear that we may not find relief there either. I think that we cannot consider searching for or depending upon magic at this time. We must focus on things that will definitely help us to survive, not pin our future on a dim hope of magic."

Minere started to protest but was cut off by Laim. "Ashmere is right, for now we must assume that there is no magic to help us and that we need to provide for our shelter and food without its benefit."

Tandeir raised her hands to get every one's attention. "I do feel, however, that Minere still has a point. Where ever we decide to make a permanent camp I believe it should not be too far from the cliff so that we can check on it occasionally and perhaps later work to see if we can uncover our magic source again."

There was general murmuring of agreement around the group. The discussion returned to the topic of where best to prepare a permanent camp. Minere drifted away from the group gathered by the fire, continuing to stare at her rock. It was drawing near evening by the time some basic decisions had been made. It was agreed that they would stay where they were at least for the time being since they already had the crude beginnings of a camp. They would break into teams starting the next day. One group would work on the problem of shelter, one on clothing and one on food.

Minere, however, stayed awake into the night contemplating her rock, certain that there was magic out there and certain that they would only survive if they could find it. Genlie, seeing her awake, joined her silently. "It is ok Minere. We will try to recover our magic in time."

Her eyes burned as she turned them on Genlie. "But in what time! Why do we put everything else first when this is the most important?"

Taken aback by her anger Genlie looked down silently. Realizing she had misplaced her anger on Genlie she too looked down and reached out with a hand to touch his arm. "I am sorry Genlie. It was not your decision. It is just so frustrating and I am so lost without magic."

Genlie looked into her tearing green eyes. "I know. It is ok. I promise I will help you to find our magic whether or not the rest do." Touched by his support she leaned into him, letting his arm come around her.

Genlie spent a long time with her, finally just holding her without speaking. The comfort offered by his strong arms was welcome. By the time she drifted off to sleep near the middle of the night, Minere had silently resolved that no matter what the rest of the tribe did, she was going on a hunt for magic, perhaps she would travel to the Maestic to see if she could use their magic source. But whatever, she was not going to waste her time making clothes and huts.

CHAPTER 28 MOUNTAIN RETREAT

The journey through their once lush plains had seemed endless for the ragged tribe of Bagnog survivors. Covered in the now stinking buck skins the Bagnog were a grizzled band smudged in black, haggard and worn by the time they reached the edge of the Black Mountains. It seemed like fights and yelling were continuously breaking out among the tribe members. Nomber could not recall a time even in the worst of circumstances when Jhirum had even yelled at each other, yet alone come to physical blows. He rationalized that it must be the dire circumstances, the loss of their magic, or the persistent headaches combined, that made their tempers so unusually short.

They had gathered additional surviving members of their tribe along the way. They now numbered about twenty members in various states of health.

Normally they preferred the open plains and spent little time in the mountains. The Black Mountains in particular were wild and little tended by their care. The denizens of these mountains had been left to fend for themselves over the millennia. Those who had ventured this far had brought back tales of unusual beasts in the mountains as well; beasts that did not recognize the Jhirum as benign healers and protectors. On this day, however, the mountains, though shrouded in mist looked like the most beautiful place on earth. Most of the trees still stood on these slopes, though there were signs of fires aplenty. Birds twittered in the trees and evidence of life abounded.

Though it was not yet the middle of the afternoon they decided to stop at the base of the mountains and make camp, perhaps sending some parties to investigate the best direction to take to find some shelter and food.

After a brief rest Nomber called the tribe together. "I think that we should break up into small groups. We need food, water, firewood and we should probably explore at least the general area to see if there are any threats or better places to camp nearby."

Nomber's jaw clenched as Thane stepped forward to speak. "We have stuck together to get to the mountains. I see no reason for us to stick together any longer."

Bashley glowered at Thane. "These mountains are unknown to us. We still do not know if we are safe. We should stick together until we are all strong and we know we have enough food."

Thane stared belligerently at Bashley. "We will better be able to find food and some shelter on our own rather than trying to find enough in a small area for all of these people."

"We are going to have to work together a while longer, Thane," Jarine retorted. "Without magic we need clothing, shelter and we need to protect each other. We can't do this on our own."

Roan nodded in affirmation. "We need to stick together a while longer. I am as anxious as you to be on my own. But frankly, I do not know if I can survive on my own without magic."

This blunt admission quieted the group as they each thought of their own uncertainties. Finally Nomber stirred. "All right, let's break up into small groups at least for now to explore nearby for danger or better places to camp. Do not go far."

Nomber also left one group to work on trying to construct some temporary shelter and to see if they could start fires to provide some warmth. Though they were now in the southern reaches of their territory, the chill in the air had not lessened noticeably. Fires would be the most difficult task in the overwhelming dampness that had soaked every bit of tinder, but perhaps somewhere sheltered, there was some dry wood and some means of setting a spark.

Nomber joined one of the groups heading up the mountain. They set off without delay. Though the mountains were steep, travel here was almost easier than in the plains. There was less ash and mud to pull at your feet and except for the occasional tangle created by fallen trees, the forest was old and clear of underbrush for large stretches. As the slope steepened the height of the trees diminished somewhat but many were still large enough around that two Jhirum together could not span their girth.

They had gone about halfway up the slope of the first line of mountains when they came across the remains of a fire. Here blackened sentinels stood in the gray afternoon amidst their fallen brethren. They ventured into the edge of this wasteland and continued up the mountain.

Though the fire had exhausted itself on the lower slope, as they reached the top of the mountain there were still smoldering piles of branches and underbrush here and there.

Nomber, after approaching one of these smoldering piles motioned to Gromand. "Gromand, can you see if you can find a branch with enough hot coals on it to start a fire? If you do you can carry it down to the camp to be used to start the fires. We will continue on for a while longer."

Nomber and Worden continued on to the top of the first peak. Everything was shrouded in mist at this height so little was revealed of the surrounding mountains. They would have to choose randomly where to go from here.

They chose to head directly down into the next valley, hoping to find a sheltered place that would provide them a good encampment. The way down was steep with rockslides where they had to leap from boulder to boulder, treacherous in the dampness. But the Bagnog had not lost their knowledge of the land, or their natural deftness at negotiating the landscape, so this presented no problem to them. Both Nomber and Worden had shed their buckskins at the camp, preferring the cold to the rotting smell and awkwardness of the heavy skins.

They reached the bottom, which provided only a small relatively flat area and then shot up again quickly to another pinnacle. Though protected from the worst of the wind by the steep sides of the valley there was little else offered by this small valley in the way of shelter, or food, so they continued on, following the valley.

The trees in this narrow valley reached high to compete for the brief light that fell between the peaks, only near midday.

As they walked, Worden glanced at Nomber. "Have you ever been in these mountains?"

Nomber did not stop scanning the valley. "A long time ago I came here, but I went not much farther than we are right now and I only stayed a short time. I prefer the open plains and even the animals here are less welcoming."

Worden looked puzzled. "Why is that?"

"They just do not know us. No Jhirum has spent much time in these mountains in millennia. The animals see us only as other animals to be eaten or be eaten by."

Worden looked around a little more uncertainly. "Is this really a good place for us to be then, without our magic?"

"We do not have much choice. I think this is about the least damaged region in our territory." Nomber fell silent as they negotiated a tangle of bushes. They had to push branches out of the way to get through, but some of the bushes were laden with fruit. They ate as they went, pausing only momentarily to fill a pouch. They finally reached a dead end where the mountains shot up all around them. With a sigh they turned to head up the steep side working their way in a zigzag pattern.

By the time they had reached the top of the next peak the light had grown noticeably dimmer. Nomber looked at the sky trying to locate the sun through the thick haze. "I think that we should head back to the camp."

Worden just grunted as Nomber turned to follow the ridge around the valley and then back down the other side toward camp. As they descended the last slope leading to their camp they could see blazing fires. Nomber picked up the pace, anxious to get dried out a little.

He could see that most of the other groups had already returned to settle in for the night. There was activity and warmth around the fires.

Nomber approached the closest fire. Reluctantly those gathered around moved aside to let him get close. "Did anyone find anything interesting?" he asked looking from face to face.

Most merely shook their heads or grunted. Clearly the fires were not enough to improve the mood of the Bagnog. Number wondered at this. Did every one still have the headache that continued to gnaw at his brain? Although he suspected that this was the case he also knew that the loss of their magic was hard to get past. He constantly felt cut off from his tribe and the world. This made him less sure of himself than he ever felt before.

He did not spend much time contemplating these questions, however, because he saw the remains of several animals spitted over the fire. The smell of roasted meat called to him. He pulled up one of the stakes with the remains of what looked like a squirrel. Though there was not a lot of meat on the small animal it still tasted like ambrosia after several days without anything but the rancid meat they had gotten from the herd of buck.

He tried again to get something out of his fellow tribesmen between bites of meat. "So no one discovered somewhere that might work better as a camp?"

Extoar finally roused himself out of glaring at the fire. "I certainly found nothing. The mountainsides are too steep and the closest valleys too narrow or devoid of water or shelter."

Tamber nodded. "I think someone mentioned a stream not far from here though that would at least give us water."

It seemed however that no one had found a suitable place to be their permanent encampment so they would have to venture out again the next day farther into the mountains.

As the food slowly filled his stomach Number's eyes began to droop. He left the fire, moving a short distance away where he propped himself up against a tree trunk and quickly fell asleep, though he briefly started awake at the howl of the giant mountain wolves that inhabited the Black Mountains and nowhere else in the land.

As he drifted off again he was all too aware of their vulnerability. A people who had feared no creature and could tame the most savage of beasts suddenly was playing the role of the sheep among wolves. With this thought running through his mind he dropped off into restless slumber.

The morning came with intermittent downpours waking them to the hissing of the fires that had been kept alive by watches during the night. They all huddled in close around the fires as they stoked them with more damp wood which initially raised clouds of smoke, choking their lungs and burning their eyes, bringing back haunting memories of the initial aftermath of the explosion. After sputtering and smoking for some time the fires blazed again, throwing some warmth against the chill, though gaining little against the dampness of their skin and clothes.

Many chose to put the skins on again, despite the smell. Number helped himself to some more of the berries and fresh meat. As he moved to the fire next to Roan who was wearing one of the skins he wrinkled his nose. "How can you stand to wear that stinking skin?"

Roan scowled in his direction. "Better to stink than to freeze." Nomber moved away from him to the other side of the fire. Soon the skins would fall apart with rot and be useless whether they could put up with the stink or not. They needed to do something because it was certainly chill enough that any coverings they had were welcome.

A sudden thought occurred to him and he glanced around to find one of the tribesmen that had been to the stream that was nearby. He spotted Floan at the other fire and still chewing on the last of his berries went to talk to her.

"Floan, you went to the stream that is near here didn't you?"

She stopped scowling at the flames of the fire for the first time noticing that Nomber was there. "Yes."

"Was the stream clear?"

"Yes, like most mountain streams," she answered a puzzled look on her face.

"But was it one of the brown mountain streams?"

Suddenly a light dawned in her eyes. "Yes. Yes it is. It is dark with tannins."

Nomber felt a small rush of excitement. "Then we should get the skins soaking in the stream before they completely rot." With a weak smile she nodded.

Nomber stepped away between the two fires and raised his voice, "Everyone, if you have untreated skins it appears the stream near here is full of tannins. I need some of you to take all of the skins to the stream and see if you can find a way to soak them in the tannic water. Perhaps you can dam up a small area and beat some more tree bark into the water."

A general murmur ran through the tribe as they realized they could perhaps make their skins usable and get rid of the stench, though without a good way to dry them first they would never be perfect. Several members volunteered to attempt this with as many of the hides as they could carry to the stream.

Nomber decided that a few of the weaker, still injured members would be left behind to tend the fires while everyone else would set out in search parties fanning out over the mountains looking for a more suitable place to set up a permanent, or at least semi permanent camp.

Before setting out Thane made it clear that he did not agree with what they were doing. "I see no advantage to us staying in a large group now that we are in the mountains. We can just as well survive on our own, and probably better."

Nomber stared Thane down, this not being the first time that he had challenged the group's direction. "We have no magic, no shelter and little food. On our own we are at the mercy of the weather and the wolves. I see no way that we are better off alone."

Dankin, whose group had rejoined them late the previous evening, strode into the conversation. "Perhaps not alone, but I think that smaller groups might be better. There is no advantage to being in one large group. We need to spread out to find what food and shelter we can."

Nomber could tell that his tenuous leadership was wavering to the point of collapse yet he felt strongly that their best chance of survival was as a single group. "At least wait until we have done some exploring and know better what our opportunities and obstacles are. You can set off on your own later."

Thane clearly not yielding everything replied, "I will wait until the end of today but unless something changes, no longer."

Nomber nodded, he had to be satisfied with this for now. He knew that he had no real right to demand their obedience, but he still had to find a way to keep them from completely falling apart to die one by one in the mountains.

With the immediate crises past the tribe broke up into groups to attend to their duties. Once again Nomber set out, this time with Bashley and Gromand to explore further into the mountains. They set out in a southerly direction which would cut straight across the range, perhaps even taking them to the other side to see what they could find.

In the beginning they stayed to the ridges so that they could see a little more of the territory around them, though the mist still shrouded everything and limited their view considerably. They had all shed their skins which had been carried off to the stream. The damp and cold slowly worked out of their bones with the exertion of climbing.

Twice on the first assent they had to pause as Gromand held his head. "I can't stand this headache will it never go away?"

Nomber who felt no better tried to sound positive. "It must get better eventually. Try to ignore it as much as you can."

"Ignore it. Can you ignore it?"

"No, not completely, but the less I think about it the less it bothers me." Gromand just shook his head and started off back up the mountain.

After walking some time in silence Bashley asked, "Nomber do you think that others will leave the group?"

Nomber stared ahead. "I cannot answer for them, but I fear many would just as soon set out on their own, though I think it a grave mistake."

Bashley was clearly trying to understand. "What is it that you fear if we are broken up?"

Nomber searched his own thoughts for a moment realizing that he had not clearly identified his concern. "I fear what we do not know. We have never been without our magic and we do not know the total impact that this catastrophe will have on the land. I do know that whatever happens, our chances of survival are greater if we stay together, at least until we know some more."

Bashley nodded, apparently reassured by his reasoning. Gromand said nothing, directing his scowl to the path ahead. The mist continued to fall raising goose bumps on their arms despite the exertion.

They were now following a ridgeline to get to the next line of peaks. Though everything was quiet, they could occasionally hear a bird call or an animal scurry out of their way. It was reassuring to hear these kinds of sounds after the desolation of the plains. Nomber could almost imagine that nothing had happened and that their lives would continue unaltered. The headache served to clear this illusion however, leaving him drawn and irritable. A wolf howled in the valley below causing them to share concerned glances and to alter their path to descend down the opposite side of the ridge.

Bashley reached for a branch and stripped the remaining smaller branches to form a crude spear. Gromand was about to say something and then began his own search for a suitable stick.

Nomber became even more somber, he had not thought of weapons. Bashley was right; they would need weapons for defense and to get food. The prospect of hunting did not please him. The Jhirum did not like killing in any form, but he knew they would need to in order to survive now.

Morning wore on, the only highlight being their discovery of a mountainside half covered in heavily laden berry bushes. They ate till they could eat no more and then vowed to return by this same route so that they could gather berries to bring back to the group. Even a full stomach did not improve Nomber's mood however. Each of them continued on wrapped in their own thoughts, scowls firmly implanted on their faces.

They proceeded on down to the bottom of the mountain where they found a narrow but fairly flat valley. As they crossed to the other side of the valley to proceed up to the next peak they saw ahead of them a black cliff. At various places there were significant overhangs and here and there a black maw opening deeper into a shallow cave. Nomber headed directly for one of these overhangs.

There was a flat enough area sheltered by the cliff for perhaps five people to lay comfortably side by side and it was about as long as four Jhirum laying head to toe. It was mostly dry though at the one end there was a trickle of water coming from a small spring somewhere near the top. They walked around this overhang to where the cliff ascended more vertically followed by another hollowed out area. This one was smaller than the first along the cliff but ran deeper ending in a short cave. This too was mostly dry though the walls were damp and moss grew over much of the surface.

Nomber stopped to consider what they had found, then walked back into the valley so that he could survey the cliff from a short distance. Gromand continued to poke around the cave while Bashley joined Nomber. "Do you think this might be a good place for us to make a camp?" Bashley asked.

"I think it might," Nomber said quietly as he continued to study the cliff and the surrounding valley. "It is not ideal, but it is the best we have found so far."

"It stinks!" Gromand exclaimed as he came out of the deepest part of the cave. "I think animals have lived in there."

"It can be cleaned," Number responded. "I think that this is the best place we have found."

"Then let's head back to camp," Gromand almost growled.

Number scowled at his tone. "We might as well continue on, we do not know what else we may find and it is not yet midday."

"I'm tired and I want to head back," Gromand retorted.

Bashley stared at Gromand as if he were from another world. The Jhirum were a peaceful and civil people, the worst among them would not speak an impatient word to another.

"What is your problem Gromand?" Bashley asked the astonishment clear in his voice.

"It's this damn headache. I can't stand it anymore. I just want to lie down until it goes away."

Though Number, too was astonished at Gromand's tone he tried to placate him. "I understand, Gromand, we have all been living with the headaches since the catastrophe, but losing our patience will not help any of us."

"Well do as you please, I am heading back." And with that he turned and headed back the way they had come. Even Number was so unprepared for this type of outburst that he just stood there and silently watched Gromand's back as he disappeared into the trees.

Bashley looked at Number as if expecting him to run after Gromand, but Number just shook his head. "Well I guess it is just you and I to continue on. I think we will need to go further down the valley to find a place that is less steep to get up this mountain." Number headed off down the valley with Bashley following, his face furrowed with concern.

As it turned out this was the last major peak before the foothills that then fell to the enclosed plane of the Valley of Mist. Though none of the living Bagnog had ever visited this valley, the name had been passed down through generations. It had earned its name because of the large swamp that covered this end of the valley. The swamp, combined with the fact that the valley was closely encircled by towering mountains, lead, according to the stories, to almost constant and incredibly thick fog. From their first glimpse the stories appeared to be true. Though the sky had been gray for many days now, from the peak they could see the mist thicken into what appeared to be a solid wall about halfway down the side of the mountain.

"It does not look very inviting," Bashley ventured.

"I see no reason for us to proceed further," Number answered reassuringly. "I doubt if we would find a place we would want to make a home there."

Bashley let out a breath, clearly relieved at this decision. Number paused a moment longer silently staring down at the forbidding wall of fog.

As he was about to turn and head back toward camp a low rumble issued from the valley followed by a piercing scream, neither of which he had ever heard the like of. More confident than ever in the decision to leave the valley unexplored he turned his back on the clouded valley and headed back toward camp. Bashley hefted his crude spear as if to test its mettle against a beast that could create such a sound, and then turned to follow Nomber.

They made sure they retraced their path to the mountainside covered with berry bushes so that they could fill their small pouches. They could not carry a lot but whatever they could they would bring.

As they left the berry bushes and proceeded up the side of the mountain Nomber noticed a number of bushes and small trees with recently broken branches. The leaf litter was also churned exposing the dark earth underneath. Nomber was certain that this area had not been disturbed like this when they had passed through before. Bashley also was looking around intently at the broken branches of the bushes, the scraped bark of trees and the ground torn up and black.

More worrisome, they next came across leaves with splatters of blood trailing off up the mountain. Nomber picked up the pace, but at the same time leveled his crude spear in readiness for anything that might await them.

They heard and saw little until they came across a smaller area similarly disheveled and more blood. Nomber was now seriously concerned, for the trail continued directly along the path that they were taking back to camp. This would also be the way that Gromand most likely would have taken earlier.

It was not until climbing the mountainside out of the next ravine that they heard ragged breathing ahead of them as well as the loud rustle of leaves. No animal of the forest that was not in distress would make this much noise. Nomber caste a warning glance at Bashley and readied his spear.

After a short time they could tell they were gaining on whatever was making the racket. Instinctively they both were in a crouch as they proceeded. Nomber caught a brief glimpse of something moving just beyond an outcropping of rocks, but still could not identify it. They rounded the outcropping cautiously, again catching a glimpse of movement, now near the top of the peak they were climbing.

As they approached the peak, at last Nomber saw a silhouette against the gray sky ahead of them. It was a Jhirum, obviously Gromand and apparently hurt. Nomber dropped his defensive crouch and bolted ahead of Bashley.

They were now within clear sight of Gromand who had turned in a crouch of his own, spear leveled ready for action, though he swayed unsteadily. It took two calls from Nomber before Gromand raised his spear upright in recognition that he was not under attack and then slumped to the ground.

Nomber and Bashley arrived together at Gromand's prostrate form. He was panting and bleeding from a gash in his arm and another in his side as well as several smaller scratches over his face and legs.

Nomber kneeled beside him and lifted his head. "What happened Gromand; can you hear me?"

Gromand opened his eyes, though they took a moment to focus. "Attacked. Beast like I never have seen." His voice faded as he grabbed for breath.

Bashley knelt beside Nomber worry in his face. "Is he badly injured?"

"I don't think so," Nomber replied uncertainly, "I think that he is more exhausted than hurt." Nomber pressed on the wound in his side to try to slow the bleeding.

After several long moments Gromand's breathing slowed to a more even tempo and his eyes fluttered open again. "Is it still following us?" he said quietly but with urgency in his voice.

"We came behind you," Nomber replied. "We saw no sign of any beast." More tension fled from Gromand's muscles and brow.

Bashley could not restrain himself any longer. "What was it Gromand, what happened?"

The answer was slow in coming. "I do not know what it was. It was low to the ground on four legs but long like a giant lizard though with hair and a blunt muzzle. It was hidden in the berry bushes. It must have just waited until I got close and then it lunged at me with razor teeth and claws as long as my hand. It was fortunate that I had the spear, or he would have had me in the first attack. I was able to get it down just enough to keep him pushed away.

We went back and forth with him attacking and me stabbing at him. He almost took the spear from me once, but while he had it in his mouth I was able to force it down his throat until he had to let go."

Here Gromand closed his eyes again, pausing to regain his breath. "I ran at that point trying to get away from him, but he was so fast that I could not gain any distance. Finally I had to turn and fight again. This time I managed to stab out one of his eyes, which infuriated him. At first I thought he would overwhelm me in his furry, but it also made him careless and I managed to stab him hard under his chin. With that he fled off into the forest, but I was still afraid that he would try to sneak up on me again so I ran as fast as I could."

Bashley looked warily around again clearly sharing Gromand's concern.

"It appears that you managed to drive it off," Nomber ventured in a reassuring tone. "It must have gone off in a different direction because we saw no sign of it. Just rest now for a while, we will keep watch."

Gromand closed his eyes again, though he occasionally threw his hand out as though swatting at flies, despite there being none around.

Nomber stood and motioned Bashley to his side. "Can you stand watch just below Gromand? I will watch the other side." Bashley nodded and they went to opposite sides of the sleeping form. Nomber had never heard of such a creature and could not guess its habits or nature, so he was not about to assume it was gone for good.

Blood had dried on Gromand's arm and side and had stopped flowing. Nomber was reassured that his wounds were not serious, but this was a good lesson for all of them regarding traveling alone in the strange mountains without their magic. He hoped that this was a lesson the rest of the clan would hear and understand.

The return trip from that point was a slow one, so it was past sundown when they arrived back at the camp. The fires were blazing and it seemed like everyone else had returned ahead of them. As they entered the camp, and Nomber scanned the Jhirum milling about he noticed that none of Dankin's group were in evidence.

Seeing Thane lurking at the nearest fire, tending some meat that was on a stick Nomber asked, "Dankin has not returned?" Thane turned noticing Nomber for the first time. "We have not seen any of her group yet. It would not surprise me if they did not return at all, particularly if they found a good campsite."

Though Nomber did not want to fall into Thane's negativism he had to agree that he would not be surprised either, but he suppressed this thought. "Can you find Jarine, Gromand is injured and needs some attention. She was good at healing with magic. We will have to test her now without it."

Thane glanced curiously at Gromand then hurried off to find Jarine.

She came hurrying over moments later, concern and uncertainty in her dark eyes. "I do not know what I can do without magic. Is he badly injured?"

"I do not think so, he has gotten on well enough during the return trip, but I think that his wounds should be cleaned and perhaps covered to keep them from bleeding again," Nomber tried to sound reassuring.

They set Gromand down by the fire, as several other Bagnog joined them. Jarine took a small piece of tanned fur from her pouch and rubbed at the wound in Gromand's side causing him to wince in pain. With a little water she cleaned the area well enough so that they could clearly see the wound, which was red and inflamed though not deep.

"This was caused by an animal?" Jarine asked.

"Yes," Nomber responded, then related briefly what Gromand had told them.

"It is likely not to heal well then," Jarine said almost to herself. "We must get some hot water to clean it as well as we can."

Nomber asked Bashley to get some water and heat it in one of their small bowls on the fire. In the meantime Jarine went on to look at the slice in his arm, which showed evidence of the heat of early infection already.

Gromand growled in his throat as she cleaned and poked at it, startling her momentarily. His teeth were clenched against the pain, but there was also anger in his face. Though puzzled by what she saw there she resumed her cleaning. When she had finished Gromand lay down where he was, panting from the pain, eyes closed until his breathing evened out and he fell asleep.

Nomber left them to circulate among the other fires taking a tally of who was there and who was not. At each group he retold the story of Gromand's encounter, hoping that it would help convince the remaining tribe members of the value of staying together.

Just as he was told, the only Jhirum missing were Dankin and her group. It did not surprise him, but still it was a disappointment to see what he was sure would only be the beginning of the disintegration of the group. After the experience with Gromand, he was more certain than ever that it would be a mistake not to stick together. They needed to be in a group for protection or they would not survive the winter.

As he stopped by the fires he asked for reports on what any of them had found. There were a few promising valleys discovered in the mountains, but on first blush none as good as what his group had found. With each group he described the overhang that they had found as well. The group that had been working on the hides also reported some success. They had left the hides in a small pool that they had closed off from the stream. They had then stripped bark off of trees and beat it on the rocks in the pool until they had a reasonably strong tanning solution. By morning they should be ready to dry the skins and to see what they might be able to fashion from them. This heartened Nomber, since even though a southerly region these mountains were prone to cool nights in the fall and the winds blew cold in the winter.

After every one had rested and eaten they all gathered around the largest fire and began to discuss what they should do next. Thane, early on asked if they should go looking for Dankin's group. "They could have been attacked like Gromand and be injured, or lost in the mountains."

"I think it is more likely that they have simply decided to strike out on their own," Nomber replied somberly. "We cannot spare the time chasing them in these mountains when we only know the general direction they followed and nothing more."

A brooding silence fell over the group Nomber could only imagine that they were each reconsidering their own decision to stay with the group. Though Nomber tried to read the answer in their faces he could not be sure which side of this argument was winning.

He decided on a conciliatory approach so as to not drive off any others who might be considering a similar decision. "I think that it will hurt none of us to stay together at least long enough to settle on a home base and establish some comforts. Even if we were to go off on our own it would be good to know that there is a safe place to return to at need. You have all heard of the places that each of us have found in our explorations. We should decide if any of them sound good enough to be our home at least for a while."

Worden who did not normally offer opinions when the group was together made a noise in his throat obviously preparing to speak. "There was ample food in the valley we discovered, though no particular shelter."

"That is good," Nomber responded. "But we also must have some shelter available."

Others in turn offered their suggestions as to which of the places sounded most promising.

The night ended with a tentative decision to move to the valley that Nomber and his group had discovered. That decision made they all settled around the fires for the night. Nomber continued to think about Dankin and what it could mean for the rest of the tribe. He was determined to do everything he could to keep the tribe together, but was not at all sure that he would succeed.

Jarine joined him where he sat a little back from one of the fires, "I think that Gromand will be all right, but we will have to watch his wounds for a while."

"That is good."

"You are concerned that more of the tribe will set off on their own aren't you?"

Nomber stopped staring at the fire to look at his daughter. "Yes I am. After Gromand's experience I think it is more obvious than ever that we should stay together, but I am not sure that others see things the way I do."

Jarine reached out and rested her hand on his shoulder. "I do, and I will do whatever I can to support you."

"I appreciate that daughter and I will appreciate any thoughts you have on how to keep the tribe together."

Jarine finally smiled. "I think that finding a secure base is important. If we have a place where people are comfortable and safe they will be more likely not to wander off. I do fear Dankin, however. I think that she would do anything at this point to undermine your leadership, though I do not understand why."

Nomber stared back at the fire. "I think you are right. I do not understand a lot of the actions of the tribe lately; all the fights and aggression. I even feel that my temper is shorter than normal."

"I feel it too. I do not know if it is the loss of our magic, or perhaps the contamination from the swamp that you feared in the beginning."

Nomber glanced back at her, his brow furrowed. "With everything that has gone on I had completely forgotten about that. Do you recall the maddened animals we encountered? All of them were covered in the same black soot."

"Well, hopefully we cleaned it off enough to prevent going mad, if that is what affected the animals."

"I do not know what else we can do anyway," Nomber replied once again turning back to the fire. "But I think we need to come up with a plan to try to handle Dankin and her group if we find them again."

Jarine nodded agreement. They talked for a while longer about various possibilities before settling in for the night. The cloud that had fallen on the Bagnog however, remained in the back of Nomber's mind, nagging at him until he fell into a fitful sleep.

CHAPTER 29 VALLEY OF MIST

As the debate continued around the fire of the main encampment of the Bagnog as to their next step, in a mountain valley that opened into the swampy plain of the Valley of Mist, Dankin, Kang and Blinan had settled in to a small cave near the floor of the valley. They had decided long before finding the cave that they had no intention of returning to the rest of the tribe.

As far as Dankin was concerned there was no advantage to being in such a large group, only the disadvantage of always having to do what someone else thought was best. So they had continued on past midday until early evening when they came upon the cave. It was not a large cave and shrank down to the size that you would have to crawl through a short distance in. But it was plenty large for the three of them, another advantage, they agreed of being in a small group. Though it was not completely dry it afforded enough protection from the elements to make them feel somewhat warmer and more protected.

Since they had not brought any coals with them, they were not equipped to start a fire, so they sat in darkness as the shrouded sun set behind the mountains and the fog began to creep up the valley from the vast swamp that lay some distance beyond their cave.

Though a headstrong and confident group, Dankin could sense that they all felt a small bit of trepidation as the mist began to swallow the dark trees surrounding them. Stories of the Valley of Mist had been past down for generations, though as far as they knew, no one currently living had ever actually visited the valley. The stories, however, told of fog so thick that only magic could keep an explorer from being lost forever. Worse, however, was the uncertain footing in the valley often giving way to quicksand, or deep pools hidden by tangled roots or floating plants.

There were also several tales, though lacking in details, of creatures that lived in this dismal valley that would snatch a person and drag them into the murky water before they could react, creatures huge and vicious.

It was these ancient stories that crept into their minds with the stealth of the fog which continued to stretch its wispy tendrils into the woods, pulling down on their mood and their resolve.

Dankin, however, refused to allow ancient stories to weaken their determination. "Why don't the two of you go to sleep? I will keep the first watch." Kang and Blinan looked at each other, then with a shrug curled up close together.

The Jhirum were not a people naturally afraid of anything in nature. Sure of themselves and their strength they boldly confronted even the largest, most vile tempered creatures, protected by their magic and their knowledge of the world. The loss of the magic affected them in totally opposite ways, depending on the character of the individual. Some felt the loss of magic as if they were stripped bare and thrown into the world as babes, unsure and frightened. Others, though aware of the loss of magic had not registered the full import of the change and walked in the world with their old confidence born of long habit, as if by refusing to acknowledge the change it could be made less real.

Dankin was of this second group, refusing to cower or even consider their new vulnerability she continued on as if nothing had changed. Thus she faced the night un-cowed as the mist drifted through the trees.

They had also reasoned that though the valley they were in seemed to open into the Valley of Mist, they were still high enough and far enough from the swamp to remain unthreatened by anything living there.

By the time her two companions were asleep the fog had completely hidden all but the nearest trees, which were left standing as ghostly wraiths against the gray mist. She had not noticed at first that as the fog crept in so had the sounds from the swamp. Eerie howls and screeches pierced the darkness. When she first noticed them she was little concerned as they clearly came from a great distance, probably from the swamp itself, which was still a good walk from where they were. As time passed however, the sounds grew closer at a rate that defied logic. Surely, no creatures could move at that speed?

With her attention heightened and despite her conviction that no creature could frighten her, she leapt to her feet when a moan that shook the very rock issued from the blackness. She was about to flee back into the cave when Blinan and Kang appeared at her side, eyes straining into the darkness.

"What was that?" Blinan asked as she stared into the blinding fog.

"I don't know," Dankin answered unable to sound as self assured as she wished. "But it was much too close for my liking."

For the first time since their decision to strike out on their own they all yearned for the company of their brethren. The thunderous moan seemed to have cleared the air of all other noise. The silence that followed strained their nerves as they listened for what would follow. Suddenly a scream that made Dankin's hair stand on end came out of the mist starting on their right and moving off to their left at an alarming rate. In its wake they could sense the movement of the fog following whatever had made the sound.

As one, they drew back into the cave slightly. Gone was their bravado, gone the confidence of years of protection provided by magic. For the first time in their lives they were confronted with their mortality in an intimate and immediate way.

Kang glanced at Dankin, the question in his eyes, though unspoken. Before anyone could voice their questions another scream erupted to their right. A dark form bolted out of the white mist almost within reach of where they stood. Whatever it was it was large, easily twice the size of the Jhirum and as fast as a buck in full flight. It had just crossed in front of them and was beginning to disappear to their left when it seemed to freeze in mid stride.

They stared in horror as they realized that the beast had been pierced through by what appeared to be a lance the end of which disappeared into the mist in the direction from which the creature had run. The next moment the beast slumped to the forest floor only to be dragged away by whatever was at the other end of the lance.

In unison they withdrew further into the cave not taking their eyes off the cave entrance. The sound of the body being drug through the leaves grated on their nerves as it approached the edge of their vision through the mist. Just as it was about to disappear into the mist the white of the mist seemed to grow dirty over a huge expanse. They could sense that there lurked just beyond their vision a huge being that was dragging the hapless victim to its final doom.

They could see no shape, however, only a shadow in the mist. Suddenly, the body on the ground was jerked into the mist and a disgusting crunching sound issued from the shadow as it swallowed its victim whole, crushing bone and flesh in one huge gulp.

Frozen in place the Jhirum dared not even breathe hoping that the creature could not sense their presence. With alarming speed for its size and the fact that it appeared to slither or crawl on its belly the shadow moved off to their left and away into the mist.

The three of them remained absolutely still for what seemed like an eternity, waiting to ensure that the creature was not going to return.

They only began to breathe when other sounds returned to the silent forest indicating that the danger had passed. Bursts of sound still emanated from the distance, either screams, or roars depending on whether it was the hunter or the hunted, but the main chaos seemed to be moving away from them.

Dazed they glanced at each other and drew further back into the cave. Dankin was the first to muster the nerve to speak, though in hushed tones. "Well, I guess this is too close to the Valley of Mist to be safe. In the morning we will move back into the mountains."

Blinan spoke so quietly Dankin and Kang had to lean in to hear. "Perhaps we should rethink breaking off from the main group. These mountains are more dangerous than our old territory and without our magic we would stand no chance against such creatures."

Kang looked to Dankin for her response as usual, unable, or unwilling to take a stand on his own. "It is the swamp that is dangerous," Dankin stated reassuringly. "We have simply gotten too close. Back in the mountains three of us will be more than enough to survive safely without the burden of trying to put up with a large group."

She clearly realized the tenuous thread by which her decision to set out on their own hung at this moment. Though she was tired and needed sleep she would do whatever was necessary to settle Kang and Blinan down. "I will continue the watch, go back to sleep for a while." Little enough concession if she could steady their nerves. Besides she doubted that she could sleep at this point. Her unwavering self-confidence had suffered a blow. They had come very close to being food for that monster and there would have been little she could have done to prevent it. They clearly had to put some distance between them and this valley in the morning. She had thought that the cave would be a good base for them, but they would have to continue the search.

The eerie noises of the Valley of Mist continued unabated in the distance as long as Dankin remained on watch. Only one other creature passed near enough to the cave to be seen and then still only as a shadow. This creature was low to the ground but massive and slow. She could not guess how it survived against the giant they had seen earlier, or what he ate, but she did not care to explore the matter further.

Well past halfway through the night she woke Kang, though still half asleep he did not wait to ask, "Any more murderous creatures about?"

"No, I think you will have a quiet watch, but stay alert." By the look in his eye she doubted that this warning was necessary. Kang moved to the entrance of the cave keeping close to one wall and Dankin settled uneasily in to sleep.

Kang woke Dankin and Blinan at first light, clearly anxious to have their company and begin the escape from the valley. The mist still clung to the trees, though it was thinning, leaving in swirls and tendrils as it withdrew back into the valley.

They picked at some left over berries from the previous day then cautiously approached the opening of the cave. The three of them stood for some time in silence listening and watching as the fog retreated, making sure that no more strange beasts lingered about.

Once they were satisfied that the area was clear, though they could still hear distant calls and shrieks of strange animals and birds, they quietly emerged into the pale early morning light. In unison they turned directly away from the valley back toward the heart of the mountains, putting as much distance as possible between themselves and the Valley of Mist.

CHAPTER 30 CAMP NOT A HOME

As the trio was leaving the valley Nomber and the rest of the Bagnog were assembling, eating their breakfast and discussing for the last time what they should do next. After much debate it was agreed that they would proceed to the valley where Nomber and his group had found the shallow cliff face caves to see if they could make an acceptable camp there.

Shortly after this was settled the group that had been sent out to retrieve the skins arrived back at camp. Though not enough for the entire group there were nearly a dozen skins of various sizes which when dried could be used as blankets or made into some form of clothing against colder weather. These were divided among the tribe, fires were smothered, after some coals were stashed in ash and secured in crude stone containers that had been picked up along the way.

Gromand was strong enough to walk on his own though the wound on his arm was a bit inflamed. Nomber raised his arms to get their attention. "I think that we should stay close together in case we encounter the beast that attacked Gromand."

He doubted that any creature would come anywhere near such a large group, but he did not know the habits of these mountain denizens and preferred not to take any chances. With this admonishment he turned and headed up the mountain.

They spent until early afternoon traveling at a steady pace until they reached the caves. They had only stopped at the stand of berry bushes to gather a solid lunch as well as to stock up on additional berries to bring with them. As they approached the cliff face he could sense various reactions from the group ranging from solid approval to downright disdain for his choice of camp sites.

He admitted to himself that the caves were not ideal, a little too shallow and a little too damp, but nonetheless providing some protection from the elements. They were also more defensible than an open encampment.

Thane of course voiced the loudest complaint. "You call this shelter? These caves are damp even in dry weather and barely deep enough to keep out the rain."

Nomber was growing impatient with the constant questioning of every decision. He understood that these people were not used to group life, but surely they could make a little more effort to support the common decisions. "They are not perfect as I said, Thane, but they are better than where we were, if at some point we find a better place we can relocate. But for now I think this will do. If the weather is dry and we are unthreatened there is plenty of flat space to camp in the open. We can use the caves only at need."

"You can bet that I will be looking for a better place, and soon," Thane responded shortly. "Perhaps I will go looking for what Dankin has found."

Nomber could feel the blood in his veins pounding in anger, which startled him, he was still in control enough to wonder at his reaction, but he let the comment go unanswered.

He called to the group to gather around again. "We should organize provisioning of the camp. We need to clean out the caves and make some bedding so that they are more comfortable, fires need to be started before we lose the coals that we have and others should gather food." He could sense Thane grimacing at his back but he continued to ignore him.

The rest of the group, with a little grumbling, broke up to tackle the various tasks. He joined a group setting out to find food. This would give him a chance to further explore the area around their camp. Thane stayed with the group ostensibly to help clean up the caves, but Nomber had little illusion that he intended to do much work. He could not trouble himself with this for the time being but he feared at some point he would have to deal with Thane, or chance the group disintegrating into factions.

CHAPTER 31 ANY HARBOR IN A STORM

The Jhirum of the Sea continued sailing to the north of their bay for the better part of a week without a single landing. The mountains continued to press up to the sea allowing no foothold that would suffice for an adequate harbor. The weather continued to be cool, with on and off rain. The sun when it appeared did so through a constant brown haze which dulled its warmth.

As he woke Shwaren thought they might arrive where the mountains retreated from the shore somewhat allowing for more level footing and small beaches. By noon they had come upon a small cove which though facing the sea directly, at least afforded a little protection.

Winfew was at the helm, Shwaren at his side. "Bring us as close as you can to the shore." He called to two Jhirum to station themselves at the bow to sound the depths to insure they did not come to ground. Their magic allowed them to sense the clearance of the boat easily.

As they were setting anchor Shwaren called out to the crew, "Let's eat some lunch then a landing party can go ashore to see if this might be a suitable harbor."

After eating some lunch a single dinghy was dispatched with four Jhirum to make a preliminary investigation of the harbor. Winfew headed up the group which guided their small boat with magic to a landing on a small beach which was only the length of their boat two or three times over. Trees crowded close to the shore leaving little open space.

Zifere jumped out to haul the boat ashore. They soon all stood surveying the beach and edge of the forest. Only a little sand filled in the cracks between small boulders and large stones. The land still fell away into the harbor at a rapid pace, prohibiting the building of an extended sand beach.

Winfew could already sense that this was not a great place to make their home, but knew they should check it out anyway. He led them to the forest's edge where he gave instructions. "Let's split up into pairs. We should not take a lot of time, but make our way as far as where the mountain begins to rise and then follow that line around so we have surveyed the level area. We should meet back here no later than mid-afternoon."

Zifere joined Winfew as he set out toward the northern edge of the beach. It was hard walking on the slippery stones near the water so they stayed up by the trees and then headed deeper into the forest and toward the base of the mountain.

The forest was thick with undergrowth making it necessary to push their way through at places and forcing them to take detours at other times. The sound of birds and animals filled the air and there was no sign of any damage from the catastrophe. There was sign, however, of the slight coloring of leaves and yellowing of grass indicative of early autumn, which should not have been evident for several more weeks.

Barely a long stone's throw from the beach the land began to rise toward the mountains and they began to circle south along the bottom of the first hills. Winfew did not like what he saw so far, there did not appear to be any natural shelter such as caves, although there could be some further up in the mountains. More importantly there did not seem to be much in the way of berry bushes or tall straight trees that would supply some of their critical needs. Instead the entire area they walked was a tangle of low branching trees and bushes. By the time they emerged back on to the beach where the other pair already waited, it was clear that this was not a suitable space for them to make a permanent camp.

As they approached Winfew looked at them expectantly, "Anything of interest?"

Bandai shook his head. "It is a pleasant enough harbor, but there are few resources. I do not think that this would make a particularly good home for us."

Madrien nodded his agreement. "It is such a tangle of brush and low growing trees that it would take us a season just to clear enough space to live."

"We saw much the same," Winfew responded. "I guess we might as well return to the ship."

Most of the crew was at the railing, awaiting their return as they pulled the dinghy up beside the ship. After climbing the ladder Winfew made his report. "I do not think there are enough resources in this small area to act as a good base. I think that we should continue on." Shwaren looked in turn at each of the others who nodded their agreement.

"The good news," Winfew continued, "is that there appears to be little damage from the catastrophe this far north and sheltered by the mountains, although there are signs of an early fall."

"We will continue north for a while," Shwaren responded. "Though I do not think we should do so for many more days. We are already getting far enough north that the climate would not be pleasant in the winter and we cannot afford to be too far from shelter if it is already turning fall."

The crew headed back to their posts to continue the journey. Shwaren knew that this far north the fall brought gales out of the west, which came upon you quickly, and violently, making extended journeys dangerous. They would have to turn south soon or risk getting caught in weather that could strand them along this rocky coast.

The end of their northern journey came several days later in another cove, this one larger than the first and cut deeper into the coast, almost forming a fjord. The deep water held to within a short dinghy trip of the shore. Of the several coves and small harbors that they had investigated this one looked the most promising. It angled into the coast providing natural protection from the direct force of the waves and wind. On either side of the cove the mountains were still high enough to block the winds but no beach awaited them. The thick forest grew to the rocky edge of the cove all around. Not even a shallow entry point existed. The bank from one end of the cove to the other was at least the height of a Jhirum above the water line. It would be difficult to access the shore, but they could pull the ship within a stone's throw and not come to ground.

Shwaren ordered the dingy overboard with six Jhirum aboard. They drove the boat to shore then stopped to survey how best to climb the steep bank. As they surveyed the bank Maerl reached down for the rope that was used to tie the boat up. "Let's see if I can get this rope around one of the rocks so we can use it to crawl up."

The rest of the group moved to the other end of the boat as she tied a loop in the rope and began to swing it back and forth. After several failed attempts it finally snagged on one of the large boulders. She tugged on it to ensure it was secure then swung herself over the side. After scrambling up the bank she adjusted the loop to a more secure position and motioned for the others to follow. After all of them were ashore they once again split up into pairs and headed off to inspect the shore.

Waymeir could see there was no completely level space around the rim of the cove. The mountains descended directly into the water, yet the slope was not so steep as to prevent walking with relative ease and it would be possible to build housing though not as easy as on level land.

She liked the look of this place though she could still see potential problems. The woods were green and dense and they soon crossed a clear stream that flowed rapidly down the mountain to the sea bubbling and splashing over the many rocks attempting to bar its path. Because of the dense canopy, however they found few berry bushes or other undergrowth. The slower slope near the ocean continued on for some distance and then rose steeply into the sky. There was, however, plenty of reasonably level space to build shelters. The biggest obstacle continued to be the last drop to the sea, which would make coming and going to the boat difficult.

They continued on around the cove, taking note of animal signs, less steep trails leading into the mountains and any other positive features of the harbor. Waymeir felt protected here with the steep mountains holding the quiet waters of the cove in a secure embrace. With the cove mouth facing north rather than directly west and out to sea all in all it was a very sheltered spot. The waves lapped lazily against the rocks making it difficult to believe that this was part of the ocean at all.

It took them till mid-afternoon to complete their inspection of the cove and return to where the rope led to their boat. As she joined the rest of the group waiting there Waymeir shook her head. "I wish there were more berry bushes or nut trees. Did any of you find any food?"

Maerl who was already working to set the rope up so it could be retrieved once they were all in the boat stopped. "I found a couple of walnut trees but that is about it." The rest of the group had found little else.

Waymeir sighed thinking of Toren. "Well I guess we should head back." They climbed back down the rope to the boat. Maerl was the last; double checking to make sure the rope was in a position that it could be flipped from the rock after they were all on board.

Arriving back at the ship they were met with anxious faces once again, it was clear that others felt safe here, including Toren. It was the first time that Waymeir had seen her eyes brighten since the catastrophe. "It is beautiful enough and well protected," Waymeir began slowly, "but the high shoreline would make supplying the ship difficult at best."

Maerl continued, "There are also few berry bushes, though there is a good stream and room to build shelters."

"What about the trees for repairing our boats," Shwaren was even now concerned with the condition of their craft and what would happen if they sustained damage this far from their camp.

"The trees are plentiful and enough are straight to make good masts," Waymeir confirmed, "and the slope would work in our favor bringing large masts to the sea."

Maerl obviously with some reluctance concluded, "The shoreline is the big weakness I fear it would make everything very difficult."

Finally Toren could contain herself no longer, "Surely we can design a way around that. Is there no place on the whole shoreline that is not low enough to make access easier?"

Waymeir hesitated, hating to be the one to break Toren's improved mood. "I am afraid not, even where the stream enters the sea it falls the last distance from a height that would require a rope to ascend."

Every one fell silent, knowing how hard Toren would take this. She did not care where they ended up, but she wanted it assured that they would not return to the old harbor, and she knew if they did not find something soon this would likely be their fate.

Finally Shwaren spoke, "We will spend the night here. There is no point going on this late in the day. I think, however that we are near the northern limit of our search. Any farther north will be bitterly cold in winter, something I do not think we need to face. We can take some more time to think about our options before making a final decision but we must think of turning south."

Toren turned and walked back to the railing away from the group, staring at the shore. Waymeir went to her, talking in hushed tones as the others stared at their backs. Shwaren knew that the decision they must make would weigh heavily on Toren. He feared for her sanity, or that she might bolt and leave the group to strike out on her own rather than return to their harbor. To stall the inevitable discussion he instructed the preparation of an early dinner. The sun was lowering toward the hill that made up the western side of the cove and a chill came off the mountains with the feel of an early fall. Their journey north had shed little light on the state of the land in general, or the nature of the catastrophe. This far from the blast there was little sign that anything had changed though he knew that this was deceiving.

A simple meal was prepared, though Toren could not be persuaded to take part. During the meal they began to debate what to do next. "It is clear that we are not finding better places here than our harbor," Winfew stated plainly. "Even with the damage it sustained, our harbor is better than this. There is no point continuing on into the colder north."

Waymeir glanced at Toren, who was as far away as she could get and still be on the boat. "I agree, I do not think that we seriously thought that we would find a better home, but we must find a way to get Toren to understand."

"I think that she will have no choice but to learn to live with our decision," Bandai said dourly. "We cannot endanger all of us to save her from facing reality."

Shwaren, though agreeing with Bandai in principal was not prepared to look at it so brutally. "Maerl, you share her memories of the catastrophe. Speak to her. Perhaps she will listen to you."

"I will try, but I cannot promise success. She is tortured by what she witnessed there and will not soon be made to forget it."

"It is time to return to our home camp," Donley said with finality. "We have explored and learned what we could, but it is growing close to fall and with the weather as cool as it has been I fear an early one. It is time to prepare for winter where we know the land and have shelter, even though damaged."

The discussion then turned to reflections on their trip and smaller matters. Maerl remained with Toren until darkness overtook the boat and the Jhirum settled in for the night.

CHAPTER 32 UNSAFE HAVEN

Dankin, Kang and Blinan spent the early morning working their way back into the mountains, away from the Valley of Mist. As they crested the first rise they each stopped to look furtively back at the still mist shrouded valley. Far in the distance, somewhere on the other side of the valley they could see a strange orange glow, occasionally flaring to brightness and then dimming again. Dankin was, however uninterested in considering the valley and its strangeness any further and quickly turned and headed into the next valley, leaving behind the nightmares of the previous night.

"What now," Kang muttered when the effect of the valley had finally passed. "Shall we return to the tribe?"

"Perhaps we shall go see how they are doing and if they have found a better place to settle. But if we come across a good place to make a home on the way back we will stop," Dankin replied shortly.

The valley into which they were now descending was a little brighter than the valley of mist, but the sun was still dulled by the constant haze, bathing everything in a shadowless feeble light. The next peak rose high into the sky and was topped by a craggy treeless point, one of the highest mountains in the region. They angled their path to take them around this formidable peak up the valley to a lower mountain further south. The air was still chill and damp, though at least there was no rain. In the distance a bird screeched a chilling song, bringing their heads up in unison. They were obviously still jumpy, a fact that angered Dankin. By shear will she forced down her apprehensions determined not to be cowed by the world they were now thrust into.

As they angled up the valley they came upon some trees that were beginning to drop nuts on the forest floor. Having eaten nothing since the previous night they stopped to open some nuts and gathered others to carry with them.

As they ate Blinan questioned Dankin. "We are headed further south, away from where our tribe is likely to be. Shouldn't we head north?"

"I am still not anxious to be back with that rabble." Dankin replied, staring a challenge at Blinan. "We will turn north on the other side of the mountain. I still hope to find a sheltering home before we must rejoin the others."

"Why are you so determined not to stay with the rest of the tribe?" Blinan retorted.

"I have no interest in doing nothing but follow Nomber's orders," Dankin sneered. "We were not made to be servants or sycophants."

Blinan, who had moved ahead of Dankin stopped and turned. "That is not what we would be. Nomber only wants us to work together for protection and to try to make the best of what has happened."

"If you are so fond of Nomber then why are you with me?" Dankin challenged her hands on her hips.

Uncharacteristic anger was building in Blinan "We originally set out in search of a better camp, not to abandon the others for good."

"And so we are, but if we find one that does not mean we need to bring the whole tribe to join us."

Blinan scowled belligerently at Dankin for a moment, then turned and walked on. Dankin stormed on after her with Kang bringing up the rear.

They continued on in silence for most of the day, slowly making their way around the base of the towering peak. They were just beginning to round the southern face when a large black smudge higher up on the base of the mountain caught Kang's eye. "Look, over there, is that a cave?"

Dankin and Blinan shook themselves from their inner storms and turned to look where Kang was pointing. The scowl in Dankin's eyes loosened a little. "It could be, let's take a closer look."

They turned to ascend toward the dark blotch. The climb was not steep or far and as they ascended it became more apparent that indeed this was the opening to some sort of cave. As they drew near the opening, they had to look up to see the top of the entrance. The mouth was easily the width of three Jhirum lying end to end and the height about the same. The other thing that became apparent as they drew near was a strong odor. At first they were unsure of its source, but as they neared the entrance Dankin saw bones littering the ground. She stopped dead in her tracks just outside the entrance. "Wolves, this is a den for wolves!" Blinan and Kang looked at her in alarm. Dankin did not wait for comments but turned immediately on her heels. "We had better get out of here."

Kang and Blinan hurried behind her, as silent as they could be. Dankin guessed that the wolves must have been out hunting, or they would have already been in pursuit, but she was taking no chances at being found near the den when they returned.

As Kang drew beside her Blinan spoke breathlessly, "Did you see the size of that cave? It would make a perfect camp."

"With the minor problem that it is already occupied by someone who would love to have us for lunch," Kang replied.

Dankin continued trotting in silence for a few more moments then slowed and turned to her companions. "But if we had the whole tribe, perhaps we would be enough to expel the inhabitants and take it over for ourselves."

Kang glanced at her with concern on his face. "That would be fine if we had our magic, but in our present state it could be a deadly battle."

Blinan, bringing up the rear had picked up enough of the conversation to know what was being discussed. She drew up to the other side of Dankin. "Surely you don't seriously think that we should try to expel an entire pack of mountain wolves from their den!"

Dankin glanced back over her shoulder briefly. "I do not know, but if the rest of the group has not found a good shelter, I think it should not be ruled out." They returned their focus for a while to negotiating a small slide, bounding over boulders in their decent back down to the base of the mountain.

When they reached the valley floor they were approaching the west side of the mountain. They slowed their pace, regaining their breath before continuing the discussion. As her breathing eased Dankin began again. "All I am saying is that if we do not find something better, then we should consider trying to take over this cave. It is too good a shelter to simply walk away from because of a pack of wolves."

As if responding to their name being spoken a lone howl rose in the distance. They glanced at each other, concern etched in their faces for a moment, but the howl was a long distance away and probably posed no threat.

"But then you are at least agreeing to go back and see how the rest of the tribe is doing?" Blinan questioned.

"Yes, unless we find another good shelter, I think that we should see what they have found. But that does not mean that I intend to stay with them, if there is no good reason." Satisfied with this Blinan fell into a more contented silence.

CHAPTER 33 INDEPENDENT MINDS

It seemed like years had passed to Jasper who could not shake the urge to explore the mysteries of the cave they now called their home. In fact, however, it had been less than a dozen days from when they first started turning the cave into a permanent living space. The transformation was considerable. Many more of the wandering Maestic had joined the group. They now numbered thirty-two, all but three of the tribe accounted for. What had originally seemed like a huge cavern just inside the entry way now seemed much smaller due to their greater numbers and the fact that most of the time fires burned in all corners chasing away the darkness that made it seem like the walls were far away.

They also had torches standing in permanent mounts around the cavern. Bastile had finally mentioned to others the strange way the sticks coated in the black effluent of the spring flared up when thrown in the fire. Others experimented and discovered that sticks and bark soaked for long periods would burn for a long time, though giving off a nasty black smoke. They had also found that they could make wells in stone or in the walls themselves, fill them with the liquid and place a strip of bark or smaller stick in the liquid and that this would burn for hours at a time without needing to be tended.

The weather had improved somewhat, though it was still unusually cool for late summer and there were not any days that the sky was the crystal clear blue that they were familiar with. They had gathered considerable quantities of fruits and nuts that were being dried and stored as best they could, though they had no bins or large containers. They did have some natural wells in the walls of the cavern and the nearby cave that served to store some of the food.

They had also accumulated and improved on their weapons. Every one now had at least one stone knife and one spear, either a simple sharpened wood stick, or a stick with a sharp stone tip tied to the end.

The Whorzen had not returned, probably having found easier prey elsewhere. As they relaxed somewhat, more of the group ventured farther out into the mountains to gather the things that they needed, though not so far that they could not return by night. Even Zeeta returned to the cave most nights, though usually as late as possible.

The most difficult task they had was to produce some form of warmer clothing. Even in the cold mountains the Jhirum normally wore only loincloths and sometimes nothing at all even in winter. Their magic had protected them from the elements, making more substantial clothing unnecessary. Now however, the chill of an early fall was enough to push them as far as the plains seeking dead animals whose skins could be used, but there really were not that many dead animals this far from the blast site and those they found were often rotted beyond use.

The Jhirum rarely killed for food or clothing, but now their need drove them to form hunting parties in search of some larger prey that would provide both food and hides. This was not an easy task however, for a people unaccustomed to hunting, and many found it distasteful. Their knowledge of the woods and the inhabitants, however, served to overcome their inexperience and poor weapons making the last hunt they had gone on very successful. They had gotten three large skins and enough meat to last for quite a while if they could preserve it. Unfortunately they had no knowledge of how to preserve meat, so they ate as much as they could in a couple of days and threw the rest to the carrion beasts.

All in all things were going about as well as could be expected. Endmere was pleased with their progress though he harbored significant fear of the oncoming fall and winter. Winter in the mountains was a cold and snowy affair, though they were nowhere near the farthest reaches to the north where even summers were cool. They at least knew how to treat the hides that they acquired since they traditionally used skins as water bags and for the loincloths they wore. But the idea of making warmer and more complicated clothing was new to them. He was not at all sure that they would be able to clothe the entire tribe warmly enough before winter.

This morning Zeeta had finally lost patience and had gone off into the mountains by herself though she promised she would not go far and would return within a week. Endmere himself occasionally felt the longing to be off on his own far away in the mountains. Unfortunately there was too much to do before he could even consider leaving the group.

Unused to living together in groups, individuals were constantly breaking away and disappearing, or dropping the job they had been assigned to pursue something else that caught their interest. Though Cragen and Lamsil frequently disagreed about specifics, they were Endmere's strongest support and understood the need to hold the group together at least until a secure and well-stocked home base was established.

Jasper could not overcome the pull of the dark maw of the cave. It drew him like a fly to flame. Several times he had drifted off to go down into the cave for some length, though never venturing farther than their initial exploration. He had taken to spending a lot of his time when not working, talking to Bastile who also felt the pull of the cave. Though their interests were somewhat different they both longed to pursue its mysteries more fully. Jasper was only interested in adventure; discovering mysteries and strange new places that he was certain awaited them in the cave. Bastile on the other hand only wanted to rediscover their magic. It had become an obsession with her. She seemed to feel the loss of the magic more deeply than any of the others and would readily throw away the security they were trying to build through their careful preparations, for the possibility of recovering magic.

Jasper sometimes feared that she would simply take off on her own one night and leave him behind. He had asked her to swear that she would not and reluctantly she agreed to at least let him know if she decided to do it. Both of them however, had obediently worked for the good of the tribe for what seemed like an interminable amount of time. He knew, however, that both of their patience was almost at an end.

They had each put aside some private stock of food and water in anticipation of a journey that they both felt was inevitable. They had brought it up repeatedly to the others, but Endmere had always objected on the grounds that they needed all hands focused on producing clothing, safe shelter and food. It seemed to Jasper, however, that they now had the most urgent needs taken care of and that they could begin to regain their freedom. After all there was no one that would actually stop them if they just left, the same way that Zeeta had left this very morning.

As Jasper was thinking these thoughts he was working on cleaning another skin that they had taken from a Boar the day before. The giant pig stood nearly as tall as he at the shoulders. It had taken five of them half an hour to finish it off. Unfortunately the long struggle had resulted in several punctures to the tough hide which would have to be worked around when making cloths.

He did not notice Bastile come up behind him as he worked. "Jasper, what do you think about Zeeta leaving this morning?" she asked. He turned and looked up at her silhouetted against the bright, though still gray sky.

"I think that I feel the way she does. We have worked hard to get a start on a safe home and food. We cannot focus only on sewing clothes for the rest of our lives." He paused as he frequently did, wondering at Bastile's beauty. She was almost twice his age, but her dark skin was smooth and taut and her reddish brown mane with just a few streaks of silver was full and silky.

Noticing that she watched him study her, he cast his eyes down with slight embarrassment. She smiled slightly and responded, "I agree, it is time for us to make our own decisions. I think that we should leave tonight to explore the caves."

Hearing her say it as if it was already decided made him start. "What of Endmere, he will not like it."

Bastile knew that Jasper could easily be swayed, as equally by Endmere as herself. "What does it matter what Endmere thinks. We have done as he wished for many days now. It is enough; it is time for us to follow our own destiny. I am leaving tonight. If you decide to join me you are welcome."

With that she turned and walked away, the discussion clearly ended. Jasper was left with his conflicted loyalties. He knew, however, that in the end he could not turn his back on the chance to explore the cave. The hair on his neck stood on end at the thought. Tonight it would be.

Endmere returned from yet another search for the early fall berries that grew everywhere in the mountains. His sack was laden with the fruit, which he intended to dry and store for later use. Now that the sun actually showed its face occasionally it had become easier to dry the fruit in one of the openings in the trees on the face of the mountain above the cave, though the haze that still shrouded the sun made it take longer than it should have. They had made an area there where they laid the fruit out in a single layer and tended it until it was dry enough to be stored.

It was difficult to know how long it would keep in the cave but at least it would last longer than the fresh fruit. They had also tried storing crushed fruit in skins and gourds, which they had in the cave. They did not know how this would work either but they had to try something. So many things they did not know which could affect their survival. This is what kept Endmere focused on keeping the tribe together and making as many preparations for the winter as they could.

As he set down his sack he watched Bastile who was talking to Jasper turn and walk away toward the cave. He was concerned about the two of them. They had repeatedly voiced their desire to explore the caves further. He had a feeling that they would not wait much longer. His hold on all of the members of the group was tenuous at best. In his gut he knew that they had more work than they could possibly complete before winter arrived. But he also knew that it was a lot to expect of nomadic loaners to simply give up their independent ways and adhere to a common purpose indefinitely.

He had to discuss this with Cragen and Lamsil. Lamsil felt much the same way as Zeeta did. Perhaps she could offer some insight and they could come up with a way to make the group hold together. If not he feared that one day he would simply wake up and be the only one left in the cave and he knew that they would regret this come winter. He decided he must find some time alone with Cragen and Lamsil but for now he hefted the sack on to his back and headed up the mountain to the clearing.

CHAPTER 34 DECISIONS

As the day drew to a close back at the main Bagnog encampment some sense of order had been imposed on the small valley. Leaves and branches had been placed under the overhangs and small caves to provide some protection from the dampness. Several fires had been started and enough food had been gathered for a reasonable evening meal as well as breakfast.

Despite this appearance of order and direction however, there was still a restiveness that was palpable, an undercurrent of tension bordering on anger. Nomber could clearly feel it, yet could not understand its source. Even he felt tense and uneasy, beyond what could be expected from having the continual headaches that they each still suffered.

Even as this thought lingered in his mind, Extoar and Tamber, both normally mild mannered men broke into argument. "I just got finished laying those branches for my bed, what are you doing sitting there!" Tamber yelled.

Extoar glared at him defiantly for a moment then stood leering over the smaller man. "You can have your pile of sticks, but be wary of pushing me around little man."

Some members refused to do their fair share of the work. Though he expected this of Thane, it surprised him about the others. All of this behavior was very uncharacteristic of Jhirum, who were a peaceful people who could disagree without rancor. Perhaps it was a combination of the headaches and the fact that the Jhirum were not used to working together as a group for this long a time.

His concerns unanswered he refocused his attention on trying to build a lean-to away from the cliff. He had strapped a branch at arms height between two trees and was now leaning other branches against this one to form a triangular shelter. He stood back for a moment to assess the design. He did not know how much weight the strapped branch could hold and how to get the gaps between branches sealed to a degree that it would keep out rain and snow. But unless the weather was bad it would still be more comfortable to sleep outside of the caves which were damp even with the improvements that had been made.

The sun or what could be seen of the sun disappeared early on the valley floor. The dull orange glow crept up the side of the sheltering eastern mountain leaving the floor in dusk. Along with the fading light came an immediate chill in the air. Though always a little cooler in the mountains, this far south and still in the late part of summer Nomber would have expected it to be warmer. It seemed like the sun had lost its ability to provide warmth. Then the clouds began to move in snuffing the last of the fading light, casting the tribe into an early night.

As the first echoes of thunder began to reverberate through the valley the tribe began to abandon their fires in the open and move under the cliff. Nomber abandoned his lean-to and headed for one of the overhangs that was not as crowded. A fire was going near the outer edge of the overhang, not completely out of the rain, but somewhat protected. The faces around the fire were grim with the prospect of facing another damp night. It felt like they had been sleeping in the rain every night without a break.

Grudgingly they huddled together as deep into the recesses of the cliff as they could. Before long water was dripping down forming a cold curtain in front of them, Nomber cringed at the cold splashes that reached him on the outer edge of the group. The fires in the valley guttered and smoked in the downpour. Roan, one of the elders of the tribe was next to Nomber. "Infernal rain, will it never clear?"

Nomber glanced sideways at him, but did not respond. He could see all of their moods turn darker until most fell into a restless slumber. He remained awake a long time after the last of his tribe fell asleep, trying to keep the fire going and wondering what was going to happen to the tribe.

The next couple of days passed with varying degrees of dampness. The strong storms of the first night lessened but left behind a cold drizzle interspersed with steadier rain. When not searching for food or working on lean-tos the Bagnog huddled back against the cliff. As Nomber had feared, the cliff afforded them only limited shelter and there was no easy way to improve upon the natural overhangs. The group became more and more restive with each day. He knew that if any of them had stumbled across a small shelter, big enough for one they would have stayed there and abandoned the group, but so far none had found better cover.

About mid morning of the fourth day in their new encampment with the mist still dampening everything, Dankin, Kang and Blinan showed up in camp. They were greeted half heartedly by most, although Thane made a big show of welcoming them with open arms. "I hope you bring good news from your wanderings. Our glorious leader has provided us with a cesspool for a camp. Please tell me you have found something better."

Nomber ground his teeth in anger at Thane's open barbs. Dankin wasted no time. "We have indeed found a noble retreat. A large cave, deep and dry, about three days walk from here." With this news everyone in the camp began to gather around expectantly. "We do have to dispose of the current inhabitants however," Dankin continued lightly. "It seems it is a den of Wolves."

This brought murmurs and some even turned and walked away in immediate dismissal. Nomber pushed his way to the front. "And how do you propose to dispose of this small obstacle?" He asked, a little more snidely than he intended.

Dankin turned to him unfazed. "We may not have magic, but we still have our brains and our muscle. Surely we can come up with a plan to remove a few wolves from a cave, even if we have to occupy it and fortify it while they are out on the hunt." Some murmured agreement while others still looked on skeptically.

Nomber stood his ground. "And why should we confront such danger when we have other alternatives. There are already few enough of us that have survived. To challenge a pack of Mountain Wolves with no magic will surely cost us more lives, if not all of our lives."

For the first time Kang moved from behind Dankin. "If you had seen the cave," Kang said scornfully scanning the damp and dismal camp, "you would think it worth fighting for. We have found nothing better, particularly this place. Do you really think to continue living like this?"

There were more murmurs from the group. Nomber even had to nod as he responded, "You are right, this is not where I would like to spend the rest of my life, but there is much of this territory that we have not yet explored, surely we can find a better camp at a lower cost. We needn't rush in to this. We can live here for the time being while we continue to explore for better places."

Gromand for the first time spoke up, "I for one would prefer not to spend another day in this camp. Perhaps we can at least send back a larger search party to stake out the cave and see what we are up against and how we might win it."

Nomber was actually surprised by how reasonable this suggestion was, coming from Gromand who was usually not so thoughtful. Perhaps he was being too hard-headed himself and was not being open to possibilities just because it was Dankin who presented them. "Gromand makes a good point perhaps we can send a larger party back to scout out the area and see how large a pack of wolves is there and whether it seems reasonable to confront them." There was a general nodding of heads and quiet agreement to this proposal.

Dankin even nodded and almost smiled. "I can lead a group back to the mountain. Who would like to travel with me?" Many hands shot up immediately. It was clear that most everyone preferred any kind of action to remaining in the damp valley.

"No more than five should go," Nomber objected. "More will increase the risk of being found out and attacked by the wolves. It would be best for a small group that can easily avoid an encounter to first investigate the situation further, before we risk more lives."

Surprisingly Dankin nodded agreement. "Since I also know the way, I will return with Dankin," Kang loudly proclaimed.

Nomber knew he had to get some of his own people in this party, "Jarine and Floan why don't you travel with them?"

Thane practically yelled, "I will go also. I am done with sitting here in the damp doing nothing." Nomber would not be sorry to be rid of Thane for a while so he did not object.

The party chosen, they all sat for a noon meal under the cliff before gathering some provisions to start them on their way. As they gathered some food to carry with them and a couple of the skins that had now been dried enough to be more useful as coverings Nomber gave one last warning. "Do not try to take on this pack by yourselves. You are only to gather more information about the number of wolves and the surrounding terrain to see if there is a reasonable way for us to claim the cave."

Only Jarine, Nomber's daughter, and Floan nodded to Nomber's comment, leaving him with a sense of unease as they disappeared up the valley into the mist.

The trek back to the cave took less time than it had taken them to get to the camp before, because they now took the shortest route between the two. On the second day Dankin stopped. "We are not far from the cave now. We should stop here and wait for the pack to go out hunting before we go any closer."

Jarine looked around the area where they had stopped. "It would probably be best for us to find a place that is safe in case the wolves come near here. Perhaps we should climb into those evergreens."

Dankin scowled for a moment but then nodded. "That is probably a good idea. Let's go. I would think the wolves would begin to hunt by sundown."

The stand of evergreens was composed of many ancient giants, thick and tall. Each Jhirum picked a different tree, but all close together. Jarine worked her way into the giant she had chosen, carefully pulling herself from branch to branch. The branches were regularly spaced making climbing easy.

About halfway up the trunk she came across a tight knot of branches that nearly formed a platform. She decided to stop here where she could stretch out across the branches and rest for the few hours left in the day.

For a while she sat there listening to the sounds of the birds and animals. Because the trees were so thick and close together she could see nothing. Even the other Jhirum were totally invisible within their own sheltering giant. Soon she became drowsy, repositioning herself so that she could lie securely across a couple of branches. Despite the fact that the branches dug in to her side she soon drifted off to sleep.

Twice she awoke to the howling of wolves, once rather close, but they did not find their scent, or were uninterested. After the wolves had passed by them the second time Jarine could here branches rustling in a nearby tree where she thought Dankin was sheltered. So she began to climb down to see if they were ready to move closer to the cave.

As she reached the ground Dankin was already waiting. She motioned her over and began in a hushed voice, "It is only a short distance around the base of the mountain from here. The cave will be easy to find even in the dark. I think that the wolves will be out for the better part of the night."

It was fortunate that it was not spring when there would be young wolves and mothers staying at the cave all day and night. This time of year the young were old enough to run with the pack so the cave was quiet and still as they approached, although Jarine immediately noticed the strong scent of the pack still lingering in the air. Though sure of its emptiness, they still approached with caution, listening for sounds either from the cave or of the returning pack.

After standing quiet for some time in front of the cave Dankin motioned them in. "Though we cannot see much inside you can sense that it is large and see how dry it is even in this rain." Jarine had to nod. The cave was indeed large and dry, worthy of some effort to wrest it from the wolves. Dankin then motioned them out of the cave.

Jarine whispered, "We should find a place nearby where we can watch the comings and goings of the wolves for a while, yet be safe from detection."

Floan added, "We probably ought to split up so that we can see more and in case one of us is discovered we will not all be trapped together."

"That's fine with me," Thane responded and immediately turned to head up the hill.

Dankin found a medium sized oak almost directly up the mountain from the cave with some lower branches that allowed her to climb into a position from which she could observe below. Kang took some time to find a suitable tree, but finally disappeared up into a pine that was almost on the level with the cave mouth. By the time the first howl arose from nearby, Floan, Thane and Jarine had also found trees to escape into, though Thane was so far from the cave that it would be unlikely that he could see anything. But this did not surprise Jarine.

The slightest glimmer of light was growing in the sky as raucous howling drew near the cave followed soon by the crashing of the pack through the underbrush of the valley below the towering mountain. Even with her excellent night vision Jarine could only see furtive shadows through the trees.

Kang, since he was level with the cave mouth had the best view of their approach. He counted ten adults and perhaps three juveniles, not a large pack, but none the less dangerous. These mountain wolves though smaller than Whorzen which inhabited the plains were still larger than a Jhirum and in a pack would pose a serious challenge to any living being, perhaps excepting some of the creatures Kang and Dankin had seen in the Valley of Mist.

The wolves trotted up from the valley stopping just short of the cave. The Alpha male paused, testing the air, making Kang freeze in his tree, hoping that he would not be detected. He was downwind, however, and it appeared that the wolves smelled their tracks where they had entered the cave. They only had to hope that their scent was uninteresting, or the wolves were tired of hunting so that they would not pick up the scent and follow it to their trees. Being treed by a pack of wolves was one thing when you could count on them eventually giving up and returning to their den, but when you are at their den it could easily turn into a deadly siege.

Several of the larger wolves continued into the cave still testing the air, unsure of the strange scent, the younger wolves however stretched out in front of the cave to await the dawn. It appeared that their hunt had been successful as they were tired and sated, quickly dropping their heads on to their paws and falling asleep. Their sleep, was easily disturbed, however, the call of a raucous bird awakening to the morning or the rustling of a squirrel nearby quickly brought heads up in curiosity.

As the light grew in the sky Jarine, who could not see much of the wolves lounging around the mouth of their cave, focused on scouting the terrain above the cave looking for anything that could aid them in taking it over. She could barely see the slide which was below her through the trees, descending nearly to the floor of the valley. At her level, above the cave entrance, the mountain began to ascend at a steeper rate forcing the trees that grew there to hug the mountainside in a jumble of low limbs and trunks, forming an almost impenetrable mass. It would be difficult for a Jhirum to get through those trees and almost impossible for one of these wolves, although she was not certain of their climbing ability. There was one very large oak directly over the cave mouth, but then below the mouth of the cave there was no underbrush and the trees were widely spaced.

With magic it would have taken little effort to convince the wolves to find another home, but without the aid of magic it would be no easy task. Jarine understood her father's concerns, and for this reason felt it her responsibility to look at the situation as critically as possible. She also shared her father's concern for the recklessness of Dankin and Kang once they were set upon a path. It did appear, however, that with some careful planning and execution it might be possible to overcome the wolves, although still at great risk. The prize of the large dry cave, however, seemed worth some risk.

By the time the light was full in the sky and the wolves were slumbering deeply she had to move to get the limb she was leaning against out of the indentation it had made in her back. All of her muscles ached from staying in a crouched position in the tree. She really wanted to stand and stretch but still feared this might draw the attention of the wolves. Finally she was able to get her legs out from under her, leaving them dangling as she sat.

This brought some blood and feeling back into them. It was going to be a long day in this tree so she had better be comfortable.

Her observation, so far had convinced Dankin beyond doubt that they should attempt to take the den from the wolves. The pack was not so large and the larger number of Jhirum should more than offset the size and ferocity of the wolves. She hoped that those with her could see what she saw and draw the same conclusion. Though this would mean that she would have to rejoin the main group, she would settle for this if it was in a comfortable cave from which she could come and go as she pleased.

Kang being the closest to the wolves, with at least one wolf always within view was the least comfortable of the group. He knew that he could not relax for a moment, or make any sound without being noticed by the pack. He had no interest in gaining such attention. Fortunately he had found two branches which together gave him a fairly comfortable, though hard, seat. So he was fine through the early afternoon.

By then he was stiff and the bark of the tree had dug deeply into his thighs and back. He simply had to move a little or he would not make it until dusk when the pack would again go out on the hunt. He slowly put his hand down on the branch and began to lift himself up so that he could move just a couple of inches. He balanced himself with his one foot on a smaller branch. Suddenly the small branch snapped causing him to lurch forward, almost head first out of the tree. Frantically reaching back he grabbed the branch he had been leaning on to save himself, but this motion made additional noise.

In seconds he could feel five pairs of eyes on him, though he was partially hidden by leaves. He froze, not even breathing, as one of the younger males got up and trotted over toward his tree. He could do nothing but remain as motionless as possible as the wolves inspected him. A second older female joined the first, testing the air with her nose. Kang remained frozen as the younger male circled the tree, nose stuck to the ground then returned to staring up into the tree.

Kang had not been able to fully resettle himself when the branch broke, so his arm was at an uncomfortable angle holding on to the branch behind him and his thighs were being dug into by the bark of the tree worse than before. Still he held on, trying not to move. Now the older female circled the tree and picked up the scent of his trail leading to the tree. He hoped that she would not follow the trail to the others in turn.

Dankin had heard the breaking branch in the direction of the tree that Kang had ascended. She watched as the pair of wolves trotted in his direction and began inspecting the tree. She froze as the female picked up his trail and headed straight in her direction, nose to the ground. The wolf followed the trail to the point where they had split up to go their different directions. Here she paused inspecting the complicated scent, and then trotted a few paces along the trail toward Jarine. She then turned back and in turn followed each of their trails in different directions for a short distance. By this time she began to lose interest and left the trails, trotting back in the direction of the den. The young male however remained intently inspecting Kang's tree.

Kang tried not to stare at the male and tried not to think of the cramp building in his arm. Much to his frustration the male chose to sit down, obviously not interested in leaving soon. Evening was coming on and soon the rest of the pack would be rousing to begin their night's hunt, he hoped that it would not begin with him. Several of the older wolves stuck their noses out of the cave and began to mill around, testing the air and nuzzling the members of their pack. As the large Alpha male exited the cave the pack came to life, the younger wolves circling excitedly as the older wolves stretched in preparation for a night of running.

Several of the wolves trotted over to the young male as if to see what he found so interesting. They too tested the air, but apparently found it less interesting, and after nuzzling and nipping at the young male they went back to the group. This seemed to distract him and soon he trotted over to the others and joined in their play.

Kang restrained an audible sigh and slowly pulled his arm back into a more comfortable position. Before long the alpha male trotted off down the mountain, skirting the edge of the slide. The others quickly followed, disappearing into the fading light.

Still no one moved or made a sound until they could hear the pack yipping and howling in the distance. Kang was the first to work his way to the ground, anxious to be out of the uncomfortable tree and to begin their journey away from this place. Dankin, Thane and then finally Floan and Jarine joined him there, each with relief clearly written on their faces.

"I thought you were going to have the whole pack around your tree for a time there," Dankin said with an effort at lightheartedness.

Kang just shook his head. "Can we get out of here? I don't want to take any chances that they will return before we are long gone.

Jarine placed a hand on his arm. "I really think we should scout around here just a little more before we leave."

Kang was about to object when Dankin cut in, "Don't you think I know that! We need to know every rock and tree in this area so that we can form a plan."

"Or make a decision that this is not a wise risk to take," Jarine added, looking Dankin square in the eye.

Dankin returning the stare responded, "Of course, though I have seen nothing to prove that this is an unreasonable plan."

Kang shuffled impatiently. "Well then let's get on with it. I do not want to stay here any longer than necessary."

With this, they split up again to cover all of the area around the cave as best they could. They agreed to gather east of the cave as it would be best to return to the camp by going around the mountain to the east since the pack had left in a westerly direction. It was completely dark with the exception of the light thrown by a rising moon through the always present haze.

Kang had searched the eastern side of the cave so when he had gone far enough he stopped to wait for the others to join him. Though they could not communicate with magic they were still knowledgeable woodsmen and so could navigate well in the dark and knew how to find Kang.

The first to join him was Floan who had searched on up the mountain just above Kang. They sat together on a large boulder waiting for the others as the moon climbed into the sky. For the most part they kept silent, listening to the sounds of the forest. Finally Floan ventured, "Without magic I do not see how we can stand against a pack of wolves." Although after his encounter earlier in the day Kang was somewhat uncertain himself he still felt confidence as if he still had magic, where as Floan had found the loss of magic almost debilitating.

With a sneer he responded, "Don't worry, Dankin will come up with a plan." Suddenly a herd of deer were flushed by Jarine's return, followed closely by Thane.

Thane grumbled, "Where is Dankin, I want to put some distance between us and those wolves before they return to their den." The others, used to his constant griping by now ignored his remark and remained silent. Disconsolately he leaned up against the boulder staring out into the darkness.

It was some time before Dankin returned, apparently more zealous in her desire to know everything she could about the area, certain that they would be returning to take on the wolves. Without even a nod Thane stood. "Let's get out of here." Even by the dim moonlight Jarine could see the scowl on Dankin's face, but they all slid off the rock and followed.

Jarine was interested in knowing Dankin's thoughts. "So, do you think there is a way this could work?"

Dankin glanced sidelong at her. "Of course, there was never any doubt. This cave is too good to give up without a fight."

Thane who was still leading at a good pace responded over his shoulder, "I would give almost anything for a warm dry place to sleep, but not my life."

"You are a sniveling coward Thane," Dankin called ahead belligerently. Floan looked nervously between them afraid that a fight might ensue.

Jarine cut off the argument, "Do you have a thought as to how this might be accomplished?"

"I have known from the beginning. The best way is to move in when they are on the hunt. They will come back to find their home occupied and defended."

"And you don't think they will put up a fight?" Jarine asked, trying to keep the disdain she felt for Dankin out of her voice.

"Of course they will put up a fight. But if we are prepared they will be no match for us." Dankin sounded as if all the decisions were already made and the outcome certain.

Floan, hesitant to even enter this discussion finally felt she must say something. "Why must we go looking for trouble? Even where we are is livable and we don't have to risk our lives."

"You are as big a fool as Thane," Dankin responded, without keeping the derision from her voice. "Be my guest and sleep on the forest floor by yourself. But don't come looking for us once we have taken the cave."

Floan looked down at the ground. Jarine pulled Dankin to a stop. "You act as if this has already been decided. The rest of the tribe will have their say in this as well."

Dankin jerked her arm out of Jarine's grasp. "They will have their say and then they will decide that I am right." And with that she stormed off after Thane.

After the initial exchange there was little further discussion and the return trip was uneventful, though longer than the journey to the den since the eastern way around the mountain was longer. Rain returning on the second day slowed their progress somewhat and dampened their mood as well. By the time they arrived back at the camp the rain had diminished to a cold drizzle.

Though difficult to tell what time of day it was with the sun continually shrouded it was sometime near noon. There were only a few of the tribe in the camp, tending to fires and working on some of the skins that they had treated. Dankin called out as they descended the valley and they looked up in curiosity.

Realizing who it was they all stood and came to meet them. Worden was the first to reach them. "What did you find? Is it possible for us to move our camp?" Clearly by the tone in his voice, conditions in the camp had not improved much even with the continued efforts to make lean-tos and dry bedding.

"I think that it is worth the effort," Dankin replied as she continued to walk, "but let's wait until all are gathered so that we can relate our information once to everyone." Worden glanced at Jarine as they left him standing there and then followed them in to camp.

Blinan was also in the camp, working to make one of the hides into some sort of cloak that could be worn over the shoulders. It was hard work with only the long needles from the locust trees to make holes in the hide, and crude strips of leather to use as thread, but she had kept the design simple and so was making some progress.

Dankin immediately drew her aside. "The cave is good and the pack is small. Clearly this is our best chance to keep the tribe together. If we have a good home then all will be happy to stay as one group." She knew that this was important to Blinan and that though she supported Dankin, she did not agree that splitting up into smaller groups was a good idea from the beginning.

"But at what cost can we win the cave?" she asked, a look of concern on her face. "We do not need to risk any lives to stay here?"

"Can you seriously consider living your life here in this open wet valley?" Dankin asked incredulously. "Surely a secure and dry home will do more to save lives than avoiding all confrontations."

Blinan studied her face for a moment, she knew that Dankin could be rash at times and was determined to weigh her reasoning carefully. "You are probably right, were we to be attacked by wolves here, there would be no good defense."

Dankin nodded. "Better to do battle at a time and place of our own choosing rather than to wait for a slaughter to be visited upon us unaware."

With the feeling that she had won an ally for the night's discussion she went to one of the fires under the overhanging cliff to dry herself and warm up, as well as to find something to eat, since they had been traveling hard and had not spent much time foraging.

As the afternoon grew old the mist lightened and the clouds lifted to the point that the sun could be seen as a bright ball through the remaining haze. As it descended behind the mountain more of the tribe returned from their various duties, some with berries and nuts, others with meat of various sorts and some with little more than what they had left camp with. All quickened their steps when they saw the wanderers returned.

Nomber returned with Gromand late in the afternoon. Upon seeing Dankin and the others he called everyone together. "Let us prepare our evening meal, and then we can sit and hear their story."

Preparation consisted of skinning the animals that had been caught, cracking and cleaning some of the fruits and nuts and gathering some fresh water from the nearby stream. By the time the animals were hanging on spits over the fires the last few tribesmen who had rejoined the group expectantly waiting for the news.

As always Dankin took the lead. "We have had a chance to go into the cave, which is large and dry. We also have seen the entire pack of wolves which currently occupy it. The pack is small, less than a dozen members in all and several of them young." A murmur went through the tribe. "I admit that this does not mean it will be easy, but we have scouted the area and I am confident we can come up with a plan."

Nomber's face was furrowed in thought. "Twelve mountain wolves, young or not is a considerable obstacle. How do you plan on overcoming them without getting us all killed?"

"I do not yet have a complete plan," Dankin replied, staring him down, "but do not think that just by staying where we are we will avoid fighting them. They hunt these woods and there may be other packs besides. Would you rather make a plan and fight on our terms, or stay here and wait for them to come for us."

A few of the tribe actually yelled their support, sounding eager for blood and battle. Nomber was taken aback by this and felt his control of the group slipping away. One way or another he would have to be decisive and strong. "Tell us more about the place where this den lies, then we can all discuss if there is a plan that would make sense."

Jarine stood to gain their attention, feeling that if she did not she would never be heard. "The cave is indeed large and dry. It would make a fine home. It sits a short way up the base of the largest peak I have seen in these mountains, looking down on a small valley. There is a slide below and to the right of the cave as you look from the cave into the valley. Except for this it is surrounded by trees, some large others small. Immediately around the cave there are few trees for a short distance. Up the mountain the slope becomes very steep with the trees and brush hugging the side making a nearly impenetrable tangle."

"Is there water nearby?" Roan interjected.

Thane responded, "Yes, a stream flows through the valley below the cave."

Nomber could sense the group focusing on how to plan an attack rather than if it was wise to do so. He shifted his focus as well, determined not to yield control to Dankin. "It would seem to be best to move in and occupy the cave when the wolves are on the hunt. Then we could fortify it to make it more defensible before they return."

Dankin stared at Nomber, having expected a fight even to consider this course of action. Before she could recover Nomber continued. "We must have considerable supplies with us so that we can wait out the wolves in the cave if they do not leave for some time. The most difficult thing will be water. We may not be able to get down to the stream if the wolves lay siege to the cave."

Roan spoke again, "How large is the opening of the cave?"

Dankin, having recovered turned to him. "It is the length of two Jhirum lying end to end and nearly the same in height."

"Difficult to defend safely," Roan mused. "We must have a way to block up the entrance so that we do not have to face the wolves directly."

Blinan who had been watching the discussion unfold finally jumped in, "We could bring rocks to block up the entrance."

Nomber thought for a moment. "I think that would take too long. It would be better if we could prepare something in advance that we could carry there to block the entrance. Perhaps we could construct a wall out of branches tied together then just carry it in and set it up."

Dankin began to realize that things were going her way, but that she had lost control and was no longer leading the group in this new venture. For a time she sat sullenly listening as the discussion focused on more details of how they could barricade the entrance, thinking of how to regain some control. But finally she decided that perhaps when they started the journey, since most of them did not know the way, she could regain the upper hand. She still had no interest in following Nomber's lead even if it was in a venture that she had suggested.

By the time the discussions started to die down it was dark, the fires illuminating only a small part of the valley where the Jhirum huddled against the chill of the mountain evening. It had been decided that they would gather supplies the next day and prepare for the journey to the cave. With this many people and supplies it would take at least four days to make the trip. Blinan had suggested that a scouting party be sent ahead, unencumbered to set up a watch on the den ahead of their arrival so that they could be certain that the patterns of the pack had not altered and to further assess the best ways to proceed. This presented a dilemma to Dankin, who wanted to be in the advance party since they would be gathering the final information in order to prepare the attack. But at the same time, being seen as the leader of the main group, the one who knows the way would put her in a leadership position.

Before she could make a choice for herself however, Nomber made his own selection. "Jarine, would you lead the advance party?"

Jarine nodded. "Certainly, how many others should come with me?"

"We will choose a few to accompany you in the morning," Nomber replied. Then he turned to Dankin. "Dankin can guide the rest of us to the site."

Dankin did not argue, deciding that her assigned place was as good as the other.

With these initial decisions made the discussion ended. A couple of fire tenders and watchers were left by the fires while the rest settled in for the night, seeking out the deep recesses of the cliff overhangs, or the few dry places in the lean-tos that had been built. As always there were some minor skirmishes over the best beds, but soon all were asleep.

The next day the advance group set out at once for the cave with explicit instructions just to watch the comings and goings of the pack from a distance until the rest of the tribe arrived. To get there as fast as possible they would take the western route around the mountain while the main group would take the eastern, taking less risk of encountering the pack since they seemed to favor the western mountains.

After the advance group had left, the rest of the tribe worked on gathering together those items which they wanted to take with them, such as the skins and any food that was reasonably portable. They would worry about gathering a larger store of food and water once they were closer to their final destination.

As the last of the preparations were being made about mid morning Dankin began to take command. "All right, if everyone is ready we will begin," She bellowed. "We will head up the valley and then turn and follow the ridge to the east."

Thane glanced from Dankin to Nomber, trying to read Nomber's reaction. Nomber remained unperturbed, but more quietly moved the group together to follow Dankin.

The whole of the first day they travelled the sky was grim, but without rain and the party made good progress. The second and third days turned worse, haunted by periodic rain and occasional thunderstorms. This slowed the tribe somewhat, although the advance group arrived near the den early on the third day.

Jarine kept her group well away from the den moving up on to the mountain, circling around and then dropping down through the tangle of trees above the den. As they approached the low growing mass of trees, Extoar who was a head taller and wider than anyone else in the group stopped short. "We are going through there?"

Jarine who was about to plunge in to the thicket turned. "This is the best way to approach during the day. We can get closer, yet they cannot get at us."

Without waiting for approval she turned and bending over to half her height disappeared into the mass of branches. Worden followed close behind leaving Kang and Extoar standing alone looking at each other and shaking their heads.

"Well I guess we have no choice but to follow now," Kang said as he tried to shrink himself down enough to fit through the small opening. Finally Extoar got down on his hands and knees and crawled through the opening cursing under his breath as a dead limb scraped across his side.

It seemed like it took forever to move less than a stone's throw into the thicket. They were all scraped and their backs ached from bending over. Finally Jarine saw a little light and pushed through to a small opening in the tangle of trees. A jumble of rocks had prevented the trees from filling the small area. "This looks like a good place to stop until it is closer to when the wolves leave for their nightly hunt," Jarine said as she sat heavily on a large boulder. By the time Extoar poked his head into the clearing he was scratched and bruised. Dirt and pine needles clung to his knees and he was scowling so darkly that no one spoke.

As the afternoon wore on with a light drizzle falling they dozed, though it was hard to find a comfortable seat on the rocks. Before the light started to dim Jarine called them together, speaking in hushed tones. "I think we should work our way to the edge of the tangle before it gets too dark so that we can see what the wolves are doing."

This time it was Kang who protested, "If we do that surely the wolves will hear us. Why don't we wait until they leave?"

"If we wait we will not be able to see the area well enough to scout out what we are going to do next and it will be much harder to get through these trees in the dark," Jarine argued.

"I don't see how it could be any harder," Kang replied brushing at one of his scrapes, "but lead on if you insist on being the leader."

Suppressing a scowl Jarine turned and plunged back into the thicket. As quietly as they could they worked their way down the steep slope taking their time to pick their way through the low branches and brush without making noise, but they had time and so did not rush.

Well before dark, however, they had reached the edge of the tangle and could peer down the mountain toward the still resting pack. They could not see any of the beasts as they were either in the cave or below the crest where they were blocked from site. The cold mist turned to a drenching rain just before dark making it even more difficult to see when the animals started to rouse themselves and prepare for their night's hunt.

Jarine noted that it was later in the day than when they had left for the hunt the last time they had spied on the wolves. She also noted that instead of heading out to the west they headed down into the valley, across the stream and almost due south. This could make it more difficult since they could not count on them going and coming from a specific direction.

By the time they were gone from view it was almost completely dark. They would have to do whatever inspection of the area they could in the chill rain which combined with the darkness of the night would limit their site and mobility. Pulling themselves from the small protection of the underbrush they stepped out into the downpour. Kang grumbled under his breath as they spread out to search the area again and to chose places to hide where they could see more during the return of the wolves and the next day.

Kang was not about to be caught anywhere near the cave mouth this time. The memory of those golden eyes on him as he hung in the tree still made his blood run cold. So before he did anything he found a tree well up the mountain from the cave which he claimed for his hiding place.

Jarine headed straight down the hill, passing to the side of the cave nearly following the trail the wolves had taken as far as the stream. Then she turned to follow the stream noting any pools and where access was protected by cliffs or brush. The water in the small stream crashed loudly against the boulders attempting to stem its flow.

After following the stream for some distance she turned and angled as directly as possible back toward the cave. She was looking for ways that they might be able to get to the creak unobserved by wolves prowling the area, if they were trapped in the cave long enough to use up their water.

There was no obvious, totally protected route, but there were brushy areas and rock outcroppings that could afford some protection. By the time she got back to the cave the rain had lessened somewhat, though there was a damp chill in the air that made her shiver in her meager coverings. The others had already congregated just inside the cave entrance having finished their immediate explorations.

Kang wasted no time making sure everyone knew where he intended to spend the next day. "I have a tree up the mountain from the cave that I will spend the day in."

Jarine had already decided that she was not going to take the safe route, but instead needed to be where she could see as much as possible of the movements of the wolves. "There is a tree between here and the creek, just to the right there that I will climb." Kang raised his eyebrows knowing that she knew she was putting herself in a risky position.

Extoar and Worden indicated they would find shelter to the right and left of the cave, about at the level with the opening. In this way they would have the cave nearly surrounded, ensuring that someone would be aware of any activity.

Without further words they split up again to find their trees and get settled before the return of the pack. The one concession to safety that Jarine had made was to find the largest tree in the area and one slightly off the path that the wolves had taken into the mountains. This way she hoped that they would not happen upon her scent and that even if they did, she could get high enough in the thick branches not to be seen. She found a point high in the ancient evergreen where several branches emerged close together almost forming a platform. Here she was actually able to lie down across the branches to watch below. She broke off a few smaller boughs to help smooth out the uneven surface and soon had formed a rather comfortable bed. It was still well before dawn so she allowed herself to doze.

She woke with a start to the sound of splashing in the creek behind her. There was just a hint of pale orange in the eastern sky shedding just enough light so that she could see shadows in the valley. The pack had clearly just returned and was crossing the creek, stopping to drink after a long night's run. The beasts looked almost benign playing and tousling in the water, but the blood stains that showed up as darker spots on some of their muzzles and legs quickly dispelled this notion.

As they began emerging from the creek to head toward their den a couple of wolves picked up a scent, the trail that she had left the night before as she walked along the creek. One wolf followed the trail, nose glued to the ground a short distance along the creek then turned back. Others picked up the trail, backtracking toward their den. Though their interest was moderated by their sated bellies they still nosed the air and the ground all the way to the den, where they then picked up the scent of the other Jhirum.

At this point confusion broke out as they all tried to pick up a trail in a different direction, becoming a whirlwind of bodies in motion. The chaos did not last long however, as their need for rest overcame their curiosity. One by one they pulled away from the trails and flopped on the ground, or trotted into the cave to sleep there.

Jarine was careful to get an exact count of the wolves. At some point it could become critical that they be able to account for every one of their enemies. There were eleven in all, ranging from two pups that were still not full grown to the dominant male that was a grizzled monster with scars to attest to each of his defenses of the pack, or his position at the top of the pack.

As the wolves settled in for the day, so did Jarine, readjusting herself so that she could lay and watch the den without having to lift her head. As the dawn broke weakly through the clouds she began to doze again.

Meanwhile the main body of the tribe was just rousing from their overnight camp on the eastern slopes of the towering mountain. They had not had a lot of shelter, so it had been a restless night out in the open with the rain varying from downpours to a chilling drizzle. They did not bother with fires despite the chill that had settled deep into their bones, for they were anxious to move on; Dankin in particular. She knew that they would arrive near the cave before the day was out. Her time was approaching, when she would show her value and leadership to the tribe.

During their trip they had continued to discuss strategy. It had been decided that they would camp near enough to the den to get there with a short morning's walk, but not so close as to alert the wolves. They would then collect the advance party and get any new information they could about the movements of the wolves. Nomber's idea to construct a wooden barrier that they could carry to the den and place across the opening to block the entrance had been deemed the most feasible so as they had hiked they gathered strips of bark, vines and anything else they could use to tie branches together. They had also used some of their valuable skins, cutting them into strips to be used as ties.

Dankin had done her best to be at the forefront of any decision making and to contribute as many ideas as possible. Nomber, was clearly aware of her ploy and tried to head her off as much as possible, but she felt that she was becoming more and more the one the group was looking to as they got closer to their destination.

Thankfully the rain had stopped and the hiking was not difficult this morning. They stayed to the side of the mountain hoping that the wolves would more likely be in the valleys and also, on Dankin's advice, so that as they came around the side of the mountain close to the wolves they could move higher up, putting the heavy tangle between them and the pack.

Nomber knew he was at a disadvantage in the silent struggle with Dankin because she knew their destination and the territory while he knew nothing. He could also sense the tribe looking to Dankin for answers and input more than him, but there was little he could do for the moment except act as a moderator of the discussions as a means of keeping his place as their leader. He also harbored mixed feelings about the struggle that was ahead of them.

It was clear that the tribe was already committed to this path and unless a major obstacle presented itself, would not be diverted. If the plan was successful this would only strengthen Dankin's position in the tribe, although with the struggle over he would once again be able to more aggressively assert himself. On the other hand if the plan failed he was certain he would lose a large part of his tribe, Dankin would lose stature, but he might as well since he did not strongly resist this plan. These thoughts weighed him down as the day wore on. But what caused him even greater consternation was that these considerations and silent battles were taking place at all. The Jhirum had never endured conflict such as they had seen since the catastrophe. Perhaps, as he had originally thought it was just because they were not used to working together for extended times like this.

They did not stop for lunch, but simply nibbled on a few berries as they walked. By mid afternoon Dankin called a halt. "We are within less than half a morning's walk of the den. We should move up the mountain and look for a protected place to wait and to make our preparations."

Nomber immediately set out angling up the mountain. Dankin frowned and followed him as quickly as she could. The mountain grew steep immediately above where they had been walking, slowing their progress. There was also a slide across their path which they traversed at an angle to get to the other side where there might be some shelter. At the edge of the slide the underbrush was thick. Nomber turned to the tribe trailing behind him and waited until most had caught up. "This thicket would make a well protected spot, if we work our way down to the lower edge so that we do not have to drag whatever we make through the densest part."

Dankin was about to protest, but could not quickly come up with a better idea so held her tongue.

Toward the lower edge of the slide the thicket thinned out and then opened up into the forest which was clear of underbrush. Nomber pushed into the thicket just above this point. The going was difficult which was just what they wanted. Not far in, there was a spot that thinned out somewhat.

Nomber paused to look around, just long enough for Dankin to announce, "This looks good, we can clear some of this remaining brush to make enough of a clearing to work and sleep. We will build our movable wall out beyond the brush so that we do not have trouble moving it once it is complete."

It was Nomber's turn to frown now but he did not let Dankin's constant attempts to assert control over the group dissuade him. "The five of you," he said pointing to a group that was together, "why don't you work on clearing this area while the rest of us work on gathering wood to be used in the wall. Branches should be as heavy and strong as possible and taller than a Jhirum so there is no chance of the wolves getting over the top."

Dankin put her hands on her hips. "I will go down the mountain from here so that I can intercept the advance party when they come and bring them back here."

And so the battle of wills continued back and forth between Nomber and Dankin. The group was beginning to grow tired of their constant jockeying for dominance. This frustration was to the point of being expressed by grumbling and angry glances. But they each set about their appointed tasks none the less.

Dankin felt good about having won this skirmish, now she would be able to bring the information the group needed and deliver it her way. Before the advance group had left they had arranged to meet up on the east side of the mountain just where the slope turned steep. This was not far below where they had their new encampment.

The light in the sky was just beginning to fade as Dankin positioned herself on a boulder right next to a large tree that she could scramble up if the wolves happened upon her. It was not long until she heard howling from the awakening pack, some distance away. She sat up alertly watching and listening in case they came in her direction. She did not however hear anything else, so continued her vigil, waiting to catch site of the advance group.

Jarine had awakened from dozing before the light of the day had begun to fade. Thankfully it had not rained all day, though it was still overcast and chill. She quietly crawled lower in the tree so that she could have a better view of the wolves as they roused for the evening. Several of the wolves still lay outside the cave, dozing. She guessed that the rest must be inside. She waited patiently for some time before a nose finally stuck out of the cave. It was a big she wolf who nosed at the wolves outside the den urging them to life.

A couple of the wolves tested the air with their noses as they stretched. She hoped that they would not pick up a strong scent of the Jhirum. The way the wind was blowing it could carry the scent of Worden from his hiding place right to the pack. Soon more of the pack ventured from the cave stretching and yawning.

A couple of the young chased each other and wrestled in the leaves. Again a couple of the wolves tested the air. It was clear that they were aware of something they found interesting in the area. Finally, one middle aged male trotted off to the left in the general direction of Worden alternately sniffing the air and the ground. A couple of other wolves followed. Jarine held her breath as they worked their way along the scent, slowly closing in on the tree where Jarine was certain Worden was hiding. She hoped that he was high enough and well enough hidden not to gain further attention.

A chill ran down Worden's back as he realized that the wolves had picked up his scent. He was well up into a fairly large oak tree and so was certain he was unreachable. But this did not mean that they would not find him interesting if they spied him. He froze in position as much behind lower branches as he could.

The first wolf arrived at the tree and circled, looking for the continuation of the trail. Two more wolves quickly joined him, circling and then looking up in the tree. The hair stood up on his arm as a low growl issued from one of the wolves. The other wolves by the cave stopped and looked in his direction. Suddenly he heard a crash coming from down in the valley, he kept himself from jerking his head up to look. The wolves, however, in unison turned in the direction of the sound. He could only guess that Jarine had thrown something to try to distract the wolves. One of the wolves at his tree trotted down the mountain in the direction of the sound. The others stood and watched. One more time the first wolf circled the tree and looked up, then trotted back to the pack.

After some more sniffing and stretching one of the elder wolves let out a long howl and the group set off toward the southeast. Worden let out an audible sigh, but continued to wait until he was sure the wolves were well away from the area. As the last distant sounds of the pack faded into the growing night sounds he began to work his way out of the tree. By the time he was on the ground Jarine was already on her way back toward the cave entrance. She waved and he turned to join her. Kang and Extoar could be heard climbing out of their trees as well.

"Thanks for the help," Worden said somewhat shakily. "I thought they might decide to stay there a while."

"No problem, it was a good thing you were well hidden," Jarine said as she turned to greet Kang.

"So I guess it's time for us to meet up with the rest of the tribe," he said without preamble.

"You're right I hope they have someone watching for us," Worden replied.

As Extoar joined them Jarine motioned them on. "Let's get going. I wonder how they are doing on their preparations."

Dankin was beginning to grow impatient as the late evening turned to night and still there was no sign of the advance party. She knew that they could not have left until after she had heard the howl of the wolves setting out to hunt, but still she could not control her anxiousness to get any news that might help her further. She was determined to wrest control of the tribe from Nomber. Earlier she would have been content to just go off on her own so she did not have to deal with anyone, but the scare they had received in the Valley of Mist had convinced her of the need for numbers to secure their safety. Particularly now with the prospect of gaining a secure dry home she had no intention of leaving the group, but likewise had no intention of following Nomber.

Her contemplation of the situation almost caused her to miss the four Jhirum as they passed in the dark just down the mountain from her position. Fortunately they were purposely trying to make noise to attract attention. The sound of Worden's voice broke her reverie and she quickly bounded off of her perch, calling quietly to the group.

Jarine was not at all surprised to find that it was Dankin who was waiting for them. Crawling off of a rock she motioned them to follow her and soon she and Kang were side by side whispering as they walked. She knew that there was trouble ahead for her father because of Dankin. She was constantly trying to overrule him, or sway the tribe against him. It was only a matter of time until she openly rebelled against his leadership.

It took them only a short time to arrive at the edge of the thick undergrowth. Dankin picked her way carefully through the thick brush and thorns until they could see the glow of fires reflected off the branches of the trees. Finally they could hear voices as they came to the edge of a clearing. It was almost cozy surrounded by the thick brush with trees overhead and several fires blazing; a house of green.

Jarine headed straight for the fire where her father was seated, finishing the remnants of a meal with several other tribe members. By the time she reached the fire Dankin was nearly ahead of her and preempted her greeting. "It appears that all is as we have seen it before, a small pack with a regular schedule. The plan we have worked out should be perfect."

Jarine stepped around Dankin. "But there are still some things to consider. It is now clear that the pack roams in all directions so we cannot predict where they will go or come from. In addition I have scouted out the stream for some distance. There are some slightly protected ways to get to the stream from the cave, but none that would allow safe exit from the cave to the stream if we are under siege by the pack. That means that we must have enough water to last however long it may take for the pack to give up and leave us alone."

"I would also not underestimate this small pack, I have looked into their eyes, they will be formidable foes," Worden added.

"We knew all of this before," Dankin retorted. "Of course we must have enough water and be prepared, but these dogs will not stay long once they realize they have lost their den."

"I am not so sure of that," Nomber spoke for the first time. "They have lived long in this cave and if it as good a shelter as you claim, they will not give it up easily."

"So, are you losing your nerve Nomber?" Dankin was standing over him glaring defiance.

"I have not lost my nerve Dankin, but caution to preserve the lives of the tribe is warranted." By now the rest of the tribe had gathered around the one fire where Dankin and Nomber challenged each other. Tension built in the group, many leaning in toward the fire as if hovering over a long awaited meal.

Finally Jarine stood to gain attention. "We do not have to decide anything tonight. We clearly have much preparation before we do anything. We have to figure out how to gather and hold water, and we need to complete the movable wall. This will take us several days at least, by then perhaps the way will be clear to us."

Still in the heat of the moment, both Dankin and Nomber glared briefly at Jarine for interrupting a battle which they had both been expecting and seemed eager to conclude. Finally Nomber took a breath and his faced smoothed somewhat. "My daughter speaks wisely. We will have time to consider this further before we must commit to a course of action. It is time we rested and thought on this quietly. We will continue our preparations tomorrow as well as continue to discuss the best way to proceed."

At first there were glances all around the fire, it was as though the whole tribe had worked itself into a motionless frenzy and now there was no way to expend the pent up energy. But at last Jhirum began to drift away from the fire in pairs, or alone to seek out a comfortable place to spend the night.

The next couple of days saw good progress being made on the wall, while the issue of water continued to prove difficult. They all had small water gourds or skins, but these could only hold enough water for one Jhirum for a day or at most two. They finally agreed to sacrifice two of the remaining hides to make a couple of larger water skins, though how well these would hold water, no one was sure.

The work on the wall and the discussions about the water were interjected with sometimes heated arguments about the plan. The entire tribe was in turmoil over this decision and sides were forming of those more inclined to plow ahead as quickly as possible, lead by Dankin, and those who felt more caution was called for, led by Nomber.

For two nights straight they had sent small parties out to check the cave and see if any more information that might be helpful could be gathered, but little new was learned until the second night. This night Extoar led a group back to the cave. As the others explored the mountain around the den, Extoar brought a still glowing brand into the cave. This was the first time that anyone had actually seen anything but the immediate opening, as little light made its way into the cave at night which was the only time they could visit. Though only a dim ember by the time he got to the cave the dull red glow allowed him some small vision. To improve the situation he ventured to bring in a few small twigs so that he could start a small fire from his brand to shed some real light.

As the small fire grew, he was able to see that the cave remained about the same diameter as far as he could see into the darkness. From the small flames he reignited his brand and ventured deeper into the cave. After a while the dirt floor turned to solid stone, uneven and dark. The cave also opened up a little, the ceiling receding into blackness beyond the reach of his weak light.

He had not gone far however, before his brand began to gutter again and die to an ember forcing him to turn around. As he retreated, staring carefully at the floor to assure his footing on the uneven surface it suddenly dawned on him. The pockets and depressions in the floor were solid rock, if filled with water they would hold it better than any skin. They could fill several of the depressions with water enough to hold them for several days at least.

As he passed the dying embers of his small fire, the first real glimmer of hope swelled in his breast. Despite the stench of the cave from dog urine and carrion, this was going to be their home. He was now convinced of it.

By the time they arrived back at camp, most of the tribe was asleep. Extoar, however, could not contain himself. Roan and Blinan were still talking quietly at one of the fires as they had been set to keep the fires going and to watch for danger. Extoar went to them beginning to talk before he seated himself. "I have found a solution to our water problem," he said excitedly. "The cave; I went into it. There are depressions that can be filled with enough water to last us several days."

Roan and Blinan looked at each other, then as one leaned forward, Roan taking the lead. "Are you sure? Will they hold the water and are they clean enough that it will be drinkable after it sits there?"

"I am certain they will hold the water, they are solid stone. I am also sure that they can be made clean enough for the water to remain drinkable."

"This is good news," Blinan said excitedly. "We are finished with the wall. We just need to cut some more branches for braces. We could be ready to move tomorrow night!"

Having shared his excitement with someone, Extoar relaxed somewhat. "Indeed we could. Should we wake Nomber and tell him?"

Blinan glanced at the other fires and the sleeping Jhirum. "No, nothing can be done tonight. We might as well wait until morning."

Extoar nodded. "I guess you are right. I am going to bed then."

He did not get to sleep late however. A rough shake brought him to a bleary eyed awareness before it was barely light. Dankin stood over him impatiently waiting for him to speak. "I hear that you have news," she said without ceremony. "So, our water fears are solved?"

Shaking his head to clear it he finally responded, "Yes, I think we have an answer. There are pockets in the rock that can hold significant quantities of water."

"Wonderful." Dankin did not even wait to hear more, turning and marching off leaving Extoar still shaking the cobwebs out of his head.

Before anyone had even eaten breakfast the camp was in a quiet uproar. Though the news was not so dramatic taken by itself; the implication, that perhaps tonight would be the night, made everyone quietly frantic. Nomber woke to the restless tribe, most of whom were already awake and obviously agitated. Bashley, as soon as he saw that Nomber was awake brought him up to date. "Extoar explored the cave last night and has found pockets in the stone floor that will hold water. We should be able to store more than enough water for a siege."

Nomber, still groggy from the night's sleep took a moment to digest the implications, along with the fact that he seemed to be one of the last to hear the news. "Is he certain they will hold water?"

"He says they are solid rock, many without any fissures. There is no doubt that they will hold water," Bashley replied.

By this time Nomber's groggy mind caught up to the fact that he was once again in danger of losing control of the situation, and the tribe if he did not move quickly. "Gather everyone here around the fire. We must plan the remaining tasks in preparation for taking over the cave."

Bashley, fire in his eyes hurried off, speaking to groups of Jhirum as he went around the camp. Dankin was already holding court at one of the other camp fires and tried to hold the group there, forcing Nomber to her, but finally relented when the rest of the tribe assembled at Nomber's fire.

Once Dankin's group arrived at the fringe of the group surrounding Nomber he began. "First of all I would like to hear from Extoar first hand so that all of us can judge the situation."

Extoar pushed his way to the other side of the fire and repeated his tale of exploring the cave. As soon as he paused dozens of discussions broke out around the group. Nomber finally had to raise his hand and his voice to command their attention again.

"This sounds like the final piece that will make our plan succeed. However, we still have work to do. We must make sure that the water skins we have made hold water and finish gathering supports for the wall. We must also make sure we have enough spears for everyone. I would suggest that we eat our breakfast and then set about our tasks. We must also gather additional food. We have enough dried food, nuts and things that will last. Now we can gather food that spoils more easily such as meat and fresh fruit or berries. These we can use first, saving the dried food and nuts for later if needed."

While he talked he could feel the tension building in the tribe, as the reality of what they were about to do sank in. As soon as he concluded they broke off into small groups heading for various fires to eat and talk more.

Jarine and Bashley joined Nomber and Roan at their fire. "What do you really think is going to happen?" Jarine asked quietly as they began to eat.

"I do not know," Nomber began. "I do fear, however that this is not going to be as easy, or as painless as many here think."

"What will we do if the wolves will not leave the area for a long time?" Bashley asked tentatively.

"We will hold out as long as we have food and water," Nomber replied looking straight into Bashley's eyes. "After that, at some point we will have to go on the offensive. But how, I cannot say until we see what the wolves do."

They each quietly contemplated the possibilities as they finished their breakfast. "Make certain that your water skins and food pouches are as full as possible by the end of the day," Nomber said as he stood. Then he headed off to pass the same word to the other groups gathered around the other fires.

Soon the camp had emptied out except for those working on the water skins and a few others attempting to sharpen heavy sticks into spears using sharp edged rocks. It was mid afternoon before Jhirum began to reappear in the camp, returning alone or in small groups, all burdened with various items, mostly food of all sorts and more stakes to be made into spears. Some brought more of the heavy branches to be used as props for the wall which lay assembled just beyond the tangle of brush where they hid.

As they returned most set about helping with the final preparations. Thane, however sat by one of the fires, ate some berries and relaxed as if nothing was happening around him.

When Nomber returned and saw this he could not contain his anger. "Thane, what are you doing?"

Thane looked at him nonchalantly. "Resting so that I will be strong enough for what lies ahead."

Nomber drew closer, towering over him like a thunderhead descending on a village. "The rest of us are actually working so that we are ready for what is ahead. Get up and help!"

Thane still remained seated staring at a berry before popping it in his mouth. "And what are you going to do if I do not?"

Without warning Nomber threw a fist straight into his face. Others around the camp stopped what they were doing to stare at the prostrate form of Thane who was out cold on the forest floor. Nomber looked at his fist a moment as if he could not believe what it had done, then looked up at the staring tribe members. "We have had enough of uncooperative tribesmen. We are facing danger for which we must all act together, so either work together or leave."

For a moment longer there was silence as the tribesmen looked around at each other, then almost in unison they turned away and went back to their labors.

As early evening set in, before the sky began to darken, Nomber encouraged everyone to stop and eat a good meal. He ignored the scowls and faces that clearly revealed their lack of understanding of his earlier actions. Thane had recovered and spent the rest of the day scowling over sticks that he sullenly sharpened, staring belligerently at Nomber every time he completed one and hefted it to try its feel. The others, however, went about their business, it would be a long and busy night and they had little time, or energy to spare on argument.

With the large wall to transport they would probably have to make a couple of heavily laden trips between their hideout and the cave as well as make several trips with water between the stream and the cave. The tension continued to build in the group, now more nervousness than anticipation as the time grew closer. Arguments broke out around several of the fires and more than once Nomber had to quell disagreements before they became violent.

Occasionally, in quieter moments Nomber still puzzled at the increase in conflicts amongst the tribe members, some like he and Thane, even coming to physical blows, something that had never occurred in the past. But now his mind was too occupied to spend much time contemplating the change that had crept over the tribe since the catastrophe.

The arguments and discussions came to an abrupt end as howls pierced the evening. Furtive glances were passed around every fire. The time had come for action.

Dankin did not pause long and was on her feet before the last howl had finished echoing off the mountains. "Let's make ready, we must leave as soon as possible."

"Wait!" Nomber's voice overrode the subsequent din. "We must send out some scouts to make certain the wolves are not headed in our direction. After all this preparation we cannot afford to be caught out in the open burdened with all of our supplies. We need two volunteers to go out now as quickly as possible and return with news that the wolves are gone."

Dankin immediately responded, "I will go, but you must start behind me, you cannot wait for me to get all the way there and back before starting, we have too much to do. I will still be able to return and warn you back if there is danger."

Nomber, wanting nothing better than to deny Dankin this lead again asked, "Are there other volunteers?" Blinan, Floan and Gromand each stood. Nomber paused only a moment. "Blinan and Gromand why don't you scout the cave, Dankin has done enough extra lately."

Dankin stared at him as if she wished him dead, but soon with obvious effort smoothed her face into passivity. This close to her victory she could not afford a direct confrontation over something that was not important.

Nomber accepted his small victory and Blinan and Floan headed off into the brush. "Now, everyone else begin moving everything out to the edge of the thicket. Once we have everything there we will decide how to divide it up."

A low din broke out as all the Jhirum moved at once. The last thing that was done was to gather some hot coals from the fires and store them in a couple of crude stone bowls that they had been using to transport coals to start new fires.

It was completely dark by the time Nomber and the last couple of Bagnog emerged from the thicket to the pile of provisions arrayed on the forest floor. The night was once again chill, though not one of the Jhirum noticed between their excitement and the exertion that they had already expended. At least it was not raining, though fog crept out of the valley trying to reach up the mountain.

Nomber briefly surveyed the group and the provisions. "We must get the wall, our coals to start fires and the supports for the walls moved first. Then we can return for the food, spears and skins."

Dankin moved close to Nomber. "We must bring the skins with us so that some of us can begin gathering water from the stream while the rest return for the remaining items."

Nomber's face grew dark, but more from the realization that she was right than from this challenge to his plans. "All right we will bring the skins as well." Groups arrayed themselves around the various items. Ten of the Jhirum positioned themselves to drag the wall while most of the others carried the large props for the wall. As soon as they started moving the noise echoed around the valley. Hopefully the wolves were far away, or they would surely hear the racket made by the wood dragging in the leaves. There was not much they could do about it, so after some concerned looks they continued on.

Meanwhile Blinan and Floan were making much better progress. Unencumbered they were nearing the cave by the time the rest of the tribe was just setting out. All had been quiet along the way, by now they should have encountered the wolves if they were headed in their direction. They hurried on, to confirm their assumption, however, not wanting to make a mistake at this late point.

By the time Blinan and Floan had reached the cave, confirmed that it was abandoned and turned around to meet up with the rest of the tribe, the wall had been hauled almost half way to the cave. As they went to join those pulling on the wall Worden stumbled, falling into Kang. Kang roughly shoved him away. "Be careful you idiot! This job is hard enough without you on top of me!"

Worden glared at Kang but Floan moved in to the position next to Kang holding the wall. Worden moved around to the other side still muttering under his breath.

The two extra hands were more than welcome as the heavy loads wore on the group's endurance. To make matters worse a drizzle had started to fall, although with the hard work they were doing it felt good, cooling their hot skin. It was nearing the middle of the night when they finally reached the cave, dropping their burdens heavily on the forest floor.

Nomber immediately gathered the exhausted Jhirum around him, allowing them to sit and rest while he spoke. "We must split up now. We have four large water skins so I would like four of you to take these skins and begin hauling water from the stream. From what Extoar told us you may have to clean out the depressions some before you fill them. I think that about six of you should begin working to position and support the wall across the cave opening, but first you will have to get a fire going so we can see within the cave. Make sure there is plenty of wood gathered inside. The rest of you should head back to our camp to bring as much of the remaining supplies as possible."

There was some arguing over who was going to do what job, but since none of the jobs was much easier than any other, only some gentle guidance from Nomber was required to get everyone set about their appointed tasks.

And so the night wore on, hauling water and supplies, gathering wood, starting a fire and finally positioning the wall. The height of the stakes they had used to build the wall left a space between the top of the wall and the cave ceiling more than half the height of a Jhirum. The top of the wall was well above the height that a Jhirum could reach, however, so it was unlikely that a wolf could get through the gap. But still Nomber insisted that they lash some stakes like bars across the remaining opening. These also served to help brace the top of the wall to the top of the cave.

The last section of wall was left folded back to allow the procession of tribesmen with provisions to pass, water skins sloshing and threatening to topple their bearers as they heaved them up the hill.

Nomber could almost feel the approach of dawn long before the sky brightened even slightly. Would they be prepared in time, would the wall hold, what would be the reaction of the wolves? In fact they had time to get all of their prepared provisions into the cave and time to gather more water than he expected as well as ample firewood.

It was still dark in the eastern sky when they began to fold back the last piece of wall. Just before they closed it however, Roan stopped them. "Wait! Perhaps a couple of us should remain safely outside in case help is needed. We will all be trapped in here when they return. Shouldn't a couple of us stay outside in case things go badly?"

Nomber was stunned for a moment, stunned that the thought had never occurred to him and stunned that they were so close to missing the chance. But he recovered quickly. "We need three or four volunteers to stay outside. You will need to hide far enough away to be safe, but be able to watch what is happening."

At first the rest of the tribe was as stunned as he had been, looking at each other with blank expressions, having never considered being left outside. But soon some of them began to realize the idea of being free and not trapped in this dark cave was quite appealing. Half the Jhirum called out to volunteer.

Nomber realized he would have to chose, what might end up being the sole survivors of his tribe. He immediately decided that it must be at least four, "Jarine, Kang, Gromand and Floan; take a few provisions and head up the mountain. Find safe places to hide where you can see what is going on. Hurry the wolves could return at any time!"

Several of the others started to protest, but the four designates were already out of the opening. Nomber, yelled, "Seal the door!"

Those outside heaved the last section of lashed branches into place. From inside the final brace was levered against the wall. Though the large opening at the top of the cave allowed plenty of air in, the cave still stank of canine urine and scent mixed with the stale odor of old bones and rotted meat. With the wall in place, the stench became almost corporeal, threatening to gag the Bagnog within.

Dankin did not let it dissuade her, however. "You five grab spears and man the wall, find holes that you can see out of to watch for the wolves."

Only a couple of them hesitated momentarily before obeying. Everyone else moved back and closer to the fire. The smoke seemed to mask the foul odor some and the warmth felt good now that their frantic activity was done. All that was left to do was wait; although a few Jhirum picked up stakes to sharpen them.

Nomber paced behind the wall and the watchers, unable to settle his nervous legs though he was as exhausted as the others. Higher up on the mountain, Jarine, Kang, Gromand and Floan had found trees to climb overlooking the valley where the cave entrance stood. As one they all froze, both in the cave and outside as snarling and yipping echoed up the valley. The time had come for all of their plans to prove themselves.

Inside the cave the tension was palpable. One of the watchers called out, "They are coming up the valley!" The next sound they heard was the splashing of the pack crashing through the stream. There they paused, lapping up water and wrestling. More of the Jhirum grabbed spears and moved to the wall. The rest waited in the firelight unable to see the approaching danger, but feeling it just as clearly in the night air.

Just as suddenly as the wolves had appeared and shattered the silence of the night with their raucous play, the silence returned. Those at the watch holes motioned for silence; the wolves had caught the scent of strangers. Some had their noses in the air, testing for the source. Others had already gone to ground sniffing back and forth along the stream bank. It did not take long for several of the beasts to follow their noses in the direction of the den. Soon the entire pack was following, pausing only momentarily to shake the water from their fur.

As those in front drew to within a stone's throw of the entrance they planted their feet, stopping dead; heads up staring at the entrance to their den. Instantly teeth showed and nerve rending, barely audible growls emanated from the leaders, as the rest of the pack drew up beside them staring at the transformed den opening. The pack leader pushed his way to the forefront and with his snarl firmly in place walked slowly but steadily directly toward the barred entrance.

The Jhirum were frozen in place; those that could see staring wide eyed, while those who could not strained to hear what was going on. Several of the Jhirum at the wall stepped back a pace as the nose of the pack leader came right to the wall, testing it for scent. The growl grew louder with each sniff. The rest of the pack began to sniff and snarl all along the wall.

At this point, even Dankin questioned her choice, hearing the low growls and the loud sounds of sniffing at every small opening in the wall.

Without warning the pack leader lunged at the wall, tearing at the stakes with his teeth. The wall pushed inward slightly, but held, with Jhirum manning each of the support stakes. Again the rest of the pack was right behind him. With the combined weight and ferocity of the entire pack the wall bulged in and the support stakes groaned in the hands of the Jhirum.

So far Nomber had held the Jhirum with spears back from counter attacking, waiting to see if perhaps it would be better not to further infuriate their opponents. As the wall bulged inward however, he yelled to the spear handlers, "Attack! Try to stab into their eyes or mouths when they bite at the wall!"

Several spears lunged through holes immediately, most missing their marks, finding only air. One loud yelp was heard as a spear struck home. Meanwhile Bashley was tugging on his spear, trying to retrieve it from a set of snapping jaws threatening to rip it from his hands. With a loud crack the spear was split in two by the powerful jaws sending Bashley sprawling on the ground. Nomber grabbed another spear and went to fill Bashley's place.

With the first blood drawn, the wolves redoubled their attack. Snarls and teeth seemed to be everywhere. One of the wall stakes splintered as a wolf tore at it, while another pair of stakes separated slightly as one of the tie ropes was cut through by snapping jaws. Another spear found its mark sending a wolf rolling down the mountainside writhing and snapping in anger and pain.

Seeing the two weakened sections of the wall, Nomber commanded Jhirum to those spots where they forced their spears through the growing gaps, trying to keep the wolves away from the weakened sections.

Just as suddenly as the attack had begun, it ceased, though growling still permeated the night. The wolves had fallen back to study the situation. These were not dumb animals simply driven by rage and brute force. These were intelligent hunters familiar with cooperative and studied attacks. Several of the wolves began to circle above the den, looking for other alternatives, or signs of their opponents.

Nomber motioned for a couple of Jhirum to try to wedge another stake in where the nearly shattered one hung. They could not see, but could hear the wolves above the cave entrance. The slope was not steep enough for them to be able to somehow drop in through the opening at the top of the cave, but they were searching none the less for alternatives to the frontal attack.

Then to Nomber's astonishment, the lead wolf lay down, eyes still intent on the cave entrance, ready to jump at any opening, yet relaxing, catching his breath, studying. This is what Nomber feared most, what if they just chose to wait; guarding their den until their enemy was forced to flee or starve. Although they had significant provisions they could not last forever in this cave without replenishing their food and water. Even if the provisions held he did not relish the thought of being trapped here for days, or longer.

Those outside the cave could only watch and listen. As the sky began to lighten the awful growling and tearing at the wall suddenly stopped. Floan peered down through the branches of the towering evergreen, watching as two of the wolves circled above the cave sniffing and listening as they went. One crossed her scent and turned in her direction for a short distance, but was too intent on rooting out the invaders to worry about others who were outside. The two returned to the rest of the pack who were now sitting or lying in front of the cave entrance, looking relaxed but with their eyes still riveted on the wall.

The sun crept up toward the horizon and though hidden by the ever present clouds brought light to the valley, while the wolves watched. Occasionally a wolf would walk cautiously up to the wall sniff and growl, only to return to the group and lie down again.

The day wore on this way until evening when the pack became restive, anxious to hunt, but still unwilling to abandon their cave. Those inside and outside the cave watched anxiously to see what the wolves would do, hoping beyond hope that they would give in and hunt, at least allowing them time to replenish water and supplies.

After milling around restlessly until it was completely dark, a group of about five wolves finally broke off and headed into the forest. Every Jhirum's heart sank as they watched the disappearing animals and those left behind to guard the cave.

Nomber could hardly believe his eyes. Surely they were not that intelligent. He had been confident that they would be driven by their basic need to hunt and their instinct to hunt as a group, but no they had split up, half the group hunting, half staying at the cave, though restless and active now.

The wolves left behind were once again alert and aggressive. One by one they came back to the impeding wall and began tearing and digging. Jhirum jabbed frantically at the attacking wolves, occasionally finding flesh, but more often than not finding only air. Several lost their spears in the process as wolves grabbed at them with their powerful jaws, wrenching them from the hands of the defenders. Gaps began appearing under the wall where the wolves were digging frantically.

Meanwhile in the trees above the cave Jarine decided that this was an opportunity to get away and replenish her water and food while the pack was diminished and busy attacking the cave. As quietly as she could she stepped from branch to branch keeping the ancient tree trunk between her and the wolves.

As she slipped to the ground she froze momentarily listening to the chaos below, then peering carefully around the tree. With the wolves close to the mouth of the cave she could not see them from the ground, nor they her, so she turned and headed up the mountain into the thicket and off into the night. The others in the trees soon did the same, each escaping unnoticed, each hoping they could get back to their tree perches the same way.

The wolves that had gone off hunting did not remain the whole night away as they normally would. Instead by just past the middle of the night they returned, sated and ready to resume the vigil. Some, although not all of the wolves that had not yet hunted headed off into the dark. The sentries that were left awake realized that there would be no opportunity tonight to escape their new home that was already beginning to feel like a prison.

Jarine had found some berries to collect on the steep part of the mountain and then circled around to the stream below the den to refill her water skin. On the return trip she encountered Floan quietly gathering nuts fallen from a walnut tree, "How are you doing Floan?"

Floan shook her head. "I am doing fine, but I do not like the way things are going with the pack. If they keep this up those in the cave could be trapped for a long time."

Jarine's face echoed Floan's concern. "I know, and I do not know what we can do to change things."

"I guess for now we just need to continue to watch for any opportunities to help," Floan answered, "which means that we should probably get back to our trees before the wolves settle in for the day."

Jarine nodded agreement. "You are right. Be careful."

With that they turned, heading up the mountain so that they could drop down through the thicket back to their trees.

As they cleared the edge of the thicket they stopped to listen carefully for what the wolves were doing. Apparently another group had returned from hunting for there was considerable commotion by the cave mouth, growling and tearing at the opening. This served to cover their return to the trees.

Days wore on with little change in the pattern. The wolves refused to abandon their home and continued to hunt in shifts, leaving no opportunity for the Jhirum trapped in the cave to replenish their supplies. The Jhirum in the trees continued their vigil, watching and slipping out occasionally for food or water, wondering all the time how their brethren were doing.

The answer was, not well. By the third day they had used up the water in their skins and had begun to use the water out of the pools in the rock which had already become contaminated with dust and soot from the fires. They still had food, but it was increasingly unappetizing as the berries dried or began to rot. Only the nuts were still at all appealing. Sanitation was also becoming an issue. From the beginning they had gone deep into the cave to relieve themselves, but the smell was beginning to grow and combined with the still strong stench of the wolves was becoming insufferable. Under these strains already short tempers flared with little encouragement.

Dankin needled Nomber at every opportunity. "Are you going to just let us die in here? We have to do something."

Nomber stared back at her in challenge, "and what would you suggest Dankin?"

"You are the leader," she responded with derision. "You must lead."

"And whose idea was it to come to this cave in the first place Dankin," Nomber responded angrily. "You are quick to condemn when things are tough, but free with your advice when it is to your advantage."

With that Nomber turned and walked away, knowing that Dankin was correct in one thing. Something would have to be done soon if the wolves did not give them an opportunity to get out of the cave for more supplies. Their wall was becoming more and more ragged as the wolves wore away at ties and dug at the earth under the wall. Meanwhile their edible food would soon be gone. The water that they drank was full of debris and stale and it was becoming harder and harder to even breath inside the fetid cave.

They had cut back their fires to preserve what little wood they had but because that was the only source of light the gloom only served to further depress the trapped tribesmen. Dankin saw this all as an opportunity to further erode Nomber's leadership position and perhaps to goad Nomber into doing something risky that might lead to his demise. More of the tribesmen each day joined her in pressing Nomber to take action of some sort, but none could agree on what to do. At this point both inaction and action could serve Dankin's purpose and so she waited and prodded.

After more days had passed with no change Nomber realized that there was no more time to wait. Something must be done. They could not simply force their way out into the middle of the pack. That would be suicide. They needed to try something when the pack was at least diminished with some of them out hunting.

At last he decided that they must agree to a plan, "Everyone come around the fire."

Many glanced at each other with dark expressions, but trudged to the small circle of light.

"Tonight when the pack is divided we must take some action. I think that we must try to enlist those outside the cave to create a diversion if we can and then get out and at least refill our water skins."

Dankin nearly pounced. "And get how many of us killed in the process? If you propose such a risky plan then you can be at the head!" Dankin knew he could not object, in which case whether the attempt was successful or not, she was bound to gain.

Nomber faced her squarely, knowing full well the game she played. "I will certainly lead those who volunteer to make the attempt and would welcome your assistance."

Dankin stared back at him in silence for a moment not wanting to risk everything but unsure of whether she could openly back out of the challenge. Finally she decided that she could still use the situation to her advantage as long as she took care. "Certainly I will join your folly, but only to help save those of my tribe who are foolish enough to follow you."

Despite the words of doubt from Dankin there were plenty of volunteers, anxious for any alternative to staying in the cave, no matter how risky. After selecting from the volunteers Nomber gathered them together. "I will try to yell instructions to those in the trees. I can only hope that they will hear me."

He strode over to the wall where he could peer up through the opening at the top of the cave. In the loudest voice he could muster he yelled, "Jarine, Gromand, Kang and Floan, if you can hear me do not answer, but listen. We must make an attempt to get fresh water."

At the sound of his voice all of the wolves were on their feet and at the wall tearing and growling with renewed ferocity, but Nomber continued. "We need a diversion. When the pack splits up tonight to hunt move up the valley some distance and find new trees that you can climb safely and then create some noise or something to draw off the beasts that remain at the cave. We will then release a party armed with spears and our water skins to refill in the creek. Try to keep the wolves occupied, but make sure you are not at risk. Once we are done we will try to draw them back here. If you have heard me make the call of the Trill."

Jarine was taken off guard by her father's yell from the cave. But as she listened she realized that they were desperate and had to do something. After he finished she whistled the simple melody of the Trill; a song bird common in their lands. Almost at the same time Gromand trilled the same song.

Nomber could barely make out the response above the snarling wolves which had been roused to fury by the sound of his voice.

Other Jhirum manned the wall again stabbing at the enraged wolves trying to limit the damage they would do to the wall. Saliva dripped from their mouths as they snapped at the spears and tore at the wall. One of the larger stakes was torn loose, falling inward dangerously.

Immediately several of the wolves lunged at the narrow opening, jaws snapping at anything. Three of the Jhirum jumped to push the pole back in place, trying to keep their hands away from the snapping jaws. Extoar put his back against the pole to hold it in place losing a chunk out of his arm in the process. Some of the other poles next to the loose one began to loosen as well with the straps that had bound them being severed.

Sweat poured down the bodies of the Jhirum as they labored almost on top of each other, some with spears, others holding stakes in place.

After long moments the wolves began to settle down again pacing just out of reach of the spears, eyes glued to the wall. Nomber hoped that the excitement had not been sufficient to keep the entire pack near the wall for the night.

Others began working on the loosened wall segments trying to tie them back together. The rest settled back to wait.

Dankin was not yet satisfied though and confronted Nomber again. "So what is the plan if they manage to draw the wolves away from the cave?"

Nomber turned and walked past her back to the fire. "Those of us that have volunteered to go out will take as many water skins as we can carry and as quickly as possible fill them at the stream and return."

Blinan glanced uncertainly at Nomber. "Is there any reason why all of us should stay in the cave? We are trapped here and the more of us there are the faster the supplies diminish."

A murmur and glances passed through the group. Several others joined those around the fire with interest.

Thane wasted no time voicing his opinion, "I agree, we do not need all of these people in the cave, it would be easier with fewer people and then we would have more people outside where we might be able to attack the wolves and weaken them."

Once again Nomber was caught with an argument that was difficult to refute, but offered by those that he would not like to strengthen. He had to accept the simple logic, but find a way to assert his own authority so that he would not further lose control of the tribe. "I agree, we can spare perhaps four more from the cave, no more or we will not have enough to maintain watches and be able to support the wall when there is a full attack."

Without hesitation he continued, pointing at a group in the corner away from the fire. "You four, if we are able to draw the wolves off and get water back to the cave you find a place to hide outside the cave where you can still see us but far enough away that you can move when necessary."

The four he had chosen pointedly did not include Thane or Dankin. Dankin approached him belligerently. "And what if I want to leave the cave as well?"

Nomber did not flinch. "You; you who's idea this whole adventure was? I think not. You will see your plan through to the end for better or worse, or do you now doubt your plan?"

Dankin glared at him. "I doubt nothing, I just do not like being told what I must and must not do. I still do not accept you as a leader that I must follow at all cost. I will make my own decisions."

"And if we all make our own decisions how long do you think we will last Dankin," Nomber said standing his ground.

She looked around the group that was watching intently. "I will follow the group's will, but not yours. If they chose to follow your orders I will stay with the group for a while yet, but make no promises for the future." With this she walked back to the edge of the light deeper into the cave.

Nomber followed her with his eyes for a while then turned to the gathered tribesmen. "Are the rest of you unhappy with the plan?"

A few glanced to others but most shook their heads, or murmured in assent. "All right then. We need to gather as many of the water skins as we think we can carry and distribute them among us. I want three of you to stay back to man the wall and defend us if need be. You must be ready to close the wall quickly when everyone gets back, or if we are caught out you must close the wall anyway and be prepared to open it again if any of us can get back to it. We must not waste any time, just get the water and then back to the cave as quickly as possible."

Nomber was interrupted by one of the watchmen at the wall. "Some of the wolves look to be preparing to hunt!" Several of the other tribesmen rushed to the wall, peering through the spaces between poles anxiously. Several of the wolves were already trotting toward the stream.

Nomber tried to count them in the dusk. It looked like five of them were heading out. "Quickly now, gather up the water skins, you three stay with the wall. Be prepared to open it when I signal and close it again when everyone is back. After scrambling to gather the skins and gourds that were scattered around the cave every one gathered again at the wall, watching and listening.

Full darkness settled in while they waited. The remaining wolves paced and occasionally sniffed, or briefly tore at the wall and then paced some more. Still they heard nothing beyond the area of the cave entrance. Nomber could feel the tension building in the tribe as time wore on.

Suddenly he heard a crash in the distance and then yelling and screaming. The wolves froze and raised their heads, staring in the direction of the racket, their ears and eyes intent. With the continuing noise two of the younger wolves bolted to investigate.

Nomber motioned for several of the Jhirum to pick up spears to take with them along with the water skins. He picked up a spear as well, although he was not sure what he could do with it when he had two full skins of water to carry.

228

The four remaining wolves stared after their brothers, straining to follow, but occasionally looking back at the cave as if debating whether it was a trick. Finally two more struck out. Nomber hoped that the Jhirum making the noise were safely out of reach of the wolves. Then he heard some more yelling that appeared to be farther away.

Nodding to himself he realized that they must have stationed themselves in two groups one closer and one farther away, to try to draw the wolves as far away as possible. The two remaining wolves had edged from out in front of the cave to the right edge of the clearing, watching and listening intently, but not leaving.

Suddenly, he heard a yelp as if one of the wolves had been injured or surprised. That was all it took, the final two wolves dashed off into the darkness leaving the cave entrance clear.

Nomber held the Jhirum manning the wall where it would be opened for a time, waiting to ensure that the wolves were continuing on and were far enough away not to hear them and turn immediately around. Then he nudged them. "OK open the end, everyone out as quickly as possible; and as quietly. Hurry now!"

The end stakes of the wall were folded back with some effort leaving an opening that the Jhirum could get through one at a time.

As soon as each Jhirum cleared the entrance they began a quick trot toward the stream, trying to be as quiet as possible while maintaining a good pace. They could still hear the distant yelling and an occasional howl from the wolves in pursuit. Everyone, however, ignored the tumult and focused on the stream.

After Nomber's message the four Jhirum outside of the cave had waited impatiently for some of the pack to leave. As soon as they saw the five wolves trot off into the gathering darkness they had all gathered together and moved off to the west side of the mountain where they discussed what to do. They had decided that it would be best if they broke into two groups one nearer the cave to initially draw the wolves off and one farther away that could then try to lead the wolves farther from the cave.

Jarine and Kang had stationed themselves nearest the cave. Finding evergreens that allowed them to climb high and to hide well enough that even if the wolves identified the trees they were in they might not be able to actually see them, which would reduce their interest in trapping them there for a long time.

Floan and Gromand had continued on around the mountain also finding large old trees to hide in.

By the time they were all in place enough time had passed that it was completely dark and they were certain that the hunting wolves were far away. Jarine motioned to Kang and began yelling and making other noises they hoped would attract the attention of the wolves at the cave.

She was beginning to wonder if their ploy was going to work when the first wolves trotted out of the darkness. They both stopped making noise. Since only a couple of wolves were there they were presented with a dilemma. If they continued to make noise the wolves would be certain of their location and might chose to stay. On the other hand they needed to get all the wolves away from the cave.

After remaining quiet for a while Jarine decided that the whole plan would fail if they did not manage to get the others away from the cave so she began to yell again. The wolves were under her tree in a flash howling and growling. Kang then began to yell as well causing the wolves to circle the two trees that were a stone's throw apart, in a constant frenzy.

Then Jarine heard Gromand and Floan take up the call, yelling and whistling. The wolves stopped their circling, staring off into the woods toward the sound. Then they turned again looking up into the trees, unsure of what to do at this point. No sooner had the others started making noise then more of the pack came into view, trotting up to the first two wolves.

At this point Kang and Jarine were silent and still, so the newcomers focused on the noise in the distance. Then they all began sniffing around the trees eventually picking up the trail of Floan and Gromand. At first just a couple of the wolves headed off into the night, but soon the rest followed.

Jarine called softly to Kang, "What should we do now?"

"Maybe we should head back to the cave and see if we can help them," Kang replied.

"But what if the wolves come back? Perhaps we should wait here in hopes that we can distract them if they return to soon."

While they each thought about the alternatives she heard a yelp as if one of the wolves had been hurt. Within moments the last two wolves trotted out of the darkness, straight past their trees and off toward the continuing racket.

Jarine's heart was pounding in her chest. They had no way of knowing how many wolves remained and had assumed that all had passed them already so they had been caught completely by surprise. They were lucky they had stayed put, but since they now were uncertain if all of the wolves had passed she decided it was best to stay where they were. So far the plan seemed to be working perfectly. She hoped that Nomber had the tribe hurrying to accomplish their end of the plan.

Back at the stream, the first to arrive had filled their skins and were heading back to the cave. Two of the four that Nomber had chosen to stay out were headed up the mountain to find shelter. Nomber had filled his skin and was working his way back toward the cave, more slowly than he had left, trying to balance two full skins and his spear.

About halfway back he stopped to measure the progress of the remaining Jhirum. No sooner had he begun to check their progress, than a howl arose from the woods beyond the stream. The hair on the back of his neck stood up and a chill ran down his spine. The hunting pack must have heard the commotion and returned to find out what was going on.

He motioned frantically for those still in the stream to head back, whether their skins were full or not. Dankin raced past him with a half full water skin without so much as a nod.

With a crash the wolves broke out of the darkness on the other side of the stream. None of the Jhirum who were just scrambling out of the water had spears and all were laden with heavy skins or gourds. There was no way that they would make the cave in time.

Nomber set his skin on the ground and charged back toward the five snarling wolves which were just splashing through the creek sending water flying in all directions. Past the last retreating tribesmen he flung himself, spear raised, as a yell of fury escaped his throat.

Dankin arrived at the cave, immediately ordering the tenders of the wall to close off the opening as much as possible just leaving an opening large enough for the last Jhirum to slip through. She watched in amazement and then anticipation as Nomber charged directly at the wolves after passing the retreating Jhirum.

He only stopped when he was nearly on top of them, his back to a large tree and his spear always in front of him. The wolves formed a semicircle around him teeth bared, growling and closing on the desperate Jhirum. He stabbed out with his spear first in one direction and then another, but the wolves kept their distance, knowing they had time. The last of the running Jhirum reached the cave and slipped through the narrow opening. Dankin ordered the wall closed.

Bashley protested, "Nomber is still out there and alone. We must go to his rescue!"

Dankin waved the wall tenders to continue. "There is no way we can help him. We will only lose more of our tribe if we send them out there. Nomber knew what he was doing. Do not make his sacrifice worthless."

Bashley stared at her in disbelief, and then dashed through the remaining crack in the wall just before it closed. Headlong he charged down the mountain.

As soon as Nomber saw him he yelled, "No Bashley, go back, you cannot help here, return to the cave!" But Bashley came on, only hesitating a moment.

Two of the wolves turned their attention on him as he called to Nomber. "Nomber begin backing up the hill. Together we can keep them at bay and back our way to the cave!"

Nomber seeing that it was already too late for Bashley simply to retreat began sliding his back away from the tree.

The wolves lunged alternately and he jabbed at them, catching one in the muzzle, causing it to back away for a moment only to come back in an angry frenzy.

Bashley continued to force the two wolves facing him down the mountain until Nomber and he were side by side backs to the cave. Then they both began to slowly retreat backwards up the mountain, their spears between them and the snapping jaws.

They had only retreated a short distance however, when the wolves realized what was happening. In one instant they broke ranks circling the two men, forcing them to stand back to back. Now they had to protect half a circle with only one spear each. Every lunge of the wolves brought the crushing jaws closer.

As Bashley stabbed at one wolf another lunged, ending too close to him for him to bring his spear around on it. He had to hit it in the head with the back end of the spear, but only after it had sunk its jaws into his calf. He stumbled with the pain and another wolf lunged at him.

Nomber brought his spear fully around to stab at the wolf attacking Bashley leaving himself wide open. Two of the wolves on his side lunged at him at once. He brought the butt end of the spear down on one of their skulls driving it nearly to the ground.

"We have got to work our way to the cave quickly, or they will have us," Nomber said as his back nudged Bashley to move up the mountain.

The going was arduous. For every step they took they had to fend off multiple attacks from the wolves still surrounding them. Their arms were tiring and Bashley was limping badly, but they had actually closed half the distance to the cave.

Inside the cave a mad argument erupted between those wanting to go out and help and those wanting to stay safely in the cave. Finally three of the Bagnog pushed their way through the opening with spears raised, yelling as they descended toward their retreating leader.

The wolves with their backs to the newcomers turned and fell away, trying to face the oncoming assault. Seeing their opening Bashley and Nomber moved quickly up the hill toward the charging tribesmen. The wolves tried to cut them off, keeping the two groups apart, but some wild jabs with the spears cleared the way for all five Jhirum to join forces.

Dankin watched; seething as the five inched their way toward the cave. She thought she had finally been given an opportunity to be rid of Nomber once and for all, but now the tide was turning and they might actually make it back to the cave.

They continued to work their way up the mountain. At times the wolves would surround them, slowing their progress, but even then they kept inching their way ever so slowly.

Suddenly one of the wolves managed to grab the spear of one of the Jhirum with his teeth. With a wicked thrash he pulled it from his hands at the same time throwing the Jhirum away from the other defenders. Two of the other wolves instantly lunged at the unprotected tribesman. One of them grabbed his arm in a bone crushing bite. The other went for his exposed side.

Nomber lunged frantically at the second wolf catching it squarely in the eye sending it yipping down the mountain. One of the other Jhirum lunged at the one holding the mangled arm. Only after two brutal thrusts with the spear did the wolf relinquish its hold.

Bashley lifted the wounded Jhirum, dragging him back to his feet. The remaining wolves redoubled their attacks. Nomber, panting and sweating yelled, "Get ready to open the wall! Bashley, get ready to help him to the cave, the rest of you, when I say so run for the cave as fast as you can but do not turn your back on the wolves. I will try to keep them off your backs. Go now!"

Without taking time to think they surged toward the cave, wildly slashing their spears around them. Only Nomber remained facing the wolves downhill while trying to back up toward the cave as quickly as possible.

The group was soon almost to the entrance. Dankin ordered the tenders of the door to open it just enough to let the returning Jhirum through and be ready to close it in an instant. She watched as Bashley thrust the hurt Jhirum through the entrance then turned back to face the wolves. In the rush a small distance had opened between Nomber, defending with his back to the cave and the rest of the group.

Within a heartbeat the wolves cut him off placing themselves between him and the safety of the cave. The other Jhirum piled through the entrance with jaws snapping at their heels. Bashley started to go back toward Nomber, but before he could even move a wolf had caught Nomber from behind, sinking his teeth into his thigh.

Dankin ordered the door tenders to grab Bashley and drag him in. Within seconds the other wolves were on top of Nomber who thrashed and yelled, not in terror, but in anger until all that could be heard were the sickening crush of bone and the rending of flesh.

Bashley almost fell back through the door, dazed and unbelieving. The stakes were rolled back into place and faces stared in disbelief. Dankin knew she could not gloat over the moment as much as she felt like doing so. "Nomber has paid a great price for us to get water so that we could carry on. We cannot allow this to dishearten us. We should find strength in his sacrifice."

Bashley just stared at the floor. He could not believe that Nomber was gone and he was not prepared to even face the prospect of Dankin taking over the leadership of the tribe.

Jarine and Kang continued to hear noises in the distance, but suddenly realized that some of them were coming from the direction of the cave. With horror Jarine grasped the reality that the rest of the pack had returned to the cave. Had they caught the tribe out in the open? The howling and growling would seem to indicate that at least some were. Now she did not know what to do. Here they sat in their trees, safe with the wolves far away. Meanwhile the tribe was in danger.

Without thinking she scurried down the tree scraping her legs on the rough bark in her haste. She ran to the tree where Kang was. "Kang it sounds like the other members of the pack have returned. We must go see if we can help!"

She could sense his hesitation and uncertainty, but after a moment she heard him working his way down the tree. By the time Kang was to the ground, Jarine was already running in the direction of the cave as fast as she could. She could hear him running after her. They both had their spears at the ready.

Though they were not that far away it seemed to take forever to get back to the cave. The sounds grew frantic and then subsided at intervals. As she topped the last hill beyond the cave she could hear her father yelling instructions. She finally came into view of the cave entrance only to see four of the wolves tearing at something on the ground. She could see no Jhirum anywhere outside the cave. She approached as quickly as she could without making enough noise to draw the attention of the feasting wolves. Her stomach turned as she heard the crunching of bones and the snarling of the hungry beasts. She knew that one of her tribesmen at least had not made it.

Kang had caught up to her by this time and together they circled carefully above the cave trying to see what was happening but also closing in on their trees in case they had to seek refuge in a hurry.

A noise caught her ear from above. She looked up to see Worden in the tree above them, motioning frantically for them to come up. Both of them grabbed branches and heaved themselves up into the tree.

As they climbed even with Worden he stared at Jarine who stared back for a moment before asking, "What happened?"

Worden did not speak for a moment and when he did, he did not begin to relate the tale, but only said, "I am sorry Jarine. Your father is dead."

Jarine sat heavily on the branch where she stood. The Jhirum did not normally count death as an enemy, only a natural part of life, but so much had changed in the past couple of months, they had come to depend on each other more than in the past. They had also come to depend on her father's leadership. She could not believe he was dead.

Kang urged Worden to tell them what had happened which he did, though he did not take his eyes off Jarine. For her part she did not hear any of it, but by the time the tale was complete her mind had taken her to the point where she had begun to realize that now Dankin would take the leadership, a prospect which was almost as frightening as the loss of her father.

Kang finally interrupted her reverie. "We should get back to separate trees so that we are not caught together."

Jarine, however, did not move. The strength had gone out of her, but a measure of anger was beginning to build. It was simply too convenient that it was her father that had been lost. She found it hard to believe that in some way Dankin had not contributed to the loss. Somewhere in the back of her mind she heard the rest of the pack return but she was aware of little else, though she did not sleep for the remainder of the night.

CHAPTER 35 RETURN HOME

The morning after their final foray looking for a suitable home base the Jhirum of the Sea set sail to return to their old bay. For two weeks they sailed without stopping except to gather some more magical fish. Donley was right about the weather. The coolness of the north seemed to follow them home bringing storms and strong winds along with the chill.

The trip, however, was uneventful with the exception of the continual nursing of Toren who would vacillate from somber and withdrawn to screaming and almost violent. Maerl made little progress with her, but as they drew nearer to the harbor Toren simply withdrew into herself.

They sailed into their home harbor midday on a cold blustery day similar to many they had experienced during the trip home. Clouds sped through the sky occasionally bringing sheets of rain with them. Though the Jhirum loved the sea in all of its tempers, none except for Toren were sorry to be turning into their sheltered harbor and the promise of a dry cave to protect them from the chill. Their magic served to keep them generally comfortable in all weather, but that did not mean that dry warm conditions did not feel better.

Even in the harbor the waves tossed restlessly, churned brown from the shore being washed away. Faren guided the ship in to shore for the first time. Though young, it was time for him to try out his skills at piloting a ship, which involved more in the way of coordinating the linked minds of the Jhirum than in actually physically steering with the small tiller he held in his hands.

Shwaren had not been blind to the young man's skill. He was quiet and unassuming but handled every task aboard ship with skill and efficiency. He did likewise with guiding the ship to the dock which had been hastily stitched together before they refitted the boat for the journey, since the old docks had been destroyed.

As they eased up next to the dock those who were not linked to control the ship stood staring inland. There were animals scattered about the remains of their village, animals of every description, large and small. This would not seem unusual in any other harbor, but here where they kept their home, there was never a large beast that would approach. The magic of the Jhirum had always kept them away from the village.

Shwaren, having satisfied himself of Faren's success at a proper docking turned to join the others in staring at this scene. Many of the beasts were plains animals normally living along the Frun or elsewhere in the valley's interior.

After the initial shock, however, Shwaren relaxed. Surely this was simply because they had been on an extended trip and had left no one behind to tend to the village as had always been the case in the past.

"Tie us up, what are you waiting for," he finally called. His voice brought them back to life with a jerk, realizing that they were derelict in their duties of securing the ship and stowing the sail.

Shwaren bounded over the railing to the dock after giving Faren a congratulatory pat on the back. He assisted in securing the ship and then turned again to face their home. The animals paid little attention to him as he left the dock and began to ascend in the direction of the caves. A few of the other Jhirum followed close behind.

The first beast they approached was a Borog which was hunting for dead crabs, fish or whatever else he could find near the water's edge. As they approached he stood to his full height easily half again the height of the Jhirum.

Shwaren reached out with his mind to calm the beast which after a brief pause went back down on all fours in a less threatening position. Next he prodded it to move away and leave the village. It turned to leave with surprising reluctance, but left nonetheless.

Shwaren turned to those following him. "I think that we should spread out and encourage the larger animals to move out of the area. If they stay, predators will be attracted which could pose a danger."

Though they did not fear or in many cases care that the animals were there, he felt it best if they were moved out. He was amazed by the number in this relatively small area. He could already see some plains cats feasting on the remains of recently killed Buck or other grass eaters.

A couple of the Jhirum approached them carefully. Shwaren could see even from a distance that the predators were even more reluctant to leave than the grazers, but eventually they started to move slowly up the hill.

By the time the larger animals had been cleared from the hillside the Jhirum that had remained with the boat were unloading supplies and were securing the boat for the night.

Fires had been started in the two caves to drive away the dampness that had accumulated there as well as to allow them to cook some fish for the noon meal. Though there were still some casual conversations about their strange welcoming party, for the most part it was seen as just that, unusual and nothing more.

As they were finishing their lunch Shwaren stood to gain their attention. "We need to get the camp ready for us to stay for some time now. I think that a few of you should work on cleaning up the caves some more while the rest of us can gather food."

Though they had cleaned up the caves somewhat from the debris the sea had washed in, they had not completed the task to the point where they would want to live in them indefinitely. Toren remained on the boat, still unwilling to consider touching the shore which had proven such a deadly trap so recently.

By evening the two caves that they occupied were in reasonable condition, the fires had driven away some of the dampness and everyone had returned with food and supplies to make their evening more comfortable. The mood had improved considerably, though several of the Jhirum who had ventured inland commented that there was still an unusually large population of animals just outside of their village.

Maerl took some fresh food to Toren and stayed to eat dinner with her on the boat, but returned later leaving her alone. Tired and content to be back, they turned in early, unconcerned for the moment about what tomorrow would bring.

Unfortunately their peace did not last long. The Jhirum of the sea never posted watches during the night, they never had need to. They used their magic to calm and control the animals that were near their village and there were never any other threats.

Donley was ripped out of his dreams by snarls that tore through the darkness. With his heart pounding he glanced around the dim cave at the other Jhirum near him who were also sitting up in alarm. A scream followed and the Jhirum were on their feet and headed toward the mouth of the cave, magic alive in their veins.

At the cave entrance Donley could see a Whorzen dragging a Jhirum from his bed and out into the night where a pack of at least a dozen of the huge beasts waited for the taste of blood. Instantly the night was lit up with fire as a dozen Jhirum attacked. The Whorzen was thrown down the hill like a leaf on the wind.

Donley rushed to the writhing figure on the ground pulling him back toward the cave. As he moved forward the other Whorzen leapt at him, sensing an easy meal. More fire burned the night throwing the Whorzen back though not completely upending them because of their mass and ferocity. They turned to attack again, but now the Jhirum had time to work together and formed a protective field that enclosed the mouth of the cave out to where Donley and the fallen Jhirum were.

Donley hastened to drag his fellow tribesman back inside the cave, where he could see that it was Nowind, his one leg bloody but appearing to be whole. By this time the commotion had drawn the attention of the Jhirum in the other cave who were now proceeding down the hill with magic glowing around them. Periodically he could see the magic stab out at an attacking animal, followed by a piercing howl.

The Jhirum were not accustomed to a direct and violent attack like this. Most animals that lived near Jhirum knew them and trusted them, even the large carnivores. Those who on occasion turned violent were quickly reminded of the strength of the Jhirum's magic and rarely had to be taught twice. For this reason the Jhirum were also not prone to killing beasts even when attacked. They were caretakers of the land and as such did everything in their power not to harm its creatures.

Tonight, however this was working to their disadvantage. Had they killed the initial attackers perhaps this would have more quickly dissuaded them. The painful blows that the magic struck only seemed to further enrage the beasts and to make them more careful in their attacks.

In fact the group coming down the hill was now surrounded by huge snarling Whorzen circling, waiting for an opening to attack. The dome of magic that surrounded the Jhirum however was impregnable and so they proceeded unfazed by the snarling whirlwind that followed them down the hill.

As they arrived at the cave mouth, without a single word the two groups joined their magic and lashed out in all directions at once throwing the beasts back with snarls and yelps. This finally convinced the Whorzen to seek out easier prey. The yelping and snarling trailed off as they passed over the crest of the hill and into the night.

The glow of protective shields disappeared with a snap as in unison all of the Jhirum turned and hurried to Donley and Nowind. Nowind was propped up against a boulder just inside the cave, breathing heavily, but without laboring. Donley was already working on repairing the damage to his leg. The gashes knitted together before their eyes, closing as the last blood oozed from the wounds.

Shwaren, who had been in the other cave, worked his way to the front of the crowd. "What happened?"

Nowind shook his head in confusion. "I do not know. One minute I was sleeping and the next a sharp pain ran through my body. I woke to find my leg in the jaws of a Whorzen who was dragging me out of the cave."

"I cannot understand what would make them so bold as to attack Jhirum right in their caves," Waymeir said, the consternation clear in her voice.

Winfew shook his head as well. "There have not even been any packs of Whorzen this near the sea in ages. They must have traveled here from inland for some reason."

Donley looking stern responded, "I suspect the reason is starvation. They have probably run out of carrion from animals killed by the blast and now find their food sources scarce inland where the effects were greater. They have come here looking for food."

"We will have to be more vigilant until these newcomers learn to stay away I am afraid," Shwaren said, half to himself. "I don't think that they will return tonight, but who knows what else is out there. We had better post guards for now."

Shwaren turned and headed back up the hill to the other cave, the rest of his group tightly bunched, scanning the darkness.

Donley settled Nowind further inside the cave where he quickly fell asleep, his breathing even and calm. Winfew took the watch. It was well past midnight so he might not take relief until daybreak. Donley along with the rest of the group settled in to resume their sleep, a little less secure than when they had first bedded down.

After silence had settled back over the cave, Winfew was left staring into the darkness. He as well as many of the other Jhirum had helped themselves to some of the magical fish in order to replenish the magic they had expended so as to be prepared for any further surprises.

For some time there was little movement in the night. His magic enhanced sight revealed only an occasional rock dwelling mammal scurrying between the rocks and the grass in search of food. Just as he was beginning to relax somewhat and had found a comfortable place to sit just outside the cave he began to see silhouettes against the night sky at the top of the hill. This brought him to his feet with concern.

The first silhouette however, proved to be a Gorgal. The lumbering Bovine though as strange a site here as the Whorzen, was not a threat. A browser, it normally fed on leaves and twigs from trees and shrubs in the plains and on the edge of the forests. It too, rarely ventured this near the ocean and never right into the village of the Jhirum.

There appeared to be three of the Gorgals together. They would find little to fill their bellies in the harbor area as it was mostly cleared of everything but a few small bushes and grass. Nevertheless they continued on down the hill, nearly to the water's edge wandering aimlessly in search of food. They also normally did most of their foraging during the day rather than at night adding to the strangeness of their behavior.

This too most likely was the result of a distressed population pushed to unusual behavior by the conditions left in the wake of the blast.

As he watched the confused Gorgals trying to figure out the ocean he felt a chill run down his spine. He turned slowly, looking back toward the top of the hill. His night vision seemed to have a hole in it. The darkness, which his magic could penetrate easily, went black in one spot, a spot that was moving slowly across the horizon, back and forth.

It did not take Winfew long to identify the shadow. He reached out to the watch at the other cave, who turned out to be Zifere. He had apparently sensed the beast as well.

The Wharecat must have spotted the Gorgals and had gone into a crouch. Winfew was amazed that any animal would even for a moment consider the Gorgal to be prey, but this cat was almost half the size of the Gorgals and Winfew had no doubt that it was capable of bringing down one of the beasts.

Together, Zifere and Winfew reached out to the Wharecat trying to prod it gently to avoid their caves. They could sense the total focus of the cat on its quarry and they could also sense the presence of magic. This was the first time either of them had ever encountered one of the legendary cats. They had heard that they instinctively sought out magical sources and would ingest the magic in large volumes until it became a permanent part of their bodies, never diminishing.

When the cat became aware of their presence he brushed aside their attempted contact as if they were a fly to be shooed away. Now Winfew and Zifere realized the true extent of the potential danger. His heart in his throat Winfew quietly slipped inside the cave. "Madrien, Faren, wake up!"

For the second time the two Jhirum jerked upright where they lay. "There is a Wharecat out here with enough magic to ignore us. Grab a couple of others and come to the mouth of the cave in case we have to defend ourselves." Before they rose he hurried back into the darkness.

By the time the others joined him the Wharecat had progressed halfway down the slope toward the Gorgals which had determined that there was no food here and had turned to head back up the hill directly toward the giant cat. The Wharecat slunk down nearly disappearing against the ground, waiting for the approaching prey.

The Jhirum stood there silently, hardly breathing. Winfew had no idea what they could do if it decided to come after them and so prayed that it would stay focused on the hapless Gorgals.

When the lead Gorgal was nearly on top of the cat it made one huge leap directly on to the back of the startled beast. The other Gorgals scattered, totally confused and unsure what was happening. The Wharecat reached around and clamped on to the underside of the Gorgal's neck. A sickening crunching sound followed by a bellow rose from the thrashing Gorgal which was running aimlessly trying to shake the cat from its back.

The Gorgal's resistance did not last long as its artery was crushed and it came to the ground with a crash. The other Gorgals were disappearing over the crest of the hill at full speed, abandoning their brother.

Silence returned to the hillside the only sound remaining, the rending of flesh by the Wharecat who was ripping huge chunks of flesh from the body. The Jhirum glanced at each other with concern, each with the same thought in their heads. What could they do to defend themselves against such a beast if it really decided to attack them? Winfew had never heard of a Jhirum being attacked by a Wharecat, but everything seemed to be turned upside down right now. It seemed that nothing could be taken for granted.

The cat continued to focus its efforts on devouring as much of the Gorgal as it could, gorging itself until the sky began to lighten in the east. Then like a shadow being chased by the sun it disappeared over the hill and was gone.

The Jhirum released an almost audible sigh as if they had been holding their breaths for the entire time the cat had been in their village. They could see the small pile of remaining flesh and bones, barely recognizable for what it had been.

There was no point in going back to sleep now so Madrien and Faren began stoking the fires, bringing them back to life to drive away the night's chill. Shortly the rest of the Jhirum began to rise; each hearing the story as they drew around the fire.

Each in turn tried to come to terms with the fact that even though they thought of their world as the sea, they could not ignore the changes that had occurred to the land.

CHAPTER 36 DRAWN TO DARKNESS

Bastile had seen Jasper visit his hidden supplies twice during the remainder of the day so she was certain that he would join her. She was glad, for though they were all loners at heart, she enjoyed his youthful company. She also did not relish the prospect of entering an entirely foreign environment without magic.

They had finished dinner and various groups broke off to talk in small groups at the fires that still burned around the cavern. She watched as Endmere cornered Cragen and Lamsil drawing them away to a far corner. He often sought their council though rarely did Lamsil and Cragen agree on anything.

Bastile located Jasper at a fire with several of the other young men. She walked by and motioned casually for him to follow. Shortly he rose from the fire and joined her under one of the lamps toward the back of the cavern. "Are you coming with me?" Lamsil asked casually.

"I would not let you go without me," Jasper responded with a small shake of excitement in his voice. "When are we going to leave?"

"I think we should wait until everyone is asleep," she cautioned. "I would just as soon not begin this with another argument." She also was not sure that such an argument would not convince Jasper to change his mind.

"Do you have enough provisions to last for a while?" Bastile asked. "We do not know when, or if we will find food and water."

"I have as much as I think I can carry," Jasper responded. "Do you really think that we will not find food in the caves?"

"Who knows," she said quietly. "It is a cave, not the kind of place known for abundant life."

She could sense Jasper waiver as he stared at the black maw of the deep cave entrance. She did not want to talk him into this out of ignorance, however, so she left him to his thoughts and his own decision.

Shortly he shook his head as if waking from a short doze and came to himself with the glow back in his eyes. "Well, there is only one way to find out."

Bastile nodded, satisfied. "I will meet you at the cave mouth after everyone is asleep." With that she stood and moved back to one of the fires where her adult son sat with several other young adults.

Jasper wondered whether she had shared their secret with her son. Not that it particularly mattered, there were few here besides Endmere, Cragen and Lamsil that would try to stop them.

Jasper rose and moved to where his pack was stored for one last look to ensure he had not forgotten something important. Like so much else that they did since the catastrophe, preparing for a trip in this way was unusual for them. The Jhirum had always traveled light, even in the dead of winter. Their magic sustained them to a large degree. Anything else they needed they found along the way.

So Jasper was understandably nervous about trying to plan for an extended journey where he might only be able to eat and drink what he had thought to pack in his bag.

Even coming up with something that he could carry the provisions in had been a challenge. Skins were in short supply and saved entirely for clothing or food storage. He had managed to find a large strip of bark from a birch tree that he tied together to form a crude pack, though it was not particularly comfortable to carry.

After looking over everything one more time, he lay down on his bed of evergreen boughs and dried grass. He could not bring himself to try to make conversation. All he could think about was the impending adventure.

It seemed to Jasper that the tribe would never settle down and go to sleep. Worst, the last group to settle, well into the night were Endmere, Cragen and Lamsil who had carried on an animated though discrete discussion since dinner had ended. He could not help but wonder what they had been discussing as they finally separated to go to their own billets.

As the fires died to embers he forced himself to wait until he was certain that all were asleep, then quietly gathered the two bark bags with slings and headed for the dark shadow that was the cave entrance. As he crossed the cavern he could see Bastile gathering her bags.

He entered the shadow of the cave and realized he had not thought about light for the first stretch of the cave where they would not want to light the runes for fear of awakening others. Just as he was about to head back to find something to use, he saw Bastile grab a torch from one of the wall mounts. She had apparently thought ahead more than he. He was glad his companion was Bastile, experienced and smart she would help to keep his sometimes impetuous personality in check.

She greeted him with a nod and continued on into the cave, not pausing for a second thought. Jasper found himself hurrying to catch up to the light that she held. They did not have to go far before they could start looking for runes to light the way.

Though it was late and both had worked a full day, neither felt the slightest bit tired. They had to search a bit in the darkness to find the first rune they felt was safe to light, but they knew that once they found it the rest would be much easier. Each seemed to lie just at the edge of where the previous light began to fail and the highly polished script sparkled in the fading light of the previous rune.

After backtracking twice they finally found the first rune. Jasper eagerly reached out to the polished stone. Blue white light leapt from the stone, growing stronger the longer he held his hand there. When he was satisfied with the intensity he withdrew his hand and stared about the cave in wonder.

Bastile dropped her torch to the floor as they turned to continue with the light to their back. Jasper wondered how far into the caves these runes went, surely farther than they were likely to travel if the stories told of explorers being gone for months. In fact he had not really thought about how long they might be gone until now. "Bastile, how long do you think we should travel?"

She did not slow her steady pace. "We have to make another important decision before we worry about how long to continue."

"What is that?" he asked with his head cocked in question.

"The first fork is only a short distance into the cave," she stated as if talking to a child. "We must decide which way to take."

He had not even considered this, assuming that they would take the main branch. The smaller size of the other fork and the fact that it angled down more steeply into the earth for some reason made him uneasy. "I wish we could decipher what these runes meant, that might give us some clue as to which would be the best way."

Bastile was quiet for a moment, thinking, and then started again, "Let's think about this logically. There are runes pointing both ways although we do not know if there are any in the smaller tunnel since no one has been down there yet."

Jasper brightened. "So we should stick with the main cave since there is more evidence that the runes continue that way. We cannot continue in the caves without the runes."

"You are right about that," Bastile replied. "On the other hand the tales also indicate that most of the exploration was probably down the main shaft and that they, as far as we know never found a pure source of magic, though they found magical creatures. Perhaps we should explore the cave where less effort was expended as there is more chance that they may have missed a magical source."

Jasper could feel his stomach turning over with anguish. "But there is also a much better chance that there are no runes to light the way in the smaller tunnel. Anywhere they did not explore we cannot explore either."

"True enough," Bastile conceded. "I hope that does not doom us from the start. Surely they would have mentioned in the stories if they had found magical waters."

Jasper shrugged. "The earth has moved many times since then. Clearly the path of our spring was changed by the last earthquake, it may be flowing somewhere completely new."

Bastile fell silent again for a moment her brow furrowed in thought as she walked. "All right, the main cave it is."

Jasper exhaled audibly and his step lightened as they came to the next rune. Bastile touched it and an orange glow crept up the wall and grew to brilliance.

They continued on into the depths of the mountain for another couple of hours until they came to where the cave split. Here they decided to rest a little before moving on. In the eternal night of the cave it mattered little what was night and day. They could decide to sleep whenever weariness overtook them and wake when they were rested.

Bastile studied Jasper for a moment under the glow of the yellow rune. "Are you still sure about this?" she asked.

Without hesitation he answered, "Absolutely, I am certain it is best for us to stick to the main cave."

"That is not what I was talking about," she coyly replied. "Are you still certain about making this journey at all?"

This time he hesitated a little, but his eyes still glowed with anticipation. "I am certain of that as well. This is much too interesting a place to leave simply as a mystery."

"Is that the only reason you wanted to come; for the adventure?"

"For the adventure and to discover what might be of use to us," he answered simply. "Why are you here?"

Bastile stared off into the darkness beyond the reach of the bright light of the rune. "I am here for one reason only; to find the source of our spring and return magic to our tribe."

Jasper considered this a moment. "Do you really think we will find it?"

"I cannot say for certain," Bastile admitted quietly. "But I think it is our best chance and one that we cannot pass up."

Jasper thought to himself that his goals in this adventure were much more likely to be achieved than Bastile's.

Bastile stood, Jasper picked up his packs to join her. They were about to venture beyond where any living Jhirum had traveled. Jasper could feel his heart pounding in his ears, his anticipation building in his veins.

Endmere woke as the first hint of light crept through the entrance to the cave, the previous night's discussion with Cragen and Lamsil still in his head. They had agreed that they had to take action before they totally lost the focus of the tribe. It was clear that although so far only Zeeta had stated she was leaving until she felt like coming back, others would soon follow. The Maestic were not used to working together except for brief and infrequent periods. They were also not used to taking direction from others.

Walking over to the nearest fire, he began to poke at the coals and add wood to bring it back to life. One of the young adults, Bastile's son, approached through the darkened chamber.

"My mother is gone," he said simply. "I am certain she went into the cave."

Endmere's brow furrowed, perhaps they were already too late. "Do you know when she left?" he asked.

"Sometime during the night, that is all I am certain of."

Endmere turned to waken Cragen, more certain than ever that their destiny was in the process of taking another turn.

CHAPTER 37 CHANGED LAND

After both camps had eaten breakfast, Winfew's group went up to the larger cave where Shwaren awaited their arrival to discuss the night's events. Though weak, Nowind was able to walk on his own to the meeting, his leg almost fully healed with only the slightest of scars to mark his ordeal.

Shwaren greeted the others with a somber nod. "We have been treated to quite a welcome home. It is clear that more has changed here than we might have thought. Inland conditions must be bad, forcing beasts out of their normal habitat in search of food and shelter. We can deal with the influx with work, and over time teach the newcomers to respect our presence, but it will take vigilance and time. We will have to keep watches posted at night and take care when venturing out alone."

"But what of the Wharecat?" Maerl interrupted, "can we defend ourselves against him if he decides to try a taste of Jhirum?" There was no joke in this statement.

Shwaren turned to Maerl weighing his answer. "We do not know what is possible against the Wharecat, but there has not been an attack by the cats on a Jhirum as far as we know, ever."

"There have also not been beasts wandering in the midst of our village in the past," Bandai practically hissed. "Do you expect us to trust to what has been before?"

"I do not expect us to trust to anything," Shwaren responded calmly. "We will take every precaution we can. What more can we do?"

"Leave," one simple word spoken by Bandai as if it were written in stone. "There is nothing to bind us to this broken land. We have looked to the North, but there are other directions in the sea. We should abandon this broken land and seek out a friendlier place."

"Where are we likely to find this better place?" Waymeir pleaded, "And when have the Jhirum run from the need of the land which is so clear. This land needs us more than ever now, to help heal and restore it."

"The land is not our concern," Bandai said cutting Waymeir short. "The sea is our charge. There are others to tend to the land."

"But how do we know that there still are others?" The concern was clear in Waymeir's face and voice. "They may have been destroyed in the catastrophe."

"It is still not our concern," Bandai said with finality turning her back on Waymeir.

"Where would you have us go Bandai?" Shwaren said turning to face her.

"To the south, or out to the deep sea." Her eyes alight at the thought. "We know of islands far from this land that are most likely untroubled by this blight. We can tend the seas as well from there as from anywhere."

Shwaren turned back to the others. "I do not think it is wise to so quickly abandon our village. True, we have some threats to deal with that we did not in the past, but we shall overcome them."

Shwaren could see the disagreement in Bandai's face, but finally the grimace smoothed out and she remained silent. It seemed that for the moment the issue was settled.

Shwaren surveyed his tribe members a moment, concluding that the discussion was ended for the time being. "I think that we should spend some more time scouting the area outside of the bay. It is clear that things have continued to change since our last sojourn. Perhaps we can move more of the animals away from our area so that beasts like the Wharecat will not find prey here."

He waited a moment for comments, but receiving none continued. "We should not travel alone given the dangers we have seen, so pair up. We will fan out inland to cover as much ground as possible.

CHAPTER 38 HOSTILE COUNTRY

Waymeir was paired with Donley. They were to scout almost due east from the village. The changes that had occurred while they were away were reemphasized as soon as they crested the hill above their village. They looked out on the rolling plains beyond, stunned by the number of animals of every size and type assembled there. Apparently they had been correct in their assumption that the animals had moved away from the desolation of the blast in search of food and better conditions. Not only the large Gorgals but, Borogs, Buck, and other hoofed animals of every description dotted the landscape in large and small groups.

With their magic they could sense the hunger and the unease of the beasts. They were also, no doubt, well aware that they had been followed by equally hungry beasts of prey.

Waymeir cast a concerned eye at Donley who just stared out across the land assessing where to begin. Most of the beasts that were visible were of no real threat to the Jhirum, but might be better kept at some distance so that large herds would not enter the village. It was the unseen that were more of a concern and Waymeir and Donley were both well aware of their presence though they remained hidden.

"Well, we had best be about it," Donley said, still scanning the landscape. "I think that we should sweep back and forth in an arc moving away from the village. There are enough animals, some dangerous that we should probably stay together." He knew that would make their task take longer, but prudence was called for in the face of the sheer numbers that they were dealing with.

Donley set out at an angle into the grassland. Waymeir could sense a pride of plains cats nearby. These cats were nothing like the Wharecat. They were much smaller though still the size of two Jhirum and deadly enough when they hunted as a group. They could run faster than a buck for short distances and their golden color blended in with the taller dead grass.

Waymeir could sense Donley reaching out to her intending to join their magic and encourage the cats to move to new territory. Linked, their awareness and strength was increased. They reached out to the cats, sensing that they had just fed and were resting with full bellies. They projected on them a sense of unease and threat emanating from the direction of the village. At first the lazy cats did not respond, but as they increased the strength of the sensation and the perceived size of the threat, they stood, appearing about a stone's throw from them.

For a while they sniffed the air and stared in the direction of the village trying to identify the threat. Waymeir and Donley continued to build the image's strength until finally the leader of the pride began to move off in the opposite direction, at first casually, but finally at a loping run.

The two maintained their projected threat image casting it about as they continued to crisscross the rolling hills. The more skittish buck took off in flight at the first touch of the sensation. The Borog they encountered took considerably longer to become concerned enough to move off. They were not accustomed to being afraid of anything except a large pride of the cats. But eventually even the Borog took the hint and strolled off over the hills.

Waymeir and Donley made sure to firmly plant the image of danger that would linger in the direction of the village. This should keep the beasts at a reasonable distance.

Donley thought of the Whorzen, he hoped that someone would encounter them so that they could be implanted as well, otherwise they might return again, even though they took a beating in their last encounter.

Donley and Waymeir did not need to go far; they simply wanted to establish a small buffer between the village and the bulk of the larger animals. As they crested one of the larger hills they stopped to survey the area. Large numbers of beasts of all sorts could be seen lumbering off away from the village. Some were already far enough away to feel secure again and had stopped to continue feeding.

As they scanned the hills Waymeir thought she saw a small dark spec in the air near the horizon. She soon sensed it as well. Though it was far away the sensation that this dot created was disturbing. Periodically it would dip toward the ground and then reappear in the air moments later. It was clearly headed in their general direction. The sensation which almost caused her stomach to turn grew stronger as it approached. She glanced over at Donley who was fixated on the same point.

Without looking away he responded to her unspoken query. "Whatever it is, it is huge. I can only imagine that it must be a Raik."

The Raiks were huge birds of prey, large enough to pluck a plains buck off the grasslands and carry it away into the mountains where they made their nests.

"There is something wrong about it though," Waymeir said quietly.

Donley nodded his head. "Yes, even its behavior is odd. They normally circle high until they have found a victim and then drop on it quickly and either stay and devour it on the spot or carry it off to the nest. This one is behaving erratically."

"Perhaps it is diseased or injured." Waymeir had to look away for a moment, so sickened was she by the sensation.

"Whatever the case, I would suggest that we repel it at the greatest distance possible," Donley responded, also looking away momentarily.

Waymeir reached for Donley's mind again and they joined, forcing their magic out with a tight focus on the rapidly growing spot. When their magic first brushed the beast Waymeir's stomach turned completely over. Then as they tried to force their way into the beast's mind they were pushed back with such violence that they both found themselves lying on their backs in the grass, staring in disbelief at the sky.

Waymeir propped herself up unsteadily on her elbows, eyes wide. "This beast has magic!"

"Yes, and not the good kind," Donley replied. The beast having been made aware of them had now set a course directly toward them, growing larger by the second. Donley looked around quickly, spotting a small copse of trees at the bottom of the hill. "Just in case we had better get to some cover, run for those trees!"

Without waiting for a second invitation Waymeir took off at a sprint with Donley close behind. As they ran they heard the first scream from the Raik, again unusual. Raik's were normally silent hunters hanging high in the sky until they spotted a victim too far from cover and then dropping silently, the victim rarely knowing their plight until the last moment before the giant claws closed around them.

The piercing cry drove Waymeir to redouble her speed without looking back. The trees were just ahead but she could sense the Raik dropping lower and closing on them. She could also sense a vileness, or madness about the beast that was entirely unnatural. The hair stood up on the back of her neck as she dove behind a tree, simultaneously stabbing out with her magic, hoping to buy Donley the extra seconds he needed to gain the refuge of the trees with her.

Her attack was thrust back at her again, knocking her to the ground for a second time and leaving her with a pounding head. But she had accomplished her intent, distracting the Raik just enough to give Donley the time to dive behind a nearby tree. The Raik crashed to the ground, ridged beak the length of a Jhirum snapping wildly between the trees. Donley and Waymeir dropped back deeper into the trees.

After several moments of thrashing, snapping and screaming the Raik took back to the air, but apparently not with the intent of moving on. Instead it circled low around the small group of trees looking for a way to get at the Jhirum. Waymeir and Donley were forced to continually circle the trees themselves in order to keep a barrier between them and the beast.

Suddenly the Raik screamed again and lifted higher into the air, circling to gain altitude. Donley and Waymeir stopped, looking upward, trying to determine what it would do next.

Breathing heavily Donley moved toward Waymeir. "Did you see the color of that Raik? I have never seen a Raik almost midnight black with only a few dirty brown patches." Normally Raiks were light gray, sometimes with a few brownish patches on their undersides.

"Yes and it is behaving so strangely," Waymeir answered, scowling. "Why would it come after us like that? There were dozens of large animals that would have been easy prey along its way to us."

"There is obviously something magical about it, though nothing good," said Donley as he maneuvered so that he could see the Raik still circling above them.

Suddenly another blood curdling scream rent the air freezing Donley and Waymeir momentarily where they stood, but not for long. Waymeir could see the beast growing rapidly larger, coming straight down on them. Both of them dove behind the trees farthest from where it appeared the beast would crash. At the last moment it slowed its decent slightly but still crashed through the canopy into the midst of the trees, breaking branches and bending smaller trees under its weight. In the midst of the chaos the razor beak lashed out blindly in every direction driving Donley and Waymeir out into the open.

Donley touched Waymeir's mind indicating that he wanted to try another attack. This time, no suggestions, but an attack meant to kill. Like a lightning bolt the magic struck out at the thrashing beast, which screamed again and struggled to free itself from the tangle of branches. Though hurt by the assault, it appeared that even this attack had not really injured it, yet alone killed it as intended.

Lifting once more into the air the beast circled, gaining altitude. Immediately Donley and Waymeir dashed back into the brush. Now the beast was enraged to the point of delirium circling erratically then diving back madly into the trees. Cowering in a thicket they maintained a meager barrier of magic. Though not strong enough to defend against a direct attack, it served as an added barrier to the tangle of trees and branches that they were under, just enough to keep the Raik at bay.

Finally screaming in frustration the Raik circled back into the sky and headed back to the open plains in search of other prey.

Donley and Waymeir watched in stunned silence as the monster diminished to a large blot in the distance. Together they stood silently and worked their way back out through the tangled mass of brush and damaged trees.

Pushing through the last cover Waymeir stopped and turned to Donley, her face pale as moonlight. "What was wrong with that animal?"

"I have never seen the like," Donley answered, concern etched in his face. "Let's circle around and work our way back to the village. We must alert the others."

Donley headed off in the opposite direction of the Raik leaving Waymeir to glance one more time at the distant smudge in the sky before turning to follow.

The sun was setting into the sea as they crested the hill that looked down on their harbor, dying in orange and yellow, purple and brown, unnatural in its haze induced beauty. The harbor looked peaceful in the fading light, deceptively tranquil.

Donley and Waymeir did not hesitate to take in the beauty or contemplate the irony of the scene. Instead they headed straight for the upper cave, hoping that none of their brethren had a similar encounter to theirs.

About half of the explorers had returned, each with their own tale of wonder, terror, or consternation. Though all the tales were different, the common thread was that an enormous change had been wrought on the land. Animals there were, in quantities never seen this close to the ocean, animals of all kinds, hunters and hunted, terrible and timid. More than a few escaped close encounters with violent beasts only through skill magic and luck.

Most of the beasts however, were of known behavior and although in some situations were more aggressive than normal; they were for the most part following their normal role in the scope of life. A few of the encounters, however, echoed Donley's and Waymeir's experience, unnatural in every respect and always violent and hate filled. Most however, were not reinforced with magic in the way that the Raik's attack had been. As Donley related the experience, faces grew long, some weary, some frightened, all concerned.

Shwaren arrived at the end of Donley's tale, as the shadows faded into darkness and the night animal's sounds began to fill the late evening quiet. He looked from face to face, each in turn seeking out his own. Never before had he seen his people frightened. Yet now to a man, fear was plain upon their faces. Even still filled with their magic, they felt diminished, inadequate to a task with no definition, boundaries or end. On the land the Jhirum of the sea rarely sought to intercede in the daily existence of life, really knowing and caring only for the sea. Now the land which was once only a way station and source of supplies had become a threat to their very existence.

For the first time ever, beasts of magic, with strength to match their own prowled the land with malice. Silence held the assemblage for some considerable time as each attempted to assimilate this awareness, to contemplate their diminished stature in a world shaken to its core.

Bandai was the first to break the silence. "There is no telling the full extent of the danger, but it is clear that we cannot, through our own vigilance guarantee our safety here. It is time to depart. The sea remains as it has always been, dangerous, yet no more or less today than yesterday, or a thousand years ago. Only it is constant. Only it is our home."

As the echo of his words died in the cave, silence returned. Now no one looked to others, all eyes and minds were turned inward, seeking out what damage and promise lie within.

Madrien did not take long to contemplate. "I agree; it is time for us to set out to sea, to find a new base from which to launch our voyages, a base far from this stricken land, where there is still health and safety."

Shwaren barely heard or registered much of the remaining discussion. His mind drifted in uncertainty for the first time in his life. But before the discussion died down and the faces turned again to him he realized that the only remaining certainty was the sea. Though he could not recall the arguments for, or against, he did not need to. There was really no argument left.

Looking around at the now expectant faces, with the growing sounds of another violent night echoing in his ears he spoke the words that all knew were coming. "We do not know how to succor the land in this state, we know only the sea and to the sea we must return. Perhaps someday we will return to these shores. When time has had a chance to heal the wounds, but our duty is to the sea and to ourselves. We must not lose any more lives to this tragedy. We are too few as it is. We shall sail west, beyond the horizon. Far from this tortured land, to where we can find peace and the safe harbor we require to allow us to continue to serve the sea."

CHAPTER 39 SAILING TO TOMORROW

Fenly awoke to another day much like the last and the one before that. It was hard to believe that it had been two months since the catastrophe that had changed their world, probably forever. It seemed to him at this moment like the only constant was Ashmere, still sleeping beside him. Healed of her wounds she was as strong and sure as ever.

He watched her sleep for a time. Like the child she had always been in sleep, untroubled and beautiful. He counted himself among the luckiest of the survivors for at least he had her and that was no small consolation.

As he sat up in the small lean-to that they shared he was thankful for the small protection that it afforded. The morning was damp as most were these days and what was early fall felt like early winter. In the chill air thin trails of smoke filtered up into the grey skies from the remnants of the evening's fires.

He wore a crude hide poncho, the best that they could do for clothing so far. It at least kept the worst of the chill out both sleeping and awake though it seemed to constantly be in the way.

As he emerged from the lean-to he went to Legolan who was tending one of the fires. He had been the watch for the last half of the night. They never slept any more without someone to tend the fire and watch for danger. Several times wild cats or wolves had ventured into their camp looking for food. There was little enough of this, and the carnivores were drawn in every time they took an animal for food.

He still found it distasteful to hunt and kill animals, but there were no longer sufficient quantities of berries, nuts and other edible plants to fill all of their bellies. Thankfully there were signs of renewed life in the blasted land. Despite the chill green shoots had emerged everywhere, forcing their way through the gray muck that still covered the land. They would barely get a start, however, before winter set in as early as the fall had come on.

He often wondered about the climate which remained colder and cloudier than normal. Given their circumstances the last thing they needed was an early or hard winter.

He nodded to Legolan as he crouched by the fire. "Was the night quiet?"

Legolan threw another stick on the fire before answering. "Yes. I heard a wolf in the distance, but he did not come near as far as I could tell."

Legolan studied Fenly a moment as if deciding whether to say more. Finally he asked, "What is going to become of us Fenly? Can we survive the winter without our magic?"

Fenly glanced briefly over at his lean-to having heard Ashmere moving about before answering. "I do not think that any of us can know. We are doing what we can to prepare. At the same time we are making some progress through the rubble at our spring. Perhaps we will once again find our magic."

"But we have not so far and we have moved nearly half the rock which fell."

"I know. That is why we must continue to make other preparations."

Ashmere joined them, nodding to each in turn before squatting next to Fenly. "There is little to be gained by wondering if we will survive. We must all just work as hard as possible to ensure that we do."

Legolan shifted uneasily before speaking again. "Has anyone seen Minere and Genlie?"

Ashmere's face clouded at the mention of the two Jhirum who had disappeared after failing once again to convince the tribe that they should travel to the Maestic to see if they could get magical water from them. A little more harshly than she intended she responded, "No one that I know of. I am afraid that they have gone to the mountains in search of magic. I just hope that they are safe."

They all fell silent then, staring at the dancing flames of the fire, wrapped in their individual visions. Ashmere was confident that they would survive. Everyone had at least crude clothing and they had food, though never as much as they might wish. This was partially because she had insisted that they store at least part of whatever they gathered for the winter. True their lives were changed, but they would survive and eventually prosper, though she was very unsure as to whether they would ever get their magic back. She had little patience for dwelling on the subject. The world was what it was and would bring them a new day whether they wanted it or not. The fate of the Natec was not in the finding of magic, but in learning to survive without it, though a different life, no less purposeful.

Meanwhile in a cave in the high mountains of the Maestic Endmere had risen, comfortable and dry. The remains of several fires still burned around the cavern that had become their home. He still scowled as he looked around at the sleeping Jhirum, counting their numbers. Besides Jasper and Bastile they had lost five others including his mate Zifere to the desire to be on their own. Though they had built up significant stores of food he was still not satisfied and wished that everyone shared his concern for how they would survive the winter.

Much deeper in the mountain Jasper and Bastile continued their journey, determined to return magic to the tribe. So far they had been fortunate.

They still had some of the original supplies that they brought with them because they had at fairly regular intervals come across fungus or animals that served to supplement their diets. They also continued to find the runes to light their way, though the novelty had long since worn off. Jasper no longer ran to be the one to touch the rune, bringing it to glowing light. Bastile recognized that in general his youthful enthusiasm for this journey had worn off. He often talked of the rest of the tribe and what they might be doing.

The one thing that still held his interest were the beautiful stones that they had come across periodically. He had a collection which he kept in his bag of gems of every color. Some he had found loose on the floor of the cave. Others he had pried or chipped from the wall. It had become nearly an obsession with him.

Bastile still clung to her hope of finding magic in the cave, though so far the only magic to be found were the runes left by their ancestors. Her craving to hold magic again and her firm belief that this was the only way for the tribe to survive kept her going through the endless, sunless days. They no longer had any concept of day and night. They would walk till they were tired, eat when they were hungry and sleep when their eyes grew weary. At what intervals each of these occurred was beyond their ken.

As Bastile day dreamed Jasper who was leading the way suddenly stopped short almost causing her to run into him. "What is the matter?" she asked a little more crossly than she intended.

"Look," was all that he answered pointing ahead.

Immediately ahead of them the cave split, one to the left and one to the right. Both were about of equal height though the right hand branch angled down a little more steeply than the left.

Finally Bastile moved ahead. "Well let's check it out."

As she approached the fork she could see the familiar glint off of a magical rune carved in the dull cave wall. This one however was composed of many symbols, longer and more complex than any previously encountered.

She reached out as they always did to coax light from the magical message. Oddly the left half of the message glowed amber and the right half red combining to form a deep orange illumination.

She stepped back to look at the message. "If only we could decipher the words."

Jasper shook his head. "It is telling something different about each direction, but what? How can we decide which is the best way to continue?"

Bastile walked slowly a short distance into the left branch then turned and did the same in the right as Jasper looked on.

"There seems to be little difference; except that the right cave descends more steeply. It also feels to me like this is headed more in the direction of our old spring."

Jasper looked at her questioningly. "I do not know how you could tell what direction anything is. We have made so many turns and twists we could be headed back toward the camp for all I know."

"I suppose you are right, it just feels that way to me."

Bastile felt that every time they were forced to make a decision like this they could be deciding the fate of their whole adventure. Down the path they did not take their magical waters could be bubbling up just out of site. Or there could be unseen danger that they were about to stumble into. But she also knew that spending more time thinking about it would not make the decision any better, or success any more lightly so finally she stepped toward the right hand cave calling over her shoulder to Jasper. "Come on Jasper, our fate lies down either path." She only hoped that the fate she led them to would not result in their early demise.

The Jhirum of the sea on the other hand headed toward their destiny united and in the fresh sea air. They had spent several weeks at their harbor gathering supplies and repairing their boat, a time during which Toren continued to refuse to step on land. Her mood however had improved dramatically with the decision to seek out a new home. The danger that they had been exposed to by the presence of multiple magical and clearly dangerous beasts had swayed those who were uncertain if they should leave their harbor. With this decision made they set about preparing for their journey and debating in what direction to travel.

Shwaren watched as the last sacks of berries were brought on board. Excitement emanated from the whole tribe, even those originally opposed to seeking a new home. The prospect of a long journey at sea was exciting to the Jhirum of the Sea, particularly under the circumstances.

Winfew bounded off the boat on to the makeshift dock a smile on his face. "We are ready to sale."

Shwaren nodded, turning one last time to look at the harbor that had been their home since he was a boy. "We had best be off. I would like to be beyond site of land before dark."

Winfew turned to the three Jhirum manning ropes. "Prepare to cast off."

Shwaren strode up the simple plank that served as a gangway. The entire tribe was on deck, the last of the Jhirum of the Sea. Some stared at their former home, some out to sea. Shwaren began to gather those together in his mind who would power the ship. One by one they linked together.

Winfew did not have to wait for a signal to know when they were ready. "Cast off!"

Those on the pier were holding their ropes which they used to climb up the side of the ship and over the low railing. The boat surged ahead into the last of the breakers toward the mouth of the harbor and the open sea. As she had been for most of the time since the catastrophe Toren stood at the bow staring out to sea. But this time the longing was gone, a smile on her face for the first time that anyone could recall.

She knew that many thought her weak, or at least immature to have not been able to overcome her fear of the land. In fact, though she still had no interest in their old harbor, it no longer terrified her, or even haunted her dreams on any but rare occasions. Her obsession with going to sea to find a new home far away, for some time now had been driven instead by her visions of a beautiful island, far away in the deep sea. The dream had recurred almost every night. She was certain that the island was real and equally sure that this was their destination as well as their destiny.

She did not pause as Waymeir did to contemplate the fate of the land and the Jhirum left behind in the violent world that had been created in an instant. As the wind whipped her dark hair and the joy of being linked with the rest of the crew sang in her veins her thoughts were only of a beautiful new home far out to sea, far away from the nightmares.

On the other hand Jarine's nightmares had only begun since the death of her father. She awoke on that day, unrested after a night of fitful sleep, filled with dark images and the death of her father. The wolves at that time were still prowling outside of the cave as she came to life high in the tree where she had sought refuge the night before. It did not take her long however to come to some decisions.

It was clear that whatever happened now, Dankin was going to assume the leadership of the tribe. She hated Dankin for constantly goading her father and probably in some measure causing his death. She could not imagine living under her constant bullying. By the time the sun had cleared the eastern ridge she knew that she was going to set out on her own. Her heart pounded a little harder at the thought, knowing of the dangers that lurked in these mountains and others that she was certain she knew little about. It did not matter, however, she was going.

That was nearly a month ago. This day she woke in a tree much has she had on that first day after her father's death, the taste of his demise still strong. From her perch she looked down a steep mountainside at a valley shrouded in fog so dense it seemed as if it must be solid. Without knowing why she had taken to staying near the edge of this valley. She knew that this was probably one of the most dangerous places she could be. Perhaps with the horrible events of the past couple of months she in some way sought the release that death would offer.

It seemed to her, however, that she was drawn by something else. Always sleeping in trees, up away from most harm, she had spent many nights listening to and sometimes watching the deadly dance of the denizens of this valley. It seemed to her that there was power here, some in the creatures she encountered and some in the valley itself. The exact form or nature of this power she could not discern, but her remaining instincts as a former creature of power told her it was there. Over the days she spent above the valley she became more and more obsessed with the thought that somewhere in this frightening demesne there was power, perhaps power that she could wield once again.

She had even taken on occasion and only during the day to approaching the edge of the deadly swamp that was the birthplace of the endless fog. She never went into the swamp itself, only to its edge. Here she had seen objects glowing deep in the murky water and strange beasts slither away into the depths.

She had also become obsessed with the small bag that she carried at her waist. She had placed the contents in this bag before they had left the area near their magical spring. She knew that her father firmly believed that the dark substance that had been blasted over the landscape by the explosion was the source of their headaches and potentially deadly. She could not resist, however, the thought that there was power here as well. The fact that it might be evil or corrupting did not stop her from gathering a pouch full of the black substance. She had mostly forgotten it until she parted ways with the rest of her tribe. Since then she had spent considerable time looking at it, handling it, trying to determine what its possibilities were.

Whenever she touched it she felt a strong nausea, but at the same time an infusion of power. She was determined to figure out how to use this power to help her survive. As she sat in the tree holding the pouch in her hand she struggled to fight the waves of nausea that it brought on, finally giving up, closing the pouch and letting it fall to her waist again.

As she slipped from her arboreal haven she felt that this was the day that she would venture past the edge of the swamp. There was one particular place that seemed to have a path that the creatures that lived here must use to navigate past the dark waters. Though her stomach fluttered at the thought her resolve was solid. If there was any chance at power in these mountains it lay in this swamp and if there was any chance she was prepared to take it.

As she walked slowly down the steep mountainside she ate a few of the berries she had stored in her waist pouch from the day before. Perhaps she could bring power back to her people and in so doing heal them and free them from Dankin. The headache that still haunted her constantly throbbed against these thoughts, her rapidly beating heart threatened to split her head as she descended into the mist and out of the world she had known.

www.ingramcontent.com/pod-product-compliance
Lightning Source LLC
Chambersburg PA
CBHW061605170626
46811CB00001B/319